THE
BURNING
GHATS

ALSO BY PAUL MANN

Season of the Monsoon
Prime Objective
The Traitor's Contract
The Britannia Contract
The Ganja Coast

The Burning Ghats

PAUL MANN

FAWCETT COLUMBINE

NEW YORK

A Fawcett Columbine Book
Published by Ballantine Books

http://www.randomhouse.com

Grateful acknowledgment is made to The Peters Fraser & Dunlop Group Ltd.
and the Estate of Hilaire Belloc for permission to reprint an excerpt from
"Verses 1910" from *Complete Verse* by Hilaire Belloc.

Library of Congress Cataloging-in-Publication Data
   Mann, Paul.
     The burning ghats / Paul Mann.—1st ed.
       p.   cm.
     ISBN 0-449-90770-8
     I. Title.
     PS3563.A53623B87   1996   96-27219
     813'.54—dc20   CIP

Manufactured in the United States of America

First Edition: November 1996

10 9 8 7 6 5 4 3 2 1

KENNEDY

FOR MARGARET O'SULLIVAN
THE GODDESS OF GENEROSITY

"And what is Art whereto we press
Through paint and prose and rhyme—
When Nature in her nakedness
Defeats us every time?"

"The Benefactors"
RUDYARD KIPLING

ACKNOWLEDGMENTS

This book would not have been possible without generous contributions of time, knowledge, and experience by the following: Dr. Pritham Phatnani, deputy coroner of Bombay; Maneka Gandhi, former Minister for the Environment; Perez Chandra, Allwyn Fernandez, Kiran Wagli, Sanjay Sitra, Vrinda Gopinath, Shiraz Sidhva, Renuka Chatterjee; former *New York Times* Delhi bureau chief Ed Gargen; and former *Globe and Mail* Delhi bureau chief John Stackhouse.

PREFACE

It has been seven years since I first went to India to research *Season of the Monsoon*. Since then I have returned twice; to research *The Ganja Coast* and *The Burning Ghats*. In that time I have seen the country transform itself from a stunted socialist economy to a booming free-enterprise economy far more in tune with the entrepreneurial spirit of the Indian people. With a population expected to reach a billion by the year 2000, and a middle class bigger than that of the EEC, India will soon rival China as the new Asian superpower.

Western banks and other corporate giants are rushing to Bombay to fuel the boom with cash and reap the rewards of expansion. Bombay is already the most important financial center between Zurich and Singapore, and Indian businessmen are learning to flex their newfound economic muscle with increasing confidence at home and abroad. India has nuclear reactors, atomic weapons, and the missiles to carry them to Islamabad and Beijing. Its aircraft carriers and submarines roam the Indian Ocean from Africa to Indonesia. It has the potential in the Agni rocket to launch its own communications satellites into space. The Bombay movie industry produces three times more movies than Hollywood annually, and the advertising industry creates slick and sexy ad campaigns the equal of anything in New York. New Mercedes and BMWs jostle with Marutis along Marine Drive. Young people wear designer clothes, drink Bacardi and Coke, have pizza delivered to their high-rise apartments, and watch MTV while their parents fret about the collapse of morality. This is not the image the West has of India. This is the new India on the brink of its sixth millennium. Affluent, modern, dynamic, eager to make up for lost time. But the old, immutable India hasn't disappeared. It looms over everything. Corrupt, chaotic, threatening, susceptible to spasms of epic violence.

India has always been a country of extreme contradictions; wealth amidst poverty, kindness amidst cruelty, candor amidst deceit, the bizarre amidst the banal. This is part of India's allure. Over the centuries, that allure has proven irresistible to many invaders. Two hundred years ago it was the red-coated mercenaries of the East India Company who conquered India with musket and cannon. Secure in their civilizing zeal, confident in the superiority of their technology, they overlaid the country with the patina of colonization and thought it was theirs forever. Modern India is built on their bones. Today the dark-suited mercenaries of Citibank, Union Carbide, and IBM seek to conquer India with Powerbooks and cell phones. Secure in their corporate zeal, confident in the superiority of their technology, they seek to overlay the country with the glitz of a new colonial power. To the world's oldest continuous civilization it is just another episode in a drama as old as time.

At the Rio earth conference in May 1992, the Indian Minister for the Environment, Kamal Nath, announced that India was the only country in the world to have increased its area of forestation. This claim was based on satellite photographs which showed that India had boosted its forest cover from nine percent of available land mass to nineteen percent in a single year. On this basis, and the understanding that satellite pictures cannot lie, the World Bank paid the Indian government $500 million for development rights to all India's forest resources. Apparently, nobody at the World Bank knew the figure of nineteen percent was provided by satellite pictures taken just before the national sugarcane harvest. Mature sugarcane reaches heights of fifteen to sixteen feet and, to a satellite camera, looks like forest. Once the sugarcane was harvested, the true area of forestation fell back to somewhere around nine percent. Some experts say a more accurate estimate of India's forest reserves would put them at around five to six percent of available land mass.

It was a bad deal and an expensive lesson for the World Bank. In India it was business as usual.

THE
BURNING
GHATS

CHAPTER 1

Raffee had never seen so many people so happy to die.

But here in the beggars' house of dying he was surrounded by them. Five on this one floor, their bodies reduced to leather rags by lives of sickness and struggle, but their faces serene and eyes eerily aglow as they looked expectantly toward death.

There were others on the floors above and below, twenty or thirty in all, and hundreds more in the hostels for the dying that crowded down upon the burning ghats of Varanasi. Others arrived all the time, by train, bus, and ox cart, by curtained palanquin and raffia litter borne along dusty roads by barefoot sons then down through the crooked streets to the banks of the sacred Ganga to await the moment of death.

At fourteen Raffee was young enough to be afraid of death and old enough to be contemptuous. He didn't believe what his father believed—that death was the gateway to a new life, a better life if you had been virtuous and your ashes were scattered upon the Ganga. Or best of all—*moksha*. Release from the

3

prison of reincarnation, an end to the cycle of suffering and a
final, blissful ascent to heaven.

Raffee didn't know much but he knew the word *bakwas*. It
was Hindi for bullshit. Something told him that when you died,
it was the gateway to extinction, a plunge into nothingness. He
had seen enough of death to know it was final. He had seen the
rat-swarmed bodies of the innocent poor in the alleys. He had
seen the broken spokes of reincarnation in the bodies of new-
born infants cast into smoldering backstreet middens.

The men he admired were not those who endured their suffering in silence in the hope of divine redemption. He admired
those who took what they wanted now, because this was the
only life there was. He had no intention of wasting his life as a
rickshaw puller like his father, a two-legged beast until lamed by
a rich man's car. Reduced to a limping fool he had spent the rest
of his life on the platforms of Faizabad station selling chai at
twenty paise a cup.

Raffee was a child of the new India, scornful of a faith that
kept its poor enslaved by superstition, taunted by the lurid symbols of consumer wealth that ringed the slums like prison
towers. He wanted designer jeans, high-top sneakers, a black
satin baseball jacket, a Japanese motorbike. He wanted girls like
the ones he saw on MTV in the stores. And the only way he
could get them was through the gangs. He had made up his
mind. When he got back to Faizabad, he would make the gangs
his family. His father would never know. He would let his father
die as he had lived—in the solace of ignorance.

His father moaned and flapped his withered arms. Raffee
folded them gently on a chest that had once boomed with life
and now looked like parchment on a broken bamboo cage. The
old man sucked at the damp night air, his cheeks molding to his
skull like wet tissue. He was fifty years old and might have been
a hundred. His breathing steadied and he seemed to settle.

It wouldn't be long, Raffee thought. People died when the
dawn came, and nobody knew why. Dawn was less than an hour

away. The doctor in Faizabad said Raffee's father wouldn't survive the train journey, but stubbornness had kept him alive. The stubborn determination to see the holy ghats that were the stepping-stones to the gods. To know a consolation at the end of his life that he had never known in its passage.

Raffee thought it would have been better if his father had died during the journey. They could have cremated him on the day they arrived and gone straight home. Dying on heaven's doorstep wasn't cheap. The beggar's house of the dying might allow them free floor space, but there were other costs. They had to pay the city for a cremation permit, they had to pay the keeper of the ghats—the richest Sudra in Varanasi—they had to pay the custodian of the sacred flame for the right to take his fire, and they had to pay for the wood that went into the pyre. There were electric crematoria in bunkers provided by Delhi to spare the nation's shrinking forests, but the devout spurned them. All around them wood pyres burned as they had every day for five thousand years.

And every day that Raffee's father clung to life drained the family's meager purse a little bit more. Food around the burning ghats sold at inflated prices. They had to buy a length of quality satin to shroud the old man's corpse before it was burned. They had to pay the barber who shaved the eldest son's head before he lit the funeral pyre. The widow had to confine herself to the widow's house so she would not be tempted to commit suttee and throw herself into the fire to join her husband on his journey to the hereafter. And the charity of the city was limited. If the old man did not die within a couple of weeks they would have to go to a hotel and pay to maintain their deathwatch.

Raffee got up to stretch his legs and walked to the balcony that overlooked Manikarnaka Ghat, the holiest burning ghat in India. Around him in the gloom people coughed and stirred behind frayed plastic sheets strung from the walls. There were no windows or shutters and during the day smoke from the funeral pyres gusted up from the ghats and filled the nostrils of the dying. Sometimes gases accumulated in a corpse's skull and exploded, sending sparks spiraling skyward. Every night the women swept the floor and picked pieces of charcoal from their cooking pots.

Raffee leaned against the soot-blackened wall and watched dawn spill over the city ramparts like molten brass; two miles of domes, cupolas, and broad-bellied towers built by hands that toiled three thousand years before the birth of the Buddha. Below the great walls, below the descending tiers of stone, the dark swath of the Ganga flowed silent and ominous. Lights glimmered on both sides of the river, electric lights, cooking fires, the lanterns of houseboats occupied by aging hippies and aspiring western mystics.

Soon the other boats would come, boats filled with tourists laden with cameras and counterfeit reverence. Other craft too. Rowboats for those who couldn't afford cremation or were spared its expense because the deceased was a holy man, a victim of snakebite, smallpox, or a child too young to have done wrong. Their modestly shrouded corpses, weighted with stones, were surrendered to the current in mid-river. Downstream, scabrous softshell turtles waited to fatten themselves till they were caught by poachers and sold to restaurants in Calcutta.

Gradually the Ganga emerged from the murk; flat, sullen, viscid as paint. No longer the mythic river of purification whose cleansing bacteria astonished European scientists, it had been waylaid on its journey from the pristine glaciers of the Himalayas to the fetid Bay of Bengal by industry, by agriculture, by the raw waste of hundreds of millions of human beings. Now it was the color of rust and smelled of corruption and decay. It was as sick as those who waited to be cast into it.

But still the faithful came to the great stone steps that lined the river bank. To worship, to bathe, to fill vials with holy water they would carefully take home to sanctify village wells. Upstream at Meer Ghat and Dasashwadh Ghat the first pilgrims had already come down to the river to cleanse themselves in its liquid filth while dhobi wallahs flailed their laundry beside gushing sewer pipes. Brahmin priests took their places under thatched umbrellas and began dispensing their blessings to the poor, reserving their most elaborate blessings for the rich. On Scindia Ghat and Lolita Ghat herdsmen drove oxen clattering down the steps to drink and wallow, while dogs and goats scavenged in the garbage at the water's edge, and high above, on the ancient parapets, monkeys capered, arrogant and obscene.

Raffee heard a noise behind him and turned to see that the family from Bihar was awake and the mother was priming a kerosene burner to make chai. He looked over to where his father lay and saw he was still sleeping peacefully.

"Is he all right?" Mushtak asked.

Raffee's elder brother was awake and sitting up amidst a tangle of blankets.

"*Acha*," Raffee said.

Mushtak scrubbed his face with his hands then crawled over to his father to see for himself. He put an ear to the old man's open mouth and listened. He felt for a pulse, first at the wrist then at the neck. Then he opened his father's eyes, studied them closely, and closed them again.

"*Laloo*," he said. It was Hindi for fool. "He's dead."

Raffee hurried over to see for himself. "He was all right a minute ago. He was dreaming."

"He was dying," Mushtak said.

▪ ▪

The old man's body burned quickly. His spirit soared exuberantly skyward with the flames, glad to be free of its earthbound misery. When it was over not a scrap of bone remained among the ash. Raffee wasn't surprised. His father had been little more than kindling when he died. They need not have wasted money on two hundred kilos of wood when a hundred would have done. To Raffee's further disgust, Mushtak insisted on tipping the kulis who built the pyre, because there was no jewelry on their father's corpse. When rich people were burned, the kulis raked through the embers afterward, claiming for themselves any rings, gemstones, or gold fillings.

Raffee thought his elder brother was too much like their father. A prisoner of superstition determined to keep the family poor while he squandered what little money there was on ceremony.

Only one final act of obeisance remained. Mushtak and his brothers would walk the short distance to Dasashwadh Ghat, where they would bathe in the river and cleanse their souls before the journey home. Their mother and sister would do the same at Meer Ghat, the women's bathing ghat. Raffee was impatient to go home, to get on the train to Faizabad, where his future waited, and he followed his brothers grudgingly, resentment weighing every step.

It was mid-morning and the ghats seethed with pilgrims, most of whom had traveled great distances and endured great hardship for the chance to immerse themselves in the embrace of Mother Ganga, where the distinctions of caste were temporarily put aside, where Kshatriya bathed with Sudra, and ash-smeared followers of Shiva bathed alongside the red-daubed disciples of Vishnu, all of them equal in the eyes of God.

Mushtak added to Raffee's irritation by making them wait while he paid a hundred rupees for a priest's indifferent blessing. Then he led them down through the noisy, jostling crowds till they were within a few steps of the water's edge. They took off their clothes and left them folded neatly on the steps with the others, magically untouched by all the milling, dripping feet. They removed everything but the dhoti and nigota, the loincloth and thread wound over the left shoulder to show the sacred connection to the universe. Only Raffee hung back, immune to the holiday mood of the crowd, and refused to take off his clothes.

"Hurry up," Mushtak said impatiently. "You won't get this chance again. Next time you'll have to pay your own way."

Raffee looked at his brother's shaven head and thought it looked stupid. A vein pulsed at the left temple, and Raffee wanted to put his thumb on it and squeeze it till his brother fainted and left him alone.

"I don't care about a next time," Raffee said.

Mushtak stared angrily at him.

"I'm not going in," Raffee insisted.

The noise of the crowd was terrific and Mushtak wasn't sure he had heard his brother right. Amar and Ramua were already in the water playing, enjoying this part of the ritual.

"What do you mean you're not going in?"

"I'm not wearing the nigota," Raffee said. "I don't wear it anymore."

"It doesn't matter," Mushtak said. "Go in the way you are. You need to cleanse your soul more than anybody."

"The water's full of shit," Raffee said. "Look at it, it's full of shit." He waved dismissively at the devotions going on around them. "It's bullshit," he said. "All of it—it's bullshit."

Mushtak looked alarmed. "Be quiet, you'll get yourself killed."

"I don't take orders from you," Raffee answered. "You're stupid, just like him. I only did it so he would die happy. I don't have to do it for you."

Mushtak sighed. He had known something like this was coming, but hoped it would keep till they got home and he could handle it properly. He couldn't deal with it here, not now on the sacred ghats. The two of them locked eyes, caught in a contest of wills amidst the unheeding swirl of people. Mushtak opened his mouth to speak but was stopped by a child's shrill scream of pain above the drone of the crowd. Like everyone else, he turned to see what was wrong.

There was a boy in the water, twenty or thirty feet out from the ghats, and he was drowning. A man swam out to him with another close behind. The boy screamed and beat at the water as if to drive off something that tried to pull him down.

A snake, Raffee thought, or a crocodile. All manner of vile creatures lurked beneath that sinister brown surface.

There was another scream and another and then a terrible cry went up all along the ghats. There were hundreds of bathers in the water and something had attacked them too. Panic spread along the riverbank as people rushed up the great steps, pushing aside those who were coming down to bathe. Children and old men fell and were trampled in the panic. Others were thrown back into the water. The river turned to foam as an unseen terror snatched at one bather after another.

Raffee stared at the frenzy that had erupted so suddenly around him. Then, in the middle of the river, he saw something. A body. Then another and another. The bodies of people and animals together, dozens of them now, drifting downstream. Then he realized that whatever was in the water would attack his brothers too.

Mushtak was ahead of him, fighting his way through the mass of terrified faces surging up the ghats. Raffee followed, shouting his brothers' names. Mushtak leaped off the bottom step toward Amar. As he hit the water he locked a hand around Amar's arm and heaved him toward the shore. Raffee was waiting and pulled him to safety. Mushtak lunged toward Ramua, but before he could close the gap something took him by the legs and he cried out in pain. He twisted and thrashed with such violence he lifted himself half out of the water. Then he slipped and vanished in the maelstrom. Raffee jumped into the water and waded quickly to Ramua, grabbed him and pulled him to shore. A powerfully built man leaned out from the bottom step and took Ramua from him.

Raffee turned around, searching for Mushtak, and a thousand tiny teeth bit into his legs and tried to tear the flesh from his bones. He struggled back to the steps but slipped and almost went under when the man who had taken Ramua seized him by the wrist and pulled him clear. The man hurried up the lower ghats, dragging Raffee with him, afraid that whatever evil was in the water would come after them. There was nothing anyone could do anymore. The only people left in the water were the dead and the dying.

Raffee lay on the steps, winded, but the pain in his lower legs spread and intensified until it became unbearable, and he had to struggle upright to look at his injuries. His legs were blistered and latticed with welts that burned as if they were on fire. There were strands of glutinous gray scum where the burning was worst, but when he went to wipe it off it sent needles of fire deep into his flesh. He gasped and his eyes filled with tears. The pain was like nothing he had ever known before. He went to wipe the tears from his eyes but beads of gray scum clung to his fingertips and were already eating through his skin. He stopped and held his burning hands away from himself. Whatever the gray scum was, it was eating him alive.

He felt a prickling sensation on his body as if flames were burning through his wet clothes. Then he saw patches of scum on his shirt. He leaped to his feet and tore off every scrap of clothing until he was naked. For the first time he saw other cast-off clothing all around him, also tainted with flecks of oily scum. There were piles of dry clothes too, left by panicked bathers. He picked up a clean shirt and dabbed carefully at his body, wincing at the pain that flared with every touch but forcing himself to continue till all the scum was gone. When he was finished he pulled on a pair of men's trousers that were far too big for him, knotted them at the waist and rolled up the cuffs so they would not chafe at his wounds.

Then he looked around for his brothers—and his breath stopped at the awful spectacle that confronted him. The great ghats that only a few moments ago were filled with ecstatic pilgrims had been transformed into a scene of horror. Naked and half-naked bodies lay everywhere. Men and boys moaning, suffering, dying. Others moved among them trying to help but were overwhelmed by the scale of the disaster. For many of the injured there would be no help. Raffee saw a man coughing up globules of scum amidst gouts of dark red blood. There was another, half out of the water, his body covered with enormous blisters that continued to expand and erupt even though he was dead, till all that was left was raw flesh.

Raffee forced himself to keep looking. He picked his way through the bodies, calling his brothers' names. Amar was close by, curled into a tight knot, whimpering while a woman dabbed at the slime that webbed his lower body. Then Raffee saw Ramua propped against a step, his arms and legs splayed out from his body as if he couldn't stand their touch. His whole body was a mottled, scalded pink, and there were so many open, bleeding blisters on his legs there seemed to be no skin left. His hair had been scorched away and his scalp was so deeply cratered that bloody patches of skull were visible.

Raffee knelt down beside Ramua, no longer aware of his own pain.

"It's me," he said. "I'm here. I'll take care of you."

He balled the shirt in his hand and dabbed gently at the clinging beads of scum. A sound came from Ramua's mouth, no more than a whisper.

"I don't want you," he said. "I want Mushtak."

The shirt in Raffee's hand soon turned dark with blood. He found another and continued to dab futilely at his brother's wounds. Then he looked back at the water, to the place where Mushtak had disappeared.

What he saw was a scene from a nightmare. The river was clogged with corpses, hundreds of them; singly, in twos and threes, sometimes dozens tangled together in grisly rafts. Some seemed still to be alive as their limbs rose and fell in the current. But no one would rescue them. All the boats had gone from the river. There was nothing but desolation as far as anyone could see.

The woman tending Amar looked at Raffee.

"Mother Ganga is angry with us," she said. "We are no longer her children."

CHAPTER 2

"Your body is exceptional."

"But wasted on an old maid like me?" Pramila glanced at the young American woman seated at the other end of the change room.

"No . . ." Annie Ginnaro smiled to cover her embarrassment. "That isn't what I meant."

Annie was a newspaperwoman and liked to think of herself as unshockable, so Pramila took a special delight in shocking her.

"I just hope I keep my figure as well as you've kept yours," Annie added quickly.

"Well, you know, diet, some exercise . . ." Pramila emphasized the word *some*. "Oh, and a chaste lifestyle."

Annie sighed. "It's already too late."

Despite an age difference of more than thirty years, the two women enjoyed each other's company. They had already squandered most of the morning at Jayans, one of the oldest and grandest sari emporiums in Bombay, while Pramila shopped for a new sari. The two of them had the change room to themselves; Pramila stood at a full-length mirror wearing bra, pants, and a short-sleeved black choli. And Annie was right, Pramila was exceptional. Her skin had the healthy sheen of betel nut, and despite a certain heaviness around the hips, she had a good figure and remarkably unblemished legs. When she moved, she moved fluidly, with the grace of a woman in her thirties rather than her sixties. The only real indication of age was her gray hair, which she wore short and uncolored.

"I don't think you need deprive yourself quite as much as I have," she reassured Annie.

"It isn't for lack of attention," Annie said. "Men still look at you. I've seen them."

"Yes, but they don't want everything that comes with it, do they?" Pramila answered. "And I'm too set in my ways to change."

She picked up a bolt of silk the color of eggplant and splashed it across the floor like a can of paint. Deftly, she took one end, passed it between her thighs, wrapped it around her hips, and knotted it to form a dhoti. The rest she wound snugly around her waist, then looped it downward to form a skirt, then upward again to cover her torso until she was left with a train that hung crease-free from her left shoulder.

Annie watched, fascinated. It was the first time she had seen anyone put on a full nine-yard sari. Younger Indian women preferred western clothes or the popular smock and pants combination known as the *salwar khameez*. It was mostly the poor and the wealthy who clung to the sari, the former from necessity, the latter for tradition. Annie owned several versions of the *salwar khameez* and one tailored sari, which she knew was cheating. But she had yet to master the art of tying the full sari, and was afraid if she tried it would unravel and leave her half naked in a room full of strangers.

"Do you ever wonder what it might have been like if you'd married General Spooner?" she asked.

"No," Pramila answered.

"Never?"

"No."

"And you never blamed him, did you, for leaving you?"

"That is a very American attitude," Pramila said.

Annie looked mildly stung. "You never worried he was just using you?"

"I think he was using me."

"And you didn't mind?"

"Not at all," Pramila said. "We used each other."

The look in Annie's eyes said she thought she deserved better. Pramila relented. Her self-assurance was the polished armor of defenses acquired over a lifetime. The glib responses were often the quickest.

"The difference is we loved each other," she said. "We were lucky to have the time together we did. You have to remember it was different then. People did what they thought was right according to the times. It's never been a question of blame."

Though mollified, Annie still wanted to know more—she always wanted to know more. It was eighteen months since she had interviewed Pramila Sansi for the *Times of India*, and her questions hadn't stopped. Pramila was a senior lecturer in Women's Studies at the University of Bombay, a longtime crusader for women's rights and the author of several books on women's issues, all of which combined to make her one of the best-known feminists in the country.

At the time of their first meeting, Annie was a month out of Los Angeles and six months out of a bad marriage. She had moved to India to force change upon herself, to confront the cosy California values that no longer worked for her. She had known of Pramila's work before they met. She was particularly struck by something Pramila had written in her book *The Gilded Cage*, that American women were struggling to break through the glass ceiling while Indian women were struggling to break out of the eleventh century. The idea for a newspaper profile was the excuse Annie needed to meet Pramila. Their personalities meshed instantly; they shared the same sense of humor, the same expressive vulgarity. Unsurprisingly, they became friends. What surprised them both was that Annie would fall in love with Pramila's son.

George Sansi was an absurdly romantic figure who belonged to another time, but in India, with its jumbled cultures and its recent colonial past, he was very much part of the present. He was the flesh and blood legacy of a love affair between Pramila and a general in the British Army during the tumultuous last days of the Raj.

Pramila was from a monied background, the eldest daughter of a Gujerati shipping broker, a Vaishya who made his fortune trading with the British. At any other time he might have welcomed a liaison between one of his daughters and a British general. After all, British soldiers had been taking Indian women as their mistresses since the early days of the East India Company. But this was 1946, the Raj was dying, and India was riven by nationalist passions. With the British gone, Pramila's father depended on the favor of the incoming nationalist government. His daughter would have an arranged marriage to a senior official in the Congress Party and thereby protect her father's business interests. He ordered Pramila to have nothing more to do with General Spooner, and when she refused, he banished her from the family home, thinking a dose of hardship would change her mind. Her mother and sisters worked earnestly to reconcile the two, but when Pramila revealed she was pregnant with Spooner's child, her father publicly renounced her and his grandchild and forbade his family from ever seeing her again.

It was General Spooner who settled on Pramila a modest annuity and bought the apartment she still occupied on Malabar Hill—sold for a pittance by a fleeing servant of the Raj and now worth a fortune. But the general was married. While his heart belonged to Pramila, his duty was to family and country. There was never any doubt that when the British left he would return to his wife and children in England. When the steamer carrying the last British troops departed India in August 1947, General George Spooner was with them, leaving Pramila to bring up their son alone without the protection of family or caste in a country united only in its hatred for all things British.

The general had tried to persuade Pramila to have their child in Singapore and to wait there till India's convulsive bloodletting ceased. But Pramila would not be driven from her own country; she was determined that she and her child would be a part of the new, independent India. She endured the threats and insults directed at her and her outcast son with a quiet courage that impressed all those who met her. Eventually the storm passed and she set about building a career for herself at a time when it was impossible for an Indian woman to have an independent life.

Nor did the general forget them. When his wife died in the early 1960s, he revisited Bombay to see Pramila and his son. He later paid for George to take a law degree at Oxford and, against the protests of his other children, insisted that he stay at Goscombe Park, the family home outside Oxford city. It was during these years that George Sansi came to see what his mother had seen in the general—that he was the kindest and most honorable man in the world.

Annie Ginnaro found that instead of becoming embittered against the two societies that disowned him, George Sansi had grown up peculiarly tolerant of both. The struggles of a lifetime had made him stronger, not weaker. She understood that she had as much to learn from him as she did from the extraordinary woman who had made him.

"But it's so nice to blame everybody else when things go wrong," she said with a mock whine.

Pramila smiled. "Was your husband good in bed?"

Annie hesitated. "At times."

"So it wasn't all bad?"

Annie knew what Pramila was saying, but she still found it hard to run a fair balance sheet when it came to an unfaithful ex-husband. She got up to examine Pramila's handiwork with the sari more closely.

"You even got this little ruche thing happening in the back," she said. "How do you do that?"

"I'll show you," Pramila said.

She gave the sari a few last tucks, then led the way back out to the store. As Annie followed she noticed how the sari was loose enough to be comfortable but how it also accentuated the contours of the female body and exaggerated the sway of the hips. Annie heard the soft rasp of silk against skin and understood that the sari worked on all the senses and not just the eye.

"I guess I know now why there's a billion people in this country," she said.

"And you never feel cheap in silk," Pramila answered.

"Not at these prices," Annie agreed.

She thought she might buy a sari too but had balked at the expense. The rest of the world thought India was a poor country, but Bombay was a rich city. The multitude of beggars in the streets were a sign of its wealth, not its poverty—they were there for the crumbs that fell from the rich man's table.

A small, slender man with glasses and a florid tie against a brilliant white shirt waited patiently for them to emerge from the change room.

"Oh, memsahib . . ." His hand went to his forehead as if to shield himself from Pramila's radiance. "You are honoring us by wearing our clothings."

"You mean it is free if I tell my friends I got it here?" Pramila teased.

Mr. Bose, the under-assistant floor manager, chuckled, unamused. "Where beauty is concerned, memsahib, price is no obstacle."

"My friend would like to look at some saris too," Pramila said.

"For the same occasion?" Mr. Bose asked.

Pramila wanted her sari for a party she was giving the coming Saturday.

"Yes," Annie said. "But I don't want to take out a mortgage."

Mr. Bose gave Annie an appraising look; thirtyish, attractive, medium-long red hair, leggy rather than busty, expensive khaki slacks and short-sleeve white blouse. His smile never faltered.

"You are American," he said.

"I live here," she countered. "On an Indian paycheck."

"We take MasterCard, Visa, American Express."

Annie sighed. To shopkeepers her white skin meant only one thing—a walking wallet.

"You are wanting the nine-yard sari or the six-yard sari?" Mr. Bose inquired.

"Six yards," Pramila answered for her.

"Please, come."

The Jayans showroom was not one large room, but a series of small, interconnected rooms on several levels with twisting staircases and shadowy landings, a vast technicolor labyrinth created by knocking down the adjoining walls of several town houses. Every room was furnished with floor-to-ceiling shelves and display cases jammed tight with multihued bolts of cloth that glowed like gemstones in a vault. Ruby reds, sapphire blues, emerald greens, platinum whites, many of them shot with threads of real silver and gold or encrusted with pearls.

Most of the fabrics were silks from the great silk producing centers of India, but not all. There were also printed cottons, gauzy taffetas, gossamer-fine organzas, and exquisite cashmeres to make scarves, jackets, and shawls. The whole place smelled of unaffordable richness, and it made Annie nervous.

Mr. Bose led his customers to another treasure cave and gestured to a wall piled high with silken ingots.

"All six-yard saris, memsahib," he said. "All Kanchivaram silk. Finest denier."

"Kanchivaram?" Annie echoed.

"Acha." Mr. Bose pointed to the sari Pramila was wearing. "Same silk as Sansi, memsahib."

"It comes from the town of Kanchivaram near Madras," Pramila said. "It's supposed to be the best silk in India."

"I think I should look at something else," Annie decided.

"Please." Mr. Bose led them jauntily to the next room.

"Maybe I should be looking someplace else," Annie whispered to Pramila.

"They have the best selection here," Pramila said.

"Yeah, and just a little out of my price range."

"They are pricey," Pramila conceded. "But I have always found them good value for money."

Annie was starting to wonder whose side Pramila was on, but before she could say anything more Mr. Bose stopped them again.

"All Benares silk." He waved at a new display. "Very fine quality."

"Benares?" Annie added.

"Varanasi," Pramila said. "It's our holiest city . . . where the pilgrims go."

"Oh."

Five months earlier the news had been dominated by reports of a chemical spill into the Ganges at Varanasi. Hundreds of pilgrims had been killed and thousands more horribly crippled.

"I don't think I could wear anything that would support industry in that town," Annie said.

"The silk comes from places all around Varanasi," Pramila said. "It could come from a factory miles away."

It was true. No one had traced the source of the spill yet and the outcry that followed was already fading. Disasters on that scale weren't uncommon in India, though Annie couldn't forget what kind of uproar would ensue if something similar happened in the United States.

"Can I see something that isn't worth its weight in gold?" she said. "Or, you know, didn't cost maybe a thousand human lives?"

Unperturbed, Mr. Bose led them to yet another room.

"Very fine quality," he said. "Not so expensive."

Annie thought she heard sarcasm in his voice. She studied the stacked bolts of material for a moment, then pointed to one that was a deep wine color.

"Can I see that one?"

Mr. Bose pulled out the cloth and threw it the length of a display case so that it unfurled with a spectacular flourish of color. Annie felt the material between her fingers then pressed it against her cheek.

"I like the color," she said. "And it feels pretty soft—what kind of silk is it?"

"Not silk," Mr. Bose announced. "Polyester."

"Polyester?" Annie smiled thinly. "I'm not buying a sari made from polyester."

"Polyester very popular," Mr. Bose insisted. "Very fine quality."

Annie thought Mr. Bose was making fun of her.

"There must be some silk here that doesn't cost an arm and a leg," she said.

Mr. Bose spread his arms expansively. "Benares, Kanchivaram, Kota, Kollegal, Mysore, Chanderi, Pochampalli . . . what you like, memsahib?"

His message was clear—they had it all. But how much was she willing to pay?

She looked to Pramila for help.

"I think you should reconsider the Kanchivaram," Pramila said.

Annie's spirits sank. Both of them had turned against her.

"Okay," she said. "Just what kind of price range are we looking at?"

Mr. Bose shrugged. "Five, six thousand for low denier. Very best denier, best design, gold thread—fifty, a hundred thousand."

Annie looked appalled. Fifty thousand rupees worked out at around fifteen hundred dollars. For something she would wear maybe three or four times.

"You don't have to spend that much," Pramila said.

"No kidding."

"You can find something very nice for between ten and fifteen thousand."

Annie did the conversion in her head. "I can't justify spending five hundred dollars," she said. "I can afford two hundred—tops."

"Why don't we just take a look," Pramila pressed.

Mr. Bose led them confidently back to the priciest selections in the store.

A scant half hour later it was Annie's turn to stand at the dressing room mirror. The sari she had chosen was a pattern of black and silver teardrops against a deep claret background with an intricate border of black and gold. Pramila had shown her how to tie it snugly so it clung to her figure with a serpentine sheen. Annie had to admit, she had never worn anything that covered so much of her yet made her feel so indecent. The sari was not only thrilling to look at, it was thrilling to wear.

"This is definitely an R-rated garment," she said.

"The other women are going to hate you," Pramila added.

"It's worth getting just for that, isn't it?"

"I think so."

"Yeah," she sighed. "But it's too much."

"To look like that?"

"Pramila, it's seven hundred dollars."

"Stop complaining, it's already taken care of."

Again Annie looked embarrassed. "I can't," she said. "I can find something else."

"Actually, it is a very good price for that quality silk," Pramila said. "And I want to get you a present."

"No." Annie shook her head. "It's too much."

"It is not just a present for you," Pramila coaxed. "I think George will appreciate it too."

"I'm sorry." Annie smiled, apologetic. "I just wouldn't feel comfortable."

"You think I am trying to buy your affection?"

When Annie was slow to answer, Pramila added mischievously: "Do you come so cheap?"

"Jesus . . ." Annie became flustered. "Look, I'll get it, but I'll pay for it."

"I would be very offended." Pramila's voice had turned serious.

Annie stood, awkward and silent.

"You think I'm doing this just because you are involved with my son?" Pramila asked.

"Well, it's understandable . . ." A little less certainly she added: "Isn't it?"

Pramila chose her next words carefully.

"You know, Annie, I have been honest with people all my life, often to my cost," she said. "I think you know that. So I hope you will believe me when I tell you this isn't only about you and George. I want you to be happy, of course, but whether you are happy together or separately is your business. What I want to do now is give you something beautiful and unique, something from India." She paused before going on. "If you don't want the sari because you don't like it, tell me and I won't say another word. But don't tell me you don't want it because you think I'm a foolish old woman and I don't know what I'm doing."

Annie felt as if she'd been mugged. She stared at herself in the mirror. Then she relaxed.

"I love it," she said.

Pramila sighed.

"Americans are so funny," she said. "You make the simplest things so complicated."

CHAPTER 3

"**G**eorge?" Annie tried to sound calm. "There are men with machine guns in the apartment."

Sansi sat on the end of the bed. He wore a pair of black dress trousers and a freshly pressed white shirt with dangling French cuffs that kept getting in the way while he put on his socks. He stopped with a sock halfway up his left foot, a worried look on his face.

"You haven't been writing about the government again, have you?"

Annie looked into his mocking blue eyes, his father's eyes.

"Don't be such a prick," she said.

Sansi finished pulling on his socks. "They are making sure everything is secure," he said. "You won't see them when the party has started."

She shut the bedroom door and turned the lock. "Who's coming, the Prime Minister?"

"Close," Sansi said. "The new minister for the environment, Rupe Seshan."

Realization dawned in Annie's eyes. She shouldn't have been

surprised. Rupe Seshan was one of many prominent women in Pramila's extensive circle of friends. She had been active in Indian political life for twenty years, first as the glamorous and outspoken wife of Mani Seshan, a member of the federal parliament for the Hindu nationalist Bharatiya Janata Party and a man seen by many as a future Prime Minister. He had been killed by a car bomb in New Delhi three years earlier, leaving Rupe a widow with two young children. Instead of retiring from public life she had sworn on her husband's ashes to finish the work he had begun to free the government from the curse of corruption. In the election that followed she easily won her husband's seat, and now that the Bharatiya Janata Party had come to power, Rupe had been given the environment portfolio.

"And neither of you said anything to me?"

"State secret," Sansi said. "I didn't know myself until today."

"But you wouldn't have told me if you had?"

He thought about it for a moment then said: "No."

He went to the dresser and poked around in a mahogany stud box for a pair of cuff links. He ignored the flimsy wafers of gold held together by chains his mother had given him one birthday and chose instead a pair of sturdy onyx ovals with clasps that he had bought for himself on his last trip to London. He fussed with his cuffs for a minute, all the while muttering under his breath.

"Here." Annie got up and fastened them for him, her eyes never leaving his face. He was older than her by twelve years, though there was a plumpness to his face that made him look young, almost boyish. His hair, worn longish and brushed back from his forehead, was still damp from the shower, making its few strands of gray stand out more. Annie noticed how much darker his skin looked against the whiteness of his shirt. She thought it uncanny how he looked darker when he wore western clothes and lighter when he wore Indian clothes, as if nature had played a trick on him to remind him and the world that wherever he was, he did not belong.

"You think you'll be able to get this new sari of yours on and keep it on?" he asked. "I'd hate to see you embarrass yourself tonight."

She wore the same blue jeans and dirty blue T-shirt she had worn all day while she helped Pramila get ready for the party. The caterers had arrived a few minutes ahead of the men with machine guns and were setting up spirit lamps on the dining room table while the cooks unpacked all the ingredients for supper in the kitchen.

"Give me ten minutes," Annie said. "Then ask Pramila to give me a hand."

"I'm looking forward to seeing it," Sansi said.

Annie smiled. Without taking her eyes away from his, she took off her T-shirt then kicked off her jeans and panties so she stood in front of him nude. Then she went up on her toes and gave him a long, open-mouthed kiss. An exciting heat radiated from her body, and he felt rather than heard the soft rasp of her nipples against his shirt. His hands went to her waist and he felt the burn of her flesh, the inviting swell of her hips. She reached down and gave him a gentle pat.

"Try not to embarrass yourself too much tonight," she said. Then she walked quickly to the bathroom and closed the door behind her. A moment later he heard the shower running and the sound of her humming unconcernedly to herself.

Sansi turned to the dresser and picked up a black silk tie. He avoided his own gaze in the mirror and struggled to tie a decent knot. It took him several tries before his fingers stopped trembling enough to get it right. By the time he had put on his shoes and his white dinner jacket, he thought he might just be composed enough to go outside.

■   ■

Sansi found his mother in the living room, wearing her new sari, talking to an army officer with a captain's flashes on his shoulders. Four or five other soldiers were visible, some inside, some outside on the roof garden watching the nearby apartment buildings. All the soldiers were armed with modern light machine guns; a lot of firepower for one cabinet minister at a party, though bloody experience said it was necessary.

"Hello, darling," Pramila said when she saw her son. "This is Captain Ramani. He's in charge of security for Rupe. Captain, this is my son, George."

The two men shook hands, Sansi aware that the palms of his hands were a little too moist, thanks to Annie.

"Darling, you're very flushed," his mother said. "You're not coming down with something are you?"

"A little warm from the shower, that's all," Sansi explained.

"Sir, your mother tells me you were in the police service?" Captain Ramani said.

"*Acha.*" Sansi was glad to change the subject.

"And I believe you had some success against the Naxalites in Tamori?"

"In another lifetime," Sansi said. Before he dusted off his law degree, Sansi had been an officer in the police service of Maharashtra, spending his first year in the remote and lawless eastern districts where he had seen action against Marxist terrorists, action that made him a hero of sorts but also left its scars and made him reluctant to discuss the experience with strangers.

"But you were decorated for bravery?" Ramani persisted. He patted a modest cluster of campaign ribbons over his chest pocket. "I had a little fun myself chasing the Paks around the Valley."

Ramani was in his mid-twenties, eyes full of ambition and a military moustache intended to make him look older.

Sansi politely waggled his head from side to side. Apparently, Ramani wanted to impress these friends of the minister with stories of his adventures against Pakistani insurgents in the Vale of Kashmir. It was understandable. Powerful friends could often assist an ambitious young army officer. Sansi wanted to tell Ramani to relax. For all their friendship with Rupe Seshan, he and his mother carried little weight with the *babus* of New Delhi.

"Well then, you know exactly how it is," Sansi said. "Long periods of boredom interrupted by sudden fright. If you're lucky you get out alive, and some people confuse that with bravery."

Ramani was not easily deterred. "A good officer makes his own luck," he said, trying to sound worldly.

Sansi smiled blandly and turned to his mother. "Annie needs your help with the sari," he said.

"Oh, of course . . ." Pramila looked guilty. "I'll go right away."

"There is someone else in the apartment?" Ramani said.

"Yes, a friend," Sansi said.

"Is she staying here?"

"No," Sansi said.

"Yes," Pramila said.

"Sometimes," Sansi added.

Ramani looked confused.

"Her name is Annie Ginnaro," Pramila added. "She's American. She stays here sometimes."

"Ginnaro?" Ramani repeated. He pulled a sheet of paper from his breast pocket. "I don't have that name listed."

Sansi looked at his mother and knew she had forgotten to put Annie's name on the list.

"I'm going to get a drink," he said. "You can tell Annie she's not invited."

He walked past the sliding glass doors that led out to the roof garden. Behind him he heard Pramila explaining to Ramani: "She is a guest but I didn't put her down as a guest because I don't think of her as a guest. She's like a member of the family only she is not exactly a member of the family, you see . . . ?"

Sansi went to the temporary bar and asked for a *stengah*. A tall glass with ice, bitters, and a half shot of whiskey topped with soda. One of the more enjoyable customs of the Raj that Indians had kept for themselves. A couple of soldiers loitered at the stone parapet. Sansi nodded as he passed them and kept going to a quiet, unoccupied corner of the terrace. Like many of Malabar Hill's residents, Pramila had turned it into a garden by stocking it with potted palms, shrubs, and a few tropical fruit trees; banana and papaya for breakfast and limes for her evening gin and tonic. She had rejected the trend set by some of her neighbors who had carpeted their terraces with turf.

Sansi sipped his drink and looked over the dark crescent of Back Bay to the brilliant skyline of a modern city on the opposite shore, its sins hidden by the discreet mantle of night. Bombay had started on the other side of the bay; little more than a fishing village on a scrubby salt flat when the Portuguese took it from the local sultan in the early 1500s. Its name came from the mouthless goddess, Maha-Amba-Aiee, which the natives pronounced Mumbai. But the Portuguese didn't stay long in Mumbai. When they realized they were marooned at the end of a chain of salt marsh islands pocked with mangroves, infested by mosquitoes, and dissected by flooding creeks, they moved north to the mainland and built their fortress at Bassein. They kept Mumbai as a trading outpost until a century later, when they yielded it to the British as part of Catherine of Braganza's dowry to Charles II. The British already had Calcutta and Madras on the east coast, but were looking for a foothold on the west. By demanding Mumbai in a marriage contract, they got it without a fight. It was only when they surveyed the malarial seven-island archipelago that they realized they'd been duped. Mumbai was uninhabitable.

When the Portuguese refused them better land, the British decided they would make a colony out of Mumbai anyway. They put their stamp on the place in a singularly British way; tin-eared officers interpreted the native pronunciation of Mumbai as Bombay, and once they had written it into their first dispatches they weren't inclined to change it.

Sansi thought it only fitting that Bombay should be born out of deception—the most constant form of human commerce and one that was woven into the character of the city from the beginning. Those other constants, vice and corruption, followed naturally. The first soldiers and traders eased their hardships with toddy, a native liquor distilled from palm sap, Indian hemp, which many Europeans found more pleasurable than tobacco, and native women. In return they contributed the spice of venereal disease to the stew of tropical maladies already rife in the colony. Drunkenness, drug addiction, and disease produced a death rate so high it seemed the Portuguese would get their wish and the rival outpost would disappear into the pestilential vapors that shrouded the peninsula.

But London decided Bombay was strategically too important to abandon, and poured in men and money. Army engineers dammed the creeks, drained the marshes, and put in clean water tanks. Roads were surveyed, farms and orchards planted, warehouses and churches built. No-nonsense administrators and church ministers were sent out to fortify the population with some much needed moral backbone. The city's future was assured when the Company of Merchant Adventurers to the East Indies, forerunner to the East India Company, declared Bombay a center of trade and the first great docks were built to refit its eastern fleets. As Bombay prospered, so the Portuguese colony of Bassein languished, until the middle of the eighteenth century when, under threat from a local warlord, the Portuguese withdrew to Goa far to the south, leaving Britain the only European power in the entire northwest.

By the early 1800s Bombay was Britain's most important city between Suez and Shanghai. The more its reputation grew, the more it became a magnet for rogues and adventurers seeking a share of the trade in silk, spices, ivory, tea, and opium, and all the other cravings of the flesh. In the boom years that followed, Bombay expanded upward through the archipelago, jumping the creeks, filling in the mangrove swamps, paving over the salt marshes, cementing the islands together with the glue of commerce. The British enhanced the city with jewels of civic architecture, and soon its clean and leafy streets, its open maidans, its palatial clubs, and its racy but elegant ambience made it the most sought-after posting in the Empire.

Now it was the biggest and richest city in India. An economic law unto itself, immune to the depressions that afflicted the rest of the country. A city state powered by its own momentum, which paid more than half the nation's taxes. It was also a victim of its own success. Built for a population of a million, it had been swollen by greed to become home to more than twelve million. Its great buildings had become crowded and soiled, its once fashionable town houses cannibalized into over-crowded tenements, its green maidans eroded by ramshackle apartment buildings and barracks-like chawls, its widest side-walks and meanest alleyways clogged with the festering shanties of the poor.

But the boom continued and fortunes were still to be made, so the rogues and adventurers came in greater numbers than ever before. The faces had changed—they were more likely to be Indian now than European—though the eyes were still the same.

Sansi's thoughts were interrupted by a blast of noise. Some-one had turned on the sound system too loud, and Mrs. Khanna, the *bai*, was yelling in her high shrill voice. The noise receded to something melodic; ghazals from Sajda, a popular album of a few years earlier. Then he heard other voices, the sound of the first guests arriving. He decided it was time to be sociable. He turned to go inside and stopped. Annie had been waiting for him to turn around.

He knew what was expected and it was easy to oblige. She looked breathtaking. Pramila had wound the sari tight so it flowed across Annie's body like liquid metal, accentuating every point and curve. She wasn't wearing a choli, so her shoulders and the upper swells of her breasts were bare. Her coppery hair was complemented by the sari's deep reds and framed a face that a scant half hour ago had been playfully lewd and was now merely provocative. She wore a necklace that Sansi hadn't seen in a long time. A fine gold mesh studded with rubies that matched the rubies in her ears. A gift from an infatuated British officer to his young Indian mistress.

"Are Bapre," Sansi breathed. It was Hindi for *My God*. "Who is it—Padma, Jaladhija, Chanchala?"

"One of those better be a compliment," Annie said.

"The faces of Lakshmi," he said. "Temptresses every one."

She smiled and did a half turn. Silken eddies glimmered beneath her breasts, between her thighs.

"You think it's tight enough?"

His mother, watching from the open doorway, answered for him. "You'd better keep an eye on her. There are movie people coming tonight, they'll take her away from you."

Sansi gave Annie a kiss on the cheek. She smelled of jasmine, his favorite perfume. She had also put a costume *thikka* in the middle of her forehead, the same shade of red in her sari.

"I think somebody enjoyed dressing you up," he said. He spoke quietly so his mother wouldn't hear, but it was a wasted effort.

"I always wanted a girl." Pramila shrugged and disappeared inside.

■   ■

By ten-thirty the apartment was jammed, the music had changed from lyric Indian folk to thumping American pop and the party could be declared a success with or without Rupe Seshan, who had yet to make an appearance. It was a party typical of both Pramila and Bombay: a chaotic mélange of cultures, castes, and creeds in which prejudices were put on hold in pursuit of the greater goal of a good time. The only tense moment came when Captain Ramani caught some of Pramila's students smoking ganja on the terrace, and Sansi made them promise they wouldn't do anything more that night to ruin the reputations of his mother or the minister.

When Annie and Sansi next saw each other, he was talking with his associate, Mukherjee, a law school graduate he had found hustling clients on the sidewalk outside the Bombay Sessions Court. Mukherjee was with a sullen-eyed beauty in a glittering sequined jacket with a black bustier and black Lycra tights, whose long hair had been teased into the fashionably unkempt look. Her name was Neisha, she said, and she was a model.

"Neisha was the jeans girl in the Bare Necessities campaign," Mukherjee explained.

Annie shook her head.

"The one with the horse," Neisha said.

"She was only wearing the jeans," Mukherjee added. "Totally topless. Very naughty."

As if at an audition, Neisha added: "I have been horseback riding since I was nine years old and also waterskiing, playing the piano, and doing the modern dance."

"I must have seen it," Annie said, knowing immediately it was the wrong thing to say.

"Neisha is planning a new career in the movies," Mukherjee continued enthusiastically. "I was telling her this party is an excellent opportunity because the bigwigs from all the entertainment fields are coming here this evening. It is possible, Miss Annie, you would consider a story in the newspaper about Neisha . . . ?"

But Neisha was already scanning the crowd for more important faces. She spotted a well-known TV director and tugged at Mukherjee's sleeve. He gave Annie an apologetic shrug and went off with Neisha in search of bigger game.

"It's always fun to see what happens when a couple of gold diggers get together," Annie said as she watched them go.

"Oh." Sansi looked surprised. "You don't think it will last?"

"I'd put money on it she leaves with somebody else."

"I don't think you should count Mukherjee out too soon."

"He doesn't stand a chance."

"He is very persuasive," Sansi added. "He knows what people want—and he's a better lawyer than me. Another year or two and I will be working for him."

"She's already got what she wants," Annie said. "She's here— she can dump him anytime she wants, and he doesn't get anything in return."

"Don't underestimate him. He has a habit of getting what he wants."

Annie looked suspicious. "You know something you're not telling me?"

Sansi smiled. "They are cousins," he said. "He negotiates all her contracts. If she gets any leads tonight, he gets twenty percent."

"Inside information," Annie sniffed. "Doesn't count."

"Mukherjee is excited by money, not sex," Sansi added. "That is why I employ him. That is why he won't sleep with Neisha— and because his uncle Bakul would very probably kill him."

The two of them sipped their drinks, Sansi trying not to look smug. Then his gaze settled on another couple.

"But that is something I don't understand," he said confidentially.

Annie followed his eye to a balding, middle-aged man with a white suit, a black open-neck shirt, and a cluster of gold chains. He was with a woman clearly half his age, sleekly beautiful in a billowy yellow blouse and a miniskirt that showed off impressively long bare legs. She pretended to listen to the bald man but her eyes were restless.

"I know her," Annie said. "I don't know her name but she's in the movies, right?"

"Anita Vasi," Sansi added. "She's not a big name. I'm surprised to see Shankar with her. I thought he had more sense."

"Who is he?"

"He's a producer at Film City. He used to be in television. He did a series of documentaries about the women's movement. That's how he knows my mother. Considering the rubbish he's done lately, he probably wishes he was back in television."

"So why shouldn't he be with Anita Vasi?"

"From what I understand, she is one of Johnny Jenta's girls," Sansi said.

Annie grimaced. Many of Bombay's gangsters had laughably melodramatic names, though there was nothing laughable about the fear they inspired. Jenta was a legend in the Bombay underworld, having been around since the 1960s, which was more a tribute to his cunning than his courage. He ran the craft unions at Film City, the state-owned studio complex that turned out three times more movies each year than Hollywood. While his name never appeared in any credits, it was impossible to make a picture at Film City without his approval—and that made him the most powerful movie tycoon in India.

"Either Jenta has finished with her or Shankar is keeping an eye on her for him," Sansi said. "For his sake, I hope he isn't doing anything stupid."

At that moment Shankar leaned closer to Anita Vasi and whispered something. She pretended to be amused.

"Maybe she's just on the make, like everybody else," Annie said. "You can't blame her for wanting to do better than Jenta."

"*Acha,*" Sansi agreed. "And that is what makes her dangerous—Shankar should remember that."

There was a stir inside the apartment and a scattering of applause. The applause grew and Sansi and Annie realized that at last Rupe Seshan had arrived. Neither of them could see her in the press of the crowd, but a moment later they heard her voice striving to be heard through the thump of the music.

"Please, everyone, I appreciate your welcome," she was saying. "But I am here like the rest of you to relax with my friend, Pramila Sansi. And as everyone knows, we are all equal in Pramila's eyes."

"Good line," Annie said.

It had the desired effect. The applause faded as those who considered themselves equal to Rupe Seshan went back to their own conversations. Rupe's arrival was also the signal for the food to be served. Dinner was usually served late at parties but this was late even by Bombay's standards. When the lids came off the silver chafing dishes and the aroma of curried meats and steaming biryanis permeated the apartment, Pramila's guests were reminded they had been partying on empty stomachs. Lines formed quickly at the buffet tables and the mood of the party sobered quickly.

Almost as if Pramila had planned it that way, Annie thought, as she put a few morsels on her plate. She found a seat in the living room where she could observe Rupe Seshan from a distance. Her first impression was how small and frail Rupe Seshan looked in contrast to her dynamic public image. She was little more than five feet tall, with fine features and tiny hands and feet. Her hair was cut short to give her an elfin prettiness that seduced every camera pointed at her. Her familiar, crooked smile was more pronounced on television than in real life. When she spoke, it was in short, confident bursts scripted for sound bites.

Though Rupe came from old money, she dressed with unusual restraint. Bombay society women tended to use parties as occasions to flaunt their wealth, competing to see who had the most gorgeous sari or the most beautiful jewelry. Rupe's sari was an unembellished sea green except for a stripe of red and gold embroidery at the hem. She wore a modest amount of jewelry, but what she wore was eye-catching. Her necklace was an antique, a gold filigree with a fringe of tiny disks engraved in Sanskrit. She wore matching disks on her ears and a plain gold stud in her left nostril. Her only rings were a gold wedding band and a diamond and emerald engagement ring, poignant reminders of the tragedy that had thrust her into the national spotlight.

Annie was also impressed by the ease with which Rupe switched from one language to another. In half an hour she moved from English to Marathi to Hindi to Bengali and back again to English. Annie had been embarrassed to find that most educated Indians were fluent in four or five languages, while she had mastered Hindi only to the point where she could trade insults with shopkeepers and taxi drivers.

Pramila made a point of drawing Annie into the conversation, and while Rupe seemed receptive, there were so many demands for her attention there was an inevitable reserve. Annie slipped back into watchful silence. It was this watchfulness that enabled her to observe a marked change in Rupe's demeanor when Sansi came into the room. Where she had been polite to everyone else, she seemed excited to see Sansi. Her smile seemed more spontaneous, more genuine. She insisted he sit near her, and when he spoke she listened more attentively to him than to anyone else. And something else. Annie had seen a look pass between them she didn't much care for. A look that spoke of a history between them, a history where Annie did not belong.

CHAPTER 4

By two in the morning all had departed except a few close friends. Rupe had taken off her sandals and curled her feet up on the sofa, her toenails like drops of blood against the pale damask. She also wore a gold chain with disks that jingled prettily on her left ankle. Only in India was it possible to meet a cabinet minister with an ankle chain, Annie thought.

"You think winning an election is difficult," Rupe was saying. "It is only the beginning. When you get to Delhi, that is when the real fighting starts."

"Because you are a woman?" someone asked.

"Because she is pretty," Pramila added.

"If that were all, then time would take care of everything," Rupe said. "The real problem is that politicians have so little power to change anything. It is only when you get inside the government you realize there has been no transfer of power at all. It is the *babus* who rule India, not the politicians—we only get in the way."

"Even Indira had to learn to live with the public service," Sansi said referring to the despotic former Prime Minister.

"Indira was a career politician," Rupe answered. "I am not. I am the *babus'* worst nightmare because I don't care about getting re-elected. I am there to get things done this time, not next time."

"Your director must be wondering what he has done to deserve you," Pramila said.

"You should have been at our first cabinet meetings," Rupe said. "They couldn't make up their minds who they wanted me to get first."

"I thought you always wanted Environment?" Pramila added.

"I did," Rupe said. "But they know they're going to have problems with Haksar at Energy, and they want to get rid of Patel at the Justice Ministry too."

"So they are using you as their hit woman?" Pramila said.

"*Acha.*" Rupe laughed. "That is exactly it. I am their hit woman."

Nobody was especially shocked by Rupe's remarks about the federal bureaucracy. It was well-known that the government was run by a cadre of about six thousand officers of the Indian Administrative Service who controlled a work force in excess of three million. All IAS officers went through the Lal Bahadur Shastri National Academy of Administration in Mussoorie, which was the crucible for an old boys network that ran more efficiently than anything else in government. Stories were rife about department directors who kept ministers in the dark or simply formulated and implemented policies without them. The idea that a novice minister, a celebrity widow elected on a wave of public sentiment, might successfully challenge an experienced and entrenched director was preposterous. Clearly Rupe was to be sacrificed in the attempt.

"And who is the lucky man at Environment?" Sansi asked.

"His name is Shukla," Rupe said. "And he knows we are in a duel to the death."

"If you get rid of him, you think the others will fall into step?" Sansi asked.

"It is the way with all bullies," Rupe said. "You first have to beat one to show the others they are not invincible."

"They will gang up on you," Pramila warned. "They protect themselves by protecting each other."

"I know," Rupe said. "That is why I have to destroy Shukla completely—his name, his reputation—so there will be no sympathy for him. So no one will raise their voice in protest."

She said it lightly, easily. But no one who heard it doubted that the dainty creature with the painted toenails was capable of doing just what she threatened.

"Does he know he is in a duel to the death?" Sansi asked.

"Oh yes," Rupe answered. "And he is doing everything he can to help me."

"He doesn't take you seriously," Pramila said.

"I am the latest in a long line of ministers to challenge him," Rupe said. "And certainly the least intimidating."

"He will underestimate you just long enough for you to get rid of him," Pramila predicted.

Rupe smiled. There were obvious pleasures to being back among friends in Bombay.

"When we had our first meeting I told him I wanted to be updated on all the key areas of my portfolio," she continued. "Forest reserves, mineral reserves, land conservation, dams, rivers, everything. He sent boxes and boxes of files to my office thinking he would bury me in information. But I knew what I was looking for. It was the figures on our forest reserves that interested me. The official figures put our reserves at around nineteen percent, and that seemed ridiculously high to me. You only have to travel around the country with your eyes open to see that it can't be true. So I asked Shukla for proof. He sent me the satellite photographs, and there it was—nineteen and a half percent forest cover. And of course satellite pictures don't lie."

Her audience waited dutifully while she sipped her coffee.

"After I had looked at the pictures for a while it occurred to me it would be useful to know when they were taken," she went on. "So I called my colleague at the Science Ministry, and it turned out they were taken two weeks before the sugarcane harvest."

There was a sigh of recognition in the room. Only Annie looked puzzled.

"I'm missing something," she said. "What does the sugarcane harvest have to do with the forests?"

"Sugarcane grows sixteen feet high," Rupe explained. "From space it looks like forest." To the others she added: "More than half the area the Environment Ministry was claiming as forest was not forest at all—it was sugarcane."

"Too much of an error even for a government department," Sansi observed.

"And it started soon after Shukla came in," Rupe added. "He has been using the sugar crop to inflate his budget allowance."

"When do you tell him?" Sansi added.

"As soon as I get the new pictures taken after the harvest," Rupe answered. "Then I will ask him to explain what he has done with the extra money he needed to manage all that imaginary forest."

"I wouldn't mind a piece of that," Annie interjected.

Heads turned in her direction.

"I'm sorry?" Rupe said.

Pramila leaned toward Rupe. "Annie is with the *Times of India*," she said.

"A reporter ?"

"An off-duty reporter," Sansi said, looking pointedly at Annie.

"We're just talking, right?" Annie hedged, looking for support and finding none.

Rupe uncurled her legs. "I didn't realize," she said. "I should have been more careful."

Annie felt the disapproval of the other guests envelop her like a rush of cold air.

"I'm sorry," she said, hastening to undo the damage, for Pramila's sake as much as her own. "I admire what you're doing and I'll keep this in confidence. I won't report it . . . if you don't want me to."

Pramila put a hand reassuringly on Rupe's arm. "You can trust Annie," she said.

Rupe smiled, but it lacked conviction.

"It's late," she said. "I'm tired, I shouldn't have kept you all up so late—and I have to fly back to Delhi tomorrow."

She got to her feet, prompting a flurry of activity between Captain Ramani and his men. Sansi and Pramila and the other guests followed to say their good-byes. Only Annie hung back, afraid she might inadvertently cause more offense.

The living room emptied, leaving her on her own for what seemed like a long time. The murmur of departing voices in the hallway ceased and the apartment fell quiet. Annie decided to go and see what was keeping Sansi and Pramila. As she turned the corner she saw Rupe and Sansi engaged in a whispered conversation in the hallway, their backs to her, their heads so close they were almost touching. The front door was open, and in the outside corridor Pramila chatted with Captain Ramani while they waited for the minister.

Annie stepped back before anyone could see her and watched. She couldn't hear what was being said, but then she saw Sansi waggle his head as if agreeing to something and heard a softly spoken *acha*. Rupe seemed pleased by his reaction. She gave his hand an affectionate squeeze. Then she stepped out into the corridor to be surrounded by her bodyguards, a green and gold figurine inside a phalanx of armed men, vulnerable and dangerous at the same time.

"A mite touchy, isn't she?"

Sansi dropped a cuff link into his mahogany stud box. "She's worried about her position," he said. "She has reason to be."

"What, is she one of those women who's afraid of other women?"

Annie sat on the bed still wearing her sari and looking peeved.

"You embarrassed her and yourself," Sansi said quietly. "You can't blame her for that."

The second cuff link chimed softly as it dropped, a genteel rebuke.

"I wouldn't have run the story till she was ready," Annie said.

"And now?"

"Are you checking up on me?"

Sansi looked surprised. "You didn't like her?"

Annie hesitated.

"I wanted to," she said. "I guess my expectations were a little high. I don't see greatness there—I see a spoiled and manipulative woman determined to get her own way at whatever cost. I'd lay money she gets hooked on the power and runs for re-election."

Sansi walked over to the bed and sat down beside her. "You're jealous," he said.

"Shouldn't I be?"

"We've been friends since we were children."

Annie took a moment to compose herself.

"There was a look, an attitude I didn't like," she said. "I think she has something for you."

Sansi didn't deny it. Instead he said: "She is manipulative. She likes to play games. She has always been like that."

"She wants something," Annie said.

Sansi smiled. "She wants me to go to her hotel tomorrow, before she returns to Delhi."

It must have been what they had been talking about in the hallway, Annie realized. "What does she want?"

"I don't know," Sansi said.

She studied his eyes, and they gazed back frankly. "Was there ever anything between you two?"

"Romantically? No."

"She must have been a man-eater when she was younger."

"A real tigress," he said. "If the sexual revolution hadn't come along, she would have started it by herself. I wasn't her type at all, too conservative, too dull. She went to the Sorbonne, I went to Oxford. That should tell you something."

Annie took his hands and drew him up so they faced each other. "Maybe she thinks you're more her type now?"

He looked amused. "I am afraid she is going to offer me a job."

"On her staff . . . with the government?"

Sansi shrugged.

"Can you say no?"

"You know how I feel about politics."

"Can you say no to her?"

He smiled. "I have been doing it all my life."

Annie went up on her toes and kissed him promisingly. She said: "I won't run away this time."

He kissed her back and she pressed herself against him, feeling him as he became aroused. She felt his hands searching the folds of her sari for an opening. He found the tuck at the waist and gently worked it loose. For a moment there was nothing, then the delicious shiver of silk as the sari slid from her shoulders down her body, leaving her naked but for the rubies at her neck.

"You didn't learn that in the back of a Chevy," she said.

"At Oxford, actually," he answered.

CHAPTER 5

A dented black and yellow taxi veered out of the traffic on
Apollo Bunder, collided with the curb at the side entrance to
the Taj Mahal Hotel, and stopped with a grinding of gears that
made Sansi wince. He got out slowly, arthritically, paid off the
driver and threaded his way through the beggars and dope
dealers who waited in ambush for the guests at Bombay's most
famous hotel, the hotel built by Sir Dorabji Tata to show the
white sahibs that Indians could run a hotel as grand as anything
in London or New York.

Sansi glimpsed his reflection in the brass-bound glass doors;
the swept-back hair, the tan suit, the dark glasses that hid eyes
bloodied by fatigue. He looked ready for business but felt as if
he were wading in glue. Annie had made sure he went to see
Rupe utterly spent.

He walked through the white marble lobby with its fanned
breezes and wished he could sink into one of its plush armchairs
and doze for another hour. Instead he got into a brass and
mahogany elevator car and pressed the button for the fifth
floor. When he got out, he was met by two armed soldiers and

a subaltern who checked his name against a list. The subaltern escorted him the length of the corridor to a corner suite, where two more soldiers stood guard, and turned him over to a liaison officer who showed him into a small reception room.

Sansi waited in the windowless room with its chintz furniture, and portraits of impressively whiskered Indian gentlemen in drab Victorian suits who looked disapprovingly down at him. He had only guessed Rupe had something in mind for him in the government. No doubt she was doing what every other new arrival in the nation's capital did—surrounding herself with friends. His problem was how to say no without offending her. She was no longer just a friend, she was a cabinet minister. Annie had been right about one thing; power changed people, and rarely for the better.

Eight o'clock came and went. The pendulum of an antique wall clock continued to count the minutes in a soothing monotone, lulling Sansi into a kind of reverie. His thoughts turned back to another time, when he and Rupe had been childhood friends. They had been neighbors in the exclusive enclave of Malabar Hill and had played with the other children when their *bais* took them to the hanging gardens. When he and Rupe were eleven years old they would find ways to sneak off together to Chowpatty Beach to see the fakirs, snake charmers, and fortune-tellers, and to eat the greasy bani puri, which tasted better than anything they got at home. Once, they saw an astrologer who told them their lives would be forever entwined. But inevitably, as they entered adolescence, they drifted apart, though they belonged to the same crowd and continued to run into each other at parties.

By the time they were in high school the parties had changed and so had they. There were new temptations to explore. They found each other again in the dangerous interlude between the end of high school and their separate paths to universities in separate countries. They kissed for the first time outside her parents' house one night when he walked her home from a friend's graduation party. It was his first open-mouthed kiss and her confidence told him she had already gone much further than him in the exploration of the senses.

A few nights later they took a path they used as children, that led to a secret cove beneath the walls of the Governor's Mansion on the outermost point of Malabar Hill. They sat on the sand and smoked ganja. He started to make love to her, but when it came to the moment when there would be no turning back, he balked. He told her it was because he was afraid he would get her pregnant, but she shocked him by taking a small foil pack containing a condom from her purse. He realized then that she had planned it, that she was ready—that she knew what she was doing and he didn't. Overwhelmed by fear, he lost his desire and was unable to continue.

He told her the ganja made him queasy, but she didn't believe him. She guessed he was afraid of her, that he thought her too bold for him, too experienced. She grew angry and accused him of thinking her a whore. That was how they parted. It was ten years before they saw each other again, and they were different people pursuing different lives.

He hadn't been at all surprised to learn she was married to Mani Seshan. He was the ideal partner for her—dynamic, charismatic, ambitious, her equal in every way. What surprised Sansi was that she seemed content to live in her husband's shadow. Outspoken and provocative on occasion, but always deferential to Mani's greater goal of cabinet power and, ultimately, the Prime Minister's office.

But her husband's karma had melded with hers in a way no one could have foreseen. He lived long enough to savor the moment of victory only to have it snatched away by the hand of an unknown assassin. Now the power he had craved all his life was hers. He had bequeathed to her the mantle of the martyr's widow, and it had become her destiny to fulfill his dream.

Sansi gave a start as the clock chimed a quarter past the hour. The door opened at the same time. An attractive young woman in a pale blue *salwar khameez* appeared and introduced herself: "I am Hemali, the minister's personal assistant. Please come."

Sansi followed her through a series of anterooms, past a number of lesser luminaries who waited with briefcases on their laps and eyed him resentfully as he passed. At last he emerged into a large sitting room with a row of gauze-curtained windows that filled the room with a milky light. Rupe was working at a large desk and didn't look up when he came in. The desk was awash with paperwork; cabinet documents, files, boxes, faxes, memos, notes and letters that cascaded off the desk onto a nearby sofa and into a spreading pool on the floor. Buff-colored folders with gaily striped ribbons bobbed like rafts as they rode the rapids over the cushioned ledges to the carpeted plain below. Upstream, Rupe's pen stroked furiously against the current.

Sansi stood self-consciously in a sunny expanse of carpet like a schoolboy waiting to see the headmistress. Carpeted was the word the British used for it. He felt as though he had been carpeted and didn't know why.

Hemali made no attempt to ease his discomfort. Instead she went to the spreading pool of papers on the floor and began sorting them into piles on a nearby bureau. Sansi thought her a younger version of Rupe. Confident, pretty, and with all the insensitivity peculiar to the upper castes.

"Done," Rupe said abruptly and put down her pen with a loud clack. She got up and used the few exposed patches of carpet as stepping-stones across the paper shallows.

She wore a white cotton *salwar khameez* that made her look fresh and rested. She studied him for a minute, amused.

"You look like a gangster," she said.

He took off his dark glasses and her smile broadened.

"Your American girlfriend keep you up after I left?"

"My duty is to serve, Madam Minister," Sansi answered blandly.

"Tea but no sympathy," she said pertly, and led him to a sunny alcove where a table was set with starched white linen and heavy hotel silverware. A curved window overlooked the Gateway to India, the monumental arch built by the British just in time for them to march through it on their way out of the country.

There were two darkly lacquered cane chairs, and Rupe took the one against the window so Sansi had the light in his eyes. A waiter wearing white jacket and gloves hovered over a serving table on which were warming stands with tea, coffee, and baskets of assorted fruits and pastries.

"Assam?" Rupe asked.

Sansi waggled his head and Rupe signaled the waiter to pour them each a cup of tea. Neither of them took milk and Sansi declined an offered wedge of lemon. The tea was scalding but he drank it anyway and felt a little better.

"Are you hungry?" Rupe asked.

He shook his head. She asked for a brioche and broke it into small pieces which she ate unbuttered.

"I suppose your American girlfriend thinks I am a bitch," she added.

"Actually, yes," Sansi said.

"Actually?" Rupe echoed. It was something Annie had done when they had first met, finding amusement in his unconscious anglicisms. "I hope you told her I'm a dangerous bitch."

"She was a fan of yours until she met you."

Rupe chewed a tiny piece of brioche. "Mani said if you can't get respect, fear is the next best thing."

"She would make a good friend and ally," Sansi said. "What my mother said is true, Annie won't breach your confidence."

"Actually," Rupe added pointedly, "I don't care what she writes about me—as long as she doesn't stop me from doing what I have been elected to do."

"If she wanted to, I couldn't stop her," Sansi said.

"No," Rupe said. "But I could."

Sansi knew what she meant. A threat to close the paper for a few days would stop any report Annie might have in mind. If that wasn't enough, there was always deportation. Governments of every party routinely threw out foreign journalists they thought unsympathetic to their cause—another of the unsubtle ways in which Indian democracy differed from American democracy.

"I'll mention it to her," Sansi said.

"Now *you* think I'm a bitch," Rupe said. She smiled her crooked smile and added: "Nothing new about that, is there?"

Sansi sipped his tea.

"I don't know how much time I've got in this job," Rupe went on. "I won't take the chance that a newspaper reporter might spoil all the good I can do just to get the little bit of glory that comes from a scoop."

"All the good you can do?" Sansi repeated. "As long as you are sure."

Irritation flared in her eyes then subsided. She *had* changed, Sansi thought.

"That is why I want you to come and work for me," she said.

"To act as your conscience? Sorry, it is too big a job for one man."

"There aren't too many people I can rely on," Rupe said. "Pramila is one. You are another."

"Then ask my mother," Sansi said.

Rupe smiled. "I would if she could do what I want. But I need you."

"To do what?" he asked.

She leaned forward and her silhouette firmed against the light. "You remember the chemical spill at Varanasi last year?"

"Of course," he said. "What was it, a thousand dead?"

"The death toll today is over eleven hundred," she said. "More than four thousand injured. A lot of them won't make it. The death toll will keep going up."

Sansi waggled his head. Disaster was industry's constant

companion in India—and the death tolls were always astro-
nomic. Mines collapsed, oil refineries exploded, chemical plants
blanketed their workers' homes with toxic waste, coal plants
spewed black sludge into rivers that supplied drinking water to
millions. Every day thousands of people were burned, poisoned,
gassed, or blown apart, and hundreds of thousands condemned
to horrible lingering deaths. Only the worst disasters attracted
attention. Everybody remembered Bhopal. Bhopal was disaster
on a world scale. But it wasn't the exception in India. It had
merely set the standard by which those industries that killed
only a few hundred a year were willing to be measured.

"You will remember we promised a full, open inquiry when
we were elected," Rupe went on. "I wanted it from the beginning. Justice was the obvious choice, but you know their record,
and the Prime Minister agreed with me so we're handling it at
Environment. I have a chairman but I need somebody to direct
the investigation, somebody I can trust."

Her voice acquired a new level of earnestness.

"I want you to direct the investigation."

"Are Bapre," Sansi sighed.

"You can pick your own investigating team," she added
quickly. "You will have the budget to do the job properly—
you've never heard anybody in government say that to you
before—you will have the resources of the federal government
behind you, unlimited powers of arrest and detention   "

"Rupe . . ." He raised a hand in protest. "You . . . I wasn't
expecting this, nothing like this."

"I will give you full backing," she pressed. "I am serious
about this, George. I want it done properly."

"I believe you are serious," Sansi said. "I admire what you
are doing and I support it in principle . . . but I think it is a mistake to ask me."

Rupe leaned back in her chair. "You support me—but you
want me to do all the fighting on my own?"

Sansi shifted uncomfortably. "It is naive to ask me. You will only make fools of both of us—and that is a much riskier prospect for you than it is for me."

"You're trying to manage me?" Rupe laughed disbelievingly. "After all these years you still think you can manage me?"

Sansi flushed. The image of the two of them on the beach at Malabar Point flashed into his mind. Surely she didn't mean that?

"It would be an appointment born of political inexperience," he persisted. "You don't put somebody like me in charge of an investigation like this. It is a job for somebody in the attorney general's office, somebody of commissioner's rank. Not somebody like me . . ." Tiredness got the better of him and his words trailed away.

"You don't think you're up to it?" she asked.

"It is a political appointment," he said. "And I think it would be politically unwise for you. Your opponents will make a meal of you."

"Hemali?" Rupe called across the room. "Could you bring me Mr. Sansi's file?"

"You have my file?"

"Of course I have your file." She looked at him as if he were stupid.

Sansi grunted. Part of him was angry. But part of him was flattered too—and interested.

Hemali reappeared and handed Rupe a pale blue folder containing a copy of a Crime Branch personnel file. Rupe pulled out a single typed sheet, a summary of Sansi's career, and began reading.

"Twenty-one years with the Maharashtra Police Service, twenty of those with Crime Branch beginning at the rank of detective constable—bit of a come-down for an Oxford law degree, wasn't it?" Before he could answer, she went on: "Seven commendations for outstanding investigative work, fifteen citations for merit, two police medals for valor. A dozen very high profile investigations including the Zafar case and the Cardus case—I remember that one, very tricky—the best conviction rate in the department, no complaints or demotions. You held the rank of detective inspector when you resigned, and were scheduled for promotion to chief inspector." She lowered the sheet for a moment and added: "My understanding is you were a long-term prospect for the joint commissioner's seat if you'd stayed."

"Your understanding doesn't take into consideration my feelings on the matter," Sansi added.

"You resigned to start your own law practice," she continued. "You are a member of the Bar Association of Bombay and the Law Society of Maharashtra, and you have no known political affiliations." She slipped the sheet of paper back into the file. "The truth is you are ideally qualified."

"Rupe—"

"Nobody is going to call either of us a fool," she interrupted. "Quite the contrary. Putting you in charge of this investigation tells everyone we are serious."

Sansi grimaced to hide his true feelings. The truth was he was flattered—and excited. He was surprised only because it was bigger than anything he had expected, but it was also a chance to do exactly the kind of work he believed in. Much as he hated to admit it, Rupe knew him better than he realized. He signaled the waiter for more tea. Rupe waited, sensing a slackening of resistance.

"Who else have you asked?"

"Nobody."

He looked skeptical.

"I had you in mind from the beginning. I knew who I wanted for chairman and I knew who I wanted for the investigation. I never considered the possibility you would refuse."

"Who did you get as chairman?"

Rupe smiled now that his interest was out in the open. "Judge Pilot."

"Pilot?"

Kursheed Pilot was a judge of the federal Supreme Court, an aging iconoclast who dissented routinely with his colleagues on the bench, all Congress Party hacks who followed the party line. Pilot too had been a Congress Party appointee, back in 1967, when Indira Gandhi rewarded him for loyal service to her father, Jawaharlal Nehru, India's first Prime Minister. But in the years that followed, Pilot had clashed often with Mrs. Gandhi, particularly during her second term as Prime Minister when she suspended civil liberties. It was only the Congress Party's defeat in the election of 1977 that saved Pilot from Mrs. Gandhi's revenge and allowed him to continue his role as the conscience of the bench and, indirectly, the conscience of the nation. Sansi had to concede that Rupe's appointment of Pilot to chair the inquiry was anything but naive.

"I didn't know he was ready to leave the bench."

"He has been ready for some time," Rupe said. "I offered him the opportunity to go out with a bang."

Sansi smiled. An open inquiry into the Varanasi disaster was an opportunity to shame a corrupt judiciary and show a cynical populace what a model of justice was supposed to be. The appeal for Pilot was obvious; vindication, the culmination of a lifetime of courageous dissent.

But Sansi had one concern that didn't apply to Pilot. Government inquiries could drag on for years. He didn't want to be stuck in a moribund investigation, especially when the Bharatiya Janata Party lost the next election as it was almost certain to.

"I do not want to make a career out of this," he said.

"If you haven't finished your investigation within one year, I will fire you myself," Rupe answered. "I want justice for the victims of Varanasi in this lifetime, not the next. I won't allow another travesty like Bhopal."

The legacy of Bhopal had degenerated from a national tragedy to a national disgrace. More than a decade after a cloud of poison gas escaped from the Union Carbide plant at Bhopal, official figures put the final toll at 4,037 dead and 240,000 maimed. Unofficial figures put it closer to ten thousand dead and half a million maimed. A government claim of $3 billion in compensation was whittled down over five years to $470 million. Ninety percent of that money never reached victims or their families because of lawyers, bureaucrats, and claims brokers who bilked the compensation process. No executive of Union Carbide was ever charged, and the company continued to do business in India

"I want quick justice," Rupe added. "It isn't only a matter of compensation—I want to see how smug those fat boardroom faces are when they are behind bars."

Sansi managed a faint smile. "What do you know so far?"

"Only what the state environmental protection agency has turned up," she said. "Police reports, hospital records, autopsy reports, eyewitness statements, that kind of thing. We know what did the damage. What we don't know is where it came from."

"What did do the damage?"

"Phosphorous," Rupe answered. "We found phosphorous residue on all the victims. It was highly concentrated and must have been discharged over a short period of time. It must have gone down the river like an oil slick."

"There can't be too many places that could produce that kind of spill," Sansi said.

"We think we are looking for a large textile plant," Rupe said. "Phosphorous is a major ingredient in the dyeing process."

"How many plants are there along that part of the Ganga?"

"We know of eighty-seven that could account for a slick of that size," she said. "There are probably more. They pay off the pollution control inspectors to underestimate their capacity. There are at least two hundred smaller plants that could have built up large accumulations over time."

"Are Bapre."

"Be grateful it isn't tanneries," Rupe said. "There are seventy thousand of them on the Ganga alone. Most of them aren't regulated at all, and they dump millions of gallons of cyanide into the river every year."

"Cyanide?"

"Undiluted, untreated cyanide," Rupe said. "But I have to leave them till next year."

Sansi closed his eyes and massaged the bridge of his nose. He could still feel Rupe's eyes on him.

"When do you need to know?"

"Wednesday," she said.

"*Bhagwan.*"

Wednesday was three days away.

"I need you in New Delhi by the beginning of next week," she said.

Sansi put down his cup. The tea had stirred the acid in his stomach and he had begun to feel bilious.

"Let me sleep on it," he said. "I'll call you tomorrow in Delhi."

He got up to go and Rupe followed. Then he stopped.

"I want to be sure you understand something," he said.

Rupe waited, confident she could handle any concern he might have.

"When you start something like this, it acquires a momentum all its own," he said. "I have to be certain you will see it through, that you won't lose your nerve when it gets bumpy."

She smiled.

"I have never lost my nerve when things got bumpy," she said. "Remember?"

CHAPTER 6

At the end of an abandoned pier, where gleaming liners once decanted starch-collared Britons into the world's greatest melting pot, a lone osprey stood atop a capstan the same rusted color as its plumage. Stirred by a restless appetite, it lifted itself skyward and began a shallow arc over the harbor, its eyes scouring the surface of the water for the metallic flicker of fish. Invisible in the muddy dawn, it glided southward from P & O pier past the empty basins of Prince's Dock and Indira Dock toward the narrow spit of land known as Colaba. Still the water yielded nothing. With a dismissive flap of its wings the bird banked into a climb that would carry it westward, away from Bombay, to the more fecund waters of the Arabian Sea.

As it flew over the darkened ramparts of the city, it was confronted suddenly by a bright opalescent disk in the sky. At the center of the disk was an indistinct black and red shape that pulsed and beckoned. The disk expanded rapidly, its glittering luminescence becoming a sunlit pool of water suspended in space. The seabird found itself drawn irresistibly toward the celestial oasis, until at the last moment the pulsing black and red shape became a threat and the bird veered sharply away, skimming the summit of the apartment building where a man completed pre-dawn laps in his rooftop pool.

Madhuri Amlani neither saw nor heard the panicked whir of wings in the darkness. All he heard was the rhythmic grunt of his own breathing as he propelled his ungainly body through the water in a slow and graceless breaststroke.

For the founder and chairman of India's sixth largest corporation it was the most precious time of the day. That quiet hour before the dawn when he could swim alone and plan the order of battle for the day ahead. The habit had begun when, as a young man, he had swum each morning in the shallows of the Gulf of Kachchh in his hometown of Jamnagar in the northwestern state of Gujerat and promised himself that one day he would swim in his own pool atop his own building in Bombay.

He had been expected to follow his father and his brothers into a secure career as a clerk on the railways, but the young Amlani knew working for the state was no way to get rich. Instead he found his own job with Indus Oil, a company owned jointly by the Indian government and a consortium of French oil producers. It was only a job pumping gas at a company service station, but he knew he could turn it into something more. Despite his unprepossessing looks, he had energy and charm. He worked hard and had a knack for getting people to do what he wanted. Within three years he was an assistant manager.

But the move to manager was always harder. Promotion rarely came easily. There was a shortcut—though it led through the Gulf states. Managers' jobs were available in the Persian Gulf for those who could stand the hardship and isolation and who were willing to be treated as second-class citizens by the Arabs.

The Gulf states were rich in oil but poor in everything else, so they offered plenty of opportunity to a man of an enterprising nature. Amlani volunteered to manage a company service station in Oman. It was the first in a series of gambles that were to transform his life.

He made friends quickly. He endured all the petty discrimi-
nations a Muslim state imposed on Hindus. He smiled at the
casual slights that came his way. He ran card games in a
back room of the service station and served the kind of good
strong coffee the Arabs liked. He sold petrol on credit. He sold
smuggled whiskey and cigarettes, and when he went back to
India he smuggled in Arab gold.

After a while it occurred to him to start a small import-
export business to cover his smuggling activities. It expanded
almost naturally as he found himself bringing in cheap cottons,
spices, pots and pans, binoculars, transistor radios, anything
that would turn a profit in Oman. He called his company
Renown Trading because Arabs disliked paperwork and preferred to take a man at his word.

His biggest coup, and the story he still liked to tell, was
inspired by the Arab love for beautiful flower gardens, the
eternal need to make the desert bloom. Because Oman was built
on sand and rock, there was an unquenchable demand for anything that would enrich the soil.

Amlani saw an opportunity. He returned to his home city of
Jamnagar, where he leased a half-dozen leaky barges and hired
kulis to fill them with river silt he knew was laden with human
waste. He spent his last money chartering an aging steamer to
tow the barges the three hundred miles to Oman, knowing he
had to sell the cargo on arrival because he had nothing left to
pay off the ship's captain. He needn't have worried. His adver-
tised premium-grade fertilizer sold as fast as he could unload it
and he made a small fortune.

Months later, when the roses of Oman bloomed fatter and
more fragrant than any English country garden, Amlani was
asked when his next shipment of premium fertilizer was due. It
was his proudest boast that he could sell shiploads of shit to the
Arabs and they would thank him for it.

When Amlani's time in Oman was up, he was making
so much money he was reluctant to leave. But he had made a

success of the service station too, chalking up the biggest sales increases of any Indus Oil outlet in the Gulf. The company made him an accounts manager in the marketing department at their head office in Bombay and earmarked him for advancement.

It was 1961, he was twenty-five years old, the economy was booming, and Bombay especially was booming. A career on the fast track at Indus Oil would have been enough for any normally ambitious man, but Amlani was abnormally ambitious—and unwilling to let go of Renown Trading. He met the demands of both companies by working eighteen-hour days, seven days a week. During the day he made money for Indus Oil. At night he went to a warehouse at Clerk Basin and a cramped first-floor office where he had a desk with two telephones, a cot, and a bathroom. He worked till exhaustion stopped him, buying anything anywhere that could be sold anywhere else at a profit.

As the year wore on he noticed how he and other brokers were shipping more and more synthetic materials into India, especially nylon and rayon, and at the same time he saw how many more textile mills were starting up in the city's northern suburbs. He saw how woefully inefficient the cotton industry was, how the middle class was expanding its buying power and changing its taste from traditional to more modern clothing, and he foresaw the coming boom in synthetic fabrics.

To the astonishment of friends and colleagues, he resigned his promising career at Indus Oil to go out on his own. He rented a bigger office on the waterfront, hired a couple of assistants and set out to see how much of the textile trade he could claim for himself. In the first six months he almost went under.

The cause was the giant textiles manufacturer, Poona Dyeing, his biggest single customer. The smaller mills paid him promptly for the yarn he shipped, but Poona made him wait for no apparent reason other than to show him who was boss. Part of it, he knew, was caste. The chairman of Poona Dyeing was Imilani Rao, whose Brahmin arrogance permeated a family empire that included mills, dye works, chemical plants, retail stores, and a publishing house that produced dozens of influential newspapers and profitable magazines. To men like Rao, small-time traders like Amlani were vulgar upstarts, useful in their way but always to be kept in their place.

Poona was so slow with its payments, Amlani was forced to borrow operating capital at high interest rates. Then his credit dried up and he found himself stuck with a cargo at dockside for which he was unable to pay the landing fees. He pleaded with the accounts manager at Poona to release a long overdue check, and the manager promised it would be ready at noon, but when Amlani went to pick it up he found it unsigned and the manager at lunch.

The manager returned late and unapologetic, claiming his missing signature was only an oversight. Amlani barely made it to the bank in time, but when he got to the dock it was to discover that his cargo had been sold out from under him to a rival shipper. He promised himself then that one day he would bring Poona to its knees.

Somehow Amlani traded his way back from the brink. He understood his prospects as a trader in synthetic yarn would always be limited by the whims of the textile producers who bought from him—but if he became a producer himself, his prospects would be limited only by the whims of the marketplace. Next to China, India was the biggest marketplace in the world.

By the mid-1960s he was in a position to leverage himself into the buyout of a small mill in the northern suburb of Sharpur. The looms belonged in a museum and he had only thirty employees, but from his office window he could see the hulking outline of the giant Poona works. That, as much as anything else, fueled his determination.

With a grand and optimistic flourish he called his new textile division Renown Industries and put it with Renown Trading under the corporate umbrella of Renown Holdings Ltd. He was the only man in India who knew it was the beginning of an empire.

By the end of the decade he had upgraded and expanded his existing mill and acquired two bigger, more modern mills. He had almost a thousand employees, and to manage them he turned to the only people he could trust—his own family. His father was gone, felled by a stroke after a lifetime of servitude to the railways, and his brothers needed little convincing that their futures were brighter with Madhuri in Bombay.

At the same time, Amlani extended his influence in other areas. He charmed and bribed into existence a network of contacts in government. He remembered birthdays and anniversaries, paid for holidays and hospital treatment, sent expensive gifts and envelopes stuffed with money to help celebrate special occasions. In return, Customs officers saw that his yarn was never delayed at the docks, and factory inspectors made sure his production lines ran uninterrupted.

He also got married. Her name was Gauri and she was the plain and compliant second daughter of the upper caste Sindhi who leased Amlani his warehouses. For Amlani it wasn't so much a marriage as a traditional Hindu alliance. What he wanted from a wife was caste, loyalty, and motherhood. Most of all he wanted a dynasty. He wanted children he could mold into a cadre of family loyalists. It was they who would be the future of the empire he was building.

Instead of cash for his bride's dowry, he negotiated a gift of land, a valuable vacant plot in Colaba where a twelve-story apartment building now stood, a landmark he named Ocean View, in whose rooftop pool he took his morning swim.

For their honeymoon they went to Italy, where Amlani bought most of the yarn for his mills and where he could conduct business between attempts to impregnate his new bride. It was while lunching with a yarn trader in Milan he heard the first whisper of a new miracle fiber from America. A fiber that was versatile, durable, cheaper, and easier to manufacture than any other synthetic. The word was that it would transform the clothing industry and render all other synthetics obsolete. Confidence in America was such that the big manufacturers were already competing to install the equipment to see who would be first into mass production. The name of the new miracle fiber was polyester.

By the time Amlani returned to India he had formulated a strategy. He knew it wouldn't be enough to be the first in India to produce clothing made from polyester. There were plenty of manufacturers bigger than him, including Poona Dyeing, who could come in later, mass produce, and take control of the market as they always had. What he had to do was unprecedented. He had to control the supply of the new fiber to India—and he had to do it before anybody realized what was happening.

Amlani learned that before polyester could be woven into fabric its fibers had to be specially texturized. Until there was a plant in India to do the work, the fiber would have to be bought already texturized. This would keep the price high because the treatment could only be done in the West.

Secretly he acquired a controlling interest in two small chemical plants in Gujerat, one in Jamnagar, the other in Surat. While his competitors speculated about the market potential for polyester, Amlani began the conversions that would enable him to texturize polyester fiber in India. At the same time he began importing untreated fiber in bulk and stockpiling it.

Amlani also understood that the only way to make sure there was a ready market for polyester was to create one. To do that would take a marketing campaign, something he had never done before. So, he set up a marketing department at Renown Industries and made his younger brother, Prakash, its manager.

Together the two of them spent weeks trying to devise the campaign that would persuade Indians to abandon other fabrics for the fabric of the future—but nothing they came up with worked. Ironically, it was during a rare moment of relaxation, on a family picnic at Karli Caves, that Amlani stumbled on the idea that would be the heart of his campaign. He was watching Prakash's six-year-old son, Vinod, playing with his cousins when the idea came to him with such clarity and completeness that he couldn't understand how it had eluded him before. The most effective marketing campaigns were those with a human face, and what could be more effective than the face of a child—the face of the future?

Amlani laid his plans with the same meticulous attention to detail with which a general prepares a military campaign. A year later he unleashed his marketing juggernaut spearheaded by the happily smiling face of his nephew, Vinod. Giant billboards, full-page advertisements in newspapers and magazines, radio jingles and TV commercials proclaimed the debut of the Vinod Line, an array of cheap family clothing in an infinite variety of colors and combinations. Pictures of Vinod bouncing happily on a trampoline fitted with a sheet of gold polyester became the best-known image in India—and Vinod himself became a star.

The reaction exceeded everyone's forecasts. The Vinod Line quickly became the clothing of choice for the common people. Sales of polyester soared while other synthetics slumped and the bottom dropped out of the cotton industry altogether. It didn't matter that polyester was utterly unsuited to the climate, that it didn't breathe, that it was hot and sticky and never quite rid itself of the taint of human sweat. It was cheap and almost indestructible and it came in the bright and exciting patterns Indians wanted.

While Amlani's mills boosted production again and again to meet demand, his competitors scrambled to catch up. The resultant rush to the same few foreign suppliers sent the price of treated polyester yarn skyrocketing. Amlani's chemical plants in Gujerat, meanwhile, turned out all the texturized fiber he needed, fueled by the abundant raw material in his secret stockpiles.

Those who were able to turn out their own lines of polyester clothing found they couldn't match Amlani's prices. For two years he enjoyed a virtual monopoly on the sale of polyester clothing in India and company revenues soared to unimaginable levels.

Still, the bigger manufacturers had no choice but to respond if they ever hoped to regain their share of the market. Several invested in their own chemical plants to treat polyester fiber. And no one invested bigger than Poona Dyeing. Imilani Rao assured shareholders personally that Poona would teach the upstart Amlani a lesson about market forces.

For his part Amlani seemed unperturbed by Rao's threats. He began spending more and more time away from his business, leaving it to his brothers to run, content apparently to enjoy the rewards of his success. He preferred to spend his time with all the new friends and acquaintances in high places made suddenly accessible to him by his acquisition of enormous wealth. He went to Delhi often and bought a small flat there. He tried to cultivate new friends in the government of Indira Gandhi but, rebuffed more often than not, gravitated downward to the disorganized coalition of opposition parties under the ineffectual leadership of fellow Gujerati Morarji Desai.

Poona's much promised counterattack came with saturation advertising and the launch of an eye-catching new line of polyester clothing that undercut even Amlani's low prices. For weeks it was impossible to turn on the television or open the business pages of any newspaper without seeing the smug face of Imilani Rao confidently predicting an end to the Renown phenomenon and the return of Poona to its rightful place as market leader. For several months Poona and Renown went head-to-head in the marketplace, and inevitably Poona began to cut into Renown's market share.

Then, in a move anticipated by no one, Indira Gandhi called a general election. Stung by foreign criticism of her dictatorial rule, she claimed the support of the electorate for her reforms

and said she would prove it at the ballot box. Given the chance
at last to voice their disapproval, the voters rejected her in favor
of Morarji Desai's opposition rabble. Within a month the Department of Industry announced it would bring in a licensing
system to restore order to the textile industry, which, it claimed,
had been thrown into turmoil by the invasion of foreign-
made synthetics. Licenses to produce the new fabrics would be
limited according to the department's view of what the market
could bear.

The only manufacturer in India given a license to produce
texturized polyester fiber was Madhuri Amlani.

An enraged Rao assailed the government privately and
publicly and sent a high level team to New Delhi to procure a
manufacturer's license for Poona at any cost.

Unaccustomed to being locked out of government deliberations, Poona's executives were cooling their heels in the corridors of the Department of Industry when a new announcement
was made by the Department of Trade only a couple of blocks
away. For the protection of the Indian chemical industry there
was to be an immediate ban on the importation of texturized
polyester yarn.

It was a double blow directed solely at Amlani's competitors,
who could now neither produce nor import treated polyester—
and it gave the protection of the government to the monopoly
Amlani had carved out for himself. Rao's Brahmin friends in
the ousted Congress Party government were in no position to
help him.

Smaller competitors folded within months and Amlani picked
up their useless, newly converted mills for almost nothing. Rao
hung on for a couple of years but succeeded only in prolonging
his humiliation.

Amlani's next move was to launch Renown on the share
market with the biggest initial public offering in the history of
the Bombay Stock Exchange. Capital flooded in from investors
eager to bet on the man who had the government in his pocket

and a monopoly on the production of polyester. Amlani added insult to injury by using the money to launch a takeover bid for Poona Dyeing.

The battle lasted only a day, and both Amlani and Rao knew the outcome before it started. The two men faced each other unseeingly across the city while the numbers ticked relentlessly over the teletype. At the close of business Poona belonged to Amlani. Publicly Rao affected a Brahmin unconcern for the fate of his now moribund textiles division and announced he would turn his attention to other more profitable divisions of his empire. Privately he vowed he would do everything in his power to bring Amlani down.

Amlani took pleasure in the humiliation of Imilani Rao and the end of once mighty Poona Dyeing. He took pleasure in going to the plant himself to watch his workers take down the famous Poona sign and put up the Renown sign in its place. He took pleasure in seeking out the accounts manager who years before had cheated him of his cargo by making him wait through lunch for an unsigned check—and telling him to clear out his office.

■　■

In the years that followed, Amlani embarked on a program of expansions and consolidations that elevated him to the ranks of the nation's mightiest industrialists. To administer his burgeoning empire he bought the old British Steamship Lines building, a triangular, six-story edifice of Aberdeen granite that loomed over the Waudy Road crossroads like the bow of a great ocean liner.

To perpetuate his empire his wife bore him three children, honoring him first with two sons and then a daughter. The eldest son, Arvind, he sent to the University of Chicago to take a degree in chemical engineering. The younger son, Joshi, he sent to Harvard to study business administration. His daughter, Rashmi, he spared the rigors of commercial life. She wanted to be an actress, a movie star, and he was prepared to indulge her.

For a while. For, just as her brothers were the seed of the next generation, she was a precious incubator of dynasty.

By the time he was in his fifties Amlani presided over an empire that threatened to eclipse that of his rival, Imilani Rao. He owned dozens of textile mills around the country. He had acquired more chemical plants and extended his range of synthetics processing. He had moved into the manufacture and distribution of petroleum products; paraffin, kerosene, butane, ethylene, propylene, and naphtha. He had controlling interests in a shipping line and two transport companies.

All of it a continuation of a strategy he called backward vertical integration—the same strategy he stumbled upon when he saw the importance of locking up the supply of polyester yarn. Whatever industry he ventured into, Amlani bought every stage of the production process until he owned everything from the source to the marketplace. Nothing could impede either the flow of product or the return of capital.

It was his move into the petroleum industry that presaged his greatest venture yet. He wanted to do something no single entrepreneur had done before in India, something no one thought possible. He wanted to move into oil and gas exploration. He wanted his own refineries. He wanted a chain of service stations and fleets of fuel tankers crisscrossing the country with the name "Renown" on their sides. He wanted his own oil company, an oil company that would exploit the weaknesses of his former employer, Indus Oil, an oil company that would protect the market from the incursions of the foreign companies that were muscling back into the country now that the economy had been thrown open. Only when he accomplished these things did the man who started out working as a petrol pump attendant believe his dreams would be close to fulfillment.

But to start an oil company took more capital than even Amlani had amassed. When he took the plan to his bankers, they balked at his grandiose vision. The line of credit they advanced was secured by his most prized corporate assets. He mortgaged

Renown House and Ocean View. He issued short-term debentures that offered a ridiculously high rate of return, thereby
double-mortgaging his assets. All he did was make the money
market nervous and dampen the return on the debentures.

Amlani realized that once again he would have to go to the
share market for money, to the millions of small investors who
had supported him in the beginning, many of whom he had
made rich. Shares in Renown Oil would be offered on every
stock exchange in India and once again it would be the biggest
initial public offering in the country's history.

It should have been easy. The economy was booming, foreign capital was pouring in, and investment was soaring.
Instead it made everyone nervous. Everyone but Amlani.

His bankers warned that he was over-extended, that he
should abandon his idea before it ruined him. But Amlani
wouldn't listen. People said his ambition had finally exceeded
his reason. Confidence in his companies sagged. The price of his
stock dropped. The sale of debentures dried up completely. At
the moment he should have been at his strongest, Amlani was
astonished to discover he had never been so weak.

It was the moment Imilani Rao chose to take his revenge.

The opening barrage came from Rao's publishing divisions.
His newspapers and business magazines carried a series of
exposés on the Amlani way of doing business, from his corrupt
dealings with the Desai government to his suspicious shuffling
of company funds to his highly leveraged foray into the oil
industry. One magazine presented a chart showing Amlani's vast
network of influence, his contacts at all levels of government.
The article went so far as to publish the names and photographs
of those politicians and government officials who had benefited
the most from their association with Amlani.

Rao followed up with a speech to the Bombay Chamber of
Commerce in which he denounced Amlani as the architect of a
vast Ponzi scheme whose companies had to keep expanding to
delay the inevitable collapse.

But his main thrust came on the floor of the Bombay Stock Exchange. First he dumped several million Renown shares he had acquired quietly and gradually over several months through a network of proxy buyers. To his amusement he made a profit. Then he started to sell Renown stock short.

Rao's plan was brutally simple and required only a willingness to risk a sizable chunk of his own money to destroy Amlani, a risk he was willing to take. His intent was to start a panic, a stampede out of Renown stock that would drive the company's value down through its debt levels so Amlani's bankers would have no choice but to seize the assets he had put up as collateral. Amlani would be unable to finance his expansion into oil, unable even to secure his twice-mortgaged debentures. The only way he would be able to meet his debts would be through the dismemberment of the empire he had worked a lifetime to build. It would be the end of him. And this time Rao would have the pleasure of picking up the pieces.

The plan worked. Renown's shares plummeted. In a few hours their price dropped from 500 rupees to 400 and was expected to crash through the 300 barrier before lunch. Once again the two men faced each other across the city, but this time the numbers that flickered on their computer screens spoke of Amlani's humiliation. Each time Renown's price plunged to a new low, Rao used the money he made to sell short again, to accelerate the slide.

By the close of business the price stood at 167 rupees a share. Renown had lost sixty percent of its face value, the biggest single drop in one day in the history of the stock market. Amlani demanded the directors of the stock exchange suspend trading in Renown because of the sinister forces behind its decline, but Rao had anticipated that too and the directors declined, claiming the market had to be free to make its own judgment. The rout would continue the following day. Amlani's bankers would have to step in.

The next morning the city awakened in a mood of heightened expectancy. Everyone knew of the drama that was being played out between two of India's biggest industrialists. The morning newspapers were filled with nothing else. Some stories already had the tone of corporate obituaries, describing Renown's meteoric rise and its equally meteoric fall. Crowds of reporters gathered outside Renown House. A titanic struggle was under way in the biggest financial arena in the country and its climax would come before noon.

The moment the trading bell sounded, Renown's price resumed its free fall. Within an hour it was below 100 and still falling. It dropped to 90, 80 . . . then it stopped. The numbers stuck at 78, and a hush spread throughout the exchange. Amlani's bankers had stepped in. The announcement would come at any moment. The Renown era was over. Then a new voice sounded on the stock-market floor. Then another and another. Amlani was buying.

Rao knew it was the desperate last gasp of a beaten man, a bluff by Amlani to stave off the inevitable. He had to have some cash in reserve for emergencies such as this. Perhaps he had done the impossible and persuaded his bankers to extend his credit that little bit further. The price would climb briefly, a final flicker of life, and then collapse.

But it kept going up. Back over 100. And still Amlani cash poured into the exchange.

A few blocks away at Renown House, Amlani went downstairs with his sons, Arvind and Joshi, and personally invited the waiting journalists to join him in the boardroom for tea. Instead of the weary, cornered figure they expected, Amlani appeared genial and relaxed. He had an announcement to make, he said. As he calmly sipped his tea from a fine china cup he promised he would buy every Renown share that came on the market.

And so he did. The price continued its slow upward climb, and by the close of business it was back above 300.

Then Amlani delivered another thunderbolt. He told the directors of the exchange he would exercise his right to have the scrip for every share he had bought delivered to his office. It had exactly the effect he wanted. The directors had to shut down the exchange while they accounted for each and every transaction in Renown stock and repatriated the share certificates to Amlani. They had to stay closed for ten days. It was all the breathing space Amlani needed. He had turned the rout. The crisis was over.

At Imilani Rao's office the phones rang unheeded. The haughty Brahmin sat alone, the numbers on his computer screen mocking him. Somewhere, somehow, Amlani had found a secret backer with deep pockets. Rao had gambled and lost and it would cost him a fortune. He also knew he would never attempt anything on such a scale again. Amlani was unassailable. He would get his oil company.

At Renown House peace returned to the top floor. Amlani called Arvind and Joshi and his brothers into his office to toast their survival with champagne. His enemies should have known; he would never make a move into the oil business without backing, without someone to share the risk. Still, the scale and the suddenness of Rao's attack had surprised him. Until an hour before he invited the gathering reporters up to his boardroom, Amlani hadn't been sure he would survive.

He had been involved in secret negotiations with the Dumont Chemical Corporation of Philadelphia for almost a year. Dumont was one of dozens of U.S. corporations seeking a foothold in the buoyant Indian economy with its middle class of 300 million and buying power equal to the EEC.

Dumont needed an Indian partner to facilitate its expansion into the subcontinent, and Amlani needed a partner to facilitate his expansion into oil. Negotiations were at an advanced stage but had stalled on the price of a twenty-one percent share in Renown Industries and the number of seats the Americans would have on the board.

Rao's attack had given the negotiations the kick-start they needed. Amlani needed money, and it was not in Dumont's interests to let him go under. He gave the Americans the deal they wanted.

For $40 million they would get a twenty-nine percent share in Renown Industries and four seats on an eleven-seat board. The bonus was a forty-nine percent share in Renown Oil and parity on the board. By American standards it wasn't a lot of money—especially for the level of access they were getting to the Indian market—but by Indian standards it was a colossal sum. It gave Amlani everything he wanted. And despite the risks of having the Americans on board in such strength, he was confident he could manage them the way he managed everybody else.

With his sons and brothers Amlani raised his champagne glass and toasted the future of Renown Oil. He put the glass to his lips and tilted back his head, and at that moment a clot of blood the size of a teardrop detached itself from the wall of his right carotid artery and joined the blood flow to his brain. It was too big to squeeze through the narrow duct behind his jawbone and it stuck there, stopping instantly the flow of blood from his heart to the right side of the brain.

The pain was instant and excruciating. Amlani dropped the champagne glass and clutched at his neck. Then he pitched forward onto his desk and lay still, his eyes open and dead.

It was Arvind who saved his father's life. It was Arvind who rushed to his father's side and moved him gently onto the floor. It was Arvind who shouted at his stunned uncles to fetch the company doctor while he pumped his father's chest and breathed life back into his still lungs. It was Arvind who brought him back to life and Dr. Ghawali who kept him alive while they rushed him to the Nehru Heart Institute where surgeons located and removed the blood clot that night.

That had been a year ago.

Amlani hadn't been back to Renown House since. In his absence Arvind ran the company with the assistance of his brother and his uncles.

Rao consoled himself with a partial victory. He hadn't

destroyed Amlani, but had crippled him nevertheless. Renown was not the same without Amlani. Everyone knew that. And the stock price reflected it. Since Amlani's stroke Renown's shares had drifted downward again and traded now between 300 and 350.

It suited Amlani to let them go on thinking as they did. For a year. He could have gone back to work after three months but he chose not to. He stayed at home, at Ocean View, and used the pretense of convalescence to plan his next moves.

Now he was ready.

He finished his last lap and rolled over onto his back to float and look at the stars. It was the most precious time of the day, the time when he could drift in his pool in the sky and feel like a god drifting through the heavens. Serene, all-powerful, immortal.

CHAPTER 7

"It's politics."

"I know."

"You're sure you want to do it?"

"I think it's worth the risk. It's a chance to do more in one year than I could in a lifetime at the bar."

"She got to you."

"It was more than I expected, much more."

"Through your ego."

They sat at a small circular table with engraved brass inlays that Annie used as a breakfast table. A sliding glass door opened onto a balcony the size of a shower stall, but it provided expansive ocean views she considered essential. An inshore breeze stirred her red hair and turned her *salwar khameez* into undulating ribbons.

Sansi thought it significant that she had chosen her apartment as the place to have this conversation. Even on her territory she seemed tense.

"You'd rather I turned it down?"

She shook her head. "I don't like it, but it's your decision."

"A chance to do something about Varanasi? To make sure there's not another travesty like Bhopal? I don't see how I could turn it down."

"You think she didn't know that?"

"It is just possible I might be the right man for the job," Sansi said, trying to ease Annie's concerns.

"You're exactly the right man for the job." She smiled wanly. "That's what bothers me."

Sansi fidgeted with his empty coffee cup. Annie got up and went to the kitchen to start a fresh pot.

Sansi called to her. "Perhaps there is not quite the degree of cynicism behind this you suspect."

"She was married to a politician for seventeen years," Annie answered. "She was at the Sorbonne in the late sixties. Now she just happens to be in the cabinet?"

"She needs friends, she needs people she can trust."

"I believe that."

He got up and walked over to the marble-topped counter that separated the living room from the kitchen. "Why are you so afraid of her?"

"You mean apart from giving you a job and throwing me out of the country?"

"She isn't going to throw you out of the country," he said, trying to sound reassuring.

"Probably not. But I'm not going to give her an excuse either."

Sansi felt relieved. "That's all she wants."

"And in the meantime, we'll both just be good little hookers and do everything Rupe wants us to do."

"This isn't America," Sansi said. "You have to work with the way things are here, not the way you want them to be."

"I know what she's doing is in a good cause," Annie said. "It's the way she's going about it that makes it feel dirty."

"I don't know any country where you can clean up a mess

without getting your hands dirty," Sansi said. "It's a matter of degree."

"What bothers me is she knows exactly what buttons to push with you."

Sansi felt uncomfortable, more uncomfortable than he should have done.

"It bothers me that she knows you so well," Annie added.

The percolator started to gurgle and steam. Annie picked up the carafe and refilled their cups. Sansi was glad of the distraction.

"She knows how to get what she wants," he conceded.

"No doubt about that, is there?" Annie said. "But what else does she want?"

CHAPTER 8

Madhuri Amlani lifted his ungainly body out of the pool and walked, streaming, up the stone steps. A servant waited with an armful of towels and helped pat him dry. Another helped him on with his robe, then knelt down to ease his slippers onto his wrinkled feet. Amlani went downstairs to the penthouse apartment that occupied the entire top floor of the building, an area so vast it provided separate, spacious apartments for him and his wife and meant they never had to see each other unless they had to.

In an overcrowded city where space was a sign of status, Amlani was profligate in its use. His bathroom alone was big enough to accommodate a mid-sized apartment.

His first stop was the massage table where a masseuse selected more for her looks than her skills oiled his skin and kneaded his muscles for ten minutes. Sometimes, when he needed additional relief, it took longer. Afterward he showered away the oil and sweat and the lingering taint of chlorine. He put on a fresh robe and sat in a brightly mirrored alcove while his barber shaved him. When he dressed there were two servants to assist him—one to help him with his shirts and suits, the other with his shoes. Though he always tied his own tie.

He ate breakfast at a white Formica countertop with gold flecks, matching swivel chairs, and a view of the harbor. Breakfast was papaya with lime followed by unbuttered toast and weak, unsweetened tea. While he ate he worked his way through the morning newspapers. Bombay supported more daily newspapers in more languages than possibly any other city in the world and he read quickly or it would have taken him most of the morning.

He had lost weight since the stroke and it suited him. He thought it made him look younger. His hair was still more black than gray but had receded in recent years to reveal more of a broad and protuberant forehead. It would have given him a forbidding look but for the legendary energy that brightened his eyes and kept his features cheerful and mobile and made him seem more physically attractive than he really was.

A few minutes before seven he heard the distant sigh of the elevator. He knew the time without looking up from his reading. His sons knew better than to be late.

The floor immediately below Amlani was occupied by his eldest son, Arvind, now thirty-four, Arvind's wife, Meher, their two young children, and servants. The floor below that was divided into two apartments occupied by Joshi and Rashmi. Both were still single. Rashmi was only twenty but Joshi was twenty-eight and a source of increasing concern to his parents. He showed no interest in getting married and ignored his mother's attempts to find him a match.

On lower floors were guest apartments, a gymnasium, another swimming pool, a private nightclub, and a games room for the children. There were servants' floors that included kitchens equipped to serve banquets for up to a hundred people; a security floor; and two garage floors for a fleet of vehicles that included a neon red American Corvette Arvind had kept from his playboy days.

Amlani also had houses in Delhi, Calcutta, Simla and Pune, a villa in Goa, and a couple of smaller apartments in Bombay where he entertained his various mistresses. He had a corporate jet and two helicopters in hangars at the domestic airport at Santa Cruz, and he was maneuvering with the city for permission to anchor a helipad in the harbor, a two minute launch ride from Ocean View.

The elevator arrived with a faint hydraulic grunt and Arvind stepped out, then Joshi. Both wore expensive suits and walked at the same synchronized pace, like a pair of executive dolls. As they came into their father's presence they stopped, pressed their hands together, and bobbed their heads respectfully.

"*Namaste,*" Arvind murmured, and knelt down to press his hands and lips to his father's shiny leather shoes. "I kiss your feet and ask your blessing for this new day."

Amlani touched his fingertips to his son's head and gave his blessing. Arvind got back to his feet and waited while Joshi went through the same ritual.

Amlani was not a devout Hindu. He lived his life with no concession to the reprimands of karma, but he liked ceremony and ritual because they emphasized the concept of dharma, the Hindu belief in duty and destiny entwined. History showed that no dynasty could endure without dharma, and dharma was the foundation of every empire.

Amlani beckoned a servant to fill two more cups then sent him out of the room. A big day lay ahead and there were matters to be discussed that were not for the ears of servants.

Amlani's first concern was the new refinery at Surat. Arvind, under his father's direction, had supervised the shipment and reassembly of an oil refinery from Mexico to India. The plant was owned by Dumont but was so dirty it had been shut down by the usually accommodating Mexican authorities. Dumont had decided it was cheaper to ship the plant to India as a pilot project for the new relationship with Renown than it was to upgrade it to meet Mexico's relaxed pollution control standards.

Dumont demanded detailed reports on its progress, company officials had been out regularly to see it, and another high level delegation was expected soon to reassure themselves that their investment was sound. It wasn't only their stake in the refinery that concerned them. It was their stake in Renown and its long-term viability as a launchpad for their expansion into India. Amlani knew it was a test to see if Renown could deliver on its promises, to see if it was capable of full partnership with a company like Dumont. He also knew that the best way to impress them was to get the refinery up and running, problem free, and ahead of schedule.

That they were a full four months ahead of schedule was due entirely to Arvind. It was Arvind who convinced the government of Gujerat that the refinery met the strictest emission control standards in the world. It was Arvind who kept officials from a dozen different federal departments away during construction. The state government was sympathetic to Amlani anyway, and once the plant was running and providing employment for hundreds of Indian workers, it would be much harder to shut down just because it didn't meet a few pollution control laws.

"I want you to go up to Surat tomorrow," Amlani told his eldest son. "I have to be sure we are ready."

"The holding tanks are ready now," Arvind answered. "We can ship in the first crude as soon as you want. We should have kerosene and diesel on-line next month, and the month after we can start processing ethylene, naphtha, and benzene. Another two or three months and we should be producing aviation fuel and all the higher grade fuels. It's all ready."

He spoke with a slight American accent, a legacy of his years in Chicago. He also watched CNN, read American newspapers, and visited the U.S. at least once a year. He kept up with the politics and could talk football and baseball. He had found it all useful in getting the measure of the people from Dumont.

"Joshi could do it," he added, a note of indignation in his voice. "I've been up there twenty times, he's been twice."

Arvind hated Surat. It was a vile, toxic place, a sprawling, industrial slum whose population had swollen from 200,000 to more than a million in a decade, where mutant strains of ancient plagues erupted regularly out of the ghettos. Arvind had spent eighty-seven days there in the past year, almost three months. He'd had the bungalows of the executive compound fitted with air filters and the water supply brought in by tanker. He had taken to wearing a face mask much of the time he was outside, but even so, for days after he came back he spat up orange phlegm.

Joshi looked unhappy. He had his father's plump, expressive face and it showed every emotion. He was getting tired of Arvind's complaints that he didn't carry his weight. He also knew what his father's answer would be and that it would only foment even more resentment in his brother.

"I have plenty for Joshi to do here," Amlani told Arvind. "You are my eyes in Surat. When you are there they know it is me who is watching them. When you speak they know it is me who is speaking. And when the time comes for you to step into my shoes, no one will question you."

Arvind knew better than to argue. His time would come. All he needed was patience.

"What about the cracking plant?" Amlani asked.

"Another four to five weeks," Arvind said. "Six at the most."

"And the converters?"

"You told me not to install them until you said so."

"I am telling you now," Amlani said. "That is why I want you up there. We will ship in the first crude next month and do a test run the month after. I want to show the Americans a working refinery."

"You're going to announce it today?" Arvind said.

Both Arvind and Joshi looked shocked.

Amlani smiled at their reaction. He knew the sensation his return would create. He was counting on it. He intended to call a press conference for midday so he could show himself to the nation, so he could prove there were no long-lasting effects from his stroke and that he was back in charge at Renown. What he hadn't revealed to anyone was that he would also use the occasion to announce the early completion of the new cracking facility at Surat. It was the first oil cracking plant in India not wholly or partly owned by the government. He just wouldn't tell them yet who had paid for it.

He knew what the effect would be on Renown's stock price. The moment word got out that Amlani was in good health, that he was back at the helm of Renown and that the first refinery in his proposed oil company was ready to go into production, Renown's share price would skyrocket.

He would initiate the buying spree himself. He had instructed his brokers to buy Renown shares the moment the stock exchange opened—three hours before he would make his announcement. At the same time he would announce a public offering in Renown Oil which would offer convertibility of existing debentures to those who wanted to get in on the ground floor of his new oil company.

Joshi had said little so far, and his response, as usual, was cautious.

"Father, I'm not so sure about this," he said.

Amlani looked at his youngest son. "Why?"

"I think it might be too soon."

"It is a miracle we kept it a secret this long," Amlani said. "We tell them today while we still have the element of surprise."

Suddenly, Arvind did not sound as confident as he had a moment ago. "We're months away from a full commissioning," he said. "Things could go wrong—"

"You will have to do it in a month," Amlani interrupted. "The Americans want to be here for the commissioning. I have to give them a date."

Both his sons lapsed into silence. Amlani looked from one to the other. It was Joshi who spoke first.

"That isn't our only problem," he said.

Amlani's brows contracted. The one thing calculated to anger him most was the thought that they might have kept important information about his companies from him.

"The Department of the Environment is going to announce a date for the Varanasi hearings," Joshi went on. "It looks like next month. We thought they would be at least another year. Nobody expected the BJP to move this quickly. They will be sitting when you commission the refinery. It could be awkward."

"Awkward?" Amlani repeated, as if the word itself was strangely unpronounceable.

Joshi shifted uncomfortably. If Arvind liked to moan about the unfair burden he carried, it seemed to Joshi that it was always he who had to be the bearer of bad news.

"If our Varanasi plant is implicated in the spill we will probably have to go before the commission," Joshi continued. "I don't think the Americans would like that. You know how public-relations conscious they are. It's not a good way to begin a partnership."

Tectonic plates of bone seemed to flex and grind inside Amlani's massive brow. Renown owned a textile mill near Varanasi under the name Patna Fabrics. It was one of hundreds of mills and dye works along that stretch of the Ganga, and as far as he knew, investigators from the state environmental protection agency had not traced the spill back to any one of them, including his.

"If we are implicated in that spill," he added quietly, "I would like to know now."

He turned his gaze back to Arvind. While Joshi helped tune Renown's corporate mechanics, it was Arvind, indisputably, who was the empire's troubleshooter, who made sure his father's will was done.

"We're not implicated in anything," Arvind said.

"Did that spill come from our plant?" Amlani asked.

"It is impossible to say," Arvind answered evasively. "It is impossible for anyone to say."

Amlani smiled the smile of a man trying to be patient.

"It is an old plant and it uses phosphorous," Arvind continued, his voice acquiring the same stridency it had when he was a boy denying he had done anything wrong. "So does every other dye plant on the river. It builds up and some of it leeches into the river. They can't say it all came from our plant."

This time when Amlani spoke his voice had a deliberate, ominous quality.

"I don't think you're listening," he said. "Joshi is right. This is the worst industrial disaster since Bhopal. It is not the public relations debut the Americans have in mind for their first venture into India."

A strained silence descended.

Then Arvind said: "Nobody will find anything to connect us to that spill."

"You are willing to stake the future of Renown Industries on that?" his father asked. "You are willing to stake your own future on it?"

"I am the future of Renown Industries," Arvind said.

Amlani smiled a more relaxed smile. Now his son understood.

"Who is the manager of the plant in Varanasi?"

"His name is Agawarl."

"Is he reliable?"

"He seems to be," Arvind answered. "He was the under-manager when we bought the company six years ago. The manager was no good and Uncle Haresh fired him and gave Agawarl a chance. The plant has shown increased profits three years out of the last four."

"What does he say?"

"He says there is nothing wrong with the holding tanks. They were repaired two years ago and the factories inspector issued a safety certificate that is still in effect."

Amlani nodded. A safety certificate meant nothing and it meant everything. It certainly didn't mean the tanks that held the phosphoric acid were safe. What it did mean was the safety inspector had issued a certificate that said they were—and that got Renown off the hook. But it wasn't something Amlani wanted to defend his company against when the Americans were watching every move.

"But there were no major leaks or breaches?"

"None," Arvind said. "Some seepage over time, of course, but that is all."

"Have the *babus* given him any trouble?"

"Two men came from the environment protection agency. They looked at the tanks and took some soil samples but he has heard nothing since."

"Did he pay them?"

"*Acha.*"

Amlani looked at Joshi to see if he was any more reassured. He wasn't.

"An investigation by the state environment protection agency is not the same as an investigation by a federal commission of inquiry," Joshi said. "Especially an inquiry set up by the BJP looking for somebody to blame."

Amlani paused. Joshi was a worrier, but he was supposed to worry about the family business and could hardly be faulted for it.

Amlani turned back to Arvind: "Can we trust this man Agawarl to deal with the commission, to keep them at a distance?"

"I'll speak to him," Arvind said, but there was hesitation in his voice.

"You don't think he's up to it?"

"We can't take the chance," Joshi said. "Agawarl may be a good plant manager, but that doesn't make him the right man to defend Renown Industries against an inquiry like this. Rupe Seshan hates us. When she knows Patna is our plant she will do everything she can to drag our name through the dirt. We are going to have to deal with this ourselves. We have to find a way to defuse it before it becomes a problem."

"Rupe Seshan hates people," Arvind interjected. "She likes only little birds and monkeys. She should stay at home with her animal shelter, mending broken wings."

Amlani smiled. Much of the publicity Rupe Seshan had generated while in her husband's shadow came from her crusades on behalf of animal welfare and endangered species. No one doubted her sincerity, but it didn't make her of sufficient caliber to threaten a man like Amlani.

"*Acha*," Joshi acknowledged. "Now she is minister for the environment and she has the power to put right everything that is wrong with the world. She will go after us because she can go after us, to make the point that she is not afraid of the big boys. If the commission recommends charges against Renown Industries while we are trying to close the deal with Dumont . . ."

He left the rest unsaid.

"Rupe Seshan." Amlani said her name slowly. "Another widow. Another Indira. Whoever heard of her before she was a widow?" He paused and then added: "Her yoni is empty so she pours all her frustrations into politics. If she had somebody to fuck her, the whole country would be grateful."

Arvind smirked. The conversation had shifted to familiar ground.

"She is a little old for me, but for the sake of the country . . ."

Amlani looked thoughtful. He understood Joshi's concern but he agreed with Arvind too. It was inconceivable that a spoiled high caste widow might pose a serious threat to the empire he had built just when he was about to embark on the greatest program of expansion the country had ever seen.

"This government won't last two years," he said. "When it goes, she goes, and so does her commission."

He turned to Arvind and added: "In the meantime we will bury them in cooperation. Tell Agawarl if anybody from the commission wants to talk to him, he is to cooperate fully. Let them have the run of the place. Tell him he is not to offer them any money. If anybody has to go before the commission, it will

be me. I will enjoy the opportunity to tell them what I think of
their little *thod jodh*."

Thod jodh was the street name for the kind of kangaroo
court the Bombay underworld used to settle scores.

Reluctantly, Joshi added: "It isn't Rupe Seshan we have to
worry about."

Amlani looked impatiently at his youngest son.

"Did you see the papers today?" Joshi asked.

Amlani gestured to the pile of newspapers on the countertop, most of which were yet unread.

Joshi plucked out that day's *Times of India*, opened it, and
pointed to a picture midway down page five, an outdated file
picture of a young man in police dress uniform. Under it was a
two column story headed: BOMBAY LAWYER NAMED TO VARANASI
PROBE.

"His name is George Sansi," Joshi said. "He was an inspector
at Crime Branch till he decided to practice law."

Amlani and Arvind scanned the story and picture.

"You know him?" Amlani said.

"I met him once at the Jehangir Gallery." Joshi smiled briefly
and added, "I was with a girl who knew him. I could find out
more."

"And you think he could be a problem for us?"

"He handled some important cases when he was at Crime
Branch," Joshi answered. "People say he never took money and
that made things difficult for him. His reputation is very *pukka*.
I think he could give us trouble."

Not to be outdone, Arvind added: "His mother is Pramila
Sansi. She was a prostitute for the British before she was a
stirrer in the women's movement. She is friends with Rupe
Seshan—that is how he got this job."

Amlani knew of Pramila Sansi. Not only because of her
celebrity, but because she helped organize a strike among
female mill workers in the mid-1970s that cost him, among
others, a lot of money.

"Perhaps his mother taught him how to make trouble," Amlani added sourly. "You say he was at Crime Branch?"

"He worked for Jamal," Joshi said. "They had some kind of falling out. That is the reason Sansi left."

"Over what?"

Joshi shrugged. His information on Sansi didn't go that far.

Amlani grunted. He knew Narendra Jamal, joint commissioner of Crime Branch, the independent investigative unit inside the Maharashtra Police Service. Jamal was a powerful, well-connected figure with political ambitions of his own. That made him a pragmatist, a man who understood the nuances of influence, the kind of man with whom Amlani could do business.

Amlani turned to Arvind and said: "Call Jamal. See what he can tell us about George Sansi."

Then Amlani gave his youngest son a reassuring pat on the shoulder.

"It may be that if we can deal with this man, Sansi, we won't have to worry about Rupe Seshan and her commission. On your word, Joshi, I will take him seriously. I will speak to him. I will give him the choice I give every man. He can be a friend of Amlani or he can be an enemy of Amlani. It is for him to decide."

CHAPTER 9

"**I** know I can count on your discretion," Sansi said, and pushed a sheet of paper across a mahogany desk as wide as the deck of an East Indiaman.

Jamal looked at the list of six typewritten names. At the top was Savitri Chowdhary, formerly Sansi's sergeant at Crime Branch and since promoted to the rank of inspector. The rest were men with whom Sansi had worked on a number of difficult cases, all of them good, dependable officers.

"They will be honored you would ask," Jamal said amiably. He leaned back in his chair, hands behind his head, ingot-sized Rolex glinting in the strip lighting. "I will inquire into their availability."

"I understand they are all available," Sansi said, equally cordial.

Jamal's expression stayed the same but his eyes hardened. Under normal circumstances he wouldn't hesitate to release six men to assist in a federal investigation. But normal circumstances were when there was a Congress Party government in New Delhi working with a Congress Party government in Maharashtra. Jamal was a Congress Party man with an eye to the chief minister's job. If he loaned six officers to an investigation initiated by the Bharatiya Janata Party and directed at corporate sponsors of the Congress Party, he might jeopardize his chances of getting party backing later when he decided to make his move. He had to be helpful enough to discharge the duties of his position but not so helpful as to risk his political future. But there was another, more personal reason why he balked. Jamal liked Sansi and admired his talents more than he let Sansi know—but he couldn't let a former subordinate come into his office and tell him what to do. Even when that former subordinate had the writ of the federal government to back him up.

"Sansi, I have five hundred men under my command," he said. "I cannot tell you what all of them are doing at this moment. But I will tell you—if pulling any one of them out of an ongoing investigation means putting that investigation at risk, I won't do it."

The two of them sat in the commissioner's office on the top floor of an elegant, two-story stone building inside the sprawling cantonment of Bombay police headquarters. The office was bright, spacious, and cooled by a rattly air conditioner over the door. On the two-tone cream and green walls was a dense foliage of maps, graphs, and charts which blossomed with multicolored flags, buttons, and pins that showed how Jamal was winning the war against crime. His furniture was almost all early Victorian, wine dark slabs of ornately sculpted wood that had proved more enduring than the Empire that spawned them.

The commissioner suffered from a form of schizophrenia not unusual among educated Indians; he was both a nationalist and an anglophile. The kind of Indian who would wear kurta pajamas and read Tagore in the privacy of his own home but who was enamored of British style and manners, especially the imperial grandeur of the Raj. Which was why he had plundered every government warehouse in the city to surround himself with the props that presented him as a man of substance.

"Commissioner, I need these men in New Delhi in two weeks," Sansi continued.

Jamal inclined his head to one side, as though puzzled.

"Sansi, you have the resources of the federal police, the Justice Ministry, and the attorney general's department at your command, and you expect to loot my department of six of its best officers at a moment's notice?"

Sansi had expected something like this. He understood perfectly the political considerations Jamal would have to weigh, and sympathized with none of them.

"You know how it is in New Delhi," Sansi said. "You don't know who you can trust." He nodded to the list on the desk. "I trust these men."

"You know too there are protocols to be followed," Jamal answered bluntly.

"The hearings begin next month," Sansi pressed on. "I have to be in New Delhi at the end of the week. I want to brief these men before I leave and I want them in New Delhi ready for work one week after me."

"Are Bapre." Jamal turned his eyes toward the ceiling as if the mere suggestion were laughable.

Sansi's gaze shifted to Jamal's expansive desk. In front of the commissioner was a pale green blotting pad with a wad of official papers turned facedown. To his left was a blank-screened computer terminal. To his right three telephones; one green, one ivory, one red. Sansi knew the green phone was for internal calls, the ivory phone was an outside line Jamal used to service his extensive network of informants, and the red phone was a direct line to the governor's estate.

"Call the governor," Sansi said.

"I am sorry ?" This time Jamal's puzzlement was genuine.

"Call the governor," Sansi repeated.

The silence that followed was the silence that follows an explosion, the ghastly suspension of reality between detonation and realization, the certainty that something had changed forever.

Jamal knew the governor better than Sansi, and the governor was a Congress Party man—but the governor took his orders from whoever was in power in New Delhi, and this particular governor was just as much a survivor as Jamal and in no hurry to give the BJP an excuse to replace him. It was possible Sansi had warned the governor in advance that Jamal might prove obstructive and if that was the case, Jamal could not doubt whose skin the governor would save first. Or it was possible Sansi was bluffing. All Jamal had to do to find out was pick up the red phone.

He smiled faintly.

"Tell me, Sansi," he said. "Do you like being back on the inside?"

CHAPTER 10

"I need you."

Annie looked up from her computer screen to see the fiercely compressed face of Alam Bajaj, news editor of the *Times of India*.

"What?"

"I need you," he repeated in the nasal cockney accent honed by a lifetime in the east end of London. "We've got a big story breaking at Renown House and I need you down there right away."

"I can't," she protested. "I'm working on a think piece for Saturday."

It was a half hour before noon, and she had come in early to finish an essay for the op-ed page. Her boss, Sylvester Naryan, wasn't due in until six o'clock and she was alone in her department with nobody to protect her against marauding editors like Bajaj.

"I don't care if you're working on a cure for fucking cancer," Bajaj snapped. "We've got a major breaking story and there's nobody else here."

Bajaj was an NRI, a Non-Resident Indian who had worked for a muckraking tabloid in London and had the pit bull personality to go with it. He belonged to a newer and increasingly prevalent breed of NRI whose family had left India decades earlier to build new lives in England, the mother of the Empire, only to see grown-up sons like Bajaj lured back to Bombay because of greater opportunities in the booming Indian economy. Bajaj was the unlovely face of a fever that had infected print journalism in the West and was now spreading rapidly in India—the fever of the lowest common denominator—and had been hired by the market-fixated son of the ailing publisher to "liven up" the once venerable *Times*.

"Why Renown House?" she argued. "I'm not a business writer. I don't know anything about business."

"Because Amlani just came back from the dead," Bajaj barked. "He's called a press conference for twelve and I've got nobody here but Sandip."

Annie looked around the newsroom and saw it was deserted but for a few copy editors, secretaries, and messengers. The only business writer available was a young graduate from Calcutta who stood nervously by the door wearing a bottle-green suit and a virulent tie Annie thought must have been conceived the same year that he was.

She got to her feet and reluctantly loaded her cassette recorder, tapes, and notebook into her leather shoulder bag.

"I thought Amlani was supposed to be a basket case," she said.

"Didn't we all," Bajaj said. "The crafty old bugger's been up to something. Been scheming, hasn't he? Now he's going to tell us what it is, and I rather think we should be there, don't you?"

"Just don't expect any in-depth analysis, okay?" she warned.

"Don't think about it too much darlin'." Bajaj grinned like a London spiv. "If you get stuck, ask Sandip. He knows a bit about the stock market, he'll see you don't make a fool of yourself."

Annie bit her tongue. It was a bad time to make trouble at the *Times*; her visa depended on her job. She was still smouldering when she reached the third floor lobby where Sandip and a photographer were holding the elevator.

"Hurry please." Sandip beckoned impatiently.

The elevator door closed behind her and Sandip gripped her arm tightly.

"This is no time to be losing your head," he said nervously. "Keep calm and everything will be all right. That is what this business is about, you know."

He was in his early twenties, looked fifteen, and had been at the paper six months. She had been in the business fourteen years, most of that time in Los Angeles. In the two years she had been at the *Times of India* she had advanced from token white woman to senior feature writer on the Insight section. While she couldn't claim to be an expert on the stock market she did know a great deal about the Amlanis.

She prized Sandip's fingers loose from her arm. "You take care of your end and I'll take care of mine," she said sweetly. "Just be sure and get your copy in on time—because that's what this business is about."

The elevator stopped and the door opened.

"Oh, and don't put your hands on me again, ever, unless you plan on a new career as a wind chime, okay?"

Sandip turned, bewildered, to the photographer. "Please, I am from Calcutta," he said. "What is wind chime?"

Their taxi careened southbound along Waudey Road, past a scrubby sliver of parkland called Cross Maidan, cleared by the British to give a clear field of fire against marauding Malabar pirates. The maidan was popular now with kite flyers who used elaborate kites to fight duels in the sky. It was a more dangerous pastime than it looked. The year before, a scooter driver had been decapitated when he rode into a kite string coated with ground glass used to cut opponents' strings.

A block from Renown House they encountered a hopeless tangle of jammed cars and milling people and had to leave the taxi behind. As they pushed their way through the crowd, they passed scrip men on the sidewalk with share certificates fanned out across the pavement like newspapers.

"What price Renown?" Annie shouted to one.

"Four hundred," he shouted back.

She looked at Sandip and his expression confirmed her suspicion. The price was up just on word of Amlani's return.

Among traders Renown House was sometimes called Fort Renown. Because the Amlanis had grown so powerful, it was said that whoever controlled Fort Renown controlled India. This morning it was a fortress under siege as a crowd of several thousand jammed the intersection under its looming prow, all of them determined to follow the TV crews and newspaper reporters into the building. Dozens of policemen armed with lathis just as determinedly beat them back.

Annie, Sandip, and the photographer had to fight their way through to the police lines and the outstretched arms of Renown security people who hauled them through the front doors. Inside it was cool and tranquil and the thick granite walls reduced the outside roar to a murmur.

Annie straightened her clothes and looked around. There was a mural on the wall from the days of the steamship line. It showed Britannia, regal and demure in her island realm, accepting tribute from dusky, bare-breasted natives. Annie wondered if Amlani had left it there intentionally.

"Are all his press conferences this much fun?" she asked.

"Amlani is like Ganesha to these people," Sandip said gravely. "His return means good fortune. I told you what it would be like."

"You should try a Thanksgiving sale at Macy's," Annie said.

More Renown security people steered them up a broad flight of stairs to the second floor and a noisy, wedge-shaped conference hall big enough for five hundred people. Rows of folding metal chairs faced a small raised stage with a lectern, a microphone, and a table set with water pitchers. Reporters and TV crews cursed, argued, and jostled each other for the best vantage points in front of the stage.

Annie went to the last row of chairs and took the seat nearest the wall. The photographer plunged into the mob at the front of the room, but Sandip followed Annie and took a seat next to her, notepad open on his lap, pencil poised.

"I thought it was every man for himself," she said.

"This is a good position," he answered defensively.

Annie smiled. It was a lousy position. They were the farthest they could be from the stage and still be in the room. Its only advantage was that it made for a faster getaway.

Despite the rush to be on time, Annie expected Amlani to be late. She had never yet been to a press conference in India that started on time. But Amlani proved her wrong. At two minutes past twelve a door near the stage opened and a phalanx of security men bulldozed into the room with a half-dozen men in suits shielded in their midst.

There was instant pandemonium and a surge toward the stage. Chairs were overturned, cameras toppled, TV lights strobed the walls and ceiling, and several people were trampled. Annie climbed up on her seat and steadied herself against the wall. Sandip looked at her and at the wild melee down front, then he too climbed up on his chair. With nothing to steady him, he stood at a half crouch like a man with a back problem, an unhappy look on his face.

Annie watched while security guards manhandled the mob into some kind of order and the men in suits stepped up to the stage. Amlani was the shortest and the most recognizable, with his bulky physique and misshapen crag of a head. He was smiling broadly, apparently pleased by the excitement his return had caused.

Annie assumed the other men were Renown executives, though she only recognized Amlani's sons: Arvind, tall and with the sensitive good looks that owed nothing to his father; and

Joshi, short, plumpish, and unmistakably his father's son. Annie recalled it was Arvind who had the reputation as the playboy and Joshi who was supposedly quiet and introspective. She noticed he was the only man onstage who looked uncomfortable.

Then, like everybody else in the room, she focused her attention on Amlani, who was smiling, rocking back and forth on his heels, trading private jokes. For a man said to have spent much of the past year in a coma, he looked very well.

At last one of the suits stepped forward and tapped the microphone. A series of loud thuds reverberated through the room.

"Everybody please be taking his seat," he said. "We are not beginning till everybody is in his seat."

Again the crowd rushed the stage. The suit recoiled and the line of security guards wavered. Amlani laughed and waved to those reporters he knew.

Annie grabbed Sandip by the shoulder. "Who's that?"

"His name is Prasad," Sandip said shakily. "He is the director of corporate relations."

She let him go and he almost fell.

Finally Amlani stepped behind the table and sat down, and the others followed. There was a moment's indecision amongst the media, then a sudden scramble for seats in the front rows accompanied by more fighting and cursing. Gradually the uproar subsided to a restless grumble. Prasad stepped back up to the microphone.

"Ladies and gentlemen of the press—" he began. The microphone shrieked and the ladies and gentlemen of the press screamed insults at him. Prasad turned down the mike and tried again.

"Today is a day of making history for Renown Industries and for India," he continued. "Today we are pleased and privileged to have with us again the gentle founder and most gracious chairman of Renown Industries, Mr. Madhuri Amlani."

He waited for applause but none followed and he added quickly: "As all of you are knowing, the chairman has suffered a long period of illness but has emerged in full fitness and in health and is returning to us today to once more take the helm of the great vessel of commerce that is Renown Industries."

This time Prasad left nothing to chance and started the applause himself. Those onstage and other Renown lackeys around the room picked it up and Amlani bobbed modestly.

"As all of you will soon be understanding, our chairman has been wasting no time," Prasad continued. "He is taking the occasion of his return today to be telling you the great visions he is having for Renown Industries as India is striding boldly into a new century and taking her place—and rightfully so—as a nation among nations."

The grumbling increased and several reporters told Prasad to shut up.

Flustered, he concluded: "It is with the greatest of honors I am presenting to you the chairman of—"

The rest was drowned in renewed uproar as everyone in the first rows leaped up and unleashed a barrage of questions at Amlani. This time the guards were rougher pushing them back. Annie saw a guard shove a woman into her seat only to have her grab his hand and bite it.

Amlani came forward with a lightness of step surprising for such an awkward looking man and spoke quietly into the microphone. It was impossible for anyone to hear what he was saying, and slowly the reporters realized that was the point. A fragile quiet spread throughout the room.

". . . and everyone was saying 'Yes, he is Amlani's son but is he as clever as Amlani?' And I am here today to tell you all that my son Arvind has not only managed the company superbly in my absence but has improved its performance to the point where I had to rush back from my sickbed before he made me totally redundant."

There were a few chuckles and like an irascible beast given a pat and a bone, the crowd settled and allowed Amlani to take them where he wanted them to go.

"Those who were waiting have missed a great opportunity," Amlani went on. "When I was speaking with our brokers a few moments ago they were telling me our share price was already over four hundred. Let me tell you all a secret—it will be a long time before the market is seeing Renown shares at such a bargain price again."

Amlani was enjoying himself, knowing that every word he said put money in his pocket.

"Prasad is right when he is telling you I have not been wasting my time," Amlani went on. "For many months now my doctors are telling me more rest, Mr. Amlani, more rest. Amlani has had so much rest he is tired of resting. But all the time Amlani is resting, Amlani is thinking."

He paused and the room grew quieter.

"The whole world is thinking India is a poor country," he continued. "Other countries are looking at us and seeing poverty, over-population, and disease, and they are thinking that is the whole story. They see our poor and they see an ocean of misery. But when Amlani is seeing our poor he is seeing an ocean of opportunity. Amlani is seeing the jobs these people can do, the industries they can build, the wealth they can create. And that is what we at Renown Industries are doing. We are building new industries, we are creating new jobs, we are creating new wealth in which everyone is sharing.

"Look at the British," he went on. "The British were once our masters and now they are a beaten people, their spirit broken. Our country was invaded many times but the spirit of our people was never broken. Today we are having our own space program, our own rockets and satellites, and the British are looking at us in amazement and asking how can we do it, how can we overtake them in less than fifty years? All of this should be telling the rest of the world something, but still they are not looking. Still they are thinking poor India, poor India."

Annie listened, thinking this was how it must have felt to be the only white reporter at a *Swaraj* speech by Gandhi in the

1930s. She scribbled in her notebook: *Amlani—corporate Gandhi for a new India?*

"India is not waiting for them," Amlani said. "The next century will be the Asian century. The world is seeing already how China is becoming a new economic superpower. Next it will be the turn of India. Renown is taking steps today to make certain that India is the economic superpower of tomorrow."

Annie felt the tension in the room heighten.

"Today Renown Industries is employing over two million people," Amlani said. "In the next ten years we will be adding two million more jobs all over India."

A murmur ran through the crowd, expectation weighted by apprehension. Annie knew they must be thinking the same thing she was—that maybe the stroke had left its mark after all.

"One year ago I announced the creation of Renown Oil . . ." There was a tremor in his voice, whether from emotion or exhaustion, it was hard to tell, and Annie noticed that Joshi seemed increasingly uncomfortable.

"Since then you have been thinking nothing is happening with Renown Oil, that the project is in mothballs, that Amlani's dreams are too big for him."

He paused for effect.

"Today I am announcing that over the next ten years Renown Oil will build ten new oil refineries to supply the complete range of fuels India is needing to continue her growth through the twenty-first century."

There was a gasp of astonishment then bedlam. This time the crowd would not be contained. Amlani's security guards pulled back and formed a tight knot around the stage. Amlani grinned under the barrage of questions, all asking the same thing: How?

"This country does not have the refineries it needs to sustain its current rate of growth," he explained. "And the government does not have the money to build them. Our own projections show India is needing thirty to forty new refineries over the next two decades. The government can let the foreign oil companies take over our economy once again or it can give Indian enterprise a chance. Big, well-managed, public companies like Renown are ready to do what is right for India. We can build one refinery a year for the next ten years, more if the government is allowing it."

One reporter's voice rang out above the others: "Who will provide the technical support for Renown Oil?"

Amlani looked amused. Everybody assumed it was impossible for an Indian company to go into the oil business without outside help. It seemed to have occurred to no one that an Indian company might go it alone.

"Oil is only another chemical," Amlani said. "A refinery is only another chemical plant. We have all the expertise we need—and the reputation of Renown Industries is extending far beyond the borders of India, so there is plenty of interest from foreign investors who know a good opportunity when they are seeing it."

Excitement coursed through the room like a rush of wind, questions pelted Amlani like raindrops in a monsoon. And clearly he loved it. He was back in his element, playing to the crowd, cupping a hand to one ear, choosing the questions he wanted to answer. He signaled for quiet but they paid no heed and he had to speak loudly into the microphone to make himself heard.

"Shares in Renown Oil will go on sale one month from today." His voice echoed throughout the hall. "In the meantime we will be offering full convertibility on all Renown Industries stock and debentures here in Bombay."

The effect was electrifying. It meant anybody who bought stock or debentures in Renown Industries during the next month would get in on Renown Oil before trading opened, before foreign investors could buy in and the price skyrocketed. It was a promise of fortunes to be made.

Annie was amazed. She had never seen such blatant

manipulation of a public stock. By comparison the insider trading scandals that rocked American markets in the eighties were masterpieces of discretion.

"Can he do this?" she called to Sandip.

Sandip shrugged, teetered, and almost fell off his perch.

"On the Bombay exchange, Amlani does what Amlani wants," Sandip shouted back.

Then a reporter, bolder than the rest, asked the question everybody wanted answered. Annie didn't see the questioner but guessed it was a reporter from one of Imilani Rao's papers.

"Mr. Amlani, what assurances can you give that your company has the resources to build these new refineries?"

Amlani couldn't have looked happier if he had planted the question himself.

"One month from today we are commissioning our first fully operational refinery at Surat," he said. "I invite all of you to come and see for yourselves."

The atmosphere in the room accelerated to the hysterical. It was history repeating itself, a replay of the polyester coup of the early 1970s, only bigger. This time it was oil, which meant service stations, aviation fuel, marine fuel, lubricating oil, and all the spin-off products like plastics, drugs, and detergents. While his enemies had consigned him to history, Amlani had been maneuvering secretly to double the size of his empire. Renown Oil wasn't a dream, it was a reality. Everyone in the room now knew that what had been a rush for Renown shares was about to become a frenzy.

Annie prepared to jump down from her position, then realized the show wasn't over yet. The hysteria ebbed only slightly, TV crews switched off their lights and put down their cameras, but nobody was leaving. She looked around, puzzled. Then the door at the side of the stage opened and a half-dozen Renown employees appeared with two trolleys stacked high with glistening bolts of cloth.

"What are they doing?" Annie shouted to Sandip.

"It's a custom," he said. "Amlani does it only on special occasions."

"Does what?"

From the corner of her eye she saw a flash of color. Amlani was passing out bolts of cloth to the crowd. All pretense of restraint vanished as reporters rushed the stage, reaching, grasping. Amlani laughed and called to his sons to help him.

"Jesus . . ." Annie said.

The cordon of security guards wavered under the onslaught. Amlani hurled a bolt of cloth out into the room, a trailing crimson ribbon. Arvind unrolled another bolt, and then the others onstage, and the air filled with unfurling banners of multi-colored polyester.

"They're fighting," Annie said. "They're fighting over it."

Sandip jumped down from his seat. "One bolt of cloth makes clothings for a year," he said.

Annie stared at him, incredulous. He seemed about to add something, then shrugged as if she would never understand, and plunged into the brawling mob.

Annie got down from her chair and walked unhurriedly to the nearest exit. She paused in the doorway to look back. Her parting image was of Amlani laughing as he hurled a bolt of lime-green polyester high into the air and Sandip pushing a female TV reporter aside as he fought to catch it.

CHAPTER 11

Anjani Agawarl kneeled on a carpet of papers in his secretary's office. It was late in the afternoon; the day shift had gone home and the night shift had been at work for almost an hour. Agawarl hoped to leave soon, as long as there were no more emergencies to command his attention.

He had been at the plant since before dawn, an hour before the day workers began their ten-hour shift. Thirteen to fourteen hours a day, six days a week, was usual for him. All part of the responsibility of management. In return his job as plant manager gave him an office, a secretary, a car, a slightly higher salary than the shift foreman, and a piece of a profit-sharing program intended to persuade all Renown's middle managers they had a stake in the company. Agawarl had yet to see a paise from it, though he had boosted profits three years out of the last four. It was all down to the continuing costs of takeover, the Amlanis told him. It would be another five years before those costs were earned out and he could expect a share of the profits he generated. But they were watching him, the

Amlanis said. He had great prospects with a company like Renown. They were always looking for talent and they believed in rewarding hard work and loyalty. Agawarl wanted desperately to believe them.

His wife complained that he was just a slave with a shirt and tie, but she was glad to have the paycheck. They had been married six years and had five children, three of them girls, and she was pregnant again. They couldn't bear the burden of more girls, so Agawarl had spent seven hundred rupees on an ultrasound to be sure of the baby's sex. They were relieved to learn it was a boy. His wife had already endured two abortions.

Despite everything, Agawarl was hopeful about the future. He was the only plant manager he knew who was twenty-eight years old. Most employees didn't get a chance like this until they were in their late thirties or early forties. He was on the way up. All he had to do was be patient and keep the profits flowing, and the Amlanis would keep off his back. Which was why he was on the floor of his secretary's office with the door locked. The moment she had gone for the day, he emptied the filing cabinets and spread their contents over the linoleum.

The files he was looking for covered the period between the first year of Indian ownership in 1947 and the year he was appointed manager. Files that showed the quantities of dyes, bleaches, solvents, and processing chemicals that were used at the plant. Between 1947 and 1973 the plant had changed owners several times. Its records were poorly kept and riddled with errors and omissions that weren't his doing and which he wouldn't have to explain. It was the twenty years that preceded his appointment as manager that worried him. Management had been more efficient and the figures for those years had been more accurately kept. They told a sinister story, a story that detailed the careless storage and disposal of millions upon millions of gallons of hazardous chemical waste—including phosphorous. Most of those figures would have to be altered, he knew. Not tonight, but gradually, over the next few weeks, so that by the time anybody else saw them, their damning message would be lost in an indecipherable maze of figures.

The ringing of the telephone reminded him that he had meant to get up a half-dozen times to turn on more lights. The plant was badly in need of refurbishing—the Amlanis had promised to spend lakhs upgrading, but after four years they still said there was no money available—and the drab, ill-lit offices hadn't changed much since the early part of the century. The floor coverings had been replaced and some furniture and electrical fittings renewed, but otherwise it was much as it had been when it opened in 1911. Back then it was owned and operated by Leeds and Orient, a long defunct textiles producer whose headquarters were in the British Midlands. It had been built on the site of an earlier mill established by the British Army a few miles upstream from Varanasi to make uniforms at a time when red coats were worn by common soldiers and not just bandsmen. The last time any real money had been spent on the plant was when its British owners had converted to electric looms back in 1937.

On his way to the phone Agawarl glanced through the windows and saw the reason for the encroaching gloom. A gusty wind from the northeast had churned up the sand flats on the western banks of the Ganga and hurled clouds of sand into the sky.

Agawarl sat on an oak desk that would have been a valuable antique in London and picked up the black Bakelite phone.

"Patna Fabrics, manager's office," he said.

"Agawarl?"

"*Acha.*"

"You are doing what I told you?"

There was no introduction, no concession to basic courtesy, and the words were a blunt command rather than a question. The slight American accent told Agawarl it was Arvind Amlani.

"Everything is under control, sahib," he lied.

"Any more visitors from the government?"

"No, no more visits."

"You will be getting some," Arvind said. "I don't want them to find anything, you understand?"

Gaunt-faced and sunken-eyed, Agawarl looked older than his twenty-eight years. His movements were rapid and nervous and he had taken to walking with a stoop, as though perpetually going uphill.

"There are no problems with the EPA," he said.

"This is nothing to do with the state," Arvind added brusquely. "This is about politics. The BJP wants its own inquiry. That little houri, Seshan, has put her own man in charge of the investigation. His name is Sansi. You can expect a visit from him or his people anytime in the next few weeks."

Agawarl knew about the federal inquiry but, like everyone else in industry, he assumed it would follow in the usual Delhi tradition and take months, perhaps years, before it got to him. He would have to start on the figures tonight, he realized. He would have to work on them every night until they were done.

"They can come," he said and hoped he sounded convincing.

"This is your mess," Arvind added. "You keep it to yourself, you clean it up down there. I don't want my family involved. I don't want my father embarrassed by this, you understand?"

"I did as you asked—" Agawarl began.

"Shut your fucking mouth," Arvind stopped him.

Amlani security had found bugs before on the phones; always at the office, never at Ocean View. Everybody assumed they had been put there by somebody working for Rao. But there was no reason why somebody inside the family wouldn't bug the phones at Ocean View, and this was one conversation Arvind didn't want to get back to his father.

He chose his next words carefully: "You handle this down there—you have a future with the company. If I have to come down and take care of it myself, you have no future. You, your family, you have no future. You understand?"

Fear soured Agawarl's gut and for a moment he couldn't answer.

"*Acha*, I understa—" There was a click followed by a flare of static. Arvind had gone. Agawarl's hand shook as he put the phone down. He looked out the window at the dust storm across the river. The dying rays of the sun had been blunted and diffused by the storm, and crimson light spread like a bloodstain across the sky. The river rushed angrily through a blasted plain, its color an eerie reflection of the sky. It no longer looked real but like an image from a dreamscape, from the time of legends, from the time when demons fought the gods for mastery of the universe. Agawarl had lived on the river all his life and had never seen it like this. Ganga was the river of life, the life of India, the life of all Hindus. But her children had betrayed her. And now Ganga was a river of blood.

CHAPTER 12

Joshi sat in front of a big screen TV in his apartment, sipping a salt lime and clicking the remote to see if there was anything worth watching on the three-hundred-plus channels the rooftop satellite dish pulled in.

First he scanned the Bombay channels, stopping briefly at a current affairs show on the government station where Renown's director of corporate relations, Prasad, was expounding the Amlani vision of the future to an earnest female interviewer. Next he tried Doordashan and Zee TV, but he wasn't in the mood for Marathi folk recitals or Hindu love sagas. He kept going; through Larry King on CNN, CNN "Headline News," the BBC World Service, channels from Oman, Kuwait, Saudi Arabia, Russia, China, all the way to "Baywatch" on Star TV, and still found nothing to suit his mood. It would have helped if he had known what his mood was rather than the odd restlessness that afflicted him more and more frequently.

He paused at MTV to watch a trio of black women in scanty leather costumes whipping a naked white man in a dog collar.

Then he shut it off. It had become just like television in America—all those channels and nothing to watch.

Unlike his brother, who watched American football and baseball on the sports channels, Joshi wasn't taken with everything American. Joshi had enjoyed his time at Harvard, but only to a point. Business management was his father's choice, not his. He found that for a country that considered itself the most advanced society on earth, there was much about the United States that reminded him of India; the crime, the corruption, the slums, the indifference of the rich to the poor who lived and died on the streets. He had considered sending care packages to shelters for the homeless in America to see if that would shame the Americans out of their indifference but he knew it would displease his father.

Joshi hadn't changed his clothes since he got back from Renown House. His shoes lay in the hallway, his briefcase unopened on the floor, his jacket and tie on the back of a chair at a dining table that could sit twenty-four but was never used. It was his habit to shower and change as soon as he got home, to discard his corporate persona as completely as a snake shed its skin, so he could relax and be the man he could be only be when he was alone. Tonight was different. It had been an especially trying day, and the spectacle in the conference room at Renown Hotel had sickened him more than usual.

Joshi was the most Hindu of all the Amlani men. His father assumed the mantle of Hinduism as a means of acquiring respectability, but Joshi knew his father was too preoccupied with money, caste, and power ever to be a true Hindu. His father's idea of piety was to hire the priciest Brahmin priests in Bombay to perform *pooja* for him.

Joshi had been increasingly drawn to the idea of pure Hinduism and had taken to reading the works of Swami Dayanand Saraswati, a Gujerati Brahmin who a century earlier had sought to free Hinduism from the burden of superstition and restore its Vedic purity. Elements of the swami's teachings had been

adopted by several militant Hindu groups who opposed secu-
larism and urged the expulsion of all Moslems and the recognition of Hinduism as the national faith. Joshi harbored a secret
sympathy for them. Economic strength was only one weapon in
the war against pernicious foreign influences. Real strength was
to be found in unity, and increasingly, Joshi believed, unity
would be achieved only through the restoration of a pure Hindu
state.

He looked at his watch. It was a little after nine-thirty.
Instead of languishing alone in his apartment he should have
been downstairs in the club room with everybody else, cele-
brating his father's triumph. There was much to celebrate. By
the close of business Renown shares had broken through the
800 barrier and his father's brokers predicted they would break
1000 the next day.

Somebody knocked hard at the door. Joshi realized his
absence from the party had been noted and he was being summoned. He prized himself out of the sofa and padded down the
hallway in his stocking feet. He paused with a hand on the door
handle, willing himself to be sociable, and opened the door.

"You always do this," Arvind said. "And it is always me who
has to come and get you."

"I'm sorry," Joshi said unapologetically. "I was coming
down."

"The rest of us have to be there," Arvind said, following Joshi
into the apartment. "You have to be there."

"Did the old man send you or is this on your own initiative?"

"I don't give a fuck what you do with your own time," Arvind
answered wearily. "But this isn't your own time. Not yet. You
go downstairs and kiss some ass and act like you're enjoying
it—then you can come back up here and finish playing with
yourself."

"You want a drink, there's fresh lime soda in the fridge,"
Joshi said. He was also the only Amlani man who didn't touch
alcohol. He had gone so far as to ban it from his apartment.

He crossed the living room into his dressing room with its neatly racked suits and brass-handled drawers filled with shirts, sweaters, and socks. He thought about wearing his white cotton kurta pajamas, but that would really annoy his father, who insisted that in public the men in the family dress like executives of a modern western company. So he chose a black silk turtleneck that hid his double chin and a light gray suit that shaved off a few pounds.

"James Bond," Arvind said. "With a belly."

Reflexively, Joshi pulled in his gut and hated himself for it. His brother was always doing this to him.

Joshi got his own back as they walked to the elevator.

"If you're going to fuck any of Rashmi's friends tonight," he said, "find somewhere else this time."

Their sister often brought girlfriends home from the studio; starlets as dim and as pretty as she was, but in awe of the Amlani mystique. Arvind treated them like party treats. One time Joshi had come home to find his brother with an actress giving an award-winning performance on the living room rug.

"Watch your mouth," Arvind said. "Meher's there with the kids."

Meher was Arvind's wife, a woman tormented by jealousy and with much to be jealous about.

"That never stopped you before," Joshi answered.

The two of them rode wordlessly down in the elevator and parted company the moment the doors opened, Arvind to his wife and children, to play the dutiful husband, Joshi to his parents, to play the dutiful son. Joshi hadn't been to the club in more than a year, since before his father's illness. The only times he came to this floor were when he wanted to swim in the indoor pool, when it was early and there was no one else around. Like everyone else, he was forbidden to intrude on his father's ritual morning swim in the rooftop pool. The rest of the time, especially on weekends, the floor shook to the noise of the Amlani grandchildren and their cousins and friends who used it for parties and birthdays.

This was one of the rare occasions when the nightclub had been taken over by those for whom it was intended. It had the look and feel of an upscale, big city nightspot. There were green vinyl booths along two walls, a fully stocked bar, and a panoramic view of the city. The diamond-shaped dance floor had floor-to-ceiling mirrors on one wall and mirrors overhead that magnified the effects of a laser projector to a level adults found dizzying and children barely adequate. Beside the dance floor was a deejay console with a computerized sound system so powerful it rippled the pool on the other side of the building.

Joshi realized why his absence had been noticed. Everybody in the Amlani clan was there; his father, his mother, Arvind, Rashmi, all his aunts and uncles and their children, all his grown-up cousins with their husbands and wives and all their children, most of whose names he could never remember. There were also many familiar faces from the boardrooms of Renown Industries: all the Amlani lieutenants and their partners, many of whom had flown in especially for the occasion. All of them were there for the same reason: to honor Madhuri Amlani in his hour of triumph. And, equally important, to be seen honoring Madhuri Amlani.

Joshi maneuvered his way through the crowd to a corner table at the farthest end of the room, where his mother and father held court amidst a coterie of close relatives and other assorted subordinates. His father was deep in conversation with Uncle Nusli on one side, while his mother, an impenetrable half smile on her face, listened to Aunt Govinda on the other. Then his father saw him coming and got to his feet with a smile of genuine delight, cutting off Nusli in mid-sentence.

"The sadhu returns," Amlani proclaimed, embracing his son as though they had not seen each other for a month. Sadhu was the word for holy man, which Amlani was inclined to call Joshi when he was annoyed with him, and it drew a few chuckles from around the table.

"I beg your forgiveness, Father," Joshi said. "I was resting and must have fallen asleep."

"You would sleep through your own wedding," Amlani rebuked his youngest son. But he was in a good mood and easily appeased. He kissed his son sloppily on the forehead and sat back down again. Everybody swayed like buoys on ripples of green vinyl.

Joshi nodded and smiled at everyone around the table, exchanging meaningless pleasantries with his various relatives and friends of the family. As he was excusing himself to leave he heard his aunt telling his mother: "You are not doing him any favors, Gauri. If you keep treating him like a child he will never grow up."

He made his way to the bar, took a seat, ordered a salt lime, and wondered how he could feel so alone in a room filled with family. But the whole day had been like that, a sense of distance and dislocation, of moving through familiar surroundings where he did not belong. He sipped his drink and looked at his watch. It wasn't quite ten. The party would go on until dawn. He was already bored. He had intended to stay an hour but wondered if anyone would notice if he slipped away after only half an hour.

"Joshi?"

He recognized the voice of his sister and his spirits sank. He forced himself to smile and turned around. She wore a black leotard with a flouncy red skirt over black tights and boots that were the latest fashion in America. He thought she looked like a water beetle.

"Hello Rashmi, are you enjoying the party?"

"It's okay," she said. She was chewing gum and drinking champagne.

"You're not drinking, are you?" he said.

"Only champagne," she said.

Joshi's eyes shifted to the woman with her. She was a few years older than his sister and was dressed in infinitely better taste—a tailored black jacket and skirt with a white blouse buttoned primly at the throat. Joshi thought she was the most beautiful woman he had ever seen.

Rashmi saw him staring and remembered why she had stopped.

"Oh, this is a friend of mine from the studio," she said. "Her name is Anita, Anita Vasi. Even you must have heard of her, Joshi. She's going to be a big, big star."

CHAPTER 13

As his plane taxied to the airport terminal Sansi glanced through a window and saw a government car with motorcycle outriders waiting on the tarmac. He wondered who was on board to merit that kind of treatment. Then he realized the car was for him.

He had flown first class by Modiluft from Bombay to Delhi, and nobody had told him he would be met on the tarmac, an honor too conspicuous for his liking. He had spent much of the past week in Bombay trying to keep a low profile. His office at Lentin Chambers had been deluged with calls from news reporters wanting to know more about the "mystery man" whom Rupe Seshan had catapulted into national prominence by appointing him to lead the Varanasi investigation. Alam Bajaj at the *Times of India* had pressured Annie to use her relationship with Sansi to get an interview. She had gone through the ritual of asking, both of them knowing what his answer would be.

That was only the beginning. The announcement brought other, more sinister pressures to bear. Lawyers, party hacks, and corporate fixers from every industry that might be targeted by the investigation had swamped him with offers, invitations, and promises of important favors to come if his investigation was "discreet."

Mukherjee wallowed in all the attention but even he had been overwhelmed. He enlisted the aid of his aunt Uma, mother of Neisha, to help him cope with the avalanche of calls and letters. Shortly before leaving, Sansi had been dismayed to find Mukherjee negotiating an advertising contract for Neisha with a liquor distillery in Bihar. Mukherjee promised solemnly not to do it again and assured Sansi that the cases of whiskey, sets of steel cookware, and Kashmiri rugs that flowed into his chambers would all be returned with polite regrets.

On his way out of the building Sansi had glimpsed, loitering on the street corner, a balding, heavyset man who looked very much like Mukherjee's uncle Bakul, husband of Uma, father of Neisha. Bakul owned a shop in Mutton Street at Chor Bazaar, the thieves market, where he traded in a range of goods that could easily include cases of whiskey, sets of steel cookware, and Kashmiri rugs. Sansi suspected he would come back from Delhi to find Aunt Uma running the office, Neisha a billboard star, and Lentin Chambers an extension of Mukherjee Enterprises.

"Mr. Sansi, your car is waiting."

Sansi looked up to see a flight attendant in the figure-hugging uniform of the airline's German partner, Lufthansa. He had still to get used to the sight of Indian flight attendants in tight skirts instead of saris—along with tight schedules, a result of the new competitiveness that followed the opening up of domestic air routes. He gathered his things together, acknowledged the good-byes of the flight crew and stepped out into the bright sunlight, glad to escape the unwelcome attention of all the other passengers. Sansi knew of few things that could impede an investigation better than the unwanted celebrity of the chief investigator.

"Most pleasurable to be seeing you again, sir," Captain Ramani said with a blur of a salute. "On behalf of the minister, I am delighted to be welcoming you to New Delhi. Please come with me."

Sansi gave him a lukewarm smile and followed him down the ramp to where the government Contessa waited, two outriders in front, two behind. Ramani opened the rear door for Sansi then got in beside the driver. He looked over his shoulder and said: "Please sir, you are staying at G Block?"

"*Acha*," Sansi said.

G Block was a residential compound for guests of the federal government. It adjoined the imaginatively named Central Government Complex, a charmless cement maze of bunkers and towers that accommodated several government departments including the Environment Ministry.

"With your permission, sir, your bags are going directly to your quarters," Ramani added. "The minister says we are bringing you first to her residence. She is expecting you will be her guest for dinner this evening."

Sansi nodded. Whatever Rupe's plans might be for him, there was much he needed to discuss with her.

He settled back and watched the dusty fields and hovels along the airport road slide past his window. Delhi was a city where the layers of history were like strata in sandstone, with slivers of the past and present chafing, blending, and often splintering against each other.

The first city had been built in a crook of the Jamuna River, a crossroads on the northern plains fought over by every army to tramp across India since the birth of the Buddha. The outskirts of the city were necklaced with the ruins of ancient fortresses, most of which had been engulfed by the scabrous mass of industry whose chimneys added to the traffic fumes, dung fires, and dust storms that turned the air into a suffocating smog.

The heart of the city beat strongest in Old Delhi, a seething medieval cauldron in the shadow of the Red Fort. It was as if all that was authentically Indian—the crowds, the noise, the smells, the life and death theater of the street—had been condensed into one sweltering pocket. Sooner or later everybody went there for something: to buy gold, guns, or ganja, or simply to taste the danger that was as addictive as any drug.

Overlooking it from a safe distance were the lofty monuments of New Delhi, a city so foreign it seemed to have been left behind by aliens, which in fact it was. Designed by the British architect Sir Edwin Lutyens to celebrate the transfer of power from Calcutta to Delhi in 1912, the shining new city on the plains was intended as an enduring monument to the glory of the Raj. It was finished just in time for the British to turn it over to their Indian successors on the eve of independence, which made it the most enduring monument to imperialist folly the world had seen. India's new rulers inherited the great halls and palaces, the elegant residences and opulent private clubs of the new metropolis and also assumed effortlessly the style of their former masters, whom they were inclined to criticize in public and copy in private.

Sansi's car turned onto the Ring Road that embraced the twin hubs of Old Delhi and New Delhi and followed the traffic eastward for a couple of miles. Some drivers pulled over when the government car and its outriders loomed into view but most didn't. Indian drivers would rather die than yield an inch of pavement, and the roadsides of India were littered with the burnt-out wrecks of buses, cars, and trucks whose drivers had laid down their lives in defense of their territory.

At Bhishm Pitamath Marg they turned abruptly northward past the Nehru Homeopathic College, then eastward again at the Love Lips Family Clothing Store. On Jor Bagh Marg they swerved to avoid a tribe of monkeys eating bananas in the middle of the road. Delhi was infested by monkeys whose tribes occupied the various parks and ruins and who came out often to raid the world of humans. One tribe had taken a fancy to the Lok Sabha, the national parliament, and armed guards now had to escort nervous parliamentarians to their offices.

At last the Contessa pulled into Lodi Colony, an enclave of

well-groomed streets with high fences and hedges shielding expensive houses situated amidst large gardens. Sansi knew which house was Rupe's before the car stopped. It was protected by an iron railing whose spikes had been draped with razor wire. Locked iron gates sealed off the driveway.

The car stopped and Sansi counted a half-dozen soldiers inside the grounds, all wearing steel helmets and flak jackets, most armed with rifles, a couple with Sten guns, the World War Two vintage British sub-machine gun still in service with the Indian Army. There would be other soldiers throughout the grounds. In half a century of independence India had never been at peace with itself. Every government had to contend with terror groups, guerilla armies, separatists, and independence movements whose followers regularly attacked buses and trains or lobbed hand grenades into crowded cinemas.

Prime Minister Rajiv Gandhi had been blown to atoms at an election rally by a Tamil suicide bomber. His mother, Indira, was shot to death by her own Sikh bodyguards. In the past year there had been car bomb attacks on two politicians in Delhi. The killers of Rupe's husband, Mani, had never been brought to justice, though a dozen organizations claimed responsibility.

Her house was one of the more modest in the street, a two-story block of yellowing stucco with a small lawn fringed by ashoka trees. There were tiny balconies on a couple of windows on the second floor, and a flat roof with a low parapet where more soldiers kept watch. It wouldn't have drawn a second glance were it not for the troops and the steel mesh screens fitted to every door and window.

A solemn-faced sergeant in a sand-colored beret emerged from the gatehouse and spoke briefly with Captain Ramani. He looked at Sansi, then signaled his men to open the gates. The short driveway ended in a parking area at the side of the house where there were two more government cars and more motorbikes. Because there was no room for Sansi's car they parked in the drive and walked the rest of the way.

"There are others here?" Sansi asked as he and Captain Ramani passed the parked cars.

"Only one, sir," Ramani answered.

Sansi waited but, uncharacteristically, Ramani offered nothing more.

"Do you mind telling me who?"

Ramani looked apologetic. "It is not for me to say, sir."

There was a mesh-screened door at the side of the house and a soldier who saluted as they approached. Ramani pushed an intercom button and spoke to someone inside. There was a moment's delay, then the sound of a lock turning. The door opened outward, a soldier with a second lieutenant's pips on his shoulders appeared, and the two of them stepped inside.

Sansi waited for a minute in the narrow, well-lit hallway until the second lieutenant beckoned Sansi into his office, where he checked his briefcase and gave him a quick pat-down. When he was finished, he asked Sansi to sign the official log. Only then did he pick up the phone and announce Sansi's arrival.

Moments later the door to the house opened and Rupe's assistant, Hemali, appeared. She looked annoyed, as if they had disturbed her in the midst of something important.

"You're very late," she said and turned away, leaving Ramani to catch the door before it closed on them.

Sansi found Hemali's manner equally annoying, but the expression on Ramani's face had changed to something approaching admiration. Sansi sighed, and Ramani caught himself. He gave Sansi an embarrassed smile, then stepped aside.

Having penetrated the final layer of security, Sansi realized the house was bigger than it appeared from the outside. The two-story hallway stretched in front of him for what looked like the entire length of the house, its stuccoed walls aglow with light from a gallery of windows that stretched from the first floor to the second-floor ceiling. The floor tiles were earth-colored and there were silk tapestries on the walls, a couple of antique chests with copper fittings, and brass side tables with bowls of fresh flowers. The glassed-in hallway formed a U-shape around a courtyard and passed the main reception rooms, offices, kitchen, and servants quarters. Above Sansi's head was a railed walkway he thought must lead to the family rooms on the second floor.

His eye was drawn by movement in the courtyard and he saw there was a small, oval swimming pool. Two children were playing, watched by a middle-aged ayah under an umbrella. The girl was about eight and the boy eleven. Rupe's children, Sansi realized. He remembered their names; Sonal and Arjun. The last time he had seen them, their father had been alive.

Then he realized Hemali wasn't waiting for him but had continued to the far end of the house, her sandals clicking her impatience. Sansi hurried to catch up with her. At the point where the hallway turned sharply left he heard voices. Hemali stopped and gestured through an open door to a sitting room where Rupe was talking with a man Sansi had never met but recognized immediately.

Judge Kursheed Pilot sat with his long, bony frame folded into an armchair, white hair cascading down to the collar of his white muslin kurta pajamas, and looked for all the world like an aged pterodactyl taking tea.

The moment Rupe saw Sansi she got up to greet him, and Pilot followed. Only when the judge had creakily extended himself to his full height did Sansi realize how dauntingly tall he was. Six-foot-seven or eight, he guessed, probably more when he was younger and not afflicted by the stoop of age.

"Madam . . . Judge . . . Mr. Sansi," Hemali announced. Without another word she turned and walked briskly back to her office, her sandals punctuating her departure like exclamation points.

"She's such a little bitch, isn't she?" Rupe said. "Did you know she's Parsi? No money but full of herself. Her father begged me to take her on. You'd think she'd be grateful, wouldn't you? She acts like she's doing me a favor."

Sansi smiled politely.

"Ramani likes her," Rupe continued. "She's pretending he doesn't exist, so I think she's interested but wants to torment him for a while to see how serious he is. She reminds me so much of me—"

Judge Pilot interrupted Rupe by stepping forward with his hand outstretched. Sansi took it gratefully. It felt like dried twigs but the grip was strong.

"So you too have accepted the dubious honor of serving your country, Mr. Sansi?" the judge said.

His face seemed to have collapsed on itself, so that the bags under his eyes descended in tiers down his cheeks, his lips and nose becoming fleshy and pendulous. His melancholy look was quite at odds with his reputation for mischief-making.

"In a manner of speaking," Sansi responded. "She threatened me."

"*Acha.*" Pilot waggled his understanding. "She might be new to the job but I think she has been preparing for it her whole life."

"She was born to it," Sansi said.

Rupe gave him a dig with her elbow, an intimacy that surprised him.

"If you have no respect for me, at least respect the position," she said.

She wore a lemon-colored *salwar khameez* and no makeup and looked so young Sansi forgot for a moment that she was middle-aged now, like him. He saw instead the girl he had known inside the woman.

"Five minutes in Cabinet and already drunk with power," Pilot grumbled amiably.

Sansi realized he had been staring, and it was his turn to be embarrassed. If the judge noticed, he gave no sign as he shuffled back to his armchair. But Rupe had noticed and it required some effort on her part to shake off the distraction.

"We will be relying on each other a great deal over the next few months," she began haltingly. "I thought it would be a good idea if the three of us got together informally at first to make sure we are all going in the same direction."

They spent the rest of the afternoon going over the agenda for the inquiry. To Sansi's relief, Rupe and Pilot were better prepared than he had anticipated. The first weeks would be taken up with the harrowing accounts of key witnesses who were on Dasashwadh Ghat the morning of the disaster. There would be postmortem reports, medical reports on the survivors, reports from SEPA—the state environmental protection agency—and the opportunity for Pilot and his fellow commissioners to grill SEPA inspectors and administrators on the agency's poor enforcement record. But it became increasingly clear they were relying on Sansi to deliver up within a month or two the first witnesses from factories that might be implicated in the disaster.

"I have arranged space for you in my building," Rupe told him. "Enough for a hundred people. You can have more if you need it."

"You have copies of the SEPA reports?" Sansi asked.

"Already in your office."

"On computer?"

"You want computers?"

"With the volume of evidence and the time constraints you have put on me?" he said. "We will need computers."

Computers were a relatively recent innovation to the bureaucracy, and notoriously expensive and difficult to procure.

"How many terminals?"

"Thirty—to begin with," Sansi said. "And they have to be fast—you have access to a good mainframe?"

"We have our own mainframe," Rupe answered. "We're not in the stone age."

"I will need reliable operators."

"Reliable as in competent or reliable as in secure?"

"Both."

She winced. "Not all our people are trained yet. I might have to borrow some from Justice. How many do you think you will need?"

"Ninety. We will run three shifts around the clock. And we will need a contact point and a secure hookup to Varanasi."

"I thought you would want policemen, not computer operators."

"I want to keep the involvement of the federal police to a minimum," Sansi explained. "They will provide the brute manpower for raids and bring in witnesses, but I don't want them at the heart of the investigation."

"They won't like that," Rupe said with a glance at Pilot.

"The federal police service was created by Congress," Sansi said. "They owe everything they are to the Congress Party—you want every piece of evidence leaked to the opposition before we see it?"

Pilot waggled his head approvingly. Nobody expected the Bharatiya Janata Party to hold power for long. Congress would find a way to bump them out of office even if it had to bribe BJP members to cross the floor. As a concession to the Lok Sabha, Rupe had been obliged to appoint six commissioners to sit alongside the judge on the inquiry; two from the Bharatiya Janata Party, two from Congress, and two from the socialist National Front coalition. The enemy was already close enough to the heart of the investigation.

"And you tell me politics is too dirty for you?" Rupe smiled.

"The difference," Sansi answered, "is that I don't enjoy it."

"Are you sure you can do this with six men and a roomful of computer programmers?"

Sansi heard the doubt in Rupe's voice and he paused before answering.

"The problem with this investigation," he explained, "is that everybody knows it is coming. They have had many months to hide whatever it is they want to hide. The only way we are going to find out who is behind this spill is to go through all the

evidence and see what has been hidden, and that means processing evidence from at least three hundred factories. We won't
be looking for clues, we will be looking for the best cover-up—
and I have no idea how long it will be before we get to anything
quite so definite as a suspect."

Rupe slumped visibly. Pilot's long reptilian face remained
impassive. Like Sansi, he knew the difference between justice
and the law—and the law was never swift.

"I can't promise success, Rupe, I can only try," Sansi added.
"If you want promises you will have to find somebody else."

She smiled faintly. "No," she said. "I've made my choice."

■ ■

"She reminds me of Gandhi."

"I'm sorry?"

"Gandhi," Pilot repeated. "I have been thinking about it
quite a lot and it's true, she reminds me of Gandhi."

"Indira?"

"No." Pilot smiled indulgently. "The Mahatma, Mohandas
Gandhi."

Sansi watched as Rupe turned down the hallway.

"It can't be the walk," he said.

"No," Pilot agreed. "Not the walk."

They had talked their way into the evening and suppertime
was approaching. Pilot had declined Rupe's invitation to stay
and eat with them, and she had gone to find Ramani to make
sure the judge's escort was ready.

"It is the spirit," Pilot went on. "All that spirit in such a
tiny body. And fearless, just like Gandhi. He was, you know . . .
fearless."

Sansi had spent just enough time in the judge's company to
get used to him as a man, to forget he was also an icon, the conscience of the nation, a man who sat at Gandhi's feet and who
spent time in jail with Nehru.

"She puts us to shame," the judge added. "The way Gandhi

did. He shamed us into conquering our fears, he shamed us into finding the courage to confront our oppressors. She does the same. Just a chit of a girl and yet she shames us into doing what we knew was our duty all along, if we could only find the courage."

Sansi looked surprised. "Your voice has been the only voice of courage in the Supreme Court for a quarter of a century," he said.

Pilot made a disparaging face. "Not courage," he said. "Sinecure. They kept me like a pet monkey on a chain, to show everyone and say, 'See, Pilot is proof the Supreme Court is free.' "

Sansi smiled. He thought Pilot was being hard on himself. Then the judge gripped his arm with a fierceness that was startling.

"We can't let her down, Sansi," he said, leaning so close Sansi could taste the staleness of his breath. "She helped us find our courage again, she has reawakened the spirit of the Mahatma, we can't let her down."

Sansi looked into the judge's age-rimmed eyes, and saw something close to panic. He was shocked. Behind the mythic image, behind the legend, was a frightened old man—and he thought Sansi was afraid too.

"We won't," Sansi said, and patted the judge's arm, wishing he would let go. "We won't."

CHAPTER 14

The courtyard was quiet except for the melodic fidget of cicadas and the drip of freshly watered shrubs. Incense sticks had been lit to keep down the mosquitoes, and lights around the pool made it glitter as if filled with coins. It was an idyll marred by a sinister, slanted shadow against one wall, the grid of a steel net suspended over the courtyard to deflect grenades and mortar shells.

Sansi sat with Rupe at a table set for dinner and the two of them tried not to talk about the inquiry. Instead they talked about the separate directions their lives had taken, about mutual friends, about who had done well and who hadn't. And occasionally they stumbled upon the intersections of their own lives and conversation became awkward as they skirted the unrealized thoughts and desires that lingered there like ghosts.

Sansi was relieved when the ayah returned with the children, freshly bathed, hair combed, looking and smelling the way only children could. It was three years since he had seen them last, and neither remembered him, but their mother told them he was a longtime friend of hers and their father's and they greeted him politely, though with a certain reserve.

He saw that Sonal had inherited her mother's fine-featured prettiness, including the angled smile, and while Arjun did not bear any strong physical resemblance to either parent, many of his mannerisms were eerily reminiscent of his father. It made Sansi uncomfortable and reminded him of the man who should have been at the dinner table.

Supper followed Rupe's vegetarian tastes: a vegetable biryani with side dishes of paneer, cubes of cottage cheese in a lightly spiced sauce, and chaat, grilled lentil balls, accompanied by fresh baked roti and an assortment of chutneys. What little reserve the children had vanished when Rupe told them that before Sansi became a lawyer he was a detective with Crime Branch. He spent the rest of the meal feeding them increasingly gruesome details about old murder cases, so that when the ayah returned at ten o'clock to put them to bed, they were desperate to know when he would be back to tell them more.

Sansi thought it time he left too, but Rupe pressed him to stay until after she had settled the children. He nursed his coffee, wondering what she wanted to discuss, but when she came back he realized it was nothing, merely that she wasn't ready for sleep yet. Touched by her need for company, he relented. When he next looked at his watch it was almost midnight. He got to his feet with a purposefulness that said this time he was serious about leaving.

Rupe looked apologetic. "I'm sorry, I do this all the time."

Sansi inclined his head. "You always liked to talk late."

"No," she said. "Hold people against their will."

He smiled. "We all get lonely," he said. "It is why we keep busy."

He wanted to say more but he felt himself straying into dangerous territory again and so said nothing.

The two of them went inside and walked down the hallway to Hemali's office. The door was open though the office was dark and empty. A few lights burned in the rest of the house but it was so quiet it seemed they were the only people left awake.

"She's supposed to check with me before she goes to bed," Rupe said. "She'll be in her room with the door locked, pretending to be asleep, afraid when you go I'll pull her out and talk at her till three o'clock in the morning."

"You do that?"

"I've done it a few times. It's why she's such a bitch around me. Sometimes I talk to Ramani. At least he pretends to be interested. But it's his job—and he feels guilty."

"Guilty?" Sansi repeated.

"About Mani," Rupe explained. "He was with Mani's security staff before me. He was away when Mani was killed, but the security staff was purged afterward and Ramani's commanding officer was demoted. Ramani replaced him and now he's terrified the same thing will happen to him. He would stay with me twenty-four hours a day if I let him."

Sansi couldn't imagine life in a cage, with secretaries, aides, and security guards in place of friends. But Rupe had spent her whole life surrounded by servants and protectors. He thought she would be used to it.

He saw his opportunity and said: "You need that kind of security, but I am not sure I do."

"You don't like it?" She sounded unsurprised.

"It is very constricting," he said. "It could impede the investigation."

She frowned. "I was thinking of giving you more, not less. You are more important than me now. If something happened to me, I know the investigation would continue."

Her response made him feel ashamed. For the first time he felt some of the burden of her isolation.

"I can live with it," he said. "It won't affect the investigation."

She smiled faintly. "Now I've made you feel guilty. See how easy it is?"

"I am glad to be here," he said. "Proud to be here."

"But you're still not comfortable with me, are you?" she said. "Not when we're alone. You've been trying to escape for the past hour. Look at you, you can't wait to get away."

"Rupe . . ." He put his hand on her shoulder. It was meant to be reassuring but suddenly seemed more like a caress. Nervously, he took it away. "Perhaps I'm just afraid," he joked.

"Again?"

She stretched up and kissed him lightly on the lips. Then she said: "You still don't know, do you?"

"Know what?"

"You were going to be my first," she said. "You were supposed to be my first. I had it all planned."

He knew immediately she was talking about the night at Malabar Point.

"I thought—"

"I know what you thought," she interrupted. "It doesn't matter. It mattered then but it doesn't matter now."

He hesitated, and in his hesitation she saw the answer she wanted. She stretched up to kiss him again. This time he kissed her back, and twenty-five years of suppressed emotion fused into simple desire.

On the far side of the courtyard a shadow moved within a cluster of shadows and the soft mechanical clicking of a camera melded with the chirp of cicadas.

CHAPTER 15

Sansi awakened from a restless sleep unsure for a moment where he was. He lay still and listened for the sound of breathing, trying to sense if she was there beside him, warm and naked from the night before.

His hand probed tentatively between the covers but the rest of the bed was cool and empty. Relieved, he opened his eyes, looked around and remembered. He was in a guest bungalow at G Block. He had left Rupe's bed around two, not wanting to fall asleep and be found with her in the morning.

The luminous green figures on the bedside clock said 5:33. He closed his eyes and tried to doze but his mind wouldn't let him. Images of him and Rupe making love jostled inside his head. Wearily he got out of bed to shower and get dressed.

When he emerged into the living room he was met by a servant who slept in a niche behind the kitchen and was on call twenty-four hours a day. An older man, probably ex-army, Sansi thought. He asked if Sansi wanted breakfast.

"Chai," Sansi said. "No milk or lemon. And two slices of toast. No butter."

He sat at a table beside a darkened window and chewed the toast mechanically, trying to neutralize the acid that burned in his stomach, eager to get to work and lose himself in the familiar routines of investigation. As for Rupe, he was certain of only one thing. He needed time to make sense of what had happened. To decide what it meant to him, to her, to their work together. And most of all what it meant for Annie.

When he stepped outside the sky had begun to lighten, but the air tasted stale and used, the way it always did in Delhi. The bungalow had a small, box-shaped veranda that looked out at a neatly kept compound of identical bungalows with the same boxy verandas, the same scrubby lawns, and the same gravel footpaths connected to a narrow central roadway wide enough to accommodate only one vehicle at a time. The compound was enclosed by a high brick wall bristling with razor wire; its perimeter was patrolled by bored-looking soldiers with rifles.

There were lights on in some of the bungalows; other government guests on other government business. But only Sansi's bungalow had its own sentry, an army corporal who wore a pale brown beret instead of the green worn by the other soldiers. He saluted as Sansi walked down the steps, and Sansi nodded to him and set off for the Environment Ministry, whose blank-eyed office tower loomed just beyond the compound wall.

He hadn't gone far when he heard footsteps on the gravel behind him. He turned, saw his sentry and sighed.

"Are you supposed to follow me everywhere?"

"Yes, sahib," the soldier said. "While you are here, Captain Ramani says I must go with you everywhere."

"What is your name?"

"I am Hassan, sahib." He turned his shoulder so Sansi could see the double chevrons. "Corporal Hassan."

He was short and wiry, and had the literal-minded earnestness of the enlisted man who knew his future depended entirely on how well he followed orders.

"Can you make a pot of tea?"

"Yes, sahib," Hassan answered solemnly.

"Well, you are perfect for the job."

Hassan seemed not to see the joke. When Sansi set off again he fell in dutifully behind.

The space Rupe had allotted Sansi for the operational headquarters of the Varanasi investigation occupied half the fifth floor of the Environment Ministry building. There were windows on three sides but the blinds were down, and Sansi left them that way. The operations center would run twenty-four hours a day, seven days a week. Whether it was light or dark outside was irrelevant.

He turned on all the lights and saw the room was empty but for a few metal desks and chairs, a dozen or so telephones scattered about the sickly green linoleum, and a row of cubicles along one wall partitioned by room dividers. There were faded posters and outdated calendars, and the smell of mildew, the smell of long-term emptiness rather than a recently vacated office. Sansi thought the Environment Ministry probably wasn't the busiest department in the government.

In the middle of the room were six trolleys, stacked high with cardboard boxes. Sansi walked over to one, picked a file at random, and saw it was a copy of the SEPA files Rupe had promised. Normally the sight of so much unprocessed raw material would fill him with dismay. Today he welcomed it.

Together he and Hassan pushed the desks together to make an island then hauled the trolley train to it and set up a couple of chairs. They unloaded several boxes, and Sansi took off his jacket, sat down, and started working his way through the files, one at a time. Hassan watched, unsure what to do with himself.

"Now would be a good time to organize the tea," Sansi said. "See if you can't find a kettle somewhere because we're going to need lots of it."

For the next several hours Sansi worked his way through one file after another, sorting them into two stacks, those he thought held something useful and those that were obvious discards—files about accidents at coal mines, ports, and nuclear power stations, alarming enough in themselves, but nothing to do with chemical spills, textiles, or Varanasi.

Buried in this mass of documents were charts that showed the Ganga's flow rate at different times of the year, the rates at which different chemical discharges could be safely dispersed into the environment, the actual rates of discharge, and lists of those mills that had been served with compliance orders requiring the installation of emission control equipment intended to impose those rates of discharge.

Late in the morning Rupe sent Hemali to see if Sansi had everything he needed. He asked for cots for himself and others who would have to sleep at the operations center at times. Wisely, he thought, Rupe did not call or come to see him personally. Perhaps, like him, she needed some distance to deal with what had happened the night before. He found himself awkward enough with Hemali, wondered if she knew and whether her polite indifference was chillier than normal or it was only his guilt gnawing at him.

In the afternoon an installation crew arrived with the computers, new Hewlett Packards. There was, however, no sign of the desks that were supposed to accompany them. Sansi had the crew set up as many work stations as they could with the furniture available while Rupe's office tried to track down the missing desks.

Around six o'clock that night the stolid Hassan was relieved by a Private Ratnan, who would take alternate twelve-hour shifts. He had the same glum detachment as Hassan, and Sansi assumed it was because Ramani, afraid of the fate that claimed his predecessor, had warned both men that their futures were inextricably linked to his.

Sansi was determined to see at least one computer terminal up and running before he left for the day, but it took longer than anticipated, and around one o'clock in the morning he was overtaken by exhaustion. With Ratnan in tow he walked dazedly back to his bungalow, where he fell gratefully into bed and the deep, dreamless sleep of the dead.

He was awakened by his alarm at six and was back in the operations center at seven. He spent most of the day partitioning the office with room dividers so that he and Chowdhary and his men would have offices and a conference room separate from the general work area. He put up wall maps, including an enlargement of the Ganga at Varanasi with every suspect factory identified by number.

In the middle of the afternoon the missing desks arrived and they completed the installation of the computer work stations. Sansi then worked all through the night helping the installation crew fine-tune the program that would drive the investigation. He finished just in time to greet the first batch of thirty computer operators to report for duty at eight o'clock in the morning. He made a brief welcoming speech and set them to work copying the SEPA files he had selected into the computer. Around eleven he lay on a cot in his office intending to take a brief nap and slept for five hours.

When he got up, the first batch of operators was ready to log off and the second batch was arriving for the four-till-midnight shift. He repeated his welcome speech and set them to work, and so it continued through the weekend, until every last file was installed in the computer. The only time Sansi saw the inside of his bungalow was when he went back to shower and change clothes. But when Inspector Chowdhary and his colleagues from Crime Branch got off the elevator on Monday morning, they walked into an operations center that looked and smelled as if it had always been there.

Chowdhary and his men knew what to expect, and Sansi put them to work immediately, each of them digging through his own coal seam of words looking for the diamonds that could be polished into clues. They spent the next two weeks sifting through spill reports, company reports, environmental impact studies, and SEPA investigations that went back ten years. They used their small army of computer operators to analyze the figures from three hundred factories to find the anomalies between amounts of chemicals purchased, amounts consumed, amounts wasted, saved, reclaimed, and ultimately discharged into the river.

At the end of that time they knew SEPA was as inept and as corrupt as every other government department in India—but they also knew which factories bought the most phosphorous, which were unable to account properly for its disposal, and which factory owners were the most consistent liars. And Sansi and Chowdhary were able to draw up a plan of attack.

With each day that passed, the opening of the Varanasi inquiry drew closer, the political rhetoric and media hype became more heated, and the pressure on Sansi became more intense. The national and international media had seized on the inquiry as the focus of a new determination by an Indian government to do what no other government in Asia had done—find a moral balance between development frenzy and ecological devastation as the third world scrambled to catch up with the first world.

Both Judge Pilot and Rupe made separate visits to the operations center to inspire the troops and see for themselves how the investigation was progressing. Pilot came alone and spent a couple of hours with Sansi and Chowdhary, but Rupe arrived with a large ministerial entourage and her usual phalanx of guards. It was the first time Sansi had seen her in the weeks since he had left her bed in the middle of the night, and it was awkward for both of them. There was no opportunity for anything but the most formal of exchanges, and the brief private glances they exchanged told him nothing new about her feelings toward him or his toward her. He was glad that the pressures of her office and the demands of the investigation had kept them apart.

Midway through the third week the investigation had advanced to the point where Sansi and Chowdhary could plan the first factory raids in Varanasi. The two of them had just sat down at the conference table to lay out a schedule when a clerk interrupted to tell Sansi he had a phone call from Annie in Bombay.

Sansi felt a chill of apprehension. He hadn't spoken to Annie since he arrived in Delhi, and that alone would have told her something was wrong. When he picked up the phone and heard her voice at the other end, he knew immediately she was upset.

"I know you're busy," she said, "but we have to talk."

"What is wrong?" Sansi asked, trying to sound calm.

"It's too complicated to discuss on the phone," she answered. "We have to meet."

"All right," Sansi said. "But we can't do it now. The inquiry opens in another week—"

"I wouldn't call you if it wasn't important," she said, her voice strained.

Sansi grimaced. "I can't leave Delhi," he said. "You have to come here."

"I can get a flight on Friday night."

"Wait till the inquiry has opened. Let me get past that."

"The day after?" she asked.

"*Acha,*" Sansi said. "The day after."

She hung up without saying good-bye, and Sansi put down the phone, his emotions in turmoil.

"Problems, sahib?" Chowdhary said.

For a moment Sansi seemed not to hear him. He felt as if his whole world was closing in on him and it was his own fault and there was nowhere he could turn for sympathy.

"Yes," he said haltingly. "Problems."

■   ■

The inquiry into the Varanasi disaster opened on a Monday morning in the central committee room of the Justice Ministry amidst a frenzy of public anticipation and media speculation even greater than what had been expected.

The crowd began gathering on the maidan near the Justice Ministry days in advance, comprised largely of the relatives of those who had been killed or maimed. Entire families had come by air, road, and train from all parts of India, in much the same way as those other pilgrims had gone to the Ganga to be purified, except these pilgrims had come to Delhi seeking the purification of justice. Thousands overflowed the hotels and boardinghouses or camped out in the parklands and maidans, come to bear witness, to hold the government to its promise of retribution against those who had poisoned the soul of the nation.

Newspaper reporters and television crews flew in from every major Indian city and around the world. They roamed the encampments, airing one horror story after another, adding to the growing agitation of the crowds. Lawyers and claims brokers pimped for business as they had after Bhopal, among them American lawyers hoping a link would be found to an American corporate parent so they could lodge bigger claims in the United States.

By the morning of the inquiry the crowd around the Justice Ministry had been swollen to more than a hundred thousand by political agitators, curiosity seekers, and troublemakers. Police lines had to be reinforced by armed troops.

The inquiry was due to start at ten, and Rupe was supposed to be present for its opening, but the unexpected size of the crowd prevented her arrival at the main entrance. Pilot delayed the start of the hearing till eleven while arrangements were made to get her in by another entrance. When word of the delay reached the crowd, it quickly translated into rumors of yet another government betrayal and a roar of outrage rolled over the maidan. A barrage of stones and animal dung followed and a section of the crowd surged toward the police lines.

Police lathis and rifle butts rose and fell like scythes in a wheat field, but weight of numbers forced the police back. For a few harrowing moments it looked as if the crowd would break through. Then more soldiers poured in from trucks at the rear of the building and gradually the crowd fell back, angry and bloodied. But the mood was volatile and the barrage of stones and filth continued, taking a toll on the defenders.

There was a bustle of activity at the main entrance to the building and more soldiers appeared at the top of the steps. Behind them were civilians, ministry clerks who hurried to set up a small speaking platform with microphones aimed at the crowd. Then the tiny figure of a woman appeared in the plain white sari and head scarf of a widow. The barrage of missiles subsided as Rupe stepped up onto the platform so she could be seen by all of the crowd.

"No more blood," she said into the microphone. "We will shed no more blood over Varanasi."

The loudspeakers crackled and boomed with distortion, but her words and her presence had an instant calming effect on the crowd. They would listen to Rupe. They would listen to her because she had suffered like them.

"I am the one who deserves your anger," she said. "I am the one who is responsible for the delay in commencement of the inquiry. I am the one whom Judge Pilot wished to accommodate."

There was a murmur of confusion in the crowd, shouts of accusation.

She went on, her voice rising: "I promised you there would be no more Bhopals, no more betrayals. I promised you justice and I am here to see justice delivered. The inquiry opens today— justice begins today."

The fury that had gripped the crowd dissipated, and the mood shifted again, to hope, to belief, as suddenly as the wind. A roar of approval echoed against the walls of the surrounding buildings.

"I have heard your cries for justice," Rupe went on. "India and the world have heard your cries for justice. Together we will bear witness to the beginning of a new era of justice for all Indians. Your voices will be heard, your testimony will be heard. I pledge you my word on it—I pledge you my life."

The crowd settled like a beast given a few soothing words from its master. There was no betrayal. Rupe Seshan, the widow of the nation, said so. And they believed her.

She stepped down from the platform and walked back inside to where Sansi waited with the rest of her fearful entourage. She stopped when she saw him, close enough for him to smell her perfume, the scent of perspiration underneath, the scent of triumph.

"We'd better give them justice," she whispered to him. "If we don't, they will tear us to pieces."

Outside on the maidan a young man near the front of the crowd watched as Rupe disappeared from view. He hadn't joined in on the assault on the police, he hadn't thrown any stones or pieces of rotten fruit. He had fought his way to the front only so he could see. So he could see the people who promised him and all the others like him justice.

Raffee intended to hold them to their word. No matter how big or important they were.

Every last one of them.

CHAPTER 16

Annie was waiting for him when he got back.

She sat in the half-lit living room smoking a cigarette. There was a book open on her lap and her face was partially obscured by a table lamp, but the cigarette was a bad sign. She had given up smoking when they got back from Goa the year before.

He'd arranged for a government car to pick her up at the airport and bring her to the bungalow, but when he looked around, he saw no sign of luggage. She must have checked into a hotel, he thought. She had come only to say good-bye. He hesitated, uncertain of how to approach her or what to say. Then he closed the door, went to a chair across from her, and sat down.

"How do you feel?" he asked tentatively.

"Shitty," she said. "How about you?"

He could see her face clearly now in the lamplight. It looked raw and pinched.

"Not . . . good," he answered.

"From what I understand, everything's going your way," she said.

Sansi's insides congealed. He knew the pain he had instilled in himself and how it must be only a fraction of the pain she was feeling. He had tried not to think about this moment, knowing that when it came, whatever he said would be inadequate. Now the moment was here and he had to confront her knowledge of what he'd done to her, and his whole being was consumed by an abject despair.

"I'm sorry—" He stopped, knowing how insulting it sounded. His eyes drifted to the open door to the bedroom and he saw her suitcase on the bed, half unpacked.

"No, I'm sorry," she said. She leaned out of her chair and put her brow to his. "I shouldn't have pushed you to let me come. There's been a lot happening. . . ."

He put his arms around her, consoling her, buying time. She didn't know, after all. He would have to tell her.

"They've given me an ultimatum," she said. "Decide who comes first, you or the paper." She leaned back and smiled wanly. "I told them I'd think about it. I can get another job, I think. I could freelance, work for the American news bureaus. The problem is my visa is up in three months, so it's not a good time to switch. I might have to leave the country and do it from outside, and the bastards know that. And this isn't a good time to be unloading all this on you either."

"Are Bapre." Sansi lowered his eyes to the floor.

Annie looked embarrassed.

"I shouldn't have come," she said. "I can imagine what it's like here. I know things can't be much better. I just needed some time out, to be with you, to know you're real. To know there's somebody left I can count on."

Sansi exhaled, a sigh from the well of his fears. "This is about the interview they wanted you to do with me?"

"We don't have to talk about it right now," she said.

"No, we do," Sansi insisted. "It's important. You are important."

Annie looked touched by the urgency in his voice. She shrugged and went on. "They know you're serious about not giving any interviews, so Alam Bajaj had the bright idea of getting me to do a general piece about you, a profile based on what I know."

Sansi nodded.

"I told them I wouldn't do it. They told me to go away and think about it for a few days."

"And if you don't they will fire you?"

"I'm not sure. They'll probably stick me with some lousy job, maybe nudge me out the door. Maybe they'll just fire me. The old paper wouldn't but it's not the old paper anymore. That lizard Bajaj seems pretty well able to do whatever he pleases."

"You don't have to put up with that," Sansi said.

"I have a few contacts among the bureaus here in New Delhi." She smiled. "It's another reason I wanted to come. It won't hurt to make a few calls while I'm here, do a little job hunting."

"I could help," Sansi said. "Give you a few tips about the investigation that no one else could get. That would make you a valuable property, wouldn't it?"

Annie looked concerned.

"I don't think that's a good idea," she said. "I don't want you putting yourself—the investigation—at risk on my account."

"I have been dueling with the media all my life," he said. "I know how little it takes to get them excited."

"No," she shook her head, resolved. "I don't have to get a job that way. I don't want it that way."

Sansi looked wretched. She still wanted to protect him.

He had to tell her about Rupe. But not now. It wasn't the moment.

Later, when they were in bed, he made love to her with an urgency that shocked her. As if he had to prove to her and to himself how much he loved her. Afterward, when he went to the living room to bring them each a drink, he passed the table where she had been reading and glanced at the paperback face-down. Makarand Paranjape's book *Playing the Dark God*. A book of poems. All of them about infidelity.

∎   ∎

Savitri Chowdhary was the finest policeman Sansi had ever known. He had felt that way since the two of them first worked together, twenty years earlier at Crime Branch, when Sansi was a detective constable and Chowdhary a sergeant. Sansi had subsequently been promoted over Chowdhary to the rank of inspector and put in the awkward position of having his former superior become his subordinate. It was a measure of the respect and friendship that existed between them that they continued to work together successfully and Sansi continued to learn from Chowdhary.

Each man knew and complemented the other's strengths and weaknesses. Where Sansi was inclined to act instinctively Chowdhary was methodical and careful. He was like the glaciers that carved their way slowly but relentlessly through the implacable Himalayas. Once convinced of the rightness of his case, Chowdhary could no more easily be deflected than a glacier from his course. These qualities would have equipped him admirably in a conventional police force, but in the corrupt milieu of the Indian police service they were impediments to advancement.

It had taken Chowdhary eight years to be promoted from constable to sergeant and nineteen years to make it to inspector. It was unlikely he would go higher. He seemed to know it was his karma to spend the rest of his days toiling anonymously on important cases that would allow superiors like Jamal to take most of the credit for work well done.

Sansi knew that much of his success at Crime Branch had been built on Chowdhary's diligent foot-slogging, and he had never been afraid to say so. Which was why he listened closely to whatever Chowdhary had to say. When Chowdhary called him at around four in the afternoon on day nine of the inquiry, Sansi knew it must be important. There was no emotion in Chowdhary's voice, no telltale tremor of excitement—there never was. When Chowdhary had something important to say, he got quieter, not louder. So Sansi turned his back on the bustle of the operations room, cupped a hand over one ear and listened intently to the words that came down the line from Varanasi.

"I think we have something, Sansi sahib," Chowdhary said. "I think we have somebody."

"Who?" Sansi said.

"You remember Patna Fabrics, sahib?"

"*Acha,*" Sansi said. Patna was one of the biggest and oldest plants on the river and among the first to be raided. Still, Sansi hadn't expected anything quite so soon.

"We raided them on Friday," Chowdhary continued. "We haven't examined all their files yet but we have found something that is most interesting."

"In what way?"

"Their figures are not like the others."

"Worse . . . better?"

"Different, sahib. The others tried to hide the quantity and the type of their chemical discharges by revising their figures downward. Some of them have installed new traps and filters where there was no emission control equipment before or where it was old or not working. Everywhere we are going we are finding backdated inspection certificates from SEPA."

"*Acha.*"

"Patna has taken the opposite approach. Instead of revising their figures downward, they revised them upward."

"Why—to show they produced more pollution instead of less?"

"Yes, sahib, that is it precisely," Chowdhary answered. "They have altered their records like all of the others but instead of trying to make themselves look better, it has been to make themselves look worse."

Sansi felt a stir of anticipation. Patna was a subsidiary of the Renown group of industries, Madhuri Amlani's empire.

"Have you interviewed anybody in management?"

"*Acha*, sahib. The plant manager. His name is Agawarl. He says the factory has always been very inefficient. He says he has been doing his best to clean it up but he has not been the manager for very long."

"How long?"

"He says four years, sahib."

"Long enough," Sansi said. "Did you ask him why he changed his records?"

"He said he was trying to make them more accurate," Chowdhary answered. "They are all saying that."

"No doubt—but not for quite the same reasons. If you are going to go to the trouble of changing your numbers and you know there is a good chance you will get caught—why would you do it to make yourself look worse instead of better?"

"That is it precisely, sahib," Chowdhary said. "We went back to the plant this morning to look at the liquid waste disposal system. The retaining tanks were at minimum levels and the sludge tanks were almost empty—which would support the manager's claim that they kept nothing, they treated nothing, they dumped everything directly into the river for years."

"But gradually, not in sufficient quantities to cause a disaster?"

"*Acha*, sahib."

"But the figures are wrong?"

"Oh yes, sahib, totally wrong. There is no doubt they have discharged some chemicals into the river over the years, but it is not the amount the manager is saying. Indeed, it is possible the contrary is true. It is possible they dumped very few chemicals into the river. It is possible they let their waste accumulate with the intention of leaving it for others to worry about."

"Like the Amlanis?"

"Precisely, sahib. And then it becomes their problem. They are the ones who have to pay for the disposal."

"Or they can tell the manager to get rid of it any way he likes as long as it doesn't cost them anything."

"You have taken the words from out of my mouth, sahib."

"Perhaps the manager of Patna Fabrics has been a little too clever for his own good."

"*Acha*, sahib. He is also a very frightened man."

"You want to bring him in?"

"I think he knows something, sahib. My feeling is if we frighten him a little bit more, he will talk."

"What do you think he knows?"

Chowdhary paused before answering.

"I think he knows what happened, sahib."

Sansi had already made up his mind. "Bring him in, hold him till I get there."

CHAPTER 17

Joshi lay in a tangle of bedsheets beneath a beam of light from the bathroom door that slanted across the room like the light of a movie projector. He lay on his back with his hands behind his head. The curtains were drawn so he could see the gaudy skyline of the city against the night sky. The city looked flat and fake, as if its lights were shining through a cardboard cutout. It made him feel even more like a character in a movie. The bedside clock said it was twenty past one in the morning. Another few hours and he would have to go to work. He wasn't at all sleepy.

The projector beam fluttered and the outline of a naked woman appeared in the doorway. She had her hands on the doorjambs and her legs were parted slightly. Shafts of light sculpted every curve and crevice of her body so precisely he could see tiny tendrils of hair between her thighs. She hurried across the carpet, an exquisite shadow, climbed onto the bed and knelt beside him. Then she shook her hair away from her face and arched her back so that her breasts rose higher, and he could see the necklace he had given her in the glow of the city. Diamonds and topaz, her favorite gemstones.

"I'll wear it only for you," she said.

"If you're going to be dressed like this . . ." he murmured and ran a finger down her arm.

Anita Vasi leaned forward and kissed him on the lips, her breasts pooling heavily against his chest. His partly tumescent penis hardened and swiveled upward across his belly. When she leaned back and saw how hard he was, she smiled.

"Again?"

"I'm hard all the time," he said. "I think of you at work and I'm hard. It's embarrassing."

"It makes me glad when you say that," she said. She lay down beside him so their faces were only inches apart and put her hand on his cock. As she kneaded it gently she watched his eyes, gaining pleasure from the pleasure she saw in him.

"When you touch me I turn into the elephant," he said.

She laughed softly. "You made me come," she said. "I never come."

His eyes shadowed, and she knew he didn't believe her.

"With others I would pretend," she said. "I know the difference."

"You will have to tell me what I am doing right."

"You make love to me—not just my body," she said.

"You are a goddess," he said. "Every man wants to lie with a goddess."

"They want only the body. They don't want to know who is inside, they don't care. You are different, you are gentle and loving, the way a man should be. That is why I come with you."

Joshi was amused. "My brother thinks I am no good with women—he calls me sadhu."

Her expression turned contemptuous. "Your brother thinks the more women he has, the more man he is. He should hear how they talk about him behind his back."

Joshi fell silent, and she saw he was still bothered by something.

"What is it?"

He hesitated, as if embarrassed to ask, and then said: "Have you slept with Arvind . . . or my father?"

She seemed neither surprised nor offended. Given the worlds they moved in, it was possible. For several years Renown's media empire had included a model agency that supplied the girls for Renown's print campaigns and TV commercials, many of which were shot at Film City. Girls shuttled between jobs at Film City and the Renown agency all the time, and the Amlani men were known to use them regularly for their own pleasure. Anita could easily have been one of them.

"No," she answered. "I have been with Johnny since I was fifteen."

Joshi had never met Johnny Jenta but knew his reputation. Jenta not only ran the unions at Film City but fancied himself a starmaker. He kept a harem of young actresses for whom he liked to find parts in the movies. Anita had never pretended to be anything but one of them; she had merely been more successful than the others. It also meant she fell more completely under Jenta's control—and even the Amlanis had to defer to the Bombay underworld.

"Do you sleep with Jenta?" Joshi asked, already knowing the answer.

"I did in the beginning," she said. "But he doesn't ask me anymore. I'm an investment now, not one of his *nautch* girls."

"But you would—if he asked you?"

She sighed. She didn't like the way the conversation was going.

"There is something you have to understand about Johnny," she said. "I know he surrounds himself with pretty girls, but it's not for the sex. The sex doesn't matter that much to him. It's for the power. He uses women to give him power over other men. It is all about control with him. He likes to control everybody and everything."

"He makes you sleep with other men?"

"I do what he tells me to do," she said. "I have no choice."

Joshi lapsed into pained silence. The love play between them had stopped. Anita leaned on an elbow and looked at him, surprised by his naiveté. For an Amlani, he seemed to know very little about the raw side of human commerce.

"Am I your first *randi*?" she asked.

Joshi winced. "Why don't you leave him?"

"Because he would kill me."

She said it matter-of-factly but Joshi knew it was the truth.

"How do you get involved with somebody like Jenta?"

"You think this is the life I chose for myself?" Her voice had acquired the dual edge of hurt and anger. "Everybody thinks that because it's the movies it's what you want to do, you'll do anything to be a star . . . and so you deserve everything that happens to you."

Joshi struggled with the emotions she aroused in him. Then he added: "I want to know how you met him."

She slumped back into her pillow and remained silent for a long time, as if she preferred not to remember, or was afraid of what it might do to them. At last she started to speak, her voice flat and detached, as if it were someone else's life she was describing.

"My family came here from Orissa," she said. "I was nine. We had no money. We lived in the chawls at Sewri. My mother worked at a mill, it could have been one of your father's mills. My father did electrical repairs but he spent all his money on *paan* and *araq*. I had one brother and four sisters. My father called his daughters his burdens. Sometimes he was drunk for days. He would beat my mother and then he would beat us for crying. I was the second oldest girl. My brother ran away when he was eleven, and when my older sister was thirteen, my father sold her to a brothel keeper. My mother tried to stop him and he beat her so badly she nearly died. I knew then what would happen to me, and so I ran away too. I decided if that was the way I had to make money I would set my own price. So I made myself up like an American whore and went up to Juhu with a girlfriend."

Joshi listened, trying not to let his emotions show. Juhu Beach was the Indian Malibu, an oceanfront enclave of fancy villas owned by movie stars, directors, producers, and other big-wigs in the movie industry. Over the years it had become a magnet for all the other hopefuls who wanted to break into the movie industry and were willing to pay exorbitant rents for rooms in the dingy apartment buildings and hotels that had sprung up in the backstreets. They took acting lessons, singing lessons, and dancing lessons, they answered ads, went to auditions, hung out on the beach, in the park, in the bars of the big beachfront hotels; they did everything aspiring actors did in Hollywood. And, like their Hollywood counterparts, they made friends with the pimps and prostitutes and drug dealers who saw more of the movie moguls than they ever would. Most went home broke and disillusioned in under a year, but others stayed on and made money by doing things that had never been part of their dreams.

"I met some hippies in the park," Anita went on. "I went with a German guy for a while, but he was into drugs too much so I went with a guy from Sweden who bought me food and gave me money for sex. And that's how I lived, going from guy to guy, until I met Johnny."

"How did you meet him?" Joshi asked, his voice neutral.

"Through a drug dealer," she said. "Johnny doesn't use drugs but he knows a lot of people who do. He was having a party and this dealer asked me if I wanted to go. I think he knew Johnny would be interested in me, so there was some money in it for him. It's funny . . ." She hesitated, her hesitation suggesting it wasn't funny at all. "When I first went to Juhu, I had no real figure. I was skinny and flat-chested, but the hippies didn't mind because most of them were junkies and that was what they were used to. But when I turned fourteen my figure went from nothing to the same as it is now . . . in one year. Then suddenly everybody was treating me differently. Suddenly I was worth something. Because I had this new body. So, I met Johnny and he asked me if I wanted to be in the movies and I said sure. It was better than what I'd been doing. So we made a deal. He would get me into the movies, and when I became a star I would pay him back."

"You don't live with him now," Joshi said. He had already spent a few nights at her apartment at Juhu.

"No, but he owns my apartment," she said. "He gets all my contracts, my jobs, and for that he gets all my money. He decides how much I keep for myself."

"How much does he take?"

"Ninety percent." She shrugged. "Sometimes he takes it all."

Joshi sighed. "Are Bapre. You must have paid him back a hundred times by now."

She smiled as if to say that at last he understood.

"And when will you be free of him?"

"When he says so."

Joshi paused before asking his next question. "Don't you see a life for yourself outside the movies?"

"I could walk out tomorrow," she answered. "And I wouldn't look back."

Again Joshi was reluctant to believe her. "Have you seen how much Rashmi envies you? All she wants is to be a star like you."

"I'm not a star, I'm a slave," Anita said. "I tried to tell Rashmi but she doesn't listen. It is a game to her, an exciting, glamorous game. Because she can leave anytime she wants. I can't. And when I complain nobody believes me. I told Rashmi I would like nothing better than to change places with her. For me that would be the greatest luxury—to be able to choose what I do with my life."

"Jenta must know he can't keep you a slave forever."

"He doesn't have to. When my looks start to go and he can't make so much money off me anymore, then he will let me go. When he has finished with me and nobody wants me."

"You could get away from him," Joshi added. "There are ways."

She smiled, as if the thought hadn't already occurred to her. "I'm saving what I can," she said. "Johnny thinks everybody is greedy like him. He has no idea how little I need to run away. Another year, perhaps two, then I'll have enough."

"Then what will you do?"

"I'll leave India for a while, come back in a few years, live somewhere else."

"Why don't you leave now?"

She looked at him, wondering if he'd heard anything she'd said.

"How much do you think Jenta would want to let you go now?" he added.

She laughed softly. "I would be the most expensive *randi* you ever had."

"How much?"

His tone told her he was serious, but her reaction wasn't what he expected. Instead of taking heart, she looked more discouraged, as if afraid of allowing herself any hope at all.

"I don't know," she said. "You would have to talk to him."

The two of them looked at one another, each trying to read the other's thoughts, each wondering how much to believe.

"What would you do if you were free to choose?" he asked.

She took a breath, as if it were an effort to keep her voice from breaking.

"I've known that since I was thirteen years old," she said. "Sometimes I think it is the one thing that keeps me sane, other times I think it is the one thing that is certain to drive me mad."

Joshi waited.

"I want to have children of my own," she added. "I want to

give them the childhood I never had, the kind of childhood every child should have. I think it is the only way I will ever be able to save myself."

For a while the only sound in the room was the background grumble of the city. Then Joshi enveloped her in his arms and kissed her face and mouth as if he could kiss away all the hurt she had known. She responded gladly, opening herself to him. Then his excitement took over and he was on top of her with his head tilted back and his eyes closed, lost in the pleasure of the moment. He felt himself building and opened his eyes so he could look at her. He saw she was watching him with a fearful longing, a longing that had nothing to do with sex.

He kissed her again and whispered: "I want to spend the rest of my life making love to you."

CHAPTER 18

High over the Arabian Sea a Gulfstream jet bearing the red, white, and blue livery of the Dumont Chemical Corporation began its descent toward Bombay. Its wings sheared through the last wisps of cloud, and the city appeared suddenly on the horizon, a glistening white ribbon between the metallic blues of the ocean and the parched browns of the land.

"Looks pretty good from up here," Bob Towne said as he looked through a porthole window.

"Wait till you smell it," Grayson said. "It's like nothing you smelled in your life before. That's when you know you're in India."

"It's got beaches," Towne added as the shoreline drew closer. "I didn't know it had beaches."

"You want to take a walk on the beach when we're there, fine," Grayson said. "Just don't stick your toe, or anything else, in the water, unless you figure on leaving it there."

"You tell that to Ray?" Towne asked. The two of them looked across the aisle to where Ray Kemp dozed with his mouth open, a strand of saliva connecting his jowls to his shirt collar.

"It's why we're here, isn't it?"

Lean and manicured, with skin like expensive leather, Tom Grayson was fifty-seven years old, had a preference for pale blue button-downs and gunmetal-gray suits. He was point man for Dumont's expansion into India. As the architect of the refinery deal with Renown, he had visited Bombay nine times in the past two years.

For Towne and Kemp it was their first visit. Others had preceded them but this would be their first face-to-face with Madhuri Amlani and their first chance to see what kind of a job he'd done setting up the oil refinery they'd given him. Officially they were there to represent the company at the commissioning ceremony, unofficially they were there to take the corporate courtship with Renown a big step further.

Towne was chief chemical engineer for Dumont worldwide. Forty-eight years old, with thinning sandy hair, he had been with the company since college and had the self-assurance of a man who could retire the next day with two houses and a yacht, a couple of million in stocks and bonds, and a pension of $80,000 a year. His trip to India was to serve one purpose and one purpose only—to give his stamp of approval to the plant at Surat. A task not expected to be insurmountable, given the considerations that governed its transfer from Mexico.

Kemp's task was a little trickier. He carried documents of intent that spelled out the terms of full partnership with Renown, terms Grayson had negotiated over the past eighteen months. If Amlani agreed, Kemp was authorized to sign an agreement in principle. All that would remain was approval by the board in Philadelphia, and Dumont and Renown would be in the oil business in India together.

On the face of it the hard work was done. But Amlani was slippery and nothing could be taken for granted till his signature was on paper. Which was why the board had appointed Kemp to close the deal. Middle-aged and balding, overweight and watery-eyed, he didn't look like he could drive a hard bargain at a cookie sale. He looked like a worrier. And he was. But he knew how to make it work for him. He worried a deal the way a dog worried a bone. He worried over every detail of every sub-clause of every appendix until he had worried his opponents into the ground and they would give him what he wanted just to make him go away.

According to Grayson, this one was going to be a vacation. Not only had Dumont saved Amlani's skin but he was forty million dollars in hock to them. As Grayson said before they boarded the plane in Philly—how hard could it be? Even so, Ray Kemp was paid to worry.

The pilot came on the intercom to announce they were cleared for landing at Sahar International Airport. In the back of the aircraft a platoon of disheveled and jet-lagged gofers stirred themselves. A pair of invincibly pert flight attendants handed out hot towels. One of them delicately wiped Kemp's chin for him.

"Have you spoken to the old man since he climbed back in the chair?" Towne asked Grayson as the plane banked for its landing approach.

"Last time I spoke to him was six weeks ago," Grayson answered. "All he told me then was he wanted to do some reorganizing before he handed things over to his son."

"He didn't say anything about another stock float?"

"Nothing," Grayson said. "I'm a little pissed about that. I know he thinks it has nothing to do with us, and strictly speaking he's right, but he should have said something—and I'm going to tell him."

Kemp had been listening without appearing to listen. "I hope he doesn't have any ugly little surprises in store for us," he said, his voice thin and phlegmy.

"Like what?" Grayson said.

"Like another potential partner in the wings."

"You know something I don't know, Ray? Because I think I'd know something like that."

Kemp looked at him as if to say he hoped so.

"He's positioning, trying to get us to sweeten the pot," Grayson added. "We've been here before."

Kemp smiled humorlessly, leaving Grayson mildly irritated.

"The old man started the company, right?" Towne asked.

Grayson nodded.

"What I've seen of guys like that, you have to cut their hand off the tiller after they're dead."

"Arvind could do it," Grayson said.

"Tough guy?"

"And ambitious."

"Went to school in the States, right?"

"Chicago. Still follows the Bears and the Cubs. He was over for the playoffs last year."

"Totally global, huh?"

"These days."

The runway rushed up to meet them, and the interior of the plane fell silent. There was a shriek of rubber, a spurt of blue smoke, and everyone leaned into their seat belts. Moments later they were taxiing toward the VIP arrivals hangar.

"Cars arranged?" Kemp looked at Grayson.

"Better be," Grayson said. He knew enough about the way India worked to make sure everything would be waiting at the hangar, including a couple of uniforms from Customs and Immigration. Their bags would follow them to the Taj Mahal later, though the air agent had spent enough money to make sure they wouldn't be held up by anything so inconvenient as a baggage inspection.

"Gentlemen, if I may . . . ?" Grayson sought the attention of his colleagues and their noisily chattering staff before they disembarked. "I know I've said this before but I can't emphasize it enough, so please indulge me one more time."

Everybody knew what was coming but they listened anyway. Nobody wanted him blaming them if the deal soured at this stage.

"This is a third world country in a hurry to be a first world country," he went on. "A lot of the time it trips over its own feet. The people we're going to be dealing with here understand we're far in advance of them in terms of technology and management systems. However, they are not unsophisticated and they are certainly not without pride. So please resist the temptation to indulge in any language or behavior that might indicate we believe ourselves to be superior beings from a superior society. These people do not like to be patronized. Do I make myself clear?"

"So, if they fall on their ass, don't laugh?" Towne said.

Laughter rippled through the cabin.

"Long as they don't try and take us down with 'em," Kemp observed.

Grayson shrugged. He had done what he could. They were on their own now.

Towne was the first to stick his head outside. Heat and fumes engulfed him like the blast of a jet engine. He looked unimpressed.

"Mexico City is worse," he said.

"Wait till you get out into that," Grayson said, and pointed past him. "That's India, right over there."

Towne followed Grayson's pointing finger to a perimeter fence a hundred yards away. Beyond the fence was an ocean of shanties stretching to the horizon in a shivering brown haze. But what held the visitor's gaze was the spectacle of human faces pressed against the chain-link fence, faces as numerous as grains of sand on a beach. What was eerie was that they made no sound. They didn't call or wave, they didn't stick their hands through the fence to beg or sell. They just watched, like prisoners, as the world of plenty went about its business without them. There was something sinister and unsettling about them, Towne thought, something he resented in those silent, accusing faces. Something to be afraid of.

"Jesus Christ," he muttered. "Can we get inside?"

Minutes later a convoy of gleaming white cars rolled through the perimeter gates with the three Dumont executives cocooned safely in the fragrant leather interior of the lead car. The ocean of mute brown faces parted obediently, then closed around them and it was as if they had never been there.

CHAPTER 19

"He is in a cell by himself?" Sansi asked.

"*Acha.*"

"Have you spoken to him?"

"Not since we brought him in," Chowdhary said. "I was waiting for you."

"So he has spoken to nobody since yesterday?"

"Only the guards. He wants to know if anybody from the company has called."

"Have they?"

"No, sahib."

"Do they know?"

"It is not possible they would not know by now, sahib."

"We will hear from them," Sansi said. "But I do not think it will be with Mr. Agawarl's welfare in mind. How is he holding up?"

"He ate a meal last night but then he was sick. I don't think it was the food. He has eaten nothing today. His wife came last night and again this morning asking when he would be released. She brought him clean clothes."

"Did you tell him? Did you give him the clothes?"

"Oh no, sahib."

"Good," Sansi said.

He had arrived in Varanasi aboard a government plane a little after one that afternoon. With him were a half-dozen scientists from the Environment Ministry who had gone directly to Patna Fabrics to help Chowdhary's men search for more evidence. Sansi had come directly to the Varanasi central police complex, where he spoke now with Chowdhary in a cramped corner of the records office, the only space the state police would allow them. Like the Union Territory police in Delhi, the Uttar Pradesh police were offended to be given no more than a supporting role in the investigation.

"Any history of violations by the company?" Sansi asked.

"Nothing recent, sahib." Chowdhary gestured to a buff folder on his desk. "It is a very old plant with many owners since Independence. There were several fines between 1975 and 1983 for breaches of safety standards. The last entry was 1991 for noncompliance on effluent control, but there has been nothing since the Amlanis took over."

"The Amlanis make their payoffs on time," Sansi said. "What about Agawarl?"

"No criminal record in Varanasi. Nothing in Bela, where he grew up, or in Allahabad, where he went to college. He is married, the father of five children. His wife is expecting another child, quite soon I would say."

"He may prefer to stay in jail," Sansi said. "What else?"

Chowdhary knew what Sansi wanted. He was looking for clues to Agawarl's personality: fears, prejudices, political beliefs, religious values, anything that would strip away his defenses and speed up the interrogation process.

"We spoke to the neighbors after we picked him up and they said he was a good husband and father. They didn't know about any drinking or drug habits, and he didn't go to the brothels or the gambling houses. There is no girlfriend we know of, no boyfriend, no major debts."

"Reason enough to be suspicious," Sansi said. "Did the neighbors ever hear any fights?"

"Yes, sahib. The neighbors said they did quarrel, usually about the long hours he worked."

"Is he clever?"

"Clever enough to try something nobody else did—he revised the discharge figures upward, not downward, remember?" Chowdhary paused to consult a worn blue notebook. "He is a chemical engineer by training. He went straight from college at Allahabad to Patna Fabrics. He was there two years and was chief chemical engineer when the Amlanis took over. They made him plant manager, his chance to show what a good company man he was."

"Any caste problems?"

"He's Vainya, mixed caste. His family was Sombatta, a local *jati*, a subcaste of rope makers, so he moved up in the world. But his wife, I think, is Sudra, so he married down."

"Or she married up. Which might suggest he is ambitious where career is concerned but she is ambitious where caste is concerned."

Sansi's observation seemed to open a whole new line of thought for Chowdhary.

"His wife seems quite devout," he noted. "She told us she spent all night at the temple praying to Durga for her husband's release, and when we would not let him go, she was very shocked. The neighbors said he wasn't as religious as his wife. He rarely went to the local temple with her. But the paan wallah said about five months ago he saw Agawarl at the temple of Shiva on the ghats and he had seen him there a few times since."

Sansi thought about all that Chowdhary had told him. The goddess Durga was one of the many incarnations of Parvati, the consort of Shiva. As Durga she symbolized righteousness.

She rode on the back of a tiger that symbolized the ego and the arrogance of man, which she struggled constantly to restrain. Shiva was the destroyer—destroyer of the universe, destroyer of man's illusions. Among the symbols that surrounded him were a circle of fire to represent the cycle of birth and destruction, a deer to represent man's inconstant nature, and a cobra to represent cosmic energy. But around his head were the waves of the Ganga, the goddess of purity. In the center of his forehead was a third eye, which represented the all-seeing eye of God, and around his shoulders a garland of skulls which represented the inevitability of death and the judgment that awaited everyone.

"He started going to the Shiva temple soon after the spill?" Sansi said.

"It would appear so, sahib."

"So his wife is devout because she wants to be reborn to a higher caste," Sansi mused aloud. "But her husband has committed a great sin, which could doom the family to an eternity of reincarnations as insects—so she prays to Durga for forgiveness."

"And he himself is going to Shiva these past months to plead for mercy for what he has done to Ganga," Chowdhary added.

"In my experience, a sudden attention to worship usually indicates a troubled conscience," Sansi said.

"He is a troubled man, sahib."

"Because he can deceive us but he knows he cannot deceive the gods."

"Perhaps he has been searching for atonement, sahib."

"Perhaps I can help him find it." Sansi paused. "What did you tell him about me?"

"I told him a very important personage was coming from Delhi to question him."

Sansi waggled his head approvingly. "Perhaps I can persuade him his prayers to Lord Shiva have been answered."

Chowdhary's melancholy face eased into a suggestion of a smile. Blue eyes in a dark face had marked Sansi as an outsider all his life—but there were times when the mark of the outsider could have a profound effect on a susceptible mind.

The police complex was a jumble of old and new buildings thrown together inside a cantonment ringed by a high brick wall. Sansi and Chowdhary followed a crumbling colonnade, where visitors on ancient wooden benches waited out the interminable delays of official business, to a narrow lane that led between two red brick buildings. They stopped at a pair of iron gates watched by a cluster of police guards, one of whom recognized Chowdhary and unlocked a smaller gate in the grillwork.

Accompanied by a guard, they continued down a short, dark tunnel that smelled of urine to another identical set of gates. On the other side of the gates was an enclosed yard the size of a tennis court, where a dozen guards with lathis watched a hundred or so prisoners. Steel bars along two walls marked an L-shaped holding cell where general prisoners awaited their day in court, some of them for years. In a corner of the yard twenty or so young men squatted in a circle chanting Shiv Sena slogans.

"Students," the guard explained as he let his visitors inside. "From the university."

The Hindu University at Varanasi was a hotbed of political unrest, and recent gains in state elections by the Hindu fundamentalist party, the Shiv Sena, had given its students another excuse to riot.

"They looted some shops, burned a few buses," Chowdhary added. "Nothing serious."

The third side of the yard was enclosed by the high blank wall of an administration building. The fourth side was occupied by a number of individual cells for special prisoners; murderers, dacoits, politicals—and the manager of Patna Fabrics.

The guard went to one of the gates and raked the bars with a lathi.

"Get up, Agawarl," he ordered.

The cell was little more than a slot in the wall scarcely five feet high so its occupant couldn't stand fully upright. There was a bare wooden bench for sleeping, and the crumbling brick roof was arched so it resembled an oven. The heat that wafted out was like the heat of an oven, and with it came the stench of sweat and excrement that attracted swarms of flies. A plate of chapatti and rice lay uneaten on the dirt floor, the glossy humps of cockroaches moving in it.

There was the sound of someone stirring, then a shape materialized out of the murk, the stooped figure of a man, eyes pouched with fatigue, face and arms scabbed with insect bites. Anjani Agawarl scanned his visitors through the bars and settled on the face he didn't know.

"You are from the company?" he asked hopefully.

Sansi made no response. He looked closely at Agawarl, studying him, seeing his fear.

"You want to talk now or do you want more time to think?" Chowdhary asked.

"I don't know what you want," Agawarl said, his eyes moving reluctantly away from Sansi. "I cooperated, I gave you everything, I don't know why I am here."

"You are here because you are a liar," Chowdhary snapped.

"I want to talk to the company," Agawarl pleaded. "There must be a lawyer here by now, I want to see my wife—"

"There is no lawyer," Chowdhary cut him off. "And you see who we want you to see."

Agawarl swayed, his fingers tightening on the cell bars. Behind them the chanting swelled to a crescendo and some of the guards shouted at the students to be quiet. Sansi waited till the racket subsided then spoke to Chowdhary in a tone of mild rebuke.

"This is no good," he said. "Take him inside, let him clean himself up then bring him to the interview room."

Agawarl's eyes swiveled back to Sansi, but Sansi had already started across the yard with Chowdhary following.

"Did you see how he looked at you, sahib?" Chowdhary said as he caught up. "He thinks you are his savior."

"I am," Sansi said. "As long as he gives me what I want."

A half hour later Agawarl shuffled into the interview room with chains on his wrists and ankles. He was freshly bathed and wearing the clean clothes his wife had brought him. Sansi ordered the guard to remove the chains and gestured Agawarl to the only empty chair. The guard stood against the closed door, the chains dangling loosely from his hand.

The interview room was a windowless cement box, cool to the point of chilliness. There were stains on the walls that could have been blood. The only furniture was three dilapidated chairs and a dented metal table with Agawarl on one side, his inter-rogators on the other.

"Do you understand why you are here?" Sansi began benignly.

"They said—" Agawarl stopped and coughed a phlegminess out of his voice. "They said there was a problem with the records."

"Yes, you could say that."

"I was trying to correct them, I knew there were errors, if you give me some time—"

"You will have plenty of time," Sansi interrupted. "You will have all eternity to reflect on what you have done."

Agawarl looked dismayed. Whoever Sansi was, however sympathetic he appeared, he wasn't to be easily manipulated.

"You are not here because you changed a few records," Sansi continued in the same uncompromising tone. "You are here because you poured enough phosphoric acid into the Ganga to kill a thousand people and to cripple thousands more. People who believed they were safe in the embrace of the holy mother Ganga. But you betrayed them—and you betrayed the gods."

Agawarl shifted nervously.

"Do you believe in Vedic law, Mr. Agawarl?"

It was like asking if he understood the difference between right and wrong.

"Yes, I believe in the Vedas," he answered dully.

"Then you know the lessons of the Srutis, the Agamas, the Darshanas, the Puranas?"

Agawarl dropped his gaze to the floor.

"Perhaps you recall the legend of Matsya, the golden fish," Sansi went on. "The Avatar of Vishnu who came to earth at the time of the great flood to save those who were worth saving?"

Agawarl continued to stare at the floor.

"How many people today would even know if they were visited by an Avatar?" Sansi asked. "How many would know enough to seize upon the chance to save themselves?"

Agawarl's head snapped up, his face riven by doubt, wondering if he had heard Sansi's suggestion properly.

Sansi smiled. "My name is George Sansi," he said. "I am in charge of the investigation into the Varanasi disaster—perhaps you were expecting Shiva himself in his fiery chariot?"

Agawarl flinched. He had told no one of his visits to the Shiva temple.

"The time when you will stand before Lord Shiva will come soon enough," Sansi added. "What you must decide is if you will go before him in arrogance and deceit or in honesty and repentance, so you may be worthy of his mercy."

Agawarl stared into Sansi's eyes, as blue as the churning ocean from which all life sprang, as blue as the once pure waters of the holy Ganga. No Indian was born with blue eyes unless his soul was touched by the spirit of the Brahman at the moment of conception, unless he had been chosen by the gods to be an Avatar.

"When Shiva comes to a man's house to judge that man's worthiness to enter heaven, he does not come as Lord Shiva," Sansi went on. "He assumes the guise of the humble traveler in need of refuge. Or, in his infinite wisdom, he sends a traveler to that man's house so he may see what transpires through his all-seeing eye."

Agawarl sat rigid, a rapid pulse in his neck the only sign of life.

"I am a humble servant of man's law," Sansi continued. "It is not in my power to offer forgiveness for all you have done. You must decide if you will take this opportunity to atone for your sins in this life, before Lord Shiva himself passes judgment on you for all eternity."

Sansi and Chowdhary watched impassively while the struggle between educated man and superstitious Indian played across Agawarl's tormented face. Slowly, the plant manager crumpled beneath the weight of his guilt.

"They said they would kill—" Again Agawarl's throat constricted, and Sansi signaled the guard to bring some water. They waited in silence till the guard returned with a metal cup filled to the brim. Agawarl took a series of swallows then shakily set the cup down on the table.

"They said they would kill me, they said they would kill my family."

"Who did?"

"The Amlanis," Agawarl said.

"Madhuri Amlani threatened to have you and your family killed?"

"Arvind, his son. I don't know how much his father knew. Arvind made all the decisions this past year."

Sansi glanced at Chowdhary, who had produced his blue notebook and was writing quickly.

"Can you protect my family?" Agawarl asked. "I don't care what happens to me, but my family shouldn't suffer."

"If you tell the truth I will do what I can," Sansi said.

Agawarl took another drink of water. The torment on his face was gone, replaced by an expression of relief.

"Arvind Amlani told me to dump the phosphorous in the river."

Sansi concealed the tremor of excitement that ran through him, the unsurpassable burn that accompanied the moment of breakthrough.

"Go on," he said.

"I told him I couldn't do it," Agawarl continued. "I told him there were other ways. I argued but he wouldn't listen. They never listened to me. All they cared about was saving money. All they ever cared about was money. Arvind said I had to flush the tanks. He kept telling me to flush the tanks. I knew what would happen. . . ." His voice faltered. "I didn't know this would happen. I thought there would be damage but I didn't know this would happen."

The air in the room seemed to charge and thicken so even the acoustics changed and their voices became flatter, duller.

"I wanted to do it in stages," Agawarl went on. "I said we could use foam to break it up, but they wouldn't spend the money on that either. They told me to flush the tanks, get rid of it all. They said the river would break it up . . . the current. . ."

"How much went into the river?" Sansi asked.

Agawarl was looking at Sansi but his eyes had an unfocused, distracted quality.

"Everything," he said.

"How much was everything?"

"It had been accumulating for years. The sludge pits were full, the tanks were full. They were leaking. If we didn't empty them, there was a risk they would burst and flood the factory. There are six hundred workers there."

"How much?" Sansi pressed.

"More than seven hundred thousand liters," Agawarl said.

"*Bhagwan*," Chowdhary breathed.

"The valves were rusted shut," Agawarl continued. "We had to break them open. When that happened, there was no stopping it. It all went into the river."

"We looked at the tanks," Chowdhary said. "The valves weren't broken. We didn't see any sludge pits."

"I made a solution of paint and metal filings and rust particles and sprayed it on the new valves," Agawarl said. "If you scrape it off you'll find the valves and the welds underneath are new. The sludge pits are underneath the tanks. They're supposed to be for the overflow, for emergencies. Their capacity is 250,000 liters. They were full when I took over as manager."

Sansi turned to Chowdhary. "Close the factory down, send all the workers home and seal it off. Don't let anybody from Renown Industries near it."

Chowdhary put away his notebook and got up to go.

"And send in a typist, a tape recorder, and a video camera operator," Sansi said. "And some chai. We're going to be a while."

Agawarl waited till Chowdhary had gone then asked Sansi: "You want me to testify at the inquiry?"

Sansi looked grimly back at him.

"At the inquiry, at the criminal proceedings that follow the inquiry, and at every proceeding and claim that follows that," Sansi said. "Testimony is the way to repentance, Mr. Agawarl— and you are going to need the rest of your life."

CHAPTER 20

"**S**he's a whore," Madhuri Amlani railed at his youngest son. "You fuck whores, you don't fall in love with them."

Joshi stiffened.

"She's not a whore."

"She's a gangster's whore. . . ." Amlani struggled to contain his temper. "She whored her way into the movie business and she'll whore herself to anybody who will keep her, including you—especially you."

"She had no choice," Joshi argued back. "She doesn't want that life, she wants to get out of it."

"Oh." Amlani affected surprise. "She wants to get off her back and onto yours?"

"She loves me for who I am, not what I am," Joshi insisted.

"She loves you because you're an Amlani!" his father shouted.

Joshi had meditated for two hours before coming to his father's study to tell him about Anita Vasi. He had put on clean white kurta pajamas to remind him of his purity of purpose. Still, his father's reaction had been worse than he expected. He stood in front of his father's desk and fixed his eyes on a place high on the chair back over his father's head where the black leather creases formed a beckoning abyss.

"No," he said stubbornly. "We love each other."

"She's an actress, a houri," his father sputtered. "She used her houri tricks to make you fall in love with her."

"You don't know her the way I know her."

"You know my health," his father added accusingly, "and you come to me with this?"

"It would have been worse to keep it a secret."

Amlani's mouth opened and closed in mute exasperation as he struggled to gain control of himself. "When did it start?"

"At the party, after the share launch," Arvind interjected. He watched from a sofa against the wall, a Limca bottle suspended between two fingers. "I saw the sadhu sniffing after the houri—"

"This is none of your business." Joshi looked contemptuously at his older brother.

"Three months ago?" Amlani asked.

"It has been almost four months now," Joshi answered.

"Three months, four months . . ." Amlani gestured helplessly. "It's nothing."

"It is long enough for us to know."

"She slept with you the first night?"

Joshi couldn't bring himself to answer. His father took it as confirmation.

"She has been sleeping with you since the night you met and she's not a houri?"

"No more than I am."

"She's leading you around by the dick." Amlani's anger drove his voice upward again. "Have you given her any money?"

"No."

"Has she asked for money?"

"No."

"Presents? Favors?"

Joshi remembered the necklace he had given Anita. "No."

"Have you made her any promises?"

"I promised to love her."

Amlani looked away in disgust. Arvind smirked and took a sip of his lime soda.

"I promised to marry her," Joshi added.

Silence expanded through the room like a shock wave. Amlani stared at his son in disbelief. When he spoke, his voice was faint and disbelieving.

"You promised her what?"

This time there was a slight break in Joshi's voice when he answered. "I promised to marry her."

Arvind sniggered.

Perspiration seeped out onto Amlani's massive forehead. "When you want to get married you speak to me first," he said hoarsely. "I will speak to your mother. That is what she is for. She knows all the respectable girls in Bombay. She knows who is the best match for you."

"I am not Arvind," Joshi said. "I won't have an arranged marriage."

Arvind's smirk broadened to a grin.

"A sound marriage is the foundation for a sound life," Amlani added sharply. "Marriage is built on respect and loyalty—it has nothing to do with love. You are still a child in your heart, Joshi. The love you are talking about is the pleasure of the senses. It makes you mad for a while and then it passes. It cannot be the basis of a lasting marriage. Marriage and pleasure must be kept apart if they are to last."

"I am not going to marry somebody as if it is just another branch of the family business," Joshi said.

"That is exactly what it is." Amlani slammed his hand down heavily on his desk. "Who you marry affects us all."

"I won't give her up."

"Keep her as a mistress, not as a wife. She has known too many men, Joshi. She cannot make a respectable wife for any man—and certainly not an Amlani."

"That is for me to decide."

"*Bakwas,*" Amlani swore. "Don't you see what is happening? She is not in love with you. She is working for Jenta. The two of them have tricked you. They have set a trap for you."

"I will take her away from Jenta."

"How?"

"I'll pay him—whatever he wants."

Even as he said it Joshi knew it was a mistake.

"Are Bapre!" Amlani was aghast. "That is what they want you to do. They want you to pay for her—or they will make me pay to make her go away."

"We're going to be married," Joshi repeated.

"She is going to get pregnant by you and you'll have to pay for her and her bastards the rest of their lives," Amlani raged. "Do you know if she is using birth control, do you know that much?"

Joshi looked bewildered. "It—It doesn't matter. . . ."

"You stupid, stupid—" Amlani's rage suddenly took over. He pushed himself out of his chair and rushed at his son, striking him repeatedly across the face with his open hand.

Joshi reeled backward, stunned by the fury of his father's attack. Arvind's smirk disappeared. He leaped up from the sofa, put himself between his father and his brother and begged his father to stop. Amlani stopped as suddenly as he had begun and walked to the far side of the room.

"Get him out," he panted. "Get him out before I kill him."

Dazed, Joshi allowed his brother to hustle him out of the study and across the empty living room to the elevators.

"I think you should stay out of his way for a while," Arvind said needlessly as he punched the elevator button and turned to go. Then, when he had gone a few paces, he stopped and looked back.

"You always do this, don't you?" he said. "You always find the one thing that is certain to spoil everything."

Joshi seemed not to hear him. The elevator arrived and he stepped inside without uttering a word, and then the doors closed behind him.

■   ■

Amlani cursed as the tiny nitroglycerine pill dropped from his shaking fingers into the sink and dissolved. He shook another from the bottle and stuck it under his tongue where it dissolved instantly.

"Are you all right?" Arvind asked from the doorway.

"He doesn't know what he's doing," Amlani muttered to his reflection in the mirror. "He can't be so stupid. . . ."

"I think you should sit down," Arvind said. He took his father by the arm, led him back out to the study and sat him down on a sofa.

"He would destroy this family," Amlani went on. "He would destroy this family and he doesn't even know it."

"Do you want me to call Ghawali?"

Ghawali was the company doctor, the same doctor who had saved Amlani's life after his stroke.

Amlani didn't answer. He leaned his head back against a mahogany wall panel, felt its coolness against his scalp and closed his eyes.

"I'm going to call Ghawali," Arvind said.

"No," Amlani said, his eyes still closed.

Arvind hesitated. His father was afraid that if word got out about another health crisis, the company's stock would plummet.

"Are you sure?"

Amlani opened his eyes and looked balefully at Arvind. It wasn't only his youngest son who tried his patience.

"All I want is to step down from the chairman's job and know Renown Industries is in good hands," he said. "So your mother and I can enjoy our *Vanaprastha* together. I thought we had earned that much. But all you and your brother do is cause chaos. Everywhere I look I see disaster. Neither one of you is ready to run the company yet. One has the mind of a child and the other tells me lies to make me feel better—I don't know which of you is worse."

Arvind looked wounded. The only reason Varanasi had gone wrong was because he had been so busy in Surat, getting the refinery up and running on his father's orders.

"I didn't want to worry you—"

"Then you tell me everything," Amlani said, stopping him.

Arvind looked away to hide his own anger.

"If we move quickly we might be able to prevent this from deteriorating into complete disaster," Amlani said. "I need to speak to Ushar. Tell him to come up here."

Arvind hesitated then went to his father's desk and picked up the house phone. Ushar was the family's chief of security, Amlani's conduit to the underworld; the world of informers, thugs, and killers for hire. Ushar was the man to whom Amlani turned when the subtler persuasions of money and favors weren't enough. He answered so promptly Arvind thought he must have been waiting by the phone.

Arvind delivered his message and had scarcely put down the phone when his father resumed his tirade.

"The two men who should never have met are talking to each other at this very moment," he went on. "Together they have the power to destroy this company."

"I can take care of it," Arvind said.

"What would you do?"

"I can stop Agawarl from talking."

"It's too late for that," Amlani said derisively. "Sansi has had him for three days now. We can assume Agawarl told him everything to save his own neck. What we have to do is find a way to discourage Sansi from using it to harm the company—or there will be no company to leave you."

There was the distant grunt of the elevator, then approaching footsteps. Arvind opened the door and beckoned Ushar inside.

The man in charge of all Amlani's security needs was physically unimposing and had a policeman's taste in clothes. He wore a pale green suit in shiny Vinod brand polyester with a mud-colored shirt and a diagonally striped tie with a synthetic gloss, all of which combined to give him a reptilian sheen. His features were bland, his ears prominent, and his densely matted hair cropped so short it moved back and forth on his scalp like carpet pile.

"*Namaste* Amlani, sahib." Ushar pressed the palms of his hands together and bobbed respectfully to his employer.

Amlani waved him to a chair. "You would like some chai, Ushar?"

"Sahib, you are most kind."

Amlani looked at his son, and Arvind frowned but picked up the phone again.

Ushar had grown up in the chawls, barracks-like apartment blocks built after the war to accommodate factory workers in the northern suburbs, where he had developed a taste for *araq*. Sometimes he shared a bottle of the locally distilled palm liquor with Arvind, who occasionally liked to hang out with the toughs on the security staff. But when Ushar was with the old man he drank chai and was careful to mind his manners.

"Ushar, I need your advice on a matter that is of grave concern to me," Amlani said, making it sound as if Ushar were a partner in the decision.

"*Acha*, sahib, I am always at your service." Ushar settled himself on one of two plumply cushioned, milky leather sofas Amlani had imported from Milan.

"You are aware of the government inquiry into the accident in Varanasi last year?"

"I have been observing it with great interest, sahib."

"You know the man in charge of the investigation, George

Sansi? He was at Crime Branch here in Bombay before he became a lawyer?"

"Of course, sahib."

"For reasons I do not entirely understand, Mr. Sansi has decided to concentrate his investigation on our factory in Varanasi," Amlani went on. "He has taken the manager there, Mr. Agawarl, in for questioning. In Mr. Sansi's opinion there has been some contributing negligence by Mr. Agawarl. It may be true—or it may be politically inspired. Do you understand?"

"The Bharatiya Janata Party is controlled by madmen, sahib."

"My son . . ." Amlani glanced at Arvind. ". . . assured me the situation in Varanasi was completely under control and that this man, Agawarl, would not make trouble for us. My son's confidence in his own judgment appears to have been misplaced."

Ushar's scalp twitched in empathy.

"Negotiations with the Americans are at a delicate stage," Amlani continued. "Three senior executives from the Dumont Corporation have arrived in Bombay to attend the commissioning of the refinery in Surat. The future of the company depends on the negotiations that will follow the commissioning ceremony. I cannot allow them to be jeopardized by the incompetence of a reckless plant manager and the politically motivated actions of an overzealous investigator."

"I understand, sahib."

It had occurred to Ushar early in his career in the police service of Maharashtra that a man who combined a willingness to wear suits and speak softly with a readiness to commit violence could become a valuable asset to the country's rich and powerful—and by extension become rich and powerful himself. The resurgence of terrorism and an increase in kidnappings of important people had led Ushar to leave the police service and start his own security business. He had come to Amlani's attention first as a security adviser and supplier of bodyguards, but it was his inventiveness as a problem solver and his preparedness to apply force when necessary that had made him Amlani's permanent security chief.

"It would be unfortunate if this man Agawarl were to appear before such a politically motivated inquiry while negotiations with the Americans were in progress," Amlani said. "I have to go to New Delhi this week on business. While I am there I will meet with Mr. Sansi and I will try to impress upon him the reasonableness of my concerns." He paused and then added: "I want you to come with me, Ushar. Mr. Sansi may be willing to listen to reason or he may not. But in all prudence I think we must deny Mr. Sansi and his commission further access to Mr. Agawarl's services as a witness. Do you understand me?"

There was a discreet tap at the study door and conversation ceased while Arvind let in the *bai* with the tea. She set down an engraved silver tray with cups of fine china, an antique silver teapot, and other silver pots containing sugar, hot milk, and extra hot water. There was also a small plate of pastries. While she served them their tea they discussed the lackluster performance of the Indian cricket team in the latest test series against Pakistan. When she had gone they returned to the business at hand.

"Did you have any particular arrangement in mind, sahib?"

"Remorse," Amlani answered. "Mr. Agawarl has brought disgrace on himself and the company. An act of conspicuous remorse is appropriate."

"*Acha*, sahib, I will make the arrangements."

Ushar picked up his cup and tried to drink without making too much noise. But Amlani wasn't finished.

"There is another matter we must discuss, Ushar. A personal matter but a matter with the potential to harm the entire family."

Ushar put down his cup.

"Joshi has become infatuated with a woman, Anita Vasi, the actress." He grimaced as if this disclosure gave him great pain. "He says he wants to marry her."

Ushar knew Joshi had been sleeping with Anita Vasi—all the
Amlani men used models and starlets for pleasure—but he
didn't know it had turned serious.

"I do not consider her a fit person to enter this family,"
Amlani said. "It is a match I could never approve."

Ushar remained expressionless. It wouldn't be the first time
he had been asked to get rid of a troublesome woman.

"It cannot be allowed to continue," Amlani said. "This
woman is a prostitute. But my son has been blinded by her
houri tricks and he has opened himself, he has opened all of
us, to her blackmail. She must not see my son again. She has to
disappear."

Ushar hesitated. Getting rid of Anita Vasi wasn't the
problem—it was what would happen afterward. He knew Vasi
was one of Jenta's girls, and assumed Amlani knew too. She was
a rising star, a valuable asset, and Jenta would be furious at her
loss. If he discovered who was behind it, he could exact payment
in blood. That would mean war against the Amlanis, the kind of
war the Amlanis weren't equipped to fight and couldn't possibly
win. Ushar would find himself in the front lines.

"Forgive my impertinence, sahib," Ushar said. "I mention
this only because of my concern for you and for the safety of the
family. This woman, Anita Vasi, is very important to the gangster, Johnny Jenta. I think he would be most unhappy if harm
were to come to her. And your most precious daughter, Rashmi,
relies on his goodwill for her own future in the movies, does she
not? Perhaps if someone were to speak to Anita Vasi, to discourage her, or to Jenta himself . . ."

But Amlani was in no mood to tolerate further argument
from anyone, and his temper deteriorated with every word
Ushar spoke.

"For all we know Jenta put her up to it," he snapped. "If
either of them is forewarned it will make matters worse, not
better." He paused, trying to curb his anger. "If you do it properly, Jenta will never know who is behind it. And don't concern

yourself with Rashmi. It is time she gave up her ridiculous notion of a career in the movies. Working with all those whores is not a fit occupation for an Amlani woman."

Ushar looked to Arvind for support, to help him reason with the old man, but Arvind said nothing and there was nothing in his expression to indicate his true feelings.

"Sahib, she is well-known," Ushar tried again. "Her disappearance will attract attention. It will have to be planned most carefully so there is no possibility—"

"It must be done now," Amlani interrupted. "Before she tells the whole world she is going to marry an Amlani. Before Joshi tells her what happened today and she goes running to Jenta for protection."

Ushar realized it was pointless to argue further. Amlani's family was sacred, his vision of their future was sacred. The idea that his precious seed might be contaminated by a casteless whore was intolerable. He would not be swayed—no matter that his actions might expose all of them to a far greater danger.

"It should happen soon, Ushar, while I am in New Delhi," Amlani added emphatically.

Ushar gave a resigned shrug.

"I will see to it before we leave, sahib."

CHAPTER 21

From the moment he stepped inside Madhuri Amlani's New Delhi house, Sansi was struck by its hollow grandeur.

A two-story palace built of white marble veined with gray, it sprawled half a block behind a spear-tipped iron railing along the eastern fringes of Lodi Colony; a reminder to the retired Prime Ministers, serving cabinet ministers, high-ranking *babus*, and old-money Brahmins on the other side of the road where the real wealth and power in India resided.

Sansi thought the house had the antiseptic feel of a hotel built for guests who never came. The high vaulted lobby was filled with bright sunlight but lacked warmth. Voices and footsteps echoed. The broad-leafed palms that flanked the front door looked oddly impermanent, as if they might be removed when the visitor had left.

"Please, come with me, sahib."

A servant in white kurta pajamas with matching turban and pugaree and a red-and-gold-striped sash at his waist—the corporate colors of Renown Industries—invited Sansi to follow him up a wide and richly carpeted staircase. On the second floor the

staircase flared outward into an immense space of interconnected pillared rooms, like a Moghul's palace designed to dazzle
and overwhelm. Sansi followed the servant along a carpeted
path that muffled their lonely footfalls. Each room they passed
through was sparsely furnished with exquisite pieces of antique
furniture and lavish tapestries that depicted scenes from the
Mahabrahta.

Sansi came at last to a room intended for human occupancy
but which in the midst of so much empty space looked like a
movie set. Four overstuffed sofas covered in silk brocade were
arranged around a silver-trimmed teak table in the middle of
which stood a massive silver bowl piled high with an array of
luscious fruits. The room was scented by bowls of fresh flowers
set on pillars against the walls. Gauzy white curtains flirted with
a breeze that wafted in from a broad, empty terrace. A number
of servants in the same red-and-white uniforms stood stiffly
against the walls. Amlani was seated on a sofa, dressed casually
in open-neck shirt and trousers. He wore bifocals on a silver
chain and appeared to be reading papers from a briefcase open
on the cushion beside him.

"Sahib, I beg to present Mr. Sansi," the servant said. He
bowed and retreated to his station against the wall.

Amlani got to his feet and came forward to greet Sansi.

"I am so delighted you accepted my invitation, Mr. Sansi,"
he said, smiling pleasantly. "It has been my experience that men
of conscience can always find a way to resolve their difficulties
when they meet in good faith."

Sansi knew what Amlani looked like from photographs, but
he had never seen India's most infamous industrialist in the
flesh. His first impression was that there was something freakish
about Amlani, that his bulbous-browed head was too large for
his body. But there was an energy about him that was absent
from his pictures, a dynamism that was both engaging and
commanding.

Sansi recognized it for what it was; the radiance of power.

Amlani used power the way a shark used the water. It was his element, the essence of his existence, the medium that gave him his momentum. He had spent his whole life amassing it, and there was no such thing as too much.

Sansi shook hands reluctantly. Amlani's hand was warm and moist. Sansi resisted the impulse to wipe his hand against his pant leg.

"I am reassured to learn that you have a conscience, Mr. Amlani," he said. "It will make my work so much easier."

Amlani smiled. He'd heard Sansi liked to spar. He invited his guest to choose a seat, and Sansi took the sofa that faced the terrace. Amlani sat down beside his briefcase and signaled a servant.

"May I offer you a drink, Mr. Sansi? I understand you like scotch whiskey."

"Only when I am relaxing," Sansi said. "I will have a glass of mineral water."

"You have a preference?"

"Perrier, if you have it."

"Ice and lime?"

Sansi gave a slight waggle of his head.

Amlani ordered iced tea for himself and the servant glided to a massive sideboard whose doors opened to reveal a fully stocked liquor cabinet, refrigerator compartments, and ice chest.

"I trust you have not been too hard on our Mr. Agawarl," Amlani added amiably.

"No more than necessary," Sansi said.

"I assume he has been cooperative?"

"He has been most forthcoming."

"And of course, I am to blame for everything."

"Your son, Arvind, actually," Sansi said. "Though it will be difficult to distance yourself from your son entirely. Would you care to acknowledge responsibility on his behalf now?"

Amlani's smile became a trifle strained. "So you believe what Mr. Agawarl tells you?"

"It is not important what I believe."

"But he will make a good witness for the commission?"

"I think so."

The servant returned with the drinks, in tall glasses clasped in elegant silver holders.

"Mr. Sansi, I would like to know what you believe," Amlani said.

"I believe your factory caused the spill at Varanasi. I believe Mr. Agawarl when he says he did it on your son's orders. I believe you should pay."

"Me, my son, or my companies?"

"All of you."

"Even if I had no advance knowledge?"

Sansi paused. There was no hard evidence Amlani knew ahead of time what his son had ordered in Varanasi.

"You don't have to convince me, Mr. Amlani. You have to convince the commission."

"But your recommendation determines who appears before the commission?"

Sansi smiled faintly. "I think you should have the opportunity to state your case directly to the commission," he said.

Amlani was silent for a moment, then roused himself and got back to his feet.

"Please, come with me for a moment, would you, Mr. Sansi. There is something I would like to show you."

Sansi did not have to go far. With his drink in hand he followed Amlani between the gauze curtains out onto the bare terrace that overlooked Lodi Road and the tree-shaded streets of Lodi Colony beyond. Amlani stood against the marble balustrade and pointed to an intersection a hundred yards away where a corner of the twelve-story Rajput Hotel was visible.

"You see the footpath down from the hotel?" Amlani asked.

The footpath that followed Lodi Road away from the hotel was bordered by a wilting chain-link fence. Against the fence were rigged a number of shelters made of palm thatch and plastic sheeting. The shelters were occupied by poor people from the country who came to Delhi to find work, to beg, and to hustle the well-heeled.

"There is a man down there," Amlani said. "In the shelter with the blue plastic roof. He's always there, watch what he does."

Sansi found the shelter but there was no one visible in the pool of shade underneath. It was late afternoon and still hot, and most of the beggars were keeping out of the sun.

"It is unfortunate that Agawarl turned out to be such a weak-minded man," Amlani said, returning to their conversation. "He might not have been so easily influenced by my son's poor judgment."

"Your son's poor judgment cost the lives of eleven hundred people," Sansi said.

"*Acha*," Amlani acknowledged. "You are right. We should pay—and we will pay."

Sansi was unable to conceal his surprise.

"Look!" Amlani pointed down the street. "You see that man, the bald man in the white shirt. Watch what happens."

Sansi saw a middle-aged man walking down Lodi Road from the hotel. He was dressed casually, a tourist rather than a businessman. His walk was leisurely though he kept close to the curb to avoid the beggars in the shelters with their out-thrust arms.

He had only walked a few yards past the shelter with the blue plastic sheet when a monkey-like figure darted out behind him, a scrawny, barefoot little man who wore a ragged T-shirt and shorts and carried a wooden box in one hand. He capered stubbornly alongside the tourist jabbering and pointing at the tourist's feet. The distance and the noise of the traffic made it impossible to hear what the man was saying but the tourist stopped, looked at his feet, and stiffened. His whole posture changed and he leaned threateningly toward the monkey man. The monkey man shook his head vigorously and there followed an antic debate lasting several minutes. Then, with obvious reluctance, the tourist followed the man to the inside of the foot-path. The monkey man put down his box, the tourist surrendered his right foot, and the man went to work scraping, cleaning, and polishing the offered shoe.

"You know what he's doing?" Amlani asked.

"Shit flicker," Sansi answered. "They're all over Delhi."

"*Acha.*" Amlani's smile returned. "Nothing goes to waste in India."

It was a street hustle common to Delhi. When business was slow, anyone with a shoeshine box could give it a boost by waiting in ambush for an unsuspecting tourist. As the tourist passed, the shoeshine man would fling a piece of excrement onto the victim's shoe then rush after him and offer to clean it off. Even those who knew it was a scam usually decided they'd rather part with a few rupees than clean it off themselves.

"The perfect industry, is it not?" Amlani said. "Low overhead, a captive market, and an inexhaustible supply of raw material."

"And no middle man," Sansi said.

"Unless he has a dog."

"I am sure he takes care of his dog."

Amlani chuckled and Sansi found himself smiling. But shared humor came perilously close to finding common ground, and Sansi had to remind himself where he was.

"You know, Mr. Sansi, I made my first fortune selling boat-loads of shit to the Arabs—and they were grateful."

Sansi had heard the story, it was part of the Amlani legend, though until now he had not been sure whether to believe it.

"A little shit goes a long way," Amlani said amiably. "You can buy it, sell it—or you can make people pay you to take it away."

He turned and leaned against the balustrade.

"I understand why the public needs to punish somebody for

what happened at Varanasi," he went on. "Somebody has to go
to jail. Somebody has to be the focus of all that anger. It is
unfortunate that Mr. Agawarl would allow the pressures of
executive responsibility to affect him in such a way that he
would act so recklessly. But I don't believe anybody held a gun
to his head."

Sansi listened impassively, remembering the death threats
Agawarl said had been made against him and his family.
Certainly Agawarl appeared to believe they were real.

"I don't see what the government hopes to gain by destroying me, by destroying everything I have built," Amlani continued, his voice and manner so reasonable as to question the
very notion of contradiction. "I have created more than two million jobs in India. In the next ten years I will create millions
more. What good will be achieved if all of that is swept away in a
spasm of mob vindictiveness? How will it relieve the suffering of
the victims of Varanasi to create more suffering?"

Sansi put down his half-finished drink on the marble
balustrade.

"Mr. Amlani, you would not be where you are today if you
were not persuasive," he said. "But you miss the point."

Amlani looked questioningly at him.

"Varanasi was terrible," Sansi said. "What is especially terrible about it is that it is only a small part of what is wrong in
India. And Agawarl is only one man. The commission is the
beginning of a much broader process intended to make sure
nothing like Varanasi happens again."

"I thought you were concerned with what is right, Mr. Sansi.
Not with the process of political vendetta."

"There has to be a fundamental change in attitude among
those who control industry in this country," Sansi said. "Eleven
hundred dead should not be just another calculation in the cost
of doing business. If it is, then the cost of business is going up."

Amlani's eyes met Sansi's directly. "I agree with you, Mr.

Sansi. I believe the company has a moral duty to compensate the victims according to its liability. I am prepared to make reparations I think you will find more than generous."

Sansi listened warily.

"I want to set up a trust for the victims of Varanasi," Amlani said. "A foundation that will not only provide immediate comfort to the victims, but a lasting benefit to everyone who has a stake in the industrial progress of the country. I want to build a hospital in Varanasi that will provide the victims with free care for as long as they need it. I also want to build a medical school, a teaching hospital, and a research center to specialize in the treatment and rehabilitation of the victims of industrial accidents. We will provide immediate financial compensation for the families of those who were killed or injured at Varanasi— without any inducement or assistance from the government, which, I think you know, Mr. Sansi, would only slow the compensation process down." He paused then added: "We will also provide scholarships for those in the victims' families who want to pursue careers in medicine. Mr. Sansi, it is my desire to give Varanasi the most advanced medical facility in the country for the treatment of industrial injuries."

Sansi smiled. "It is most impressive. I hope you follow through with it."

"But you see it as an attempt to buy off the government?"

"I see it as an attempt to circumvent the judicial process."

"The commission is hardly neutral in its objectives, Mr. Sansi. Rupe Seshan has harassed my family's business interests for years. Now the Bharatiya Janata Party has given her the tools of government to continue."

Sansi wondered if Amlani was being disingenuous or if he really didn't understand the idea of executive accountability.

"If you hire a man to burn down your neighbor's house and his children die, you think you should be pardoned because you offer first aid?"

"More than first aid, Mr. Sansi. The Renown Foundation will be a national asset."

"And a considerable asset to Renown Industries."

Amlani smiled indulgently. "You know, Mr. Sansi, I understand your skepticism. And I anticipate considerable public skepticism also—until people see how serious we are. That is why I must appoint the right person to administer the Renown Foundation. Someone whose abilities are ideally suited to the position and whose scruples are above reproach. Don't you think it would be better for everyone if you were to do something constructive for the nation, to create a worthwhile legacy for the victims of Varanasi instead of allowing a discredited government to use your talents to settle a few old political scores?"

"Would I be expected to resign from the investigation immediately or would the position be held open?"

"Of course you should finish the investigation," Amlani said. "Only after we have buried the past can we build for the future."

"What sort of salary would we be looking at?"

"For an enterprise of this stature?" Amlani said. "What do you feel would be appropriate?"

Sansi gave it a moment's thought. "My price has gone up from a roll of carpet and a case of brandy."

Amlani frowned, realizing Sansi was toying with him. "There is a great deal to be considered here, Mr. Sansi. The implications of your decision will be considerable. You should take a few days to think it over—but not too long."

Sansi leaned away from the balustrade. "I will see you at the commission, Mr. Amlani," he said, and started back across the terrace.

Amlani followed with a sigh. "I will not accept a decision now, Mr. Sansi. I believe when you have had time to reflect, you will reconsider your position."

"Believe what you will," Sansi replied. "You have told me everything I needed to know."

He passed between the gauze curtains and continued across the big open room.

"Not exactly, Mr. Sansi."

Amlani's tone had changed dramatically. Sansi stopped, curious. He had seen the carrot, he may as well see the stick. Amlani went to his briefcase, extracted a large brown envelope from under a sheaf of papers and handed it to Sansi.

Sansi opened it and looked at the contents. Shock coursed through him. There were four eight-by-ten color prints, blowups evidently and slightly blurred. But there was no mistaking the people in the photographs or what they were doing. The first showed Sansi and Rupe leaning together in a moment of intimacy in the hallway of her home. The second showed them kissing. The third showed the kiss had advanced to a close and passionate embrace. The fourth picture showed Rupe leading Sansi by the hand to the stairs that led to her bedroom.

Sansi felt a sudden nausea sweep through him.

"My relationship with Rupe Seshan has no bearing on the investigation," he said.

Amlani looked sympathetic.

"There is no need for anyone but you and I to know of the existence of these photographs," he said. "I understand your commitment to Rupe Seshan. She is a beautiful woman, a long-time friend. More than that now, it would seem. You feel an obligation to her, a sense of duty. These are admirable qualities, but under the circumstances, misguided. You should not allow yourself to be manipulated by a personal involvement with someone so politically motivated. You must make your own decision, Mr. Sansi. You must do what is right for you—and for the country."

Anger mixed with revulsion flooded through Sansi, threatening to overwhelm him.

"Show these pictures to whoever you want," he said. "They will embarrass me a little, and the minister perhaps a little more. But they will make no difference to the deliberations of the commission."

"I think they will," Amlani responded. "It is not illegal to sleep with your employer, but it is certainly, what is the word—reckless? Especially when you are the chief investigator in a government inquiry and she is the minister who hired you. I think it will raise one or two questions about personal bias, don't you?"

Sansi turned and forced himself to keep walking, the pictures clutched sweatily in his hand.

"Remember what I said, Mr. Sansi," Amlani called after him. "A little shit goes a long way."

■   ■

Anita Vasi waited for her cue.

It was a simple scene: a party at a restaurant where she was to meet the swaggering leading man for the first time and reject him with just a hint of promise. It was the kind of scene she had played in a dozen movies before, so predictable she no longer needed a script.

Everything was as it was supposed to be: all the actors were at their marks and the cameras were rolling. One by one the other actors went through their moves and delivered their lines. But when it came to her, she couldn't speak. She was held fast by a terrible force that prevented her from moving or saying her lines. She felt a suffocating pressure bearing down on her and realized she could no longer breathe. She tried to scream but her mouth wouldn't open.

She saw herself as if from a distance, saw her eyes staring in terror, her arms thrashing, and people all around her watching but doing nothing to help. Then she heard a familiar, reassuring voice say: "It's all right, don't scream."

She opened her eyes and she was in her bedroom. A dark figure stood over her, his hands pressed over her face.

"Don't scream," the voice said again. "Everything's all right, just don't scream."

The hand lifted and she could breathe again.

"Joshi . . . ?" she said between frightened breaths. "What are you doing?"

He knelt down beside her and whispered urgently: "Get dressed. Don't turn on the light. You have to come with me now."

She looked at the bedside clock. It was past two-thirty in the morning. She pushed back the covers and sat up.

"What's going on, what's wrong?"

"Is your passport here?"

"My passport? Yes," she answered. "Why do I need my passport?"

"You're leaving Bombay, tonight."

She froze. "I can't, I can't leave Bombay. I'm working on a movie, I start another one in two weeks."

"You have to." He grabbed her shoulders and pulled her to her feet. "My father wants you dead. I have to get you out tonight."

"Your father?"

"He has sent somebody to kill you. It could happen tonight, tomorrow—"

"No . . . no . . ." She pushed her hair back from her face. "Take me to Johnny, he'll know what to do."

"Jenta can't stop this," Joshi said. "My father has gone mad, he won't listen to anybody."

"Johnny will kill him when he finds out," she said, anger mixing with fear. "Doesn't he know that?"

"Don't tell Jenta anything."

"He knows I've been seeing you."

Joshi looked increasingly desperate. "Let's just keep you alive," he said. "I'll talk to Jenta and my father later."

She pulled off her nightdress and put on a pair of jeans and a shirt. Then she went to a large and ornate dresser with dozens of different-sized drawers. She opened a drawer with a hidden panel, took out a wallet containing her passport and traveler's checks and put them in her purse. Then she rummaged through her jewelry drawers, picking out her favorite pieces and stuffing them into her purse. She opened her makeup drawer, picked up a heavily jeweled hairbrush and started to brush her hair.

"There's no time!" Joshi swatted the brush from her hand. "We have to leave now."

He pulled her out of the bedroom and across the apartment. Outside, the waters of Juhu Beach gleamed innocent silver in the moonlight.

"I can't leave everything," she pleaded. "I have to take some things. . . ."

Joshi ignored her. He dragged her down the back stairs and out into the alley where his green BMW waited. He pushed her into the passenger seat then climbed in beside her and accelerated away, heading south out of Juhu in the direction of Sahar.

Beside him Anita stared blankly at the passing streets lined with the forms of sleeping bodies lit by the occasional cooking fire.

"Where am I going?"

"I've got you on a flight to Kuala Lumpur," he said. "The plane leaves at four-fifteen. When you get there, go to the U.S. Embassy and get a visitor's visa for the United States. Go to New York, you can lose yourself there."

"New York?" she repeated. "I don't know anybody in New York."

"That's the point."

He flipped open the glove compartment, pulled out a bulging airline wallet and handed it to her.

"There's seventeen thousand American dollars in there," he said. "It's all I could get my hands on. I'll send you more later. When you get to New York, get an apartment. Use any name but your own. Contact a man called Wasserman at Premier Investors Group in Manhattan. He will help you. We knew each other at Harvard, he is a good friend and he can get a message to me without anybody knowing. Just let me know you're all right. We'll work things out from there."

"My God . . ." Her voice shook. "I can't believe we're doing this. I can't believe your father would do this to me."

"It wouldn't be the first time he's had somebody killed," Joshi said. He eased his foot off the gas pedal, afraid he might draw the attention of the police.

"Your family . . ." Her voice filled with contempt. "They're no better than gangsters."

"We are gangsters," he said. "It's all we've ever been."

They reached the airport a few minutes after three. Anita pulled her tangled mass of hair into a knot and put on a pair of sunglasses. Then she and Joshi plunged into the crowded departures terminal. Joshi led her to the MAS counter and waited nervously while she checked in.

The clerk seemed suspicious that Anita had no luggage, but then the woman next to her whispered something and the clerk smiled. Movie stars did things like this all the time.

"Thank you for flying MAS, Miss Vasi," the clerk said, and handed Anita her boarding pass. "Would you like someone to escort you to our first-class lounge?"

"No." Joshi snatched Anita away before anybody else recognized her and started to make a fuss. "Go through Customs now," he said to her. "Nobody can touch you once you're on the other side."

He dragged her, half running, through the busy terminal till they came to the entry gates to the Customs hall. Then Anita took off her sunglasses and wiped tears from her eyes.

"How long do you think it will be before I can come back?"

"I don't know." Joshi felt his own composure cracking. "Perhaps only a few months."

"Oh Joshi . . ." No longer able to hold back her emotions, she put her arms around his neck and clung to him, trembling.

Joshi held her briefly then pushed her away. "I'll find a way," he said. "Or I will see you in New York."

"You'll call me. Promise you'll call me?"

"You have to go now," Joshi said and pushed her toward the gate.

But she stopped and would go no farther. She stared pleadingly at him, and he was afraid she would break down completely.

"Go on . . ." he urged.

"Joshi, I have to tell you something," she said, and took a step back toward him. "I was going to tell you soon. . . ."

"No, there's no time—"

She shook her head, refusing to be silenced.

"I'm pregnant," she said. "You have to know before I go—I'm pregnant."

CHAPTER 22

Amlani took pains to make sure his American guests saw only what he wanted them to see.

He told the helicopter pilot to keep to the coast for the 150-mile flight northward to Surat. Instead of flying directly across the city as he usually did, he was to loop in from the north to avoid the worst of the slums before he put down at the refinery. But even with these precautions it was impossible to pretend Surat was anything but a nightmare.

The historic port city of the Moghuls had been obliterated by the crust of heavy industry. The first indication they were getting close was an excremental stain across a clear blue sky, a nicotine-colored stratus so long it followed the curvature of the earth. The city itself was obscured underneath, though its effluents could be seen in the estuaries that drained into the Gulf of Khambhat, turning the creeks and marshes pastel shades of yellow, orange, and mauve with brushstrokes of virulent green.

The pilot began his descent over a scorched plain where the skeletons of trees were all that remained of a once dense jungle. Gradually the city materialized through the murk: a malevolent archipelago of smelters, dyeworks, chemical plants, tanneries, fertilizer plants, and munitions factories whose smokestacks poured endless ribbons of filth into the infected sky.

The helicopter slid beneath the gloomy canopy, and the cabin was suffused by a sickly yellow light. The Americans appeared not to notice. Scudding beneath them like waves on a tainted ocean were the shanties of the workers who supplied the giant industries with muscle power, India's cheapest, most dependable source of energy. Among the shanties was an anonymous blur of upturned faces, the women, children, and infants who ate, slept, and played around the crayon-colored streams that wound through the alleyways like toxic lace.

"This where they had that outbreak of plague a few years back?" Bob Towne shouted into his helmet mike.

"When we're on the ground, just try not to screw any rats," Grayson responded.

The air in the cabin turned rank, the smell of unfettered industrial power.

"The smell of money, gentlemen," Grayson said, speaking for them all.

"No medical insurance, no overtime, no benefits, no worker compensation, and an average daily wage of five bucks," Bob Towne recited. "This place is paradise."

"We should bring some of our union people here around contract negotiation time," Ray Kemp said. "Show them how things are done in the real world."

"Globalization," Towne added. "Greatest innovation since the assembly line."

In his seat beside the pilot Amlani listened to the banter on his headset and relaxed. Some foreign visitors had weak stomachs and were upset by what they saw around India's industrial complexes. This time he needn't have worried.

"Please, gentlemen," he interjected. "If you look to the right you can see the plant now."

The Americans strained to distinguish one fuming profile

from another. The helicopter hacked through the last layers of
smog, and the steel minarets and cupolas of the refinery
appeared suddenly on their starboard side. Beyond them a row
of gas vents like flagstaffs trailed banners of flame.

"Our landing zone will be at the main gates to the left,"
Amlani added.

His guests shifted their attention to the entrance of the
refinery and a large open area in the midst of what looked like a
crowded fairground. As the helicopter maneuvered for landing,
the Americans saw tents, food stalls, a red-and-gold-striped
pavilion, and a bandstand with a brass band in red-and-gold
uniforms and high cockaded hats.

"Gentlemen, I welcome you to the Renown Petrochemical
Complex, Surat," Amlani announced grandly.

The helicopter bumped and settled, and the rotors had
scarcely stopped turning before it was swarmed by company
officials and security guards. Amlani and his guests climbed out
as liveried servants squeezed forward with enormous, tasseled
umbrellas to protect the VIPs in their tan linen suits from
drifting flakes of soot. In the background the band played a
barely recognizable version of "Hello Dolly."

Amlani led his guests toward the pavilion with the pomp of a
royal procession, smilingly acknowledging the cheers of a crowd
made up of Renown employees lured by the promise of free food
and entertainment. Under a blaze of flash cubes they ascended a
flight of red carpeted stairs to a platform occupied by every
important official in the state of Gujerat, a sizable contingent of
Renown Industries executives, and the rest of the American contingent, who had flown in earlier by charter aircraft. Amlani
walked the three Americans along the front row of officials,
introducing them in turn to the governor of Gujerat and his
wife, the chief minister, the deputy chief minister and most of
the state cabinet, the local Congress Party representative to the
Lok Sabha, the mayor of Surat, the president of the Chamber of
Commerce, and all their wives.

As they took their seats alongside the governor and the chief minister, Grayson made a point of introducing his two colleagues to Amlani's docile wife, Gauri, along with Arvind and his less docile wife, Meher, all of whom he knew from his previous visits. Unaccountably, there was no sign of Joshi, whom Grayson privately considered the smarter of Amlani's sons and woefully underrated by his own father. When he asked innocently about Joshi's absence, he was puzzled by Amlani's evasive response and by the way Gauri would not hold his gaze.

At last all took their seats and Renown's director of corporate relations, Prasad, went to the microphone to begin what the Americans knew was to be a long afternoon of speeches. Amlani was first with a welcoming address in which he acknowledged each and every VIP guest by name, praised them for the individual roles they had played in making Renown the company it was, and emphasized the roles they would continue to play in its future success. He was followed by the president of the Chamber of Commerce, the mayor of Surat, the state minister of development, the minister of industry, the minister of finance, the deputy minister, the chief minister, the federal assemblyman, and finally the governor. When it was over, the Americans were in no doubt that there would always be a warm welcome for American capital in Surat—nor was there any doubt about who wielded the real power in the state of Gujarat.

Grayson responded with a speech he had refined over several weeks, a speech he intended to be the keynote of the Dumont visit. He began with a measured but thorough denunciation of past evils, from the excesses of the Moghuls to the territorial expansions of the European powers to the cruel exploitations of the Raj. He paid tribute to the courage of the Indian people, to the uniqueness of Hindu culture, and to the genius of a civilization that had endured five thousand years. He compared India's Independence movement with the American Revolution, Mahatma Gandhi with George Washington, the Indian melting pot with the American melting pot, and Indian republicanism with American republicanism. He made brief mention of India's dismal experience with socialism and lauded the vision of the later statesmen who committed India to the ideals of free enterprise.

The commissioning of India's first privately owned refinery was an historic occasion, he said, an occasion at which all those fortunate to be present stood at the threshold of a bold new era of cooperation between India and the developed world. The Dumont Corporation was committed to India for the long term, he said, not as a colonizing foreign power, but as an equal partner in the economic development of the nation. The refinery at Surat was just a beginning. There were other, bigger projects ahead. The benefits would be immense—to investors, shareholders, workers, and government treasuries. The next logical step, he concluded, was the exploration of an expanded partnership between Dumont and Renown and the realization of all the glittering promise such a union would bring.

It was a speech intended to appeal to Amlani's ego, to flatter him, to enhance his reputation before the local audience and the national audience. It was a speech intended to appeal to Amlani's particular brand of corporate nationalism, the kind that said what was good for the company was good for the country—and to persuade the country that was indeed the case.

But it was more than that.

It was the public expression of a secret deal. Grayson had a hold over Renown, and he didn't intend to let Amlani forget it. Amlani owed Dumont $40 million in hard currency and had put up half of Renown Holdings as collateral. But he owed Grayson a lot more. He owed Grayson a debt of gratitude for saving the Renown empire when it was on the brink of surrender to Imilani Rao. These debts had now come due. On Dumont's terms. On Grayson's terms.

It was a speech that brought all on the platform to their feet.

Grayson lingered at the microphone enjoying the loud and prolonged applause that cascaded over him. He turned to acknowledge the loud whoops of the American contingent and caught a nod of approval from Ray Kemp. At that moment a broadly smiling Amlani walked over to Grayson, clasped his hands, and shook them vigorously. Then he hoisted both their arms in the air and turned toward the crowd as cameras flashed and the applause reached a new crescendo.

It was several minutes before the applause subsided and those on the platform resumed their seats. The large media contingent at the front of the platform continued to buzz with excitement. Grayson had confirmed what many suspected was true. Despite repeated denials, Amlani had a secret backer all along—the Dumont Corporation of America. And it was Dumont that would bankroll Amlani's expansion into oil.

"Taking a bit of a chance, aren't you?" Towne whispered as Grayson returned to his seat. "You could have pissed him off."

"Does he look pissed?" Grayson answered through tautly smiling lips.

Towne had to admit Amlani didn't look too unhappy that Grayson had come so close to stealing his thunder. It augured well for the negotiations that would take place in the days ahead—and Amlani would still have the pleasure of making the formal announcement once the ink on the contracts was dry.

Grayson basked in his success. The skeptics could say what they liked about declining American influence in the world, about the risks of venturing into volatile Asian markets and India in particular. Here was a country with a fifth of the world's population, on the brink of a boom unprecedented in its history. Grayson had seen it coming years ago when other American companies still thought of India as a nation of rickshaw pullers. He understood the pride that drove India, the anger that gave the country its determination to be taken seriously in the world. He saw the scale and the rapidity of India's advancements in technology, in computers, in space, in nuclear energy. He knew the gains that were to be made by any company bold enough and far-sighted enough to invest in India in a big way. He had seen it and he had done it. He had handed India on a plate to Dumont—and the price was peanuts.

The sound of Amlani's voice intruded on Grayson's thoughts. It was time for the governor to formally declare the plant operational and to unveil the bronze commemorative plaque that would be mounted on the front gates. Grayson got to his feet with the others and joined in the applause as the governor pulled the cord and the curtains fell away. At the same time the band launched into another showtune which, after some confusion, the Americans decided was: "There's No Business Like Show Business."

Then there was a swelling roar from the crowd and all heads on the platform turned as a magnificently caparisoned elephant lumbered into view. Mounted on its back was an ornately carved howdah whose canopy and skirts were fringed with gold and silver tassels. The elephant's head, ears, and trunk were painted with intricate patterns and symbols, its tusks blunted and capped with brass and its toenails painted gold. Its harness was garlanded with gold and white marigolds and studded with nuggets of colored glass that flashed with the reflected fires of the refinery. Astride the elephant's neck was a uniformed mahout who guided the beast with his knees and the occasional sting of a long cane. Behind him was another gorgeously ornamented elephant, then another and another, making up a procession of twelve in all.

Descended from war elephants bred to face cannon, lance, and musket fire, the great beasts seemed unperturbed by the noisy crowd or the flash and roar of industry all around. The lead elephant maintained a steady pace until it was abreast of the VIP pavilion and then stopped, the door of its howdah level with the platform. At the mahout's command, the elephant raised its trunk in salute and waited for its passengers to board, its eyelashes like giant combs flicking soot and dust from its placid brown eyes.

Amlani rode in the lead elephant with the governor, the chief minister, the deputy chief minister, and the assemblyman. Arvind and his wife rode in the second with the Americans. The other guests followed behind according to a pecking order set out in their printed programs.

Grayson was surprised by the plush interior of the howdah. The walls were padded, the plum velvet seats snug and comfortably upholstered. There were also brass handrails for nervous passengers and the added precaution of gold-painted rope netting which enclosed the howdah entirely.

"My father took over the stables of the Nawab of Cutch a few years ago," Arvind explained. "They cost a great deal to maintain but the Nawab can't afford it anymore and the government won't do it. My father believes it is important to preserve our traditions."

The mahout barked an order, the elephant lurched forward, and the Americans clutched at the handrails. Slowly, the elephant train wound its way around the crowded fairground and in through the refinery gates. The Americans found they adjusted quickly to the rhythmic sway of the howdah. There was something stately and soothing about the elephant's gait, and they were soon confident enough to relax their grips on the brass rails.

Arvind leaned forward and unfastened a metal clasp at the front of the howdah. A trapdoor swung down on a chain to reveal a row of neatly packed steel flasks and cups secured by metal clips.

"Brandy, gentlemen?" he offered. "I find it takes away the taste of Surat."

The Americans each accepted a small cup of brandy as they began their tour of the refinery. The route was easy to follow. To keep down the dust, a track had been laid out and covered with wet sawdust which the refinery's fire unit kept damped down from water trucks. In addition to the brilliant electric lighting that bathed the plant in perpetual daylight, the track was lined with brightly burning torches that acted as markers and provided an extra touch of theater.

The flames from the torches were mirrored and magnified in every gleaming surface, every shiny arch and plane. In the background black-tinged fireballs erupted from roaring gas vents in a syncopated vision of hell, filling the metal canyons with shards of reflected fire. The noise and fumes and heat were ghastly, but the elephants remained unperturbed. They plodded along the damp yellow carpet, oblivious to the inferno, a bizarre juxtaposition of the medieval and the modern, a detail in a surrealist tableau.

Towne leaned closer to Grayson so he could make himself heard.

"Tell you one thing," he said. "We're not in Kansas anymore."

The gloomy pall of night was falling when they returned to the pavilion. White-gloved servants waited with glasses of chilled champagne as the guests dismounted from each arriving elephant. Chairs had been moved back and tables set out with refreshments. The bandstand adjoining the pavilion was occupied by a children's choir which sang Gujerati folk songs as the VIPs drank and mingled. The choir was followed by dancers, acrobats, and jugglers, and then the band returned and played more unlikely showtunes.

After an hour it was time for most of the guests to begin leaving for the airport and the flight back to Bombay. Only Bob Towne would stay behind for two days to conduct a closer inspection of the plant with Arvind.

The Americans huddled together in a corner before they parted company, Kemp worried by something he had seen on the elephant tour.

"They're cracking," he said. "Amlani just confirmed it for me. They've got the cracking plant up."

"I know," Towne affirmed. "Arvind says they shipped in the first tanker load of crude last week."

"We didn't figure they'd be cracking this soon," Kemp said. He looked accusingly at Grayson. "You said it would take them at least another six months to a year."

"They moved a lot faster than I expected," Grayson admitted.

"What else didn't you expect?" Kemp asked.

"I'll check it out tomorrow," Towne said. "It could be they're exaggerating their progress to impress us. If they're not cracking in volume they're still working the bugs out."

Kemp didn't look reassured. "What about the son, what's his name—Joshi—where's he, what's he doing?"

"I asked," Grayson said. "Amlani didn't want to talk about it."

"Great," Kemp said. "What if he's talking to somebody else someplace?"

"I don't think that's it," Grayson said. "Something's going on, but it doesn't have to have anything to do with business. I asked the mother and she looked pretty unhappy. I think it's family business. There's no way Amlani would let Joshi handle discussions at that level. This whole thing is his baby. It's always been his baby."

"If they're cracking, they could be talking to somebody else," Kemp insisted. "They could be screwing us here."

"They're not screwing us," Grayson answered. "You saw the way Amlani reacted to my speech. I think it's a family matter. I think the whole thing is a coincidence but I'll find out."

"Good," Kemp said, unimpressed. "Because when I sit across the table from that son of a bitch two days from now I want to know everything that's going on here—everything."

"I'll find out," Grayson repeated firmly, as much to reassure himself as Kemp.

At a distance, hidden by the crowd, Amlani watched the Americans. He thought it was a day that would give them something to talk about. Grayson's speech had been something of a surprise, but even that would still work to his advantage. All things considered, Amlani had reason to feel pleased with himself. Everything was going exactly as he wanted.

■ ■

"I'm not sure which is worse," Rupe said. "When you reject me and run away or when you use me and run away."

"It is not a question of running away," Sansi said, irritated by her flippancy. "If I go, I will take the blame with me. Chow-dhary will take over the investigation and it will proceed without the taint of scandal. Damage to the inquiry will be minimal."

"You think so?"

"The evidence is good," Sansi answered. "It deserves to be considered on its merits. If I stay, Amlani's lawyers will claim I manipulated the investigation and pressured Agawarl to give false testimony because you wanted me to—because you and I are lovers."

The two of them sat in the untidy sprawl of Rupe's top floor office at the Environment Ministry. Her office door was closed. In the beginning she had left it open so her staff could come and go as they pleased, but not anymore. The atmosphere of open-ness and informality that had been her style had been replaced by suspicion and paranoia. Her phone lines were swept and monitored and her aides had to buzz her on the intercom when they wanted to see her. Hemali's desk had been moved outside, so there would no longer be anyone hovering in the background to eavesdrop.

"They will do that anyway," Rupe said. "And with you gone they will be free to focus their energies on me and Pilot, to try and pick us off one at a time. It isn't as if we didn't expect some-thing like this, George. We have to stand firm." She paused, then added with a small smile, "You aren't going to get out of it that easily."

If anything, Sansi was relieved. He felt duty bound to offer his resignation, but Rupe's response was the response he wanted. He knew that once the scandal broke, the only way he would salvage even a shred of his reputation was by finishing the investigation and making the evidence against Amlani stick.

"They will make us look like fools," Sansi said. "We have made ourselves look like fools."

"What happens between us personally is irrelevant," Rupe responded. "If the evidence is as good as you say, people will make their own judgment, regardless of any scandal Amlani can generate."

"Is that what Pilot said?"

For the first time she looked slightly abashed. "He thinks it is unfortunate," she admitted. "But he shares my opinion—it is a personal matter, and our approach will be no public comment on personal matters."

"What do you want to do about your staff?"

"I will let them all go," she said. "It's a pity, some of them have been with me a long time."

"Do you have any ideas?"

"About who it might be?" She paused. "Probably Hemali. She's been with me the shortest time and she's very mercenary. I think she would do it for the money."

"Don't get rid of anybody just yet," Sansi said.

Rupe looked doubtful. "You want me to go on living with a spy in my house?"

"If you let them all go, you will never know who it was. Most of your staff is loyal—keep them. If you hire new people, Amlani has a better chance of finding somebody among them to betray you all over again."

"I don't know." She paused. "I can't pretend everything is all right when somebody in my house is informing on me."

"Don't," Sansi said. "Whoever gave Amlani those pictures knows now that we know. Getting rid of everybody is just the reaction they expect. Keep everybody and it puts the pressure back on them."

"Try and make them crack, you mean?"

"We could help them along," Sansi said. "Somebody might give himself—or herself—away."

"How?"

"We will start with a search. Go through everybody's belongings. I doubt we'll find anything, but it will make everybody nervous, make them suspicious of each other."

"The atmosphere is bad enough already," she said. "That will make it unbearable."

"That is the idea," Sansi said. "We will check their movements over the past few weeks. Bring them in to be interviewed, one at a time. Somebody might remember something—and our spy is going to want out before anyone does."

"I don't want the children around for that," Rupe decided. "I'll send them back to Bombay, they can spend a few weeks with my parents."

Sansi sighed. He could deal with the professional consequences of his indiscretion with Rupe, but he wasn't so sure about the personal consequences. And it had to start sometime.

"You are going to have to tell them why," he said.

"I have already told them," she said.

He looked surprised. "How did they react?"

"They're fine," she said. "They like you."

Sansi felt a growing dismay. She didn't seem to realize yet that what had happened between them would only happen once.

Before he could respond she said: "You haven't told Annie yet, have you?"

"Not yet."

"You should tell her soon."

"I will," he said, knowing he had already waited too long.

"I'm sorry," she said.

"So am I," he answered.

"How do you think she will take it?"

"I have absolutely no idea."

Rupe smiled faintly. "I think she will forgive you. The question is—do you think there is anything to forgive?"

Sansi glanced out the windows at the rooftops of Delhi, which radiated outward like fields of checkered rubble. After half a mile they started to dissolve into the encircling brown haze, like a tapestry unraveling.

"I am in love with Annie," he said. He looked back at Rupe and, partly out of nervousness, partly to remove all doubt, said it again. "I am in love with Annie."

He saw disappointment in Rupe's eyes. She dropped her gaze to the floor, but when she looked up again her eyes were clear, her emotions stowed safely until later.

"And to think, all those years I thought you were saving yourself for me," she said.

Awkwardly, Sansi searched for the words that might somehow make the moment more tolerable. "Rupe, it was my fault—" he began.

"Don't," she said, stopping him. She was smiling slightly and had raised her voice a fraction. "There are times when that noble streak of yours can be just a little bit irritating." She inclined her head slightly to one side. "I think we both knew what we were doing."

Sansi looked chastened. He had made his decision. He had chosen Annie over Rupe. There was no need to diminish what had happened between Rupe and him.

"Just do me one favor," she added. "And Annie and yourself."

He waited.

"Don't tell her it didn't mean anything."

CHAPTER 23

Her name was Zarine, she said.

Grayson didn't believe her.

She said she was twenty-seven years old and came from Bhandara in East Maharashtra. She had been in Bombay since she was nineteen, most of that time as a model with the Renown Agency, though she was in the second year of a business degree at the Bombay College of Higher Education. She was getting too old to model, she said; she had to look to the future. Arvind Amlani had promised her when she got her diploma he would find her an office job at Renown Industries.

Grayson thought the rest was probably true except for the bit about Arvind Amlani getting her a real job, though she seemed to believe it and Grayson saw no need to spoil her illusions.

It didn't really matter what he thought. What did matter was that she was pretty and she had offered to have sex with him—the prettiest woman to offer to have sex with him in the past twenty years. If he was honest with himself, the only woman to offer to have sex with him in the past twenty years, including his wife, and he had stopped asking her.

But tonight Madhuri Amlani had made him a gift of this lovely, eager-to-please young woman. And Grayson wanted desperately to accept. If he could only manage it without Kemp or Bob Towne knowing. Which would be difficult because both of them were seated next to him, albeit with equal temptations of their own.

There was little doubt that Towne would take advantage of the girl who had been offered to him, despite the wife and family he had at home. But Kemp was different. Kemp would go only so far. He would enjoy the girl's company, he would enjoy the evening—it would be one more corporate war story to tell when he got home—but he wouldn't take the bait. And unlike Grayson, it wasn't a question of image. Kemp was the only one of them free to act with a clear conscience because he was the only one who was single. It was because he liked to keep business and pleasure separate. As far as he was concerned, this evening of decadent pleasures arranged by Amlani was still business.

Grayson knew it too. It was he who had warned his colleagues what to expect. Evenings like this were designed to get under their guard—to disarm and distract, to seek out weaknesses that could be exploited later. If nothing else, the fine food and liquor, the exotic entertainments, the blandishments of beautiful women that extended late into the night, would wear them down before the hard bargaining began.

Amlani was like many successful Indian businessmen—he took pride in his mastery of western business practices. But he also liked to see how western businessmen adapted to eastern business practices. And western businessmen were often embarrassingly eager to assist in their own downfall.

In their arrogance, in the latent racism that gave them confidence in the superiority of western culture, they were rarely as well-prepared for Asia as they thought. Certainly not as well-prepared as Asians who came to the West to do business.

Centuries of colonization had given Indians, in particular, a

close familiarity with western ways, a comprehensive understanding of the caliber and peculiarities of the western mind.
But apart from scholars and eccentrics, western visitors rarely
brought the same degree of understanding to the Indian mind.

Educated Indians spoke several languages. Fluency in English, the international language of commerce, was axiomatic.
Many Indian businessmen conversed knowledgeably about
western politics, sports, and entertainment. The proficiency of
some Indians was such that they could mimic regional accents,
recite cockney rhyming slang to a Londoner or adopt a New
York accent with an American. But it was a rare western visitor who could speak a word of Hindi, who could converse
knowledgeably about the films of Satyajit Ray or the fortunes of
the Bharatiya Janata Party, who could name the captain of the
Indian cricket team—or tell a joke in upper-class Hindi about
the boorishness of Punjabis.

This one-way bridge across the cultural chasm made it easy
for someone like Amlani to maximize the advantage of home
ground. Western minds were often jarred by the foreignness of
India. The most worldly of visitors could be easily tripped and
kept off balance. It was easy to exaggerate their slights and mis-
demeanors, real or perceived, to embarrass them and incur their
indebtedness.

Even to the most sophisticated traveler, India offered temptations far beyond anything that could be had in the West. There
was no pleasure devised by the mind of man that could not be
easily procured by India. There was no vice that did not have its
own industry. There was no human appetite, however bizarre or
depraved, that could not be satisfied.

Grayson knew the dangers. Among the American contingent
he was the most familiar with India. He knew the Amlanis best.
He knew Madhuri Amlani would seek an advantage by any
means—and temptation was the easiest way to measure
an opponent's mettle. But he had kept the upper hand in the
relationship with Amlani. He had anticipated all Amlani's moves

and outmaneuvered him at every turn. And he had set up a deal
that would secure Dumont's future in India for years to come.
His job was done. It was up to Kemp now to do what he was
supposed to be good at, and Kemp had no right taking out his
nerves on him.

Towne's confirmation that the cracking plant was operational only confirmed further the advisability of Dumont part-
nering up with Renown—and the sooner the better. Kemp
would just have to roll with it. Maybe up the price another five
million. He was authorized to go up another ten. And it wasn't
like he wasn't getting paid enough to handle this kind of thing.

Grayson also knew that if he did take this beautiful girl back
to his room, everything he said would find its way back to
Amlani. But that was a two-way street. He could feed her any
line he wanted and that would get back to Amlani too—and it
might even do Kemp some good when the negotiations started
tomorrow.

"I was in America once," Zarine said.

"I'm sorry?" Grayson said.

"California," she continued. "I went to Disneyland. It was
beautiful, so clean."

"With Arvind?"

She lowered her eyes in a way Grayson found even more
arousing. He could get this girl to do anything, he realized.
Anything.

"I would like to live in America," she said. With a smile she
added: "Maybe you help me get a green card? Maybe I work for
you in America? Executive secretary . . . personal assistant?"

Grayson could see her in Philly. There were Indian commu-
nities in every city on the eastern seaboard now; restaurants,
shops, clothing stores, newspapers, radio stations, temples; doctors, lawyers, computer programmers, garage owners, cab drivers. A conspicuous component of the Asian archipelago that
had displaced the old Italian and East European neighborhoods.

He could picture her in an apartment somewhere. A world

apart from the women he knew: his arid wife, flinty career women, the crass hookers he bought from time to time, secretaries who examined every remark for sexual innuendo. She was thirty years younger than him. Just a girl. He loved even the sound of the word with its soft, fleshy undertones, its promise of generously given pleasures. He remembered a time when women had been glad to be called girls. There were no women like that in America anymore. Only fantasies. Or memories. Or they had to be imported. Like Zarine. She was perfect. Good for another ten, maybe fifteen years. A sound investment. His mistress. Exotic, pliant, dependent on him for everything.

She sat on the sofa beside him with her feet curled easily beneath her in a way that accentuated the curve of her hip. She wore an aqua-toned sari and a matching *thikka* on her forehead, but her hair was cut young, gamine. Like most Indian women, she wore plenty of jewelry but, he was pleased to see, no studs or rings in her nose. The sari, he knew, was on Amlani's orders. All the girls in the room wore saris. When she wasn't entertaining VIPs, he thought, she would dress young.

"What clothes do you prefer to wear?" he asked.

"I keep a lot of the clothes from work," she said. "The Vinod Women's Line, of course. Lavanya, Hunza. Shailja Hemdev is very popular. You know of her?"

Grayson shook his head.

"Expensive." Zarine giggled. "I like expensive."

Grayson felt slightly giddy. It wasn't the drink, he had been careful to have very little, but the almost adolescent intensity of his desire for her. Her scent, her softness, her nearness. He looked around the room searching for equilibrium and finding none.

At Amlani's request the men all wore black tie, though they reclined in the Indian manner on low, padded divans littered with bolsters and silk cushions. To Grayson there was something delicious about sprawling in a thousand dollar tuxedo across a piece of furniture that was essentially a large bed with a lovely young woman to keep him amused.

Amlani had hired the crystal ballroom at the Taj Mahal Hotel for the evening, though its stolid Edwardian grandeur had been subsumed by an effusion of silk wall hangings and tapestries that transformed it into a maharajah's court. The ceiling was hidden by billowing sails of scarlet and gold which fanned out from the great crystal chandeliers that gave the ballroom its name. Fluted support columns were encircled by trellises draped thickly with roses, marigolds, and orchids. Carved mahogany screens inlaid with glittering lapis lazuli surrounded the dance floor, creating a chamber within a chamber, adding to the atmosphere of opulent intimacy. Squads of security guards stood at every doorway to ensure privacy.

The divans had been arranged in a U shape on the dance floor, and in front of each divan was a lacquered bamboo table of matching height with an array of dishes containing chutneys, condiments, and curds to both complement the food and salve inflamed palates. The centerpiece of each table was a large brass dish filled with floating rose petals. The plates, serving dishes, and cutlery were antique silver and brass. Drinks were served in silver goblets of varying sizes spangled with semiprecious stones that blazed with the reflected brilliance of the chandeliers.

In the center of the U was an island of carpet ringed with bolsters, where a pair of musicians played ragas on tabla and sarod. Each corner of the carpet was anchored by an enormous bronze statue of a naked and bejeweled goddess whose polished curves and exaggerated breasts seemed intended solely to stir the male libido. Their bodies were warmed and enlivened by the flames of jasmine-scented candles veined into phalluses by beads of molten wax.

The musicians finished a piece with a flourish and there was a smattering of applause from the guests. Most of them were familiar by now, senior Renown executives, a few politicians

and assorted Congress Party bagmen. Dinner had straggled to
its epic conclusion a few minutes earlier, and waiters hurried to
clear away the remaining dishes while others brought decanters
of whiskey and brandy. There were also trays containing wads
of crushed betel nut, tobacco, and spices wrapped in moist
green leaves, which Zarine explained was *paan*, a digestive. The
Americans declined the *paan*, though Towne accepted a shot of
brandy. While the food had been magnificent and the wine had
come from France, the three of them had eaten and drunk selec-
tively, determined not to let hangovers or stomach upsets keep
them from the negotiating table the next day.

Grayson estimated there were around eighty guests, all of
them male, and an equal number of girls. Cultural ambassadors,
Amlani had said, their hostesses for the evening. Amlani himself
sat at the head of the U, with his brothers and his son Arvind
nearby. Apart from a brief welcoming address when he had
exorted his guests to relax and put aside all talk of business
for the evening, he had circulated very little, though he was in
the company of a very beautiful girl and seemed to be enjoying
himself.

"You get anything out of the old man?" a voice whispered.

Grayson eased himself around so he could face Kemp, who
was leaning close to him. He noticed how Kemp seemed uncomfortable on his divan and his pants kept riding up to reveal
bleached and hairless expanses of calf.

"It's a family problem," Grayson said. He hadn't been able to
pursue the matter at all with Amlani, but he had spoken to
Arvind briefly during drinks before dinner, and Zarine had filled
in some of the blanks with gossip she'd heard, though he didn't
attach too much importance to it. "I don't know the whole story
yet but it looks like Joshi got mixed up with some girl in the
movie business and the old man isn't happy about it."

"Why would that be a problem?" Kemp asked.

"You have to understand, the movie business here is run by
gangsters," Grayson said. "I don't mean crooks, like Hollywood,

I mean gangsters. Amlani doesn't want his family mixed up in it."

"I thought his daughter was in the movie business?"

"Yeah, kind of . . ." Grayson made a pained expression. "She's a kid, she's been playing at it. From what I understand, the old man was prepared to let it go for a while. This is different. Joshi got serious on him, and Amlani decided he had to put an end to it."

"So where is he now, the son?"

"He's here, in Bombay," Grayson answered. "But he's not doing anything connected with the business, not till the thing with the girl blows over."

"You believe that?"

Grayson began to get annoyed. "I know Joshi. He's not somebody who can easily be dissuaded when he gets his mind set on something. If he was serious about this girl, the old man had to treat it seriously. And he did. The girl got out of town, walked out on a movie she was making."

"No shit!"

"That's what—" Grayson glanced at Zarine and lowered his voice further. "That's what my lady friend here says. Apparently there was a piece in the papers about it. I'll try and dig it up. It doesn't say why she left, it just says she left. But that's how serious it is."

Kemp looked slightly more reassured. "So I'm not going to find out the son has been talking to Shell or Dow?"

"He's locked up in the fucking tower," Grayson said. "I told you, it's a family affair. That's why the old man doesn't want to talk about it."

Kemp was about to say something more but was stopped by an explosive pounding from the tabla player followed by the piercing notes of the sarod. Zarine tugged Grayson's sleeve and he leaned gladly back toward her.

"Watch," she said. "It is the dancer I told you about."

The Americans settled back as a tiny figure in red and gold

ran lightly out onto the dance floor and stopped in front of the musicians. She wore a gold-speckled choli with diaphanous red pants that reached upward into a sash that looped over her left shoulder. Over her pants she wore a filmy red skirt with open pleats and a heavily brocaded gold tongue that extended down between her legs to her knees. Her hair was oiled and pulled back from her face into a tight braid that was tucked into a gold belt at her waist. On the back of her head was a tiara with a gold and ruby pendant that extended forward and matched the bloodred *thikka* on her forehead. Around her neck was a long, four-stranded necklace of pearls divided into sections by gold clasps. Her earrings were enormous sculpted curlicues of pearlescent gold, there was a heavily ornamented ring in her right nostril, and a jeweled disk that dangled from her septum. Her arms and wrists were banded by red and gold amulets and she wore tiny cymbals on the fingers of both hands. Around her ankles were chain anklets of seven or eight tiers with dozens of tiny bells attached that tinkled with every step.

She struck a pose in the center of the floor, her arms arched in front of her, one hand cupped, three fingers of the other hand extended, the thumb curled over the folded forefinger. The heel of her right foot rested lightly against her left knee. Still as a statue, she waited for her cue.

The tabla player lightened his drumbeat and the sarod player took precedence, slowing his playing so that every note could be caressed, stretched, and manipulated into a keening echo. Slowly, gracefully, the dancer uncurled her hands and began to turn on one leg. She flexed her raised leg and turned her foot so the bells jingled melodically. At the same time she moved her head rhythmically from side to side and with a series of rapid, fluid movements her hands traced patterns in the air. Then she stopped in a new pose and froze again. Her audience applauded appreciatively.

"This kind of dance is called Bharatanatyam," Zarine whispered to Grayson. "You have seen pictures of statues on Hindu temples?"

He nodded.

"She is bringing them to life," Zarine said. "Every pose is another statue, another story. But the dancer gives her own interpretation to each story. That is what makes it interesting. Each dancer is different, each time she dances is different."

The dancer changed from one leg to another then back again, hopping, twisting, sculpting her limbs into impossible shapes and angles, describing a sensuous semaphore that held the men in her audience entranced. The poses continued for several minutes, shifting, changing, and stopping again, each new position bringing fresh applause.

Without any apparent signal between dancer and musicians the music changed and clattered into a boisterous raga. The dancer slipped out of her still life as if shedding a skin and ran across the floor with a series of short, skipping steps. Her hands fluttered, her finger cymbals chimed, and her steps were punctuated by a succession of loud, jangling stamps.

Several men in the audience clapped their hands and called out in recognition. Grayson glanced at Towne and Kemp, noting their polite, blank expressions, suspecting they mirrored his own. He couldn't recall an occasion when he had felt quite so much like a stranger in a strange land.

The music picked up tempo and the dancer's movements became increasingly expressive and energetic, her gestures broader, more dramatic, her stamping louder. She used the whole floor, running, swooping, skipping, her face contorting into exaggerated expressions of anger, surprise, and fear.

Grayson looked questioningly at Zarine.

"It is a kind of play," Zarine said. "She is playing the child, Krishna, stealing butter while his mother Yashodhara chases and scolds him."

"She's playing two roles?"

"*Acha*, the dancer plays all the parts." She smiled apologetically. "I think it helps to know the story."

The music became faster and faster. The hands of the tabla player blurred over his odd-sized drums like the wings of a hummingbird. The fingers of the sarod player seemed scarcely to touch the strings of his instrument but to draw the incredible flood of notes magically from its burnished bowl, while his other hand flew up and down the frets teasing an insistent, lingering resonance from the cascade of sound. The dancer's movements became increasingly fast and frenetic until they too were an intricate, dizzying blur. Then the music and the dancer stopped on precisely the same beat and there was a sudden startling silence. The dancer remained quite still, her face sheened with sweat, her chest rising and falling.

The silence lasted barely a second and then was swallowed by an eruption of applause and a chorus of approving cries. The dancer pressed her hands together and bobbed her head in acknowledgment.

Grayson looked at Zarine and saw she was quite solemn. Then she realized he was watching her and she turned to him with an instant smile.

"It was beautiful, was it not?" she said. "She is such a beautiful dancer."

"Yes, yes it was," Grayson said.

But something told him the rest of her sentence remained unsaid. " . . . if only you could appreciate it."

A few pieces of colored paper fluttered over the dance floor like drunken butterflies, and Grayson realized that some of the guests were throwing money. More guests joined in, littering the floor with big bills, trying to outdo each other with their generosity.

The applause swelled as Amlani got up from his sofa, walked over to the dancer, embraced her and pressed a large wad of notes into her hand. Then he went to each of the musicians to shake their hands and give each of them a tip too.

"Gives you a hard-on just watching it, doesn't it?"

Grayson looked up to see Towne, hands in pockets, grinning at him. A few feet away his girl gathered her things, getting ready to leave. Others too were getting up, an indication that the evening was over.

Kemp struggled awkwardly out of his divan, his hostess guiding him by the elbow. When they were on their feet, Kemp shook her hand formally and thanked her for a lovely evening. He seemed not to realize that his left trouser leg was concertinaed up his calf. Grayson looked at his watch. It was half past midnight. Time he left too.

Towne stepped in closer. "You keeping the babe for the night?"

Grayson flushed.

Towne looked at him with amused disbelief. "How many chances are you going to get like this?" he said. "Stop worrying what other people might think and do what you want."

Grayson only felt more uncomfortable. Behind him Zarine smoothed her sari and picked up her purse.

"You can't give a shit what Ray thinks?" Towne continued. "What are you scared of, that he'll tell your wife? Christ, he'd be doing you a favor."

"Thanks for your input, Bob." Grayson squeezed Towne's shoulder just hard enough to let him know he should drop it.

Towne stared at Grayson a moment longer then shrugged and turned away. "See you guys in the morning," he called back, and took his girl by the arm. "Sleep tight."

Kemp watched disapprovingly then turned his attention back to Grayson and waited. Grayson smiled at Zarine and with insincere grace he too thanked her for the evening, wished her luck in her future career and shook her hand. Together he and Kemp sought out Amlani, thanked him for a wonderful evening, then made a farewell circuit of the room on their way out.

"You'll feel better about it in the morning," Kemp said as they rode up in the elevator.

"I doubt it, Ray," Grayson said, staring straight ahead. "But as long as it keeps you happy."

Grayson closed the door to his room, leaned back and expelled a regretful sigh. He unfastened his bow tie and walked through his empty, silent suite to the bedroom. He hung up his jacket, took off his shoes and, safe from Kemp's disapproving eye, poured himself a large whiskey.

Not at all tired, he wandered out onto the balcony and sipped his drink, savoring its restorative burn as he gazed at the floodlit Gateway to India on the quayside. The streets were still noisy with traffic. Young toughs loitered in the shadows, hookers hustled the tourists, dope dealers pushed heroin and hashish. Even though it was late, gangs of young children still played along the waterfront—orphans of the city chasing each other, laughing as they jumped into the filthy floodlit water.

He heard a soft tapping sound from inside. He put down his glass and walked quickly to the door. Zarine waited outside. He looked up and down the corridor but no one was watching. Relieved, he let her in.

"Did anybody see you?"

"Nobody cares, except your boss," she said, amused apparently by the need for secrecy.

"He's not my boss," Grayson said edgily.

He led her into the sitting room and she dropped her purse onto an end table and sat down on the sofa next to it. Grayson retrieved his scotch from outside then stood self-consciously in the middle of the room.

"Can I get you a drink?" he offered.

"I'd like a smoke," she said and opened her purse.

Grayson didn't know she smoked. He didn't much care for it but said nothing as she opened a small silver cigarette case. Then she took out a thin, torpedo-shaped cigarette with tightly twisted ends and put it to her lips.

"Is that what I think it is?" he asked.

"Ganja," she said. "It helps me relax."

"Marijuana? Jesus Christ, you can't smoke that in here."

"It is nothing," she said. "We put it in our children's milk."

She produced a lighter, put its flame to the joint and took a series of rapid pulls to get it going. Pungent blue smoke gusted toward him, a smell he knew and didn't know. He'd graduated from college in the 1950s. Only beatniks and jazz musicians smoked marijuana then.

"Zarine, put it out," he said. He crossed to the balcony doors, closed them, thought better of it and opened them again. He looked pleadingly at her. "Please, Zarine, I don't care if it's a big deal here or not. It's a big deal to me. I can't get caught with drugs in my room."

She smiled indulgently at him, took a couple of extra pulls then pinched the end of the joint with her fingers and put it back in her cigarette case.

"Nobody will come," she said.

Grayson took a drink of scotch and wondered if it wasn't a mistake after all to have her in his room.

She saw the doubt in his eyes, saw him wavering. She got up from the sofa, walked over to him and kissed him on the lips. Her mouth was hot and dry and tasted of something alien and unknown. He wanted to touch her hair but resisted, then his hand went up anyway and he traced the curve of her cheek with his old, white fingers. He thought they looked like dead man's fingers against her darkly glistening skin, warmed from within by the radiance of youth.

"You're safe here," she said coaxingly. "Quite safe."

She kissed him again and played the tip of her tongue along the edges of his lips. Desire stirred in him, drowning the fear. He kissed her back, feeling awkwardness in the purse of his old man's lips. She was the first woman he had kissed with honest passion in twenty years. Desire flooded through him, enervating and irresistible. His fingers started to tremble, then his knees. He felt like a boy of fifteen confronting his first fuck.

Her eyes seemed to smile at him. She took his hand and held

it, stopping its trembling. Then she led him to the bedroom, a woman leading a boy. She sat him on the end of the bed, turned on the bedside radio and dimmed the lights. Then she stepped back from him and undressed herself, her eyes never leaving his. Her sari unfastened easily and slid from her body in a liquid rush. Underneath she wore only a bra and pants, pale brown, the color of eggshells. On a white woman they would have been flesh-colored. They made Zarine's skin look darker. Grayson didn't know why but he was surprised she wore western underwear.

She unhooked her brassiere and dropped it on top of her sari. Her body was slim-hipped and slender, which made her largish breasts seem larger still. Her nipples and aureola were a deep purplish color. Grayson felt a constriction in his throat. She was black. The thought hadn't occurred to him before now. He was going to fuck a black woman.

She pushed down her panties quickly, leaving her naked except for her jewelry. Until she was naked it was impossible to know that her necklace extended downward into a mesh of finely engraved silver disks that lay across the upper swells of her breasts. She wore several gold and silver bracelets on each wrist and on her left ankle was a silver anklet with charms that tinkled softly. Also invisible until now was her belt of fine gold mesh with dozens of beaded chains that trailed down over her hips and brushed the dark curls between her thighs.

She stepped toward him so that her breasts swayed temptingly only inches from his mouth. She stood there for a moment, saying and doing nothing, teasing him with the musky perfume of her body. Then she put her hands on his shoulders and pushed him back onto the bed. She followed, straddling him, her thighs forming dark inviting hollows to her crotch. She undressed him deftly, unfastening his shirt buttons and the waistband of his trousers, sliding his clothes off easily until he lay naked beneath her, ghostly and gray in the dim light.

"I . . . I don't know what to do."

"Let me do it," she said. "I am here to give you pleasure."

She started by running her fingers lightly over his body, tickling, teasing, pressing and pinching, sometimes hard enough to make him gasp.

"It awakens the senses," she said. "Increases the pleasure."

His penis lay half tumescent on his belly, the best he could do. It was never hard enough for him to enter a woman. Pleasure could only be delivered to him by mouth or by hand.

She kissed him on the lips again then lowered her hips and pressed her moist cleft against one thigh, then his cock, then the other thigh. Then she changed position again and lowered her head so she could kiss his neck, his chest, his nipples. She increased the firmness of her kisses and used her teeth to give him quick, fleeting bites that left welts on his skin. But he didn't complain. His body was coming alive.

She moved her head down to his crotch, her hair brushing his skin. He arched his back expectantly for the delicious envelopment of his penis in her mouth. Instead he felt something else. A teasing, fluttering sensation. A delicate tickling and scratching that excited and inflamed every nerve. Then he realized what it was. She was fluttering her eyelashes against him. In the instant of realization his cock pulsed and semen spilled out of him, puddling on his pallid belly.

"God . . ." He pulled the bedsheets over himself, embarrassed. "I'm sorry."

She sat upright and smiled at him. "No, it's good. Now you are relaxed. Next time will be better."

"Next time?"

"Wait here," she said.

She got up and disappeared into the living room. When she returned she had her purse. She opened it and took out a plastic baggie.

"That's not drugs—" he began.

"Be quiet," she admonished him gently. "This is India, not America."

She found a couple of brass ashtrays and set them on each side of the bed. Into each ashtray she shook a small mound of what looked like wood shavings and used her lighter to start them smoldering. Smoke wraiths coiled up to the ceiling and an exquisite, sweet perfume spread through the room unlike anything Grayson had ever smelled before.

"Sandalwood," she said. "It is beautiful, *nahi*? Good for funerals—and for sex."

She pulled the bedcovers away from him and threw them onto the floor. Grayson turned on his side and moved a leg to hide himself.

"Pleasure is for all the senses," she said. "I like to look too."

"You can't like looking at this old body," he said.

She lay down facing him and gently moved his leg so he was exposed to her again.

"How else can I see if I excite you?" she said.

"You excite me," Grayson said. "All night I was thinking how you would look, like this."

"And now we are here," she said. "We should make it last. The only way you know real pleasure is when you make it last."

Grayson smiled feebly. "That's a young man's prerogative, I'm afraid. I can't make love twice in one night anymore. I'm too old."

"Then tonight I will make you young," she said.

She leaned over to the radio and switched it from piped Muzak to something Indian. Then she reached into her purse and took out a couple of small makeup jars and put them on the nightstand. She also took out her cigarette case, and he was afraid she was about to light another joint. She didn't. She broke the joint open and sprinkled the contents onto the burning mounds of sandalwood.

The bittersweet perfume of marijuana merged with the sandalwood to create a new and intoxicating aroma. Grayson sniffed tentatively, afraid of what it might do to him.

"It won't drive you mad," she teased him. "It will relax you a little, that's all."

She opened the bedroom window and the night sounds of the city flowed in on the warm tropic air, another aromatic. She poured him another whiskey and a smaller one for herself. Grayson felt a gradual ease steal over him, a comfortableness with what he was doing, with his nakedness. His body no longer looked quite so ugly or felt quite so stiff and awkward. It was the way it was, he thought, neither good nor bad. The liquor was getting to him, he realized, robbing him of his inhibition. He was glad.

Zarine brought a couple of towels from the bathroom and asked him to move while she spread them on the bed.

"I'm going to give you a massage," she said. "A massage you will remember."

He went to lie down on the towels but she stopped him and made him wait by the bed. She looked around and saw a padded footstool. She brought it closer to the bed and told him to stand on it. He did as she asked, feeling a salacious thrill as he put his nakedness on display. She sat on the edge of the bed, opened one of her makeup jars and smeared her fingers with a viscous amber gel.

"Sandalwood ointment," she said. "Very nice, very sexy."

She started with his hands, smearing his fingers, playing lewdly with them one at a time, then working her way up his arms to his shoulders. She made him turn so she could work on his neck and back. Then she worked on his feet, legs, and buttocks. She asked him to turn again so she could coat his inner thighs, his flaccid, tired genitalia. The feel of her hands on him, the sight of her face so close to his crotch, the feel of her eyes on his cock excited him and he felt a responsive stirring.

"See." She smiled up at him. "Your lingam doesn't know how old you are."

When she was finished she made him get down and then she stood on the footstool.

"Now you do it to me."

Grayson smeared the ointment over her, savoring the

roundness of her young limbs, her firm buttocks and belly. He cupped each breast separately in his hands, aroused by their fullness, their heaviness. Her nipples, shiny and purple as egg-plant, became engorged. He ran his hands between her thighs again and again, feeling her heat, her pleasure, stretching out the dream as long as he could.

When he had finished she was as shiny as marble. She told him to lie on the bed facedown. He waited for her to straddle him again, to feel her fingers working at the muscles in his back and shoulders. But again she surprised him. She lay facedown on top of him, pressing the length and weight of her body against his. He felt her breasts on his back, the hard trace of her nipples, her belly, the firm push of her pudendum against his buttocks. She started to writhe and squirm on top of him, undu-lating her body so he could feel every tactile inch of her skin against his. He moaned, exulting in the ecstasy of the moment, fearing it would ever end.

She asked him to turn over, and when he did he saw his penis was hard, harder than it had been in years. She was right. It was a young man's cock. He waited eagerly for her to lie on top of him and repeat the process but instead she leaned back and opened the second jar. She put in her fingers and extracted a creamy white ointment. Then she began smoothing it thinly over his genitals. It felt cool and soothing on his swollen mem-ber, almost a relief.

"What is that?" he asked, scarcely caring anymore.

"Palang-tod," she said. "Cocaine paste."

He tensed. "You're putting cocaine on my dick?"

"I told you, pleasure should be made to last."

"What will it do?" he asked, fearful again.

"The sensation you are going to feel is so strong you will come very fast," she said. "Too fast for me to enjoy. This will make you last longer."

Grayson surrendered. She had already shown him more pleasure, more surprises, then he could recall in a meager lifetime of sexual experiences. He watched, catching his breath as she eased herself across his body. She took a moment to position herself then reached between his legs and guided him into her. Then she lowered herself smoothly, gently, until she held him completely inside her. He gave a gasp of excitement as he felt the hot, moist clench of her muscles on him—

She began moving on him, rocking rhythmically, back and forth, rising and falling, changing sometimes to a lewd circular sway. He closed his eyes and let the pleasure radiate outward from where their bodies were joined. She changed again and he opened his eyes and saw she was lifting herself into a new position, bringing her legs up while holding him inside her.

"What are you doing?" he breathed.

"You'll see."

He watched disbelievingly as she drew her legs up in front of her and crossed them into a lotus so she was balanced perfectly on top of him. She swayed slightly and used her fingertips against the bed to keep her balance. Then she began to turn.

Grayson heard himself groan as she turned herself slowly on him. The confluent sensations of pleasure were so intense as to be almost overwhelming. He understood now why he needed a drug to help him keep his erection. Slowly she continued her turn. Flexing, bracing, easing herself up and down on him, changing the sensation with every exquisite movement.

He found himself staring at her back, the primal elegance of her curves. He reached out so he could hold her breasts from behind. Then he ran his hands down her body, squeezing her hips, pressing her harder against him. She giggled softly then started to turn again. A little faster this time, the movements a little harder as she found her balance, her rhythm. Then she stared down at his astonished, sweating face.

"Where in the hell do you learn something like that?" Grayson panted.

"There are many different ways to take pleasure," she said. "This one is called the top."

She began to move on him again and he felt himself building to another climax. He closed his eyes and allowed himself to dissolve into the sensations that enveloped him. Immersed in his waking dream he heard her say something more.

"You have only begun to learn," she said. Her voice seemed to have a slight mocking tone.

But he knew she was right.

CHAPTER 24

Sansi woke up early, his mind too restless to allow sleep beyond the quenching of exhaustion. He switched on the bedside radio and tried to doze to the lilt of a sitar. He managed only a few minutes before he had to get up.

He winced at the old man's aches that troubled him after two nights on a cot in the operations center, and thought how much worse he would feel if he hadn't slept in a real bed last night. Instead of showering he went to the kitchen and made himself a pot of chai. He sent the house servant back to bed, insisting he would rather be left alone.

He drank the tea clear, sitting at the table by the window in his undershirt like a kuli, savoring the calm before the storm of another day. There was an easing of the gloom outside though the smog was so oppressive it could scarcely be called dawn. He saw the silhouettes of the soldiers against the perimeter lights, heard them coughing, the crunch of their boots on gravel. A light came on in the bungalow opposite and someone passed in front of it.

"Good morning, sahib."

It was Chowdhary at the screen door. Sansi looked at his watch. A few minutes before six and the day couldn't wait to get started.

"Chowdhary, you are a typical policeman," Sansi groused as he opened the door. "Always where you are not needed."

"I am sorry, sahib," Chowdhary said, not always certain when Sansi was kidding. "I can come back in an hour."

"Come in, have some chai." Sansi nodded at the teapot on the stove. "I will only be a few minutes."

He had asked Chowdhary to be there early so they could meet with Agawarl and review their progress. Agawarl was due to make his first appearance before the commission the following Monday and his testimony was expected to take up the whole week. They had to be ready, and they had to be sure he was ready. They intended to call Amlani immediately afterward, when the impact from Agawarl's testimony was at its greatest.

Sansi emerged from the bedroom freshly showered and shaved and wearing a fresh suit but still looking tired. Chowdhary finished his tea and got up.

"Has he come up with anything new?" Sansi asked.

"He remembers something every day, sahib. I am certain he will be telling Judge Pilot things he hasn't told us yet."

Sansi frowned. Agawarl had no idea how vital some of his information was when it came to making charges stick. He knew the big things, the obvious things, but there was a wealth of other evidence about Amlani business practices, their constant cutting of corners and disdain for basic safety standards which showed a history of recklessness that went back long before the Varanasi spill. It was as if Agawarl had been so browbeaten by the Amlanis, had grown so inured to their callousness, it was only the most heinous of their crimes that made any impression on him.

Sansi and Chowdhary stepped out onto the veranda. The morning air was rank with the smell of dung fires. At the bottom of the steps Corporal Hassan stood to attention.

"Anything happen last night?" Sansi asked.

"Nothing, sir," Hassan replied.

There had been much debate over where Agawarl should be kept until it was time for him to go before the commission. There wasn't a jail in India where security was not compromised by some level of corruption. In the end it was decided he would be safest as Sansi's neighbor at G Block, another VIP guest of the government, under the protection of the army.

They walked down the steps and continued toward Agawarl's bungalow, Hassan falling in behind them. The guard at Agawarl's bungalow saw them coming and saluted. Sansi looked at his watch. It was past six-thirty now and the bungalow was still in darkness.

"I see no reason why he should sleep any better than the rest of us," he said and trotted up the steps. The door was unlocked and the moment he opened it he was enveloped by a bitter chemical smell.

"*Bhagwan.*" Sansi stepped back, his eyes tearing.

Chowdhary looked at him in alarm.

"Agawarl?" Sansi called. "Are you all right?"

There was no answer. The blinds were all down and the living room was in darkness. Sansi took out a handkerchief and held it over his nose and mouth. Chowdhary did the same.

Sansi went in first and turned on the light. The living room was tidy. They walked quickly to the rear of the house. The bedroom and the kitchen were empty. So were the servants' quarters. There were dishes washed and stacked in the sink, but the bed hadn't been slept in. The smell seemed to be coming from the bathroom. A foul, frightening smell.

Sansi turned the handle slowly and gave the door a gentle push to see if there was anything blocking it. There wasn't. The door swung open easily and noiselessly to reveal a floor coated wall-to-wall with blood. The blood was drying and had acquired a gluey, plastic sheen.

Agawarl lay naked in the bathtub, immersed to the chest in blood. His head rested on the edge of the bath and was turned toward them, one eye closed, the other half open. On his forehead there was an open cut but no bruise. His mouth was open, the lower jaw skewed to one side. Oozing from his mouth and extending down the side of the tub to the floor was a thick column of bloody gruel, the liquefied remains of Agawarl's insides.

Sansi looked away from the corpse, his eyes scanning the rest of the bathroom. On the bloody floor, trapped between the tub and the toilet pedestal, was a plastic bottle on its side. It was a quarter bottle of bleach, empty, where it might have rolled after it had slipped from Agawarl's fingers.

"Maderchod!" Sansi issued a muffled curse through his handkerchief and stepped back into the kitchen.

Agawarl would have died screaming, or trying to scream. There must have been some noise, the sound of a struggle, something. How could nobody have heard? But the cut on the forehead wasn't an accident. It had happened just before death, so there was no time for it to bruise. He had been hit, hard enough to knock him unconscious, so he wouldn't make any noise, so he wouldn't put up a fight. And then they had poured the bleach down his throat, turning his organs to the foul pulp that gushed from his mouth and anus.

"Suicide," Sansi muttered disgustedly. It was supposed to look like suicide. He looked past Chowdhary at Hassan and the other soldier watching dumbly from the front doorway.

"Put them under arrest," Sansi said. "And every other man who was on duty last night. Then call Ramani. Tell him we've got another traitor."

■   ■

From the corner of her eye Annie saw Alam Bajaj approaching.

Her spirits sank. It had taken her most of the morning to get into the piece she was writing, and now he had to come and spoil her concentration. Screw it, she thought. She'd done her best. She'd been patient. She'd put up with his crap and all the crap that filtered down through the subordinates too scared to stand up to him. She didn't want to leave the paper, but she had an out if she wanted it. If Bajaj dragged her off this piece to do something else, if Sylvester wouldn't stand up for her this time . . .

She kept typing as Bajaj walked up beside her. There was something in his hand, photographs. He dropped them on the desk beside her. She kept her eyes on the words that marched across the screen of her word processor.

"Something here you might want to look at darlin'," he said in his annoying cockney accent, the accent that was supposed to tell everybody he was big time.

"I'm working on deadline, Alam," she said. "Take it up with Sylvester. I work for him, not you."

"I don't think you understand." Bajaj jabbed a finger at the pictures. "I would assume these are of very great interest to you."

Reluctantly, Annie stopped typing. She looked up at Bajaj and became aware for the first time that there was a pool of silence around them. Others nearby had stopped working too and were watching. She sensed a peculiar tension in the air.

She looked down at the pictures and saw why. There were three, slightly blurred but good quality prints. All showed Sansi with Rupe Seshan in what looked like the well-lit hallway of a house at night. There was some glare between the camera and the subjects, suggesting the pictures had been taken from out-side through a window. It gave them a furtive, authentic quality.

The first showed Sansi and Rupe close to each other in what

looked like intimate conversation, very much the way she had glimpsed them in the hallway at Pramila's apartment. On its own it was unsettling but not especially compromising. The other two pictures were damning. One showed Sansi and Rupe embracing and kissing with obvious passion. The third showed Rupe leading him by the hand to a stairway.

Annie felt a deadening chill seep through her body, dread mixed with disgust.

"Where did you get these?" she asked.

"Came in the post this morning," Bajaj said. "The envelope was postmarked New Delhi CPO."

She turned over the pictures but there was nothing on the back to identify them, no photographer's stamp or processor's address, no codes to be traced.

"Anonymous," she said.

"Somebody in the right place at the right time," Bajaj gloated. "Now do you think there's a story here?"

"Has everybody seen these?" she asked, her voice strangely calm.

"From what I understand, every newspaper and TV station in the city got a set of these this morning," he said. "By tonight I imagine everybody in the country will have seen them."

"You're going to run them?"

"All three, sweetheart. Front page. It's a major story, in case you can't tell. Didn't they teach you anything in America?"

Anger vied with humiliation inside her.

"So you tell me," Bajaj continued. "You think there might be something you want to talk to your boyfriend about now?"

Everything that followed felt to Annie as if it were happening to someone else, as if she had stepped outside her body and were floating some distance away, near the ceiling, watching herself.

She stood up, and Bajaj snatched the pictures and stepped back, a sudden apprehension on his face. She smiled at his reaction then shut off her computer and calmly and methodically went through her desk drawers, putting everything that was hers into her big leather shoulder bag.

"You're right, Alam," she said. "There is a story here—but you'll have to find someone else to write it."

Then, without a glance at the silent, watching faces all around, she walked through the newsroom and out of the office for what she knew was the last time.

CHAPTER 25

She was there when Grayson woke up in the morning, a naked provocation in the ruined sheets.

He watched her sleeping for a moment. Unable to resist, he ran his hand down her back in a light caress and was astonished by the inner heat of her. She stirred and mumbled something, words in a language he didn't know, and he was reminded how utterly foreign she was to him.

He went to the bathroom, turned on the light and tried not to look at his ugly body in the harsh glare. His limbs felt heavy and stiff and he nicked himself a few times while shaving. When he applied aftershave the pain was searing. The shower failed to relieve an incipient headache, and he rummaged in his travel kit for an aspirin. He had to expect a hangover. He'd had two or three large whiskeys after leaving the dinner the night before. Not to mention the lack of sleep, the marijuana and the cocaine. Good God almighty—cocaine! How much of that had penetrated the soft genital tissue and been absorbed into his bloodstream?

She was still sleeping when he looked in on her before

leaving. He thought about waking her to make sure she was gone when he came back, in case Towne or Kemp were with him. But part of him wanted her to stay, wanted more of her. Part of him wanted to know what else she knew.

Her face was hidden in the pillow, so he kissed the black, perfumey tangle of her hair. When he stood up he felt a warm longing in his groin. If he stayed he would want her again. Despite the hangover, despite the guilt.

In the sitting room he checked his briefcase and the contents of his wallet. His passport and the bulk of his money were in the hotel safe but he counted his Indian bills and his travelers checks all the same. It was uncharitable, he knew, but this was India. It paid to be careful.

Before opening the door he checked himself one last time in a full-length mirror in the hall. The iron-gray suit, the neat gray hair, the gray skin. The reflection of a gray man. The consummate corporate warrior. He removed the smug look from his face. There was a press conference to attend, an image to maintain. And that afternoon—the opening of negotiations to determine the details of full partnership.

Kemp waited impatiently in the hotel lobby. Outside two hotel cars were idling; their staff were crammed into the second.

"Bob isn't with you?"

"I haven't seen him since last night."

"Son of a bitch. I called him when I got up. He said he'd be here."

Grayson felt the ominous bass pulse in his head increase its tempo. "Ray, relax. It's not nine-thirty yet. The press conference is at ten. Renown House is five minutes from here."

"He shouldn't have taken that broad back to his room," Kemp fretted. "Call him on the hotel phone, would you? Tell him to get his ass down here. I'll wait with the car."

He bustled off without waiting for an answer, and Grayson watched him go thinking how much better it would be for all of them if Kemp were to have the heart attack now that everybody knew was long overdue. Then he could step in, breeze through the final negotiations, and reap the glory that was rightfully his. Grayson went to the house phones beside Reception and picked up a handset. Then he saw Towne ambling toward him, a mudslide under each eye, a haggard smile on his face.

"Good night's rest?" Grayson said, putting the handset back.

"What there was of it," Towne answered. "You?"

"I don't sleep well on the road," Grayson said.

"Me neither," Towne said. "Must be the stress."

The two of them fell in step together and continued toward the main entrance.

"You know, I like this country," Towne continued amiably. "After everything you said, I thought the whole place would be a shithole, but it has a lot of class too. They've got a style all their own, a real style, don't you think?"

"In some ways."

"Did you know you grunt like a pig when you fuck?"

Grayson jolted.

"Your bedroom window was wide open," Towne continued in the same amiable tone. "Me and my broad were out on the balcony having a joint and listening to you guys. All the fun you were having, I nearly leaned over and asked if you wanted to swap."

Grayson saw Kemp beckoning impatiently to them. He smiled a tight, uncomfortable smile.

"Shut the fuck up, Bob," he said.

"You know the problem with you, Tom," Towne said as they stepped outside. "You just don't know how to unwind."

Grayson bore Towne's leering silence stoically on the drive to Renown House. Kemp continued to fret, scribbling notes on a briefcase on his lap, crossing out and making additions. By the time they pulled up at the entrance he was sweating heavily, and Grayson again wondered how he had ever been given the job of lead negotiator.

"There's nothing you left out, nothing more I need to know?" Kemp asked him.

"Nothing," Grayson said as a Renown security guard opened the car door.

"You gave me everything . . . you're sure?"

"You've had everything on your desk for weeks, Ray."

Renown's director of corporate relations, Prasad, waited inside to greet them. He took them upstairs to a hospitality room adjoining the conference hall where a table had been set with pastries, juices, mineral water, and coffee. All the by now familiar faces in Renown Industries were there, including Amlani's three brothers. Only Amlani and Arvind were missing, but they would be along soon, Prasad said.

Kemp looked nervously at Grayson, and Grayson deliberately put as many people as possible between them. Half an hour passed in pleasant, innocuous conversation. Ten o'clock came and went with no sign of Amlani and no apparent concern to anyone but Kemp, who sidled his way determinedly toward Grayson.

"This is India, Ray," Grayson said, anticipating his question. "Nothing starts on time, remember?"

Almost as he finished speaking the door opened and Amlani appeared with Arvind, both of them smiling and relaxed. Amlani made a point of going around the room to greet everyone individually. He was especially attentive to the Americans and expressed the sly hope that they hadn't found the entertainments of the previous evening too tiring. When he was finished he signaled Prasad they were ready. As Prasad opened the door to the conference hall, Grayson saw a tangible relief in Kemp.

With Amlani in the lead they ran the gauntlet of flash cubes and TV lights to the stage and took their preassigned seats at a long table facing the hall. The Americans had been warned that Renown press conferences could be boisterous affairs, but Amlani had taken pains to ensure there would be none of the pandemonium that attended his last press conference. Then he had wanted frenzy, now he wanted order.

Admission was by invitation only and had been enforced zealously, so the room was only three-quarters full. Apart from an area set aside for TV cameras, everyone was required to remain seated, and there were enough security guards in the aisles to see that they did. The whole mood in the room was different. Instead of the usual pushing and shoving and a barrage of shouted questions, there was a discreet buzz of anticipation.

There was also a sense of anticlimax. Everybody knew the main event was over. Renown and Dumont were in bed together, Surat had set the seal on the marriage, and all that remained was the thrashing out of the prenuptial agreement before the contract was signed. Then it would get interesting again—when the Americans were on board and battle was joined to see who held the upper hand at Renown Oil.

Prasad stepped up to the microphone and got the conference under way in a brisk, businesslike manner. He ran quickly through the introductions, pausing only to make special mention of the Americans, who bobbed politely to the cameras that reeled in their file footage. With uncharacteristic brevity, he introduced Amlani, who was filled with such energy he seemed to bound from his chair to the microphone.

"My dear, dear friends and colleagues, " he began, his massive face illuminated by an expansive smile, "I hope I can convey to you the pleasure it gives me to stand before you today on this most historic of occasions."

His pleasure was so evident, his smile so infectious, it seemed almost churlish not to share in his good humor. While it wasn't likely to be the biggest news day of the business year, obviously it was one of the biggest days of the year for Amlani, and it was impossible not to be touched by his excitement.

"Many years ago I went to America for the first time, and I went there expecting to find a great and dynamic society," he went on. "I was not disappointed. The United States of America is the industrial and economic engine of the twentieth century. An engine so powerful it was pulling the rest of the world along in its train." He paused. "Until now, unfortunately, many of us were riding in the caboose."

There was a ripple of laughter. The Americans smiled uncertainly.

"What I was seeing in America was the future and the promise of the future," Amlani went on, his voice growing serious. "A future I wanted to share in, a future I wanted my countrymen to share in. And that is why I was sending my own two sons to be educated in America, to acquire the knowledge and the skills that would enrich our company and our country.

"The twentieth century has been called the American century," Amlani continued. "The twenty-first century will also be the American century—but with a difference." He punctuated his next few words with a jabbing finger. "India will be there to share in it."

There was a burst of applause from Renown's directors and some of the assembled media.

"Today we face the future together, two great and enterprising public corporations from two great and enterprising nations. Those of you who were with us in Surat this week saw the reality of that vision. With the assistance of the Dumont Chemical Corporation of America, the first privately owned and operated petroleum refinery in India is now in production, with full production only a matter of months away. And that, my friends, is only the beginning."

Kemp leaned forward slightly and gave Grayson an approving nod.

"In the future, I am hoping there will be many such joint ventures between us of even greater magnitude and importance. We have nine more refineries to build, more if this government can be alerted to the opportunities available. I am telling you all here today, I am telling you for the record, I could not wish for a better, a more generous partner in those ventures than my friends at the great Dumont corporation."

He turned and gestured to Grayson, Kemp, and Towne and invited them to stand while he led his directors in a protracted round of applause. The three Americans smiled and nodded their appreciation. As they sat down again Amlani reached into an inside pocket and took out a long white envelope.

"That is why it is giving me the greatest satisfaction today to be recognizing in public my great debt of gratitude to Dumont. Would Mr. Kemp please join me here?"

Kemp looked blankly at Grayson then pulled out his chair and walked around the table to stand with Amlani at the microphone. Amlani stood on his toes so he could put an arm around Kemp's shoulders and squeeze him warmly. The first cameramen hurried down to the stage and a couple of security men moved to intercept them, but Amlani waved the guards away and invited the cameramen closer so they could record the moment.

Smiling broadly, he turned to Kemp and said: "It is with great pleasure I present to you this company check in the amount of forty-two million dollars, which is representing payment in full, with interest, of all Dumont advances against Renown Oil stock."

There was a collective gasp from the media. It wasn't just the enormity of the sum, it was what it represented to those who knew. Cameras flashed and TV lights strobed as every Renown executive got to his feet and started to applaud. Kemp looked at the envelope in his hand as if Amlani had presented him with a used condom.

Grayson sat numb with shock.

"What happened?" Towne asked, knowing only that some kind of disaster had taken place.

Grayson knew what had happened. It was a setup. Amlani had set them up and Grayson hadn't seen it coming. He never

dreamed Amlani would find the money to pay Dumont back
before the start of negotiations. He never dreamed Renown
would get the refinery, especially the cracking plant, up and running in under twelve months. But Amlani had done all that and
more. He had found a way to use Dumont's money against
them—not just to save his company, but to manipulate the
market and make his company stronger. He had used it to
underwrite Renown Industries stock, to support Renown debentures and to push up the share price of Renown Oil's initial
public offering—and he had siphoned enough money out of the
market and back into the company to pay Dumont off.

Grayson knew all along that $40 million—even $50 million—
was a steal for half share of an oil company in a market the size
of India. He knew that ten times that amount would be a fair
price. So did Amlani. And he had suckered them all. Now that
he had the first refinery up and running, he could sit back and
wait for offers from Dumont's rivals, who would be laughing
themselves sick when the news flashed over the cable services
about an hour from now. All Grayson had done was win his
company first place in line. A half share in the one refinery they
had given Amlani. That would earn them the honor of opening
the bidding on the nine remaining refineries, on the rest of the
Renown Oil empire. Other bids would follow. All Amlani had to
do now was sit back and watch the money roll in.

"What the hell happened?" Towne whispered fiercely at
Grayson.

Grayson hardly heard him. He was listening to Zarine's
mocking voice from last night. "You have so much to learn," she
was saying. " . . . so much to learn."

"We just got fucked again," he said.

■ ■

Sansi slumped in the back seat of his government car as it drove
through the fetid New Delhi night.

He had been unable to reach Annie. He had tried her

apartment at Nariman Point several times but all he got was her answering machine. His secretary had called the *Times of India* but they said she no longer worked there. Nor had she called Pramila in several days, which was unusual. And the conversation with his mother had been difficult, the disappointment in her voice worse than any anger. It seemed Annie had cut herself off from them all, from the India she loved and which had turned on her.

The pictures had appeared sooner than Sansi expected. He had been so embattled by one crisis after another he had forgotten the passage of time. They had been used far more widely and their impact been far greater than either he or Rupe had anticipated. The newspapers, especially, had feasted on them. The *Hindustan Times* had run a scathing editorial about government morality under the title "Conduct Unbecoming."

The day had been a torment of sideways looks and awkward exchanges, of whispered conversations in the hallways abruptly ended when he appeared. And all of it made worse by the knowledge that he deserved it, that he had brought it on himself.

Sansi had the unsettling feeling he was losing his way, that events were slipping out of control and the compass that gave him guidance through the chaos was no longer true.

Annie was right. This case was changing him. He was turning into someone he didn't recognize anymore, someone he didn't like. She had warned him the stakes were too high to think he could get in and out without it taking a piece of him. He had promised her the cesspool of politics would not drag him down. Now he had been exposed across the front pages of the nation—foolish and feckless as any politician. How could he distinguish himself from the rest of them now? How could anyone?

The car slowed and turned into the gateway of the army detention center at Ashoka Barracks. Sansi pushed his personal

fears to the back of his mind. They were an indulgence in the
face of a far greater crisis. Annie would have to wait. He would
have to wait.

The death of Agawarl was a critical blow to their case. Without
him they had no eyewitness testimony to support the evidence
against the Amlanis, no single thread to show the deliberate
hand of the Amlanis behind so many crimes, nothing that would
connect them directly to what had happened at Varanasi. With
Agawarl gone they needed a new star witness. They needed to
prove a link between Hassan and the Amlanis, to show that the
Amlanis ordered Agawarl's death because of what he knew
about them. They had to make Hassan talk—and soon. They
needed to find out where Hassan got his orders and who else in
New Delhi was on Amlani's payroll. They needed to know the
name of the spy in Rupe's household.

All the other guards on duty that night had talked, either to
protest their innocence or to blame one another for what happened at G Block. The sentry assigned to guard Agawarl insisted
he had seen nothing unusual. He claimed that the only time he
left his post was around eleven when he went to eat and Hassan
had watched both houses. And Hassan hadn't uttered a word
since his arrest.

Despite six days of round-the-clock efforts by interrogators
working in relays to break him he had maintained the same
stubborn silence. To keep him disoriented he hadn't been
allowed to sleep more than twenty minutes at a stretch. He was
allowed four cups of water a day and a single chapati and rice,
enough to keep him functioning but not enough to relieve the
pain of thirst and hunger.

There had been no shortage of suggestions, from electric
shock to chilis rubbed in the eyes. Sansi had no stomach for tor-
ture and he knew a tortured confession was worthless in court.
But he was running out of options. Hassan came from the
lowest levels of Indian society. He was used to hardship and
deprivation and seemed possessed of a fanatic determination to

hold his silence. He knew, just as well as Sansi knew, that if he said nothing they could prove nothing. There was nothing to implicate him directly in Agawarl's murder and nothing to implicate the Amlanis. The worst that would happen to him was a dereliction of duty charge, a short prison term followed by a dishonorable discharge—with a fat payoff waiting for him when he got out.

The interrogation room was at the end of a long basement corridor whose cement walls were coated with condensation. After the warm night air the basement air was chill and dank, something else that should have sapped Hassan's will to resist.

A small group of soldiers stood at the interrogation room door taking turns looking through a thick glass porthole. Sansi recognized a couple of guards, an interrogation officer, and Captain Ramani.

"Anything?" Sansi asked.

Ramani shook his head. "He doesn't even ask for food."

The others stepped aside so Sansi could look through the porthole. The interrogation room was a cement box empty of furniture but for a single metal chair. Hassan was naked, cuffed ankle and wrist to the chair. He was conscious, his face gaunt, his eyes blank. The interrogation officer was shouting into his face, insults about his manhood, his family, his betrayal, anything to provoke a response. The porthole was scratched and slightly opaque but there seemed to be welts on Hassan's face and chest.

Sansi frowned. "How long has he been in there now?"

"Two, two and a half hours."

"Take him back to his cell," Sansi said. "Tell him he can have a couple of hours' sleep. Give him five minutes then bring him back and I'll take a turn."

Ramani seemed about to argue, as if resentful that Sansi thought he could achieve what the army could not, but then he did as he was asked. They stood back while the guards half dragged, half carried Hassan to his cell. When he was gone, Sansi went into a huddle with Ramani and the two interrogation officers.

"You told him all the others have given him up?" Sansi asked.

"Four days ago," Ramani said.

"Does he respond to the name Amlani at all?"

"We tried that."

"It is like trying to get a dead man to talk," the newly relieved interrogation officer said.

"We should fry his balls," the other said. "If you know what you're doing, it doesn't leave marks."

"It would loosen his tongue," Ramani said. "It's worth it if we get just a couple of names out of him."

Sansi knew the methods the army had used against captured Pakistani insurgents in Kashmir. They hadn't done much good there either.

"His family?" Sansi asked.

"He is not married," Ramani said. "His mother is dead. His father and two brothers are living, but there is no leverage there, he has had no contact with them in many years. The army is all he knows."

"He's Muslim?"

"The family is Muslim. I have never known him to pray."

"There must be something," Sansi said.

A guard returned to tell them Hassan appeared to be sleeping. Sansi told them to bring him back, then he and Ramani went into the interrogation room together.

Hassan winced as the guards cuffed him to the hard-edged metal chair again but he offered no protest, no resistance. His wrists and ankles were bloody and the underside of his thighs raw. There were already fresh splashes of blood around the legs of the chair.

If Hassan recognized either Ramani or Sansi, he gave no

sign. He sat with his head tilted to one side, his eyes blank, his face expressionless.

Ramani walked around him slowly, appraising him, then stood behind him, a silent threat. Sansi knew Hassan must have expected to be tortured. He had to know they were running out of time and patience. He had to know it could come at any time.

Sansi leaned down and looked directly into Hassan's eyes. Hassan looked through him.

"You hate us all so much, Hassan?" Sansi said. "You hate us so much you would turn traitor for money?"

Hassan might have been deaf.

"You hate your comrades, the men you lived with, trained with these past eleven years? You hate your country—the country you took a sacred oath to protect?"

Still there was nothing.

"Who was it promised you the money?"

Sansi stood back.

"How much did they say they would pay you?"

Hassan's chest rose and fell slowly, the only sign he was alive.

"You know the power I have, don't you? You know the importance of this case to the government?"

This time he didn't wait for a response.

"Let me tell you what is going to happen to you. Whatever you have been promised, whatever Amlani or his agents told you would happen, what they would do for you—however you think the army and the government will handle this—put all of that out of your head for now and think about what is really going to happen."

His voice was a low monotone so Hassan would know it wasn't a bluff.

"When the army is finished with you, when you've done your time, what's left of you will be turned over to us to face treason charges. If you are lucky you will be hanged. If you are unlucky you will go from an army prison to a civilian prison and you will never see the outside again. You won't get a chance to spend your money. You will spend the rest of your life in a place like this."

He paused and then added: "You are nothing to Amlani. He is using you the way he uses everybody. You have served your purpose and now you will be thrown away, like garbage into the river."

There was a change in Hassan's eyes, a glimmer of something, doubt or anger. His jaw worked under his taut skin, his lips moved as he tried to say something.

Sansi used his open fist to hit Hassan as hard as he could. Hassan's head jolted sideways, then he clamped his mouth shut again.

"His mouth," Sansi shouted. "Open his mouth."

Ramani stared, uncomprehending.

Sansi locked an arm around Hassan's head and tried to force his thumb between Hassan's tightly compressed lips. Hassan rocked back, twisting his head, trying to break free.

"Help me get his mouth open," Sansi shouted again.

There was a soft crunching sound and Ramani realized what was happening. He leaned down, grasped Hassan's lower jaw with both hands and tried to prize it open. Hassan grunted, a snuffling, animal sound. Mucus bubbled from his nostrils and a thin stream of blood ran out between his lips.

"*Bhagwan!*" Sansi grunted.

The crunching sound continued, loud and sickening.

Sansi hit Hassan again, and again Hassan's head snapped back and forth but his mouth stayed shut. Blood poured down his chin onto his chest, staining his belly red, running in rivulets down the chair legs to form a puddle on the floor.

"Move away," Sansi shouted.

He clenched his fist and swung at Hassan with all his

strength, determined to break Hassan's jaw. Hassan grunted and spasmed. His mouth opened and blood gushed out. He made a sound that wasn't quite human, the cry of a wounded beast.

Sansi groaned and looked down at the spreading pool of blood on the floor. At its center was a glutinous curled lump of flesh. What remained of Hassan's tongue.

CHAPTER 26

Amlani came to the commission alone.

He came without bodyguards, without his brothers, without his sons, without colleagues, without lawyers, without even a personal assistant to carry his briefcase for him.

His driver delivered him to the front entrance of the Justice Ministry alone. He walked up the steps, between the police lines, past the muttering crowd, alone. He threaded his way through the crowded lobby and into the central committee room alone. Because he was alone, because he came without a corporate cavalcade, without a bristling phalanx of lawyers, he went unnoticed by most of the media until it was too late. He took his place on the witness benches, one man against a hostile government and an irascible judge.

Despite its name, the central committee room of the Justice Ministry was not a drab reminder of India's socialist past but a remnant of the Raj at the height of its glory, a lofty chamber as tall as it was long, with columns and arches, gilded with gold leaf and shafts of sunlight streaming through a vaulted glass ceiling. For the purpose of the commission, the room had been divided in two. One half was crowded with wooden benches, the first few rows sectioned off for the world's media, correspondents from every major Indian newspaper and TV network, every foreign wire service and news bureau, and observers from a dozen environmental organizations including Greenpeace.

Behind them sat the families of those who had perished at Varanasi; parents who had lost children, husbands who had lost wives, brothers who had lost brothers. Among them some of the survivors, their bodies crusted with molten flesh, waited with the patience of the dispossessed, the way India's poor always waited for justice.

Circling them, watching them, swooping in for furtive, whispered conversations were the human vultures, the brokers and the lawyers looking for victims whose wounds could be picked that little bit cleaner.

The other half of the room was reserved for the business of the commission. Against a curved rear wall where a mural of the British victory at Plassey had been painted over by a representation of the great Mauryan king Chandragupta, the commissioner's bench reared up in ramparts of polished oak. Behind it were seven red leather chairs, the center chair a little taller and a little grander than the rest. Beneath the ramparts was a smaller embrasure where the clerk of the commission sat with the recorder and his assistants. To their right was a long, wide table furnished with word processors and recording devices for the clerks and typists who logged the minutes and kept the commission documents. Against the opposite wall was a table of equal size reserved for friends of the commission. Marooned in the middle of the room like a two-man life raft was a small, square table with two chairs facing the bench: the witness table, big enough to accommodate one witness at a time and a lawyer.

The two halves of the room were divided by a velvet rope supported by brass stands, which separated the audience from the players. Between the rope and the public benches were a dozen uniformed policemen. Other policemen patrolled the corridors and halls and watched every entrance and exit. The only armed policemen guarded the doors at the back of the room through which Judge Pilot and his fellow commissioners would enter and leave.

Sansi and Chowdhary were seated at the table reserved for friends of the commission. In the seats beside them were a half-dozen well-known assemblymen, senior officials from the Justice Ministry and the Environment Ministry, and a couple of high court judges, all of them come to watch Pilot and Amlani duel.

Sansi had watched Amlani closely since he arrived. He had expected Amlani to come in strength, to make a show of force equal to the forces arrayed against him. To come alone was cunning. It cast him in the role of underdog. But it was more than that. It was a silent statement to the commission, to Rupe, to Pilot, and to Sansi. It said Amlani did not fear them, that he was stronger than they were, that he could walk into their midst alone and defeat them all.

If Amlani noticed Sansi, he gave no sign. He sat on the witness benches, relaxed and impassive, oblivious to the photographers who leaned out of their benches to get his picture, his eyes fixed on some indeterminate place in front of him. Sansi regarded him with implacable loathing. Somewhere in the preceding months he had lost the ability to detach himself from his emotions, to pursue the case and not the man. The pursuit of justice and the pursuit of vengeance had fused within him into a single cause—to bring Amlani down, whatever the cost.

He couldn't say exactly when it had happened. He couldn't isolate the single moment or event that changed him. It wasn't just that Amlani put himself outside the law. Any common pickpocket did that. The difference was the pickpocket used stealth, deception, and a swift hand because he knew what he did was wrong. He weighed risk against gain and knew if he was caught he would be punished. Amlani saw no wrong in what he did, so the very notion of accountability was an affront. His crimes were not crimes because they were committed in the name of a higher calling—the paramountcy of his own desires. The legal apparatus of the state was an encumbrance for others, not him.

His arrogance was evident in the way he promoted the corruption that crippled every aspect of Indian life while holding himself aloof from its consequences. It was evident in the contempt he showed equally for the judges, lawyers, and politicians who served him as well as those who did not. It was evident in the detachment with which he determined the fates of men, whether they should be rewarded, ruined, or deprived of life itself.

Sansi's hatred was the product of all that and more. It was fomented by the disgust he felt at the way Amlani used the wash from his vile wallow to smear Sansi and all those Sansi held dear. It was fomented by the rage Sansi had turned in on himself for the single lapse that enabled Amlani to shame him so publicly, so completely. And it was hardened by the image of Agawarl immersed in a bath of his own blood, by the image of a man's ragged tongue on a jail cell floor, by the image of a river filled with corpses. And all of it in the name of business as usual.

A door at the back of the room opened and the clerk of the commission appeared, a government lawyer robed in black with a forked white collar and a gray periwig. He was followed by the recorder, similarly robed, a couple of assistants, and a half-dozen female clerks burdened like porters with accordion files and stacks of documents bundled with string.

The clerk went to his hutch in front of the commissioners' bench, rapped the gavel loudly and called for everyone to stand. There was a mass shuffling and scraping of feet and all eyes turned to the rear doors through which the commissioners would enter. All eyes but those of Sansi and Amlani. At the last crack of the gavel Amlani turned his head and met Sansi's gaze directly. Amlani smiled.

The door on the left opened a fraction ahead of the door on the right and the lanky, white-haired figure of Judge Pilot ducked into the room followed by two assemblymen from the Bharatiya Janata Party and an assemblyman and assembly-woman from the National Front coalition. The two Congress Party assemblymen entered through the door on the right, unable to do anything without making a political point.

The judge wore a long gray vest over his usual white cotton kurta pajamas. He carried a sheaf of papers in one hand and acknowledged no one as he made his way to the center chair. He dropped his papers onto the bench with a slap that his micro-phone carried around the room then sat down to a corre-sponding chorus of scrapes and shuffles. He put on his glasses and briefly studied the papers in front of him before consulting with his colleagues on the bench.

There had been a distinct tension in the room before Pilot entered, an expectation that today would bring a turning point in the life of the commission. Today was the day when they would see if the commission had any teeth. When they would see if the government was serious about making a man like Amlani pay for his misdeeds. When they would see if Pilot, in the twilight of his career, was the man to defeat Amlani in a public battle of wills. Now that moment had come and the ten-sion in the room had increased to the point at which it was almost crystalline, so the air itself seemed to crackle.

At last Pilot glanced around and appeared to notice there were others present. He signaled the clerk to proceed and the clerk smacked his gavel once more and pronounced day seventy-five of the Commission of Inquiry into the Cause of Death and Disability Arising from Chemical Contamination of the Ganga at Varanasi in session. Then he called the name of Madhuri Amlani.

Amlani got to his feet. "I am Madhuri Amlani," he said.

There was a loud murmuring on the public benches and

amongst the media. Those in the back seats and the open doorways jostled for position and craned their necks to see. Pilot put
a hand over his microphone and spoke to the clerk, who called
for order. Then he invited Amlani to step up to the witness table.
Amlani walked forward and set his briefcase down on one of the
empty chairs. The clerk handed him a printed card and Amlani
recited the affirmation that his testimony would be truthful and
that he understood it could be used in whole or in part against
him or others in future proceedings. Then he took his seat,
folded his hands on the table in front of him and leaned toward
the microphone.

"Mr. Amlani, you do not appear to have brought an attorney
with you," Pilot began, his manner almost avuncular. "I doubt
that decision was due to the natural reticence of any member of
the bar that I know."

Amlani smiled. "Your honor, I come here today to serve
justice. I do not believe that process would be assisted by the
presence of another lawyer."

There was an amused stir on the media benches.

Pilot smiled thinly. "The commission welcomes any initiative by you that would expedite a finding of guilt, Mr.
Amlani."

"Then we are united in the same cause, your honor," Amlani
rejoined. "God grant us the courage to see it through, wherever
it leads."

There was a pause in which each man seemed to take the
measure of the other. Then, with the same deceptive geniality,
Pilot added: "Mr. Amlani, would you tell the commission your
occupation?"

"I am chairman and chief executive officer of Renown
Industries."

"Are those your only positions?"

"I find them sufficient, though I am also a major shareholder."

"Renown is a publicly listed company, is it not?"

"It is, your honor."

"And what percentage of shares do you hold personally in Renown Industries?"

"I own eight percent of Renown Industries stock."

"Common stock?"

"Yes, your honor."

"And your family?"

"To the best of my knowledge each of my brothers holds between two and three percent and my sons each have five percent, though they have all traded on their holdings in Renown and various other of our companies on their own initiative and those figures may be higher or lower."

"And how many companies does Renown Industries control in total?"

"Seventy-three, your honor, spread over five divisions; textiles, chemicals and petrochemicals, transport and shipping, marketing, and communications. Our newest division is Renown Oil, which is still in the early phases of development."

"Does that include subsidiary holdings?"

"No, your honor. With subsidiaries, the figure would be closer to one hundred and thirty companies."

"And what would you estimate is the full extent of your family's holdings in Renown Industries?" Pilot continued patiently.

Amlani had to think before answering: "Somewhere between twenty-two and twenty-six percent."

"Neither your wife nor daughter holds shares in your companies?"

"They have never expressed the desire." Amlani shrugged as if deferring to a higher logic. "Like most women, they prefer their assets in a form they can wear."

There was another ripple of amusement from the media.

"So the figure of twenty-six percent represents the full extent of your family's holdings in Renown Industries?"

"That would be the high end, your honor."

"All common stock?"

"Yes, your honor."

"So your exposure to risk is the same as every other shareholder?"

"Greater when you consider the proportion of my family's wealth that is tied up in stock."

"But that is not the case with Renown Holdings?"

"Your honor?"

"Renown Holdings. The corporate parent of Renown Industries. You do remember it?"

"Renown Holdings was established sometime after Renown Industries, your honor. It was never the corporate parent."

"For what purpose was Renown Holdings established?"

"To hold shares in various companies."

"To hold a controlling interest in various companies?"

"In some cases, at some times."

"And Renown Holdings is a private holding company entirely owned by whom?"

"It is no secret that Renown Holdings is my company, your honor."

"Its existence has not been included in any of your corporate literature over the past thirty years?"

"Renown Holdings is a private company, your honor."

"Quite," Pilot acknowledged. "And as long as its existence is not a secret you won't mind telling the commission what percentage of Renown Industries stock is held by Renown Holdings?"

Amlani saw where Pilot was leading but it was too late for him to do anything about it.

"I believe about twenty-four percent," he answered.

"Twenty-four percent?" Pilot paused to let the number linger in everyone's minds.

There was a murmur on the public benches. Sansi was gratified by the sight of scribbling pens on the media benches and faces that no longer seemed so entertained.

"Which combined with your personal holdings in Renown Industries and the holdings of your immediate relatives puts the Amlani family's total shareholding in Renown Industries somewhere between forty-six and fifty-two percent?" Pilot added.

"Of which at least twenty percent is in common stock," Amlani added quickly.

"And the shares in Renown Holdings?" Pilot sprang his trap.

Amlani hesitated then answered: "The shares in Renown Holdings are in preferred stock."

"For the benefit of those who may not know, would you explain the difference between common stock and preferred stock, Mr. Amlani?"

Amlani seemed about to protest then thought better of it. Resignedly he admitted: "Preferred stock has priority over common stock in the payment of dividends and the distribution of assets."

"And issues of preferred shares have been strictly limited over the life of Renown Industries, have they not?" Pilot continued.

"By their nature preferred shares are limited issues," Amlani countered.

"In the case of Renown Industries limited exclusively to yourself and a few immediate relatives," Pilot added.

Amlani looked pained. "Your honor, there has to be some protection against risk."

"In fact, according to the records I have examined, there has never been a public offering of preferred stock in Renown Industries," Pilot pressed on.

"Your honor, preferred stock is a very marginal form of insurance," Amlani insisted. "Not every investor requires that kind of insurance."

"It is remarkable to me that the thought seems never to have occurred to the directors of the Bombay Stock Exchange that the investing public should at least be given the opportunity to make up their own minds," Pilot replied.

"Your honor, my companies' offerings have always been conducted in accordance with the strictest requirements of the exchange."

There was a groan from the public and media benches alike. The Bombay Stock Exchange was the wildest, most sloppily regulated share market in Asia, and claiming respect for its rules was like respecting the rules of a bear garden.

"Mr. Amlani, this is an arrangement which would appear to make Renown Industries a public company only in the most nominal sense," Pilot went on. "In actuality it is a very efficient mechanism for dredging funds out of the share market directly into your pockets while limiting your exposure to the risks of the market. At the same time, control of the company and direction of its policies remain very much in your hands and you enjoy little or no accountability at all to either your board or your shareholders."

"Your honor, I believe my company enjoys the support of all its shareholders and of the market too if the increase in our prices over the years is any indication," Amlani responded.

"It would appear you have been amply rewarded for your efforts," Pilot observed.

"The bulk of our profits goes into the business of creating new industries, your honor, new jobs, new wealth. I don't ask what other shareholders do with their dividends."

"So Renown is something of a philanthropic endeavor for you—and it is a privilege for shareholders to participate?"

"Renown is a success, your honor. I have never seen the need to apologize for that. It is not as if our country has been overburdened with success stories these past forty years."

It was a jibe at Pilot's leftist loyalties and the mess socialism had made of the Indian economy, but it missed its mark. Pilot seemed more amused than offended and Amlani seemed to be losing his composure.

The sparring continued for hours, the two men circling each other like fighters, probing, feinting, blocking, and countering.

But piece by piece Pilot extracted the testimony he wanted, testimony that showed the extraordinary degree of control Amlani wielded over his empire, the sinister extent of his reach, the oppressive personality behind the smiling facade. The way nothing escaped his attention, the way no decision, however small, was made without his approval. And piece by piece Pilot laid the groundwork for the evidence that was to come—that however much he pretended to be removed from it, Amlani must have known in advance about the events that led to the spill at Varanasi.

Around two o'clock Pilot decided to adjourn for lunch. Before rising, and only partially in jest, he advised Amlani that he might reconsider his decision to appear before the commission without a lawyer. And from the conversations Sansi overheard in the corridors and stairwells, it seemed everyone agreed that Amlani was losing and losing badly.

The commission reconvened soon after three-thirty amid the heightened expectation that Pilot would bring the uneven duel to a close, that he would deliver a knockout blow before the end of the day, if only to make the evening news.

Pilot seemed to have other ideas. If only to keep Amlani off balance, the judge ceded the microphone to his colleagues so that they might take their turn at questioning, so they might task Amlani for a while before Pilot resumed his questioning.

As Sansi expected, the two Congress Party assemblymen threw Amlani soft questions that enabled him to expound on Renown's good industrial relations record. The assemblymen from the Bharatiya Janata Party made up for it to some extent by pressing Amlani on employee safety standards and Renown's woeful environmental record. Even so, Amlani easily made the point that safety and environment inspectors who worked harder at soliciting bribes than doing their jobs were more a product of corruption in government than corruption in the private sector. For its part the National Front seemed more interested in Amlani's foreign dealings, and the only female commissioner on the bench seemed particularly anxious to know about Renown's stalled negotiations with Dumont. Sansi suspected that the socialists, like many politicians, secretly had shares in Renown.

Pilot regained the microphone a little after five and a current of electricity ran through the room. It descended to anticlimax when Pilot conferred with his fellow commissioners on the prospect for early adjournment, but the decision was made to continue until six o'clock.

"Mr. Amlani," Pilot began genially, "would you tell the commission when you acquired Patna Fabrics?"

Amlani fidgeted for a moment then answered: "In early 1993, I believe, your honor."

"And did you play an active part in the acquisition of that company?"

"It was researched by our textiles division in the same manner we use to research all potential acquisitions."

"And who is in charge of the acquisitions arm of your textiles division?"

"At that time my son, Arvind, was responsible for all executive decisions in textiles, including research and acquisitions."

"And to whom did your son report on the matter of acquisitions?"

Amlani smiled faintly. "To me, your honor."

"And did he recommend to you that you proceed with the acquisition of Patna Fabrics?"

"Yes he did."

"And did you approve that acquisition?"

"I did."

"And what did you know about the plant you had acquired?"

"I knew it was an old plant," Amlani acknowledged. "It had been allowed to run down over a period of years but it was my understanding it could be upgraded on a cost-effective basis to become a productive and profitable unit of our textiles division. One of the things Renown Industries has always done best is take old, unproductive plants and turn them into productive—"

"This isn't a shareholders meeting, Mr. Amlani," the judge rebuked him. "Would you tell the commission if you were aware of any problems with the factory at Varanasi in the three years of your ownership that preceded the spill?"

"There were many problems," Amlani acknowledged. "The situation was much worse than we were led to believe by the owners. They concealed many things from us. There was much exaggeration and deception."

"Exaggeration and deception?" Pilot repeated the words slowly, as if savoring their familiar taste. "In what way?"

"With the machinery, your honor, all of it. But most particularly so with the condition of the waste disposal equipment."

"Chemical waste? Phosphorous waste?"

"Your honor, that is why we are here, is it not?"

Pilot seemed surprised by Amlani's response.

"You are saying you were aware of the dangers posed by the poor state of the disposal equipment at Patna Fabrics?"

"Absolutely, yes," Amlani answered. "The holding tanks were badly deteriorated and close to capacity. Many of the valves were rusted shut and there were signs of metal fractures and seepage. We knew the tanks and the sludge pits underneath would have to be drained and replaced."

"You knew that?" Pilot asked.

"Of course we knew that." Amlani took confidence from the judge's apparent confusion. "We have been in the chemicals business a long time. We knew what the dangers were."

"And you did nothing to stop it getting worse?"

An awed silence settled over the huge room, the only sound the wheezy rattle of the air conditioners. The public and media benches were eerily still.

Sansi felt a growing unease. He had warned Pilot to expect something like this, and still the judge had been caught off guard. He had grown too confident. Amlani had weathered the initial onslaught, yielded Pilot his modest victory, and now it was Amlani's turn. He had prepared his own trap. And all Sansi could do was sit and watch as Pilot unwittingly surrendered the last vestiges of their case.

"Of course we dismissed the factory manager immediately," Amlani continued in the same reasoned tone. "For letting the equipment deteriorate to that level in the first place—and for concealing it from us. It was concealed from us when we did our own pre-purchase inspection and through the six month transitional phase when we would have been protected by the terms of the buyout. When we discovered the extent of the deception, we got rid of the manager and replaced him with Mr. Agawarl, the assistant manager. We thought Mr. Agawarl was a good man."

"This would be Anjani Agawarl?" Pilot said, searching through his papers for the threads of a case that moments ago he had held securely in his grasp but was now slipping through his fingers.

"Correct . . . your honor," Amlani said. "We asked Mr. Agawarl to look at all the options for the safe disposal of the phosphoric acid waste and the repair or replacement of the holding facilities."

"Did Mr. Agawarl make any such recommendations?" Pilot asked, snatching at a vanishing twist of thread.

"He did, your honor." Amlani reached into the briefcase on the chair next to him and produced a thick file of papers. "Mr. Agawarl sent us several memorandums detailing various options and their cost."

Sansi watched, helpless to intervene, as Pilot stepped further into the trap.

"Why then did you ignore all of those options?" the judge asked. "Why did you allow the situation at Patna to continue to deteriorate?"

"We didn't, your honor." Some of Amlani's old bellicosity reemerged. "We have all of Mr. Agawarl's memorandums here and copies of our replies that show we authorized him to make the necessary arrangements for the safe disposal of all chemical waste and to proceed with the replacement of the deteriorated holding equipment. We transferred funds to the Patna Fabrics account in late 1994 and again in early 1995 to pay for it. We have several memorandums from Mr. Agawarl advising us the work was in progress." Amlani brandished the sheaf of papers in the air. "The records are all here, your honor."

Sansi had no doubt the documents Amlani waved under the commissioners' noses were just as he said. Bank records, purchase authorizations, cash transfers, all correctly dated and easily verified. Memorandums from Agawarl filled with lies but with his initials reproduced perfectly at the bottom. And hidden somewhere, but not well enough to escape detection, would be a bank account in Agawarl's name with funds equal to the amounts Amlani said had been wired to Patna. There wasn't a document in the world that couldn't be forged by a company with Renown's resources. More than that, Amlani could produce an army of bank managers, clerks, and secretaries to swear before any court that the documents were all genuine and the paperwork was executed exactly as he had described.

"I remember it well because it was a very difficult and very expensive undertaking," Amlani continued. "But Mr. Agawarl assured us he had it all under control. We were under the impression the work was in progress when the spill took place."

There was a confused muttering on the public benches as an assistant to the clerk of the commission took the papers from Amlani and delivered them to the bench.

"Of course we know now the money was withdrawn from the Patna account but never spent on the work we approved," Amlani continued. "It is obvious to us, your honor, that Mr. Agawarl misappropriated those funds for his own use and vented the tanks into the Ganga himself, thinking it would not be noticed."

The muttering in the room swelled into uproar, cries of anger and betrayal; people argued with each other, shouted insults and accusations at Amlani and the commissioners.

Cameras flashed capturing the turmoil. The clerk banged his gavel and policemen moved into the aisles to restore order. Sansi and Chowdhary exchanged looks of dismay. Everywhere there was doubt and confusion—all the demons Amlani wanted unleashed.

Pilot had to threaten to have the room cleared before a tenuous calm was restored. When he addressed Amlani again the judge sounded strained, as if he could feel his authority slipping away and did not know how to regain it.

"Mr. Amlani, given the degree of control you exercise over your companies, do you expect the commission to believe you had no knowledge of Mr. Agawarl's conduct in the period prior to the spill at Varanasi?"

"Your honor, the commission would have known this months ago if your investigators had come to us and told us what they wanted, if they had been at all interested in conducting an impartial investigation." Amlani raised his hands in a gesture of resignation. "But this is not an impartial investigation, the whole country knows that."

"I will remind you, Mr. Amlani, laws of contempt apply just as effectively to this commission as they do to a court of law," Pilot snapped back, though there was a tremor in his voice that seemed to stem more from desperation than anger.

Adjourn, adjourn, adjourn. Sansi recited the word over and over in his head, all the time staring at Pilot, willing the judge to look his way. But Pilot's eyes were on Amlani, watching him the way a cobra watches a mongoose, knowing he was in a duel to the death.

Pilot pressed on: "Would it surprise you to learn, Mr. Amlani, that before he died Mr. Agawarl gave detailed testimony to this commission that you denied all his requests for funds to make the necessary repairs to the disposal facilities at Patna

Fabrics, that you pressured him to find other means of disposal and threatened him when he refused—and it was in fear of you that he discharged the holding tanks into the Ganga?"

Amlani shook his head as if wearied by a lifetime of false accusations.

"Your honor, I am sure it surprises no one. Just as it would surprise no one that Mr. Agawarl would lie to save himself from prosecution. Mr. Agawarl is the perfect witness, is he not? He provides the investigators with exactly the testimony they want then dies mysteriously but conveniently in custody so he cannot be questioned again."

There was increased agitation on the public benches and a renewed stirring among the media, though this time it was harder to read. From the beginning Sansi had noticed glances and whispers directed his way, but for the first time he heard his name spoken openly and people began to point and stare at him. Sansi gazed stonily ahead, preparing himself for what was coming.

"Mr. Amlani, I have warned you once about contempt," Pilot was saying.

"Your honor . . ." Amlani half turned in his chair so he could appeal to the packed media benches. ". . . how can I speak the truth when every time I try you threaten to put me in jail?"

For a moment Pilot was too stunned to respond, and Amlani moved quickly to take advantage.

"This inquiry has been biased against me from the beginning," he added belligerently. "The only reason it exists is because Rupe Seshan wants to make political capital out of a national tragedy, to show how tough she is against polluters, as if pollution was something new. She wants to make an example out of me and my companies. . . ." He jabbed a finger in Sansi's direction. "And that man, the man she put in charge of the investigation, will do anything to help her. The whole country knows they are in bed together. . . ."

The room erupted in uproar. People spilled out of the

benches and into the aisles, many of them screaming their frustrations at Amlani. But there were others who directed their
rage at the commissioners, at the police, at Sansi. Those who
knew all about government betrayal, about sellouts, about corrupt politicians, corrupt police officers, and corrupt judges.

Brawls broke out between some of the spectators and the
police. Camera flashes added to the hysteria. Reporters got nervously to their feet when it seemed the crowd would spill out
onto the commission floor. Sansi looked at Chowdhary and woefully shook his head. It was a shambles. Amlani had taken the
hearing away from Pilot and turned it into a shambles.

Several minutes passed before order was restored. Scores of
people were ejected, the doors were closed and more police
called to line the walls of the committee room. Sansi knew that
those who remained were trapped in a nightmare of Amlani's
making. Amlani had done what he wanted, had seized the initiative and with it the day's headlines. Pilot couldn't adjourn now
until he'd done something to salvage his position—and with that
came the prospect of fresh assaults from Amlani.

"Mr. Amlani, you have made grave allegations before this
commission," Pilot said, his voice wavering somewhere between
outrage and anguish. "If you have anything of substance to offer
in support of those allegations you should present it now. But
you will not make speeches, you will not play politics, you will
not issue personal slanders. You will confine yourself to the evidence at hand. Or I promise you this—you will end this day in a
prison cell."

"Your honor, I did not come here to pick a quarrel with
you," Amlani responded, conciliatory. "I did not come here by
choice. I came because I was summoned. I came alone, armed
only with the truth. And I came because I am chairman of
Renown Industries and it is my dharma to be here." He paused
and lowered his voice a level. "I came here to accept responsibility for what happened at Varanasi."

There were gasps on the public benches. A tense silence took hold, as if people were afraid to breathe, afraid of what they might miss. It had been a day of high drama and sensational disclosures, and now it seemed the most sensational was yet to come.

"Renown Industries is not without a conscience, your honor," Amlani added solemnly. "We don't want another Bhopal. We are not Union Carbide. We do not need the government to make us do what is right. We know where our duty lies. Renown stands ready to cooperate with the government in any endeavor that will help with the healing process. That is why the Renown Trust was formed, your honor. That is why we are building a new hospital in Varanasi and a medical center and a research facility. That is why we are funding scholarships for the benefit of the victims—"

"Mr. Amlani, I warned you about speeches," Pilot admonished him.

"Your honor, I know what matters to the commission. I know what matters to the victims. I have concerned myself with little else these past months. That is why I can pledge to you now, without any direction from the government, that Renown Industries, on its own initiative, has invested the Renown Trust with sufficient funds to begin making compensation payments to the victims of Varanasi immediately. We are ready to begin the processing of all legitimate claims now . . . today. And I give you my word before God, before everyone present here today, payments on those claims will be made no later than two weeks from submission—so people can get on with the business of rebuilding their lives. . . ."

The mood in the room changed yet again. Astonishment turned to excitement, excitement to relief, and relief to calculation as minds turned to thoughts of the money that would flow.

Even Sansi had to acknowledge its brilliance. Amlani was bribing the entire country, out in the open, with Pilot's blessing. It put the whole purpose of the commission in doubt. Without the fuel of public indignation, the commission's role would be merely punitive. Eventually—and Amlani, with his genius for public manipulation, would see to it—it would be seen as something worse, as something that was pointlessly vindictive.

"You are only half right, Mr. Amlani," Pilot said, his amplified voice cutting through the commotion. "This commission will ensure that the victims of Varanasi are adequately compensated for their suffering. But I will remind you, the commission is also concerned with matters of criminal liability."

Amlani seemed to relish Pilot's remarks the way an actor relishes a cue.

"Then the commission would not deny me the right to speak the truth in my defense," Amlani demanded. "I will submit to the demands of dharma but I will not submit to the demands of a corrupt investigator."

He turned and pointed at Sansi and every eye followed the accusing finger: "That man is a disgrace to the process of law."

Sansi felt his face burn with impotent rage. He lowered his gaze against the blaze of flashbulbs, and to some it must have seemed like a look of shame.

"When the existence of the Renown Trust was known only to a few, your honor, that man came to my house here in New Delhi to seek a position with the trust. He came to ask for a job that paid higher than this one. Another job that would help him enrich himself on the suffering of others, to continue gorging himself off this tragedy like the parasite he is—"

"Mr. Amlani . . ." Pilot shouted into his microphone. But his voice was scarcely heard through the new uproar that engulfed the room.

"He told me the minister was out to get me and it was up to him to decide if she pressed the investigation . . ."

The public benches erupted in turmoil as people who had come to the commission as allies now turned on each other.

". . . and when I refused him, he said he would destroy me. . . ."

Reporters surged from their seats, past the restraining rope, shouting questions at Sansi. Police pushed them back. Beside him Sansi heard another voice shouting the word "liar" at Amlani. Even the stolid, imperturbable Chowdhary had been pushed beyond the limits of tolerance.

"Check with his office in Bombay," Amlani urged the swarming reporters. "He has been taking gifts and bribes ever since he got this job. . . ."

Somewhere in the distance Sansi heard Pilot order the room cleared. But it was too late. Amlani the rabble-rouser had won. Sansi shut his eyes against the blinding barrage of flashbulbs and saw only the damning calligraphy of accusations that burned into his brain.

CHAPTER 27

"**D**id you read the newspapers this morning?" Rupe asked.
"I decided I would deny myself the pleasure," Sansi
answered.

"You have to do something about that guilty look of yours,"
she said. "You haven't acquired the brazen stare of the politician
yet. If you are going to have a career as an advocate, you'll have
to work on that."

"I didn't think I had a reputation to worry about before yesterday," Sansi said. "Till I saw what Amlani did with it."

"It was you who warned me it was going to get dirty," Rupe
reminded him.

"I haven't seen any demands for your resignation yet," Pilot
told Sansi. "I have had three already, one from the *Times*. I must
be doing something right."

It was a little after eight and the three of them sat around
Rupe's desk drinking coffee. She had called an early meeting to
discuss the fallout from the previous day's debacle before Pilot
returned to the Justice Ministry to chair that day's session.

"It's not all bad," Rupe added. "Not everybody was taken in by Amlani's little act yesterday."

"A lot of people will be," Sansi said, "because they want to be."

"Well, I have been up since five and I've read all the papers." She looked pointedly at Sansi. "And my staff taped all the TV and radio newscasts. There is plenty of criticism for the three of us, but it is not so much because of what Amlani did as because of what we are not doing. We are not making a case against him. He is making us look bad because we are making ourselves look bad." She pushed a sheaf of newspapers toward Sansi. "Most of them agree Amlani is long overdue for some sort of action by the government—the consensus is we aren't up to the job."

"We have a substantial body of evidence to show complicity," Sansi said. "Without at least one witness to testify directly on criminal misconduct, the bulk of the evidence is circumstantial, but convictions have been won in the past on circumstantial evidence less compelling than this. And we are trying all the time to find other witnesses." He paused, reluctant to criticize Pilot but knowing it had to be said. "A public inquiry is a showcase for somebody like Amlani—he won't find it so easy to disrupt a court proceeding."

Rupe didn't look convinced. "Who's coming up today?" she asked.

"The factory manager before Agawarl, I believe," Pilot answered. "And the woman who was the secretary to both of them."

"What will they say?"

"They will contradict much of what Amlani said yesterday," Sansi said. "The manager was pressured by Amlani and his son, Arvind, to dump the phosphorous before he was replaced by Agawarl. The secretary will testify about the pressure the Amlanis put on both of them."

Rupe shook her head. "One person's word against another—

and Amlani has all that documentation supporting his version of events. I assume it looks authentic?"

"We're going over it," Sansi said, but his tone wasn't hopeful. They all knew Amlani wouldn't surrender any document without knowing it would withstand close forensic examination.

"I want him arrested," Rupe said. "I want him out of circulation before he does any more harm to the investigation."

Sansi glanced at Pilot but the judge's eyes, hidden in the folds of his face, revealed nothing.

"On what charges?" Sansi asked.

"He admitted liability on behalf of his corporation yesterday," Pilot suggested.

"That won't keep him in jail an hour," Sansi said. "He must have filed for anticipatory bail by now."

Anticipatory bail was another anomaly of the Indian justice system. It allowed suspects to avoid the inconvenience of a remand to custody when they were charged. It was intended, among other things, to cut back the number of cases in which a defendant languished in jail for years on trivial charges while waiting for his case to come to trial. It had instead become a favorite tool of the rich, who used it to make sure they never spent a night in jail.

"Obstruction of justice," Rupe said. "I spoke with lawyers from the Justice Ministry last night. Involvement in the death of a witness will allow us to hold him for ninety days. That should give you enough time to find other witnesses who will talk."

"We can't prove involvement," Sansi said. "Not yet."

"Suspicion is enough," Rupe said. "Other people have been held on lesser charges. Justice will issue the warrant. Just send them the paperwork."

Sansi grimaced.

"You don't like it?" There was an edge to her voice.

"It presents problems."

"What kind of problems?"

"I want to win this case," he said. "But not like this."

"But you're not winning it," she said tersely. "And you won't win it as long as he's free to bribe, intimidate, and kill witnesses. If we detain him, if we put him behind bars, it might reassure those potential witnesses we know are out there."

Sansi realized it wasn't just her confidence in Pilot that was waning. She was getting desperate. And this was exactly the kind of maneuver he was afraid she would try when she got desperate. He also knew that if he didn't go along with Rupe's decision, there was every chance he would lose Amlani. Rupe had all the power of government at her disposal and she was ready to use it. He had to decide if he was willing to lend his hand to hers, to wield the blunt instrument of power to suit his own ends—precisely the kind of thing he had despised Jamal for doing at Crime Branch.

"If we don't find something in ninety days we will have to go with what we've got," he warned. "And it could prejudice the entire case. He could beat us on conspiracy."

"Then you have ninety days to come up with something that will stick," she said.

Sansi's mind went back to the meeting with Rupe in the Taj Mahal Hotel when she had first asked him to direct the investigation. He remembered the misgivings he'd had, the certainty that a moment like this would come, and wondering then which way he would lean. Whether he would have the courage to resist the pressures that would be brought to bear on him, whether he would be able to resist the temptations of power. He remembered the crude appeal to ego—the opportunity to do something important for India and for justice. And he remembered Annie's warning that however noble his aspirations might be, in the end it would still come down to politics. He had made his decision back then, he realized, and hadn't even known it. But Annie had.

"I will make the case," he said.

"Prove obstruction and you've proved the case," she

answered. "Then everybody will congratulate us for putting him in jail early."

"When do you want us to make the arrest?" he asked.

"Get the paperwork over to Justice as soon as you can," she answered. "I will speak to the Prime Minister and let him know it is coming."

"You think Amlani will try to get to the Prime Minister?" Pilot asked.

"He'll try," Rupe said. She paused and seemed to consider how much more she should tell Pilot and Sansi. Then she made up her mind. "You remember the Tripura scandal, the no-confidence vote when eight members of the BJP crossed the floor to keep Congress in government?"

Both Sansi and Pilot remembered. It was the lowest point in the history of the BJP and kept them out of power another six years.

"That was Amlani," she said. "He paid them enough so they wouldn't have to worry about giving up a career in politics."

"Are Bapre," Pilot murmured. "He bought the government?"

"One of them was supposed to be Mani," she said. "Kanchi Patel, Congress's bagman in Bombay, came to our apartment one night. He said Amlani would pay two hundred thousand American dollars to any bank account anywhere in the world if Mani would cross the floor. Mani said no. The others couldn't."

Sansi thought that Amlani seemed to have a talent for bringing out the worst in everyone.

"So Amlani was telling the truth," he said. "It is personal."

Rupe smiled faintly.

"It is personal for all of us now, isn't it?" she said.

■   ■

Amlani swam beneath a layer of cloud so hot and oppressive it seemed to weigh on the city like a giant hand. When he was finished he felt worse, not better, and when he stepped from the pool he was so light-headed he had to rest for a moment on a servant's arm.

His doctors had warned him that stress would kill him, that diet and exercise alone wouldn't save him. He knew he was in a race with death. He could hear its footsteps in the blood that pounded in his ears, feel its vibration in his clotted arteries. But it was a race he had to finish; he would rather die than abandon it.

If he could only last another few months—long enough to get the government off his back, to secure a huge new infusion of American capital, to bring the Americans on board as full partners, to assure the success of Renown Oil. Then he could step down. Then his empire would be strong enough to withstand anything, including the bumbling of his own children.

A shower didn't make him feel any better, and when he peered closely at himself in the mirror, he saw a worrisome sallowness under his skin. It was enough that he decided to ignore the advice of his doctors completely. He had his coffee with condensed milk and disdained the dry toast for a fatty paratha with onions and chilis. With death such a close companion, he decided he was due some pleasure in the time he had left.

A little past seven he called Ushar; moments later a bell announced his arrival. Ushar wore a shiny bronze suit with a bile-colored shirt and a gold-and-red-striped company tie. He twitched his carpet pile hairline and wished his employer a good morning but Amlani only grunted as he got into the elevator. Ushar guessed it was going to be a very unpleasant day for a great many people and he would have to tread carefully to avoid being one of them.

The garage had no windows and was brightly lit twenty-four hours a day, 365 days a year. It was equipped with security cameras and a guard booth that was always occupied by at least two men. When the elevator doors opened, two black Mercedes waited, their engines running. In the lead car were a driver and two bodyguards. A third bodyguard opened the rear door of the second car for Amlani. Ushar got in after him and the bodyguard closed the door then went around to the other side so that Amlani had a man on either side. As an added precaution the doors on Amlani's car were armored and the windows shatterproof.

The first car led the way down the ramp to the street exit, where a half-dozen guards saluted as the security door cranked open and Amlani's little convoy drove out onto Cuffe Parade. The sun was struggling to break through the deadening cloud, so the street was drenched in a sepia haze. Early cooking fires glimmered among the huddled forms of the poor. Kulis with barrows moved slowly through the murk in the direction of Sassoon Dock and old women crawled on the pavement on bony knees, laying out fish scales to dry.

"Ushar, I need your advice on a matter of great concern to me," Amlani said as his car hissed down the center of the road in the direction of Renown House. "It will be necessary for Arvind to be there, so after we—"

Something hit the lead car, there was an explosion, smoke poured from the hood and the car shimmied violently. Instinctively the driver of Amlani's car stepped on the brakes.

"Don't stop," Ushar yelled. "Pass him, keep going."

He grabbed the back of Amlani's neck and pushed him down to the floor. Amlani grunted under the sudden exertion. Beside them the bodyguard, pistol in hand, twisted in his seat looking for the source of the attack, but saw no one.

The lead car veered wildly from one side of the road to the other, its driver blinded by the fumes pouring up from the hood and over the windshield. The car bounced over the curb, its wheels snatching a sleeping figure off the sidewalk, dragging it under the car and spilling it out behind, limbs flailing.

"I can't get past," Amlani's driver shouted, panicking. There was a loud crack on the roof on the driver's side; a burst of shrapnel and what looked like water cascaded over the car. The water turned instantly to milk, smearing the windows and wind-shield. Then the milk started to smoke and a bitter stench filled the car.

"Maderchod!" The driver turned on the wipers but they only streaked the smoldering milky fluid, spreading it, blinding them too. Crumbs of molten rubber flew from the wiper blades and the windshield started to crackle and star. A hole appeared in the glass and the liquid ran inside. The driver put up a hand to stop it and it ran across his fingers and down his arm. He con-vulsed and screamed in agony. He took his other hand off the wheel and clawed at his arm as if trying to tear away the flesh.

The car swerved and rocked and there was a shriek of metal as they careened along a brick wall. Sparks spumed up from the side of the car. More holes appeared in the windshield and holes appeared in the roof, like bullet holes, only ragged and smol-dering. More of the lethal liquid splashed inside onto the driver's scalp. He tore at his hair and clothes then lunged across the seat, opened the passenger door and threw himself out onto the street. The car swerved, hit something and jolted to a stop, trapped between a building and a palm tree.

Ushar kicked open the rear window and together he and the bodyguard dragged Amlani out of the car to an alleyway filled with shanties. Everywhere people were screaming, running. Ushar saw their driver run to the harbor wall and throw himself into the water to douse the invisible flames that consumed him. But there was no crack of gunshots, no shrapnel, no explosions. Just the clamorous sounds of terror.

Together Ushar and the bodyguard hauled Amlani into the alleyway, out of sight of the street. They pushed into a shanty, propped Amlani against the wall and crouched inside the doorway, guns ready. But no one came.

After several minutes Ushar walked cautiously to the end of the alley and peered into the street. He scanned the rooftops of the surrounding buildings, but their attackers could not be seen.

Amlani's car stood fifty feet away, where they had left it, its engine racing. The street was deserted though hundreds of people stood in side roads and doorways watching. There was no sign of the lead car. Ushar thought it must have escaped, its occupants with it, forgetting whom they were supposed to protect. If they were wise, he thought, they wouldn't come back.

He put away his gun, walked to the car and shut off the engine. The silence was immediate and eerie. Then he stood back and surveyed the damage.

The windshield was gone, little more than a rind of broken glass around the edges. The driver's side window too was no more than jagged remnants. The holes in the roof had expanded into a ragged gash. There was a dent in the roof and the paint all around it was scorched and peeling. New paint blisters appeared as he watched and milky traces of smoke wisped upward. Fragments of thick green glass, what he'd thought was shrapnel, left a crooked, smoldering trail along the road like green jewels. The smell was enough to burn his eyes and throat. He knew what it was. He had smelled it before.

It was acid. Sulfuric acid.

A few onlookers ventured tentatively back out onto the street, then more, and the silence was replaced by excited chatter as they surrounded the wrecked car. From the corner at the end of the block, a young man watched with his new goondah friends. Raffee had missed this time. But he would try again. And next time he would make sure.

CHAPTER 28

Rupe's car hissed across the wet tarmac of Palam Airport shielded by a gauntlet of army jeeps. The lights of the lead jeep swept the fuselage of an aging Tupolev cargo jet then veered sharply off into the rainy New Delhi night, settling on the perimeter fence a quarter mile away and the sodden shanties beyond.

The convoy stopped with Rupe's car beside the boarding ramp, and she waited while the soldiers threw a protective cordon around the plane and Ramani checked inside the aircraft. He returned a moment later with an air force captain carrying an umbrella to shield the minister from a sooty rain that stained everything it touched.

It was late, and Rupe would have preferred not to be flying to Bokaro Steel City at all. But she had delayed the trip twice already, and had to be there at ten the next morning to broker a meeting between the two sides in a dispute between the steel plant and a government power station. Both plants were on the Damodar River, which had the distinction of being the most polluted river in India. Eighteen months earlier the steel plant had spilled seventy thousand gallons of furnace oil into the river. The oil had ignited inside the boilers of the power plant, which used water from the Damodar in its cooling processes. The resulting explosion and fire had shut down the plant and set the river ablaze, which in turn had threatened to ignite the Ranigunj coalfields. The death toll was minor by Indian standards; fewer than a hundred. What was important was that both sides were now close to an agreement which, at Rupe's insistence, was to include a new filtration plant for the five million people who got their drinking water from the Damodar.

Rupe hurried up the ramp, followed by Hemali and a couple of ministerial secretaries, and into the Tupolev, which had changed little since it was converted to a ministerial transport in the late 1960s. The color scheme was Aeroflot drab and the furnishings vintage sixties, with foam rubber cushions whose contents spewed from the many tears and rents like vomit. Senior cabinet ministers flew in marginally better style, their decor upgraded to the 1970s, while the Prime Minister enjoyed the airborne comforts of the almost contemporary 1980s.

Rupe and Hemali went directly to the tail section, where there was a sitting area with a couple of vinyl-backed chairs at a bench that doubled as a meal table and a work station. The two secretaries took their seats in the forward section of the plane with Ramani and the rest of Rupe's escort.

After takeoff a late supper was served, then Rupe settled down to some paperwork with Hemali. But it was close to midnight, Rupe found it hard to keep her eyes focused on the pages in front of her, and it was obvious Hemali wanted to be with the others in the forward section, where conversation was more lighthearted. Rupe let her go. Hemali's flirtation with Ramani had advanced to full-blown romance in the past few weeks and Rupe thought it churlish to stand in their way. Ramani had gone so far as to give Hemali a new overnight bag for all the trips she took, and there had been jokes among the staff about the real purpose of the bag.

Rupe decided she would call Sansi on the radio phone. She hadn't spoken to him since their meeting with Pilot ten days earlier—it had taken that long to get a private meeting with the Prime Minister. Finally, she'd seen him for half an hour that morning, and it was pretty much as she had feared. The Prime Minister was nervous at the thought of jailing Amlani prematurely and on insufficient evidence, no matter what mayhem Amlani wrought on the investigation and all those who cooperated with it. Reluctantly he had agreed, but she was afraid he would change his mind if someone else got to him in the next few days, and she wanted to make sure the request for Amlani's arrest warrant would be at the Justice Ministry in the morning.

When she got through to the operations center, Chowdhary said Sansi had just left, but when she tried the bungalow at G Block, there was no answer. She decided to call again in a few minutes and closed her eyes. She was startled to be awakened two hours later, when they commenced their descent into Allahabad for refueling. The stopover at Allahabad was ninety minutes of tedium. The only blessing was that they had left the black rain of Delhi behind and were able to stretch their legs and enjoy the clear night air for a while.

Soon after they were airborne on the final leg to Bokaro, she tried Sansi again, but the weather in Delhi was still bad and it was hard to get a clear link. At last the communications officer patched her through to Delhi control tower on a secure wavelength and they relayed the call to Sansi's number. She heard the phone ring and smiled when she saw the time. It was five minutes to four in the morning. He was going to be annoyed.

A brilliant arc of light appeared in the forward section of the plane, expanded till it filled the entire fuselage and rushed toward her with a roar. The plane juddered and dipped and all sound ceased. Then she saw patches of night sky and bodies tumbling against the stars. She felt her breath torn from every recess of her body and a cold, scouring wind that stripped away all flesh and feeling. The memories of a lifetime were discarded in a blur until only one remained, the faces of her children, Arjun and Sonal, luminous and uncomprehending, soundlessly mouthing her name. Then they vanished too. Rupe was consumed by the chill black vacuum of space and all consciousness stopped.

Conditioned to bad news in the middle of the night, Sansi awakened quickly and picked up the phone on the third ring. There was only a deafening blare of static on the line. For a moment he thought he heard something more, a distant scream. Then the connection went dead and there was nothing.

■   ■

It was the biggest funeral Delhi had seen since the funeral of Indira Gandhi.

A million mourners watched Rupe's funeral procession make its way down the broad avenue of Rajpath, through the high sandstone arch of India Gate, along Mahatma Gandhi Marg, past the black marble slab at Raj Ghat where the Mahatma was cremated, to Vijay Ghat on the western shore of the Yamuna River.

What remained of Rupe's body was sewn inside a white cotton sheet and wrapped in a gold and white silk shroud. It rested on a bier covered with gold and white marigolds, which was carried on a gun carriage drawn by six horses and escorted by troopers of the president's bodyguard. Security in the capital was the heaviest Sansi could remember. Armed soldiers stood every few feet along the funeral route to protect the mourners who walked behind, including the Prime Minister, the cabinet, chief ministers, governors, and ambassadors from more than fifty nations. Armored cars guarded every intersection and trucks filled with soldiers in full combat uniform stood in the side streets. Air traffic at both Delhi's airports was suspended while the funeral was in progress.

The day was as somber as the ceremony, the sun shrouded by layers of leaden cloud, the enormous crowd subdued. There was no hysteria, no wailing, no mass outpouring of grief or anger. It was as if the country had given up on itself. As if a mass awareness had taken root that India was beyond hope, that it was a country that could never be saved from itself. Rupe's karma was India's karma, and its destiny was what it had always been—corruption and chaos.

A platform with a white canvas awning had been set up at Vijay Ghat. In the front row were the Prime Minister and the president, too frail to walk the funeral route. With them were Rupe's family and Mani's family, remnants of a dynasty denied its promised greatness. With them were Rupe's children; Sonal with shadows under her eyes that should never have been seen on a child, and Arjun with his head shaved, trembling in the heat, determined to do his duty—to carry the lighted brand that would ignite his mother's funeral pyre. Near the back were Sansi with Pramila and Pilot, all of them dressed in the white robes of mourning.

Soldiers carried the bier to a granite slab at the top of the burning ghats, where a pyre of sandalwood logs had been built shoulder high. Brahmin priests in white robes descended from the platform and circled the pyre, sprinkling incense to purify Rupe's remains in preparation for *moksha*.

The eulogies went on long into the afternoon and ended with the Prime Minister, who spoke longest of all. He ended with a solemn vow that evil would not be permitted to triumph, that Rupe's spirit would be preserved and her work continued. Sansi listened numbly, scarcely able to believe she was gone.

With a start he realized the Prime Minister had finished speaking. In front of the platform a priest lit a torch from a flaming urn and held it aloft. Silence bore down on the great crowd like a thick cloud. Rupe's father got up from his seat, took Arjun's hand and led him down from the platform. The torch dipped when the priest handed it to Arjun, and for a moment it looked as if it might drop, but his grandfather steadied his hand. He paused for a moment then walked to the pyre and circled it in short, rapid steps, almost running, as if in a hurry to get it over with before he lost his nerve. On the third circle he stepped forward and pushed the brand into the kindling under the logs.

The flames leaped up violently and seemed to reach out for Arjun, but his grandfather grabbed him, pulled him away and walked him quickly back to his seat. Arjun sat beside his sister quite still, but then his eggshell head bowed forward and he began to cry. In the space between the chairs Sansi saw Sonal take his hand.

The fire flared into an inferno and a thick column of smoke leaned up into the clouds. There was a moan from the crowd and, despite the press of people, a feeling of great emptiness. Sansi waited till it was dark and the last embers had died. Then he went down to the pyre and filled a small vial with some ashes.

■ ■

A cleansing wind gusted down overnight from the distant Himalayas and swept the city of its dirt brown mantle. The morning was sunny and seemed unnaturally bright as Sansi got out of his car at Judge Pilot's house.

The judge lived with his wife in a narrow, two-story town house in the dowdy but upscale Kailash Colony in the south end of the city. Sansi was concerned to find only three soldiers at the front gate. After Rupe's death he thought security would have been increased, not decreased.

An elderly manservant greeted Sansi at the front door and took him to the judge, who waited in his study. The study was dark and surprisingly small for a big man, its smallness emphasized by ceiling-high shelves stacked with legal reference books and bound editions of historic judgments. A pair of glass doors looked out at a tiny, walled-in lawn which added to the feeling of closeness.

The judge was pouring himself coffee from a stainless steel flask when Sansi appeared.

"You drink coffee in the morning, don't you, George?" the judge inquired.

"Not at the moment," Sansi said.

The judge waggled his head. "Something else, perhaps? Chai, fruit juice, a glass of water?"

"I can't stay long," Sansi said. "I'm on my way to the Justice Ministry and then on to Bombay. I want to make the arrest personally tomorrow morning."

The judge was half turned away from Sansi but his silence suggested something was wrong. He turned and gestured Sansi to take a seat.

"You may as well sit down," he said. "I don't think you'll get anywhere at Justice today."

There was an inflection to the judge's words that gave Sansi pause. He sat down while the judge maneuvered his awkward body into the swivel chair behind his desk.

"They haven't told you, have they?"

"Told me what?" Sansi said.

Pilot sighed. "The Justice minister called me this morning. The commission has been suspended. If it resumes, I won't be chairman."

Sansi slumped back in the chair.

"Most of my guards were stood down this morning," Pilot added. "That is the good news, I suppose. I am no longer a threat to anyone so I am no longer in danger."

"The investigation?" Sansi asked, already knowing the answer.

Pilot shook his head. "They are such cowards," he said wearily. He prodded his coffee cup with his long, bony fingers, looking for the words. "The investigation will be turned over to the federal police. You will be notified officially in a day or two, I suppose."

Sansi put a hand to his forehead. "What about yesterday? What the Prime Minister said about continuing Rupe's work?

The government wanted her to get Amlani—it was why she was brought into the cabinet."

"Politics," Pilot said. "Just politics."

"Bhagwan," Sansi moaned softly. "He's won. Amlani's won."

"Perhaps we deluded ourselves from the beginning," Pilot said. "Perhaps we never were a threat to Amlani, we or the government. The most we were able to do was inconvenience him a little. That's all we are, I think—the police, judges, government. We're only an inconvenience to a man like Amlani. It's people like him who really run India, not people like us."

Sansi got up abruptly, startling the judge.

"This is an emotional time for all of us," Pilot said anxiously. "Please don't do anything in haste—"

"I have to go," Sansi muttered, distracted.

"Where—" Pilot began, but Sansi was already at the door.

"To collect our evidence," he said. "Before somebody else does."

CHAPTER 29

Sansi walked into his office at Lentin Chambers feeling as if he had been away six years rather than six months.

His first impression was that he didn't belong there, that it wasn't his office anymore. Or perhaps it was the imposing presence of Mukherjee's aunt Uma, who had set up her desk front and center like a barricade so she could receive or repel visitors at her pleasure. Uma was a big woman with a girlish smile and eyes that said she would throw him to the ground and sit on him if he gave her trouble. But there was no sign of Neisha and, Sansi was relieved to see, no piles of loot.

He introduced himself to Aunt Uma, who came out from behind her desk and lunged at him. It was intended as a bob of respect, he realized, and it was only her size that made it threatening, but still she reminded him of a trained elephant going down on one knee.

"Sansi, sahib," Mukherjee said, striding out from his office, teeth and hair shining. "How happy I am you are seeing me, now the old place is being quite the same."

"Yes, sorry about that," Sansi said. He continued through to his office and was met by the reassuring smells of disuse and stale linoleum. Gratefully, he set his heavy briefcase down on the desk.

"Not enough excitement around here to hold Neisha's interest?" he asked.

"Neisha is having many irons in her fire," Mukherjee answered. "This week she is doing very exciting things with horses."

Sansi pushed the image from his mind, slid into his chair, and turned on his computer. "How is our caseload?"

"Oh, plenty of work, sahib." Mukherjee grinned. "Always plenty of work."

"For you perhaps," Sansi said. "How many calls for me?"

Mukherjee looked apologetic. "Not so many calls, sahib."

"As in none."

"Now you are back, and as soon as the word is getting out, sahib, I am sure—"

"I doubt it," Sansi said, cutting him off. As soon as the gifts started going back, as soon as word spread that he had bungled the investigation, that he was just the latest in a long line of Amlani victims, he knew the offers would dry up. He had no power, no connections, no influence. He wasn't worth bribing anymore.

He was relieved to be left alone even though it was the loneliness of the pariah. He had his future to consider, he had to talk to Annie—and there was unfinished business with Amlani. He had to move soon, before Amlani moved against him. And it would come soon, he knew, within days, not weeks.

He spent the rest of the day downloading onto his computer the diskettes he had brought back from Delhi, all the evidence he and Chowdhary and the investigative team had accumulated over the past six months. Then he made two copies of each and wrote a summary for the benefit of the lawyers who would see them. By the time he was finished it was getting dark, and

Mukherjee and Aunt Uma both stopped by his office to wish him good night.

When they had gone he locked the door and secreted the original diskettes in various places around the empty office so if Amlani's people came looking they might assume they were the only copies. Not for long, perhaps, but long enough for Sansi to do what he needed.

Finally, he packed both sets of copies into his briefcase and let himself out. There were a couple of lightbulbs missing in the top floor corridor, so the area at the top of the stairs was tented in darkness. The building was quiet and felt empty. The usual scrape and banter of the security guards four floors below was absent. Sansi walked warily to the lift, poised for the touch of a hand, the sudden rush of footsteps. He checked the lift cage before getting in, and on the way down every grunt and clang sounded like a threat. When he opened the gate, the ground floor corridor was empty, the guards' metal stools unoccupied and the door to the street open and unattended. It felt wrong. Then he recognized the sound of laughter from outside. Both guards were out front on the sidewalk, sharing a smoke, chatting with a guard from the building across the street.

Sansi bid them good night and walked quickly to the junction of Mahatma Gandhi Road and Nariman Road, where he waved down a taxi from the passing stampede. He told the driver to take him to the departures terminal at Sahar International Airport. There, he gave further directions, and at the Federal Express air freight terminal paid the driver off and told him not to wait.

Inside, he put the two sets of diskettes into separate express packs, both to go out that evening to separate addresses in Europe. The clerk guaranteed they would go directly from the terminal to the plane with only Customs in between. Sansi gave him two thousand rupees to get around the Customs check.

Back outside he walked to the passenger arrivals terminal,

his step and his briefcase lighter, and took a taxi back to Malabar Hill. But he wasn't ready to go home yet. One more thing remained. When they reached Walkeshar Road he told the driver to keep going past his apartment building, toward Malabar Point. He got out a scant hundred yards from the front gates of the governor's estate at Raj Bhavan.

Sansi watched the taxi pull away, then stood conspicuously on the busy footpath and checked the oncoming cars and passing faces for any sign of interest or evasiveness. But no one avoided his gaze, no one turned around abruptly, no one drove too fast or too slow. He turned and continued up the road, past the expensive apartment buildings, another businessman heading home after a long day at the office.

Between the last two apartment buildings before the governor's estate was an alleyway barely wide enough for two men to stand abreast. Sansi turned into it and broke into a run. He had to be careful when he reached the end because it was slippery and there was a spiked iron railing to stop people from getting in off the shore. But there was a nook where the wall ended. Sansi tucked himself in and looked back down the alley. No one followed, no one seemed interested in the man who had darted suddenly down the darkened alleyway.

While the main entrances to all the apartment buildings were on the Walkeshar Road side, the fronts all faced the other way, their gardens and balconies overlooking Back Bay and the city skyline on the opposite shore. Every garden was protected against waterborne thieves and intruders by high, well-maintained fences. The cement ledge where Sansi perched was the foundation for a chain-link fence wrapped around a scrubby patch of lawn with a few scuffed white plastic chairs and tables scattered around. The ledge continued out over the rocky shoreline.

When Sansi was young, he and his friends had been able to clamber around the ledge with the speed and agility of monkeys.

They had to. Residents who saw them would rush out and poke them through the fence with broom handles.

Sansi was relieved there was no moon and the night sky was cloudy. It took him almost twenty minutes to make his way around the ledge to the drop-off down to the path. The drop was about six feet, and he was afraid that in the intervening years a spiked railing had been placed there too. With one hand holding the fence, he eased himself down the cement wall. He probed clumsily with his feet but felt nothing and let himself go. There were no spikes, but the rocks were slippery and he turned his ankle. It would make getting back harder—and getting back had always been the hardest part.

The footpath was where he remembered it: a stone and shingle track that followed the shoreline beneath the ramparts of Raj Bhavan, blocked by occasional boulders that had to be climbed over. He limped and climbed his way through the treacherous darkness, stumbling occasionally, grazing his knees, streaking his suit trousers with seaweed.

At last he was near the cove. He stopped and listened for voices, afraid the place might already be occupied by teenagers doing exactly the kinds of thing he used to do. But he heard nothing, and when he peeked over the last ledge, he saw the cove was empty. A darkly glistening scallop in the shoreline with a thumbnail crescent of sand at the top big enough for a half-dozen people if they sat close enough, or for two if they were lying down.

Sansi crunched the last few feet over the shingle then sank down into the sand to get his breath. He couldn't remember the last time he had been there. At least thirty years ago. He propped himself against a rock and watched the milky surf rush up the beach toward him then recede with a clatter of stones. Behind the black basin of water were the lights of Marine Drive, only their amber glow visible from this position.

In the darkness, between the eternities of land and sea, it

was easy to drift back, to imagine himself youthful again, unafraid of the future and all the harms it would bring. The dampness in the sand leached through his clothes and he shivered despite the warmth of the night.

Quickly, he took off his shoes and socks and rolled up his pant legs. Then he opened his briefcase, unzipped the inside pocket and took out a metal vial. The shingle bit at his feet when he walked down the beach, and the water felt warm and greasy on his skin, like dishwater. He had to tread carefully because the beach sloped steeply and the shingle shifted under his feet. He felt the water slop over his rolled-up pants and thought he would make quite a sight walking home.

He unscrewed the metal cap and paused, wondering if he should say something. It was only sandalwood ash, he knew. It was hardly likely there was even an atom of her mixed in with it. But he'd wanted to do something, some kind of private ritual to show respect for what had passed between them. She would enjoy seeing him like this, he thought. Sentimental and ridiculous. About to be slapped into the surf by a wave if he didn't get on with it. He turned the vial over and scattered the gray powder in a single arc. It vanished instantly.

When he got home it was after midnight and Pramila was waiting for him out on the roof garden. She looked at his wet clothes, the green-brown stains and crumbs of seaweed clinging to his trousers, but she didn't ask where he had been.

"Annie called," she said.

Sansi stared numbly at his mother. "How did she sound?" he asked.

"She's leaving for America," Pramila answered. "If you have anything you want to tell her you'd better hurry."

■   ■

"Friday," Annie said. "The three fifty-five to Tokyo, then on to L.A."

Sansi looked around her apartment. It already appeared

unlived-in, perhaps because it was the first time he had seen it tidy. Annie left things lying around—wine bottles, plates, clothes, newspapers, magazines, books, pictures, letters, tapes, souvenirs, parcels from home, the usual flotsam of the expatriate. Now the floor was clear, cushions were in their proper places, flower vases and fruit bowls were empty. She'd even taken the funny newspaper clippings and snapshots off the refrigerator.

"It's bigger than I realized," he said.

"That's what I thought," she said. "Do you want a drink? I've got beer, mineral water—there are a few limes left somewhere, I think. I could make tea if you want?"

Standing in the middle of the living room with his hands in his pockets, he felt like an uninvited guest. He looked at all the familiar things that now felt unfamiliar because he had lost the right to make himself at home. The carpet under his feet where she had given him a massage, the sofa where they first made love, the tiny balcony where she once stood naked in the monsoon.

"Are you coming back?" he asked.

"I don't know," she said. "That's what I have to decide."

She wore jeans and a red T-shirt, and stood barefoot in the doorway to the kitchen. She seemed far more relaxed than him, but the distance between them now was emphasized in every word and gesture.

"The lease is up in two and a half months," she said. "The rent is paid till then. I'm putting a few things in storage just in case. The super said he'd send them on."

"Do you have to go?"

"Yeah," she said. "I do." She leaned against the doorjamb. "There's too much shit here for me to think clearly. I have to put some distance between me and everything that's happened before I can even start to figure out what I want to do."

"Including me?"

She laughed softly.

Sansi sighed. "Can I sit down?"

"Sure, do you want that drink?"

"No, thank you."

The enormity of all that had happened in the past few months bore down on them suddenly in weighted silence.

"Did you resign from the paper?"

"Three weeks ago."

Sansi grimaced. "I'm sorry."

"About what in particular?"

"That you didn't . . . feel you could call me."

"I knew you had your hands full."

She smiled slightly at the unintended irony.

"Have you looked for anything else?"

"There's stuff around . . ." Then she shrugged. "No. I stopped."

He paused to take a breath. "Annie, it wasn't planned. It wasn't something I expected. But it happened. I wish an apology were enough. I wish I could go back and undo it, but I can't."

From her expression he saw she had already pulled back considerably in the time they had been apart. She might already be inaccessible.

"I told Rupe afterward it wouldn't happen again," he added. "I told her I was in love with you."

Annie nodded, and there was something almost matter-of-fact in the gesture.

"Are you sure about that?" she asked.

"Yes, I'm sure," he answered.

A kaleidoscope of emotions swirled behind her eyes then stopped as suddenly as they had appeared.

"It's not the sex. I don't mind that as much as you might think," she said. "I knew my husband was cheating on me a long time before I did anything about it. But I hung in because I wanted to give him a chance, I wanted to trust him again—and in the end it cost me a lot more." She paused. "You can't say it won't happen again. There's no way of knowing. And I don't know if I want to take the risk."

"I don't want you to go," he said. "I don't want you to give up on India because of me."

"Oh, everybody gives up on India sooner or later," she said, only half joking. "If you think about it, there's not a lot to keep me here, is there?"

"Stay for me," he said.

She folded her arms as if to buttress her resolve. "That's the problem isn't it? Who would I be staying for?"

"Am I so terrible?" he asked.

She shook her head. "You're not terrible. Sleeping with Rupe is only part of it. You've changed this past year, and I don't think you know how much. I watched you get more and more frustrated with the practice because it wasn't working out the way you hoped. I thought things would get better when you started getting better cases. Then this job with the commission came along and I saw the way you jumped at it. I knew then what it was."

Sansi listened dismally.

"You were so glad, so grateful to be back on the inside, back where the power was," Annie went on. "And everything else just kind of slipped into the background. Me included. I don't even think you knew it was happening. But I remember the way you were when I first came here. You were convinced you could beat these assholes without becoming like them. You wanted to make a point of it. But somewhere along the line something happened—it was too hard, you got tired, I don't know—and now you're turning into exactly the kind of person you used to hate."

She was right about everything but one thing, Sansi thought. He knew what was happening to him. He'd felt it and there didn't seem to be anything he could do to stop it.

"Annie, this isn't America," he said. "In America enough of

your institutions work enough of the time that people can still have some hope. Here, nothing works. The courts, the government, the Prime Minister, everybody can be bought or intimidated. In India if you have no power, you have nothing . . . you are nothing."

"I think you're right," she answered. "I think maybe the only way to do anything here is to be as bad as the people you have to beat. And I know I'm still in love with you. So if I stay here I'm going where you're going. And I don't know if I'm ready to do that."

CHAPTER 30

"Sahib, rupee, sahib."

The beggar stirred in a nest of shadows at the doorway to Sansi's apartment building. Sansi went to drop his taxi change into the outstretched hand but the beggar grabbed Sansi's wrist and pulled him down hard. Sansi grunted in surprise and stumbled. The beggar leaped nimbly to his feet, wrapped an arm around Sansi's neck and threw him to the ground. Sansi fought but then there were more hands on him, grabbing and lifting. He felt himself being carried swiftly through the darkness and thrown roughly into the open trunk of a waiting car. The door slammed shut behind him and the car accelerated away.

The whole thing had taken seconds. They were on a busy Bombay street in the early evening, and nobody had done a thing to stop it. Where were the security guards who were always at the front door? A couple of them had worked there since he was a boy. They were like family friends. Had Amlani bought them too?

He fought the motion of the car, feeling his way around the

trunk in the darkness, searching for a safety latch, a tire iron, a tool of any kind he could use to get out. There was nothing.

He lay on his back, pulled up his knees and tried to brace the soles of his feet against the trunk. He pushed with everything he had but there was no give. He squirmed around and used his heel to kick at the trunk lock, again and again. He kicked so hard his shoe heel chipped and split, but when he felt the lock he had made no impression at all. It wasn't an Indian car, he realized. It was solid, perhaps reinforced. He was trapped. They would let him out when they were ready, and then they would kill him.

The car slowed and turned and the noise of the street stopped. The car started to shudder and vibrate and there was the whiny rasp of tires on corrugated pavement. The trunk tilted backward and he rolled against the rear wall. They were going up a ramp. Soon, he realized. He squirmed around onto his knees and braced himself. He wouldn't go without a fight.

The car turned a few more times then stopped. The engine was shut off. He counted three doors closing, heard voices, footsteps, then nothing. For several long minutes there was only the thump of his heart, the sound of his own rapid breathing.

There was a click, a gentle hydraulic sigh, and a widening sliver of yellow light as the trunk opened. He pushed it hard but it insisted on opening at its own gentle pace. He saw a shape against the light and launched himself toward it, but whoever it was was ready. Sansi hit the floor badly, and before he could recover, powerful hands grabbed his arms and legs and splayed him flat against the cold cement, face down.

Nobody spoke to him and nobody moved him. He twisted his head and looked around. He was in a garage, empty and well-lit. The car was just visible behind him—a black Mercedes. He let his face rest against the floor, felt the cold of the cement against his skin, felt it seep into him, cold as death.

There was the distant clank of an elevator car, the moan of

wind in the shaft, and moments later the bump of its arrival. He heard the men who held him talking to each other in low voices then stop at the sound of approaching footsteps. The footsteps came to within a few feet then stopped.

"Let him up," Amlani said. "Hold onto him."

Sansi felt himself plucked from the floor as if he weighed nothing and set on his feet with dizzying suddenness. His knees buckled; the hands on his arms gripped tighter and he grimaced at the pain. When he opened his eyes again he found himself looking not at Amlani but at the face of a dead man.

Captain Ramani looked blankly back at him.

Amlani smiled, pleased by the expression of shock on Sansi's face.

"You see, if you were my friend, you would know I have the power of life and death," Amlani said.

He wasn't going mad, Sansi realized. Ramani was alive and standing in front of him. He hadn't died in the plane wreck after all. Then the pieces tumbled into place in front of him.

"You were the spy," he said weakly. "You were working for Amlani all the time."

"Captain Ramani's duty is to me, not India," Amlani said. "He knows I will take care of him. His country won't."

"All those people, your own men, people you swore to protect . . ." Sansi's voices was an echo of his disbelief. "You must have got off the plane at Allahabad—after you put the bomb on board."

"Hemali put the bomb on board," Ramani said matter-of-factly. "She carried it on herself in Delhi. It was in the lining of the bag I gave her. I didn't have to do a thing."

"And Hassan took his orders from you the night Agawarl was killed. You told him not to talk or the same thing would happen to him."

"Hassan is a dumb animal," Ramani said. "I didn't tell him to bite off his tongue."

"Everybody who trusted you," Sansi mumbled. "You betrayed them, you betrayed your country. . . ."

"My country is rotten," Ramani said. "Every politician in India is rotten—and they expect me to give up my life to protect them?"

Sansi's head lolled forward. He shook it, trying to clear it of the horrors that crowded in. Then a final dreadful realization . . .

"Mani . . . you killed Mani too. You killed both of them."

"Some people don't learn, Mr. Sansi," Amlani interjected. "You are one of them."

He signaled to someone standing to the side, out of Sansi's view. A man appeared with a canvas drawstring bag. He opened it and handed it to Amlani, who shook the contents out at Sansi's feet—all the computer disks he had copied at his office two days earlier and delivered to the airport, all his evidence against Amlani.

"The World Court in the Netherlands?" Amlani said, mockingly. "And Oxford, England? You have family in Oxford, don't you? Your father, I believe. A half brother and sister—they're not too fond of you either, are they? But your father paid for that law degree at Oxford, didn't he? He must be quite old now." He paused, enjoying himself. "I have friends in England too, Sansi. In London. Only an hour's drive from Oxford. You really have no shame, do you? You will use anybody, drag all the people you care about into your problems."

Sansi stared mutely at the diskettes scattered around his feet. Everything had stopped, all feeling, all sensation. He felt only a bitter, consuming hopelessness.

"Take them away with you," Amlani said. "Send them wherever you want. Do whatever you want. Waste the rest of your life trying to fight me if that's what you want. This is India, Mr. Sansi. In India I decide what happens to me. Not you. Not Pilot. Not the Prime Minister. Not anybody else."

Sansi looked uncomprehendingly at Amlani, not believing that he was to be let go, that he could take his evidence with him.

Amlani smiled a smile of satisfaction, his victory complete.

"You think I want you dead?" he asked. "You aren't important enough to kill, Mr. Sansi. You are nothing. I want you to spend the rest of your life knowing you are nothing. I want you to know that everything you've done and everything you do from this moment forward means nothing." He paused. "And I wish you a very long life, Mr. Sansi."

CHAPTER 31

Sansi slid into despair.

He called Mukherjee to say he would take some time off. Cheerfully, with more truth than tact, Mukherjee assured him no one would know he was missing. The truth was Sansi didn't know when he would be back.

He spent his time on the terrace, watching the weather change over Back Bay, turning the events of the past months over and over in his mind, analyzing where he had gone wrong, what he would do differently, and always arriving at the same answer. He had been out of his depth from the beginning. He had understood too late the extent of the evil he was up against. And it had cost him everything. It had cost him the woman he loved and the woman he might have loved. It had cost him his dignity and his name. He would have sold his soul to get Amlani—now he didn't even have that to sell.

Whenever he picked up a newspaper he was taunted by Amlani's success; the progress of the bidding war for Renown Oil, the winning bid of $470 million from Dumont, the soaring price of Renown stock. Tucked away on the inside pages he found reports of the newly reconstituted Commission of Inquiry into Varanasi scheduled to resume the following month with a new chairman, a career bureaucrat no one had ever heard of. Judge Pilot had stepped aside due to failing health brought about by the strain of the inquiry, the report said. He would not return to the bench. The man who replaced him said the commission would focus its energies on a regulatory overhaul of the environmental bureaucracy, especially SEPA. The new chairman added that, in order for the commission to do its job properly, there would be no deadline for a report on its findings. There was a quote from Prasad, Renown's director of corporate relations, welcoming the government's new, constructive approach to the Varanasi problem.

Whenever a newspaper or TV reporter called for Sansi's reaction, he had Mrs. Khanna put them off.

One day there was an item about Rupe. A terrorist group in Tamil Nadu had claimed responsibility for the bombing of her aircraft because she had failed to oppose a dam that would displace several million peasants. It was the eighteenth or nineteenth group to claim responsibility so far. In the Lok Sabha the Justice minister said the federal police would pursue all leads.

Pramila watched Sansi with growing concern. He was often on the terrace when she left for the university in the mornings, and still there when she got back at night. He deserved to stew, she thought. For a while. But she feared he was sliding into something deeper.

Then, after supper one night, when she switched on the television to catch the evening news, she saw something that might lift her son from his torpor.

"George," she called out to the terrace. "There's something about Amlani on the news—something that might interest you."

Sansi wandered into the living room looking doubtful, assuming it was something on the Renown-Dumont merger or some slick political maneuver that would concentrate even more wealth and power at Fort Renown. But it wasn't. It was something quite different.

Sansi was just in time to see the report switch from the studio to video footage of a smoking, burned-out car in a Delhi street. Sansi recognized the street and the house behind. It was Amlani's house.

". . . the driver and two bystanders were killed by the blast and at least a dozen other bystanders were seriously injured," the voice-over was saying. "Several windows in Mr. Amlani's Delhi residence were blown in by the force of the explosion and pieces of metal from the car were scattered over a wide area. Mr. Amlani was in the house at the time but was not hurt. A spokesman for Renown Industries said Mr. Amlani was cutting short his visit to Delhi and returning to Bombay immediately. It is believed Mr. Amlani was in New Delhi for high level meetings with the government concerning the merger of Renown Industries with the Dumont Chemical Corporation of America . . ."

"You are not the only one who wishes him harm," Pramilla observed.

"Who doesn't?" Sansi murmured.

He went back out onto the terrace and sat down. Part of him was gladdened by the news, mostly he was indifferent. It didn't surprise him there would be an attempt on Amlani's life. There had been others; it was likely there would be more. It was more likely that Amlani would die violently than peacefully, given the state of the Indian judicial system and the way scores were invariably settled personally. He would like to see Amlani exposed first, exposed for what he was, to the nation and to himself, so there could be no more lies and posturing, so some sort of truth would prevail. Then, Sansi could kill him and rest easy.

He heard the phone ringing and a moment later his mother stuck her head outside and said: "It's for you."

"If it's the newspapers—"

"It's Commissioner Jamal from Crime Branch," she interrupted. "He says it would be to your advantage to speak with him."

Sansi hesitated, remembering the last time they had talked, before he went to Delhi to take up the investigation. He picked up the extension beside his chair.

"Did you see the news?" Jamal asked.

"About Amlani?"

"*Acha.*"

"I have an alibi."

"Would you like to know who is behind it?"

"Isn't that your business?"

"Not yet," Jamal answered. "But it will be. And after all the work you've done, I thought you might like to be involved. Meet me at Chowpatty in half an hour."

Chowpatty was a twenty minute walk from Sansi's apartment. He decided he had better get dressed. It would be the first time he had been out of the apartment in two weeks.

The grimy arc of sand known as Chowpatty Beach was wedged between the fuming traffic of Marine Drive and the turbid waters of Back Bay. What charms it once had as a relaxing enclave in the heart of the city had long since been eclipsed by the demands of commerce and the dispossessed. The palm-studded sidewalk that followed the outside curve of the beach was encrusted with souvenir stands, trinket sellers, and food stalls. Strollers who came down at night ran a gauntlet of beggars, pimps, and drug dealers to get to a beach where masseurs, astrologers, and snake charmers competed for space with refugees from the countryside who spent their first weeks in Bombay camped on the sand.

Sansi found Jamal, the only man on the beach in a cream linen Italian suit, buying bani puri at a food stall.

"It is something about Chowpatty at night," Jamal said, offering the bag. "I cannot come here without wanting bani puri."

Sansi took a savory puffed rice ball and popped it into his

mouth. It vanished in a sizzle of chili and left a greasy aftertaste. It tasted better when he was a kid, he thought. Jamal led the way out onto the footpath and the two of them followed the curve of the beach, keeping to the shadows under the palm trees.

"You know the Americans thought they were going to get Renown for forty million dollars?" Jamal said, biting into another rice puff. "They made a deal with Amlani to give him the refinery at Surat and the money to start Renown Oil in exchange for a half share in the company, and he used it to leverage the stock price up and buy them out. Clever, don't you think?"

"*Acha,*" Sansi agreed. "It is hard not to admire a man like that."

Jamal smiled. "Chowdhary told me what happened. He said you never recovered from the loss of your chief witness."

"Or the loss of security, or the loss of Judge Pilot, or the loss of Rupe Seshan," Sansi said.

"What are you going to do now, sit at home and feel sorry for yourself because you got beaten up by the big boys?"

"I thought you were going to tell me."

"You should have called," Jamal said.

"*Acha.*" Sansi stopped and faced the commissioner. "You were right, I tried to do it my way and it didn't work. What would you have done?"

Jamal popped another rice ball in his mouth. "You'll never get Amlani playing fair. He doesn't play fair, why should you?"

"I had these old-fashioned ideas about the way the law should work," Sansi said. "Principles or something."

"Yes, but you are wiser now, aren't you?" Jamal said. He wasn't mocking Sansi, he wasn't gloating. He was waiting to see Sansi's reaction.

"Yes, I suppose I am," Sansi said.

Jamal watched him a moment or two longer then waggled his head. They started walking again.

"I play tennis at the Willingdon Club with Imilani Rao,"

Jamal continued. "He told me a few of the things that have been happening inside Renown this past year."

Rao was still a major force in Indian industry, though he had kept a much lower profile since his costly batterings by Amlani over the years. Sansi wasn't surprised to learn that Rao still had informants inside Renown.

"Did he try and blow up Amlani in Delhi today?"

Jamal smiled. "Your presence around Crime Branch has been missed, Sansi."

"And what have Rao's sources at Renown been telling him that he told you that you could have told me but didn't?"

"Well, it wasn't much at first," Jamal answered, ignoring the jibe. "It seems the refinery at Surat that was supposed to be fitted with the most advanced pollution control technology in the world was actually equipped with very little. The real reason Dumont moved it from Mexico to India was because the Mexican government closed it down. It was cheaper for the Americans to give it to Amlani and take a share of whatever it made here than to let it rust in Mexico."

Sansi shook his head. "I could have used that, a couple of months ago, before Amlani came to the commission and made fools of us all."

"It would have been rather a waste, don't you think, considering what a leaky vessel the commission was?"

"So why are you telling me now?"

"It might do some good."

"It's not enough on its own," Sansi answered. "And in case you hadn't noticed, I am no longer in a position to do anything with it."

"I wouldn't have given it to you while you were running an investigation for the BJP."

Sansi gave a grunt of disgust.

"Don't get precious on me, Sansi," Jamal said. "You were on shaky ground from the beginning. You don't know your way around Delhi, neither did Rupe Seshan, and neither does the present government. That's why I didn't want you dragging my men into it. The Lok Sabha is Amlani's chessboard. You were all just pawns to him. Amlani buys and sells governments."

"Including Congress," Sansi said.

"You see, that is the typical misconception of the amateur," Jamal said. "Amlani doesn't own the Congress Party. It is easier for him to influence a party like the BJP than it is to influence Congress. Congress is too big, too diverse, too difficult to control. And there are too many individuals in Congress who will stand up to Amlani. He can buy some politicians, he can influence decisions, sometimes too much, but he can't intimidate Congress as easily as you might think, and certainly not the way he intimidates the smaller parties."

"Still, enough reason for you to help him," Sansi added.

Jamal's own ambitions to be chief minister made him much more of a political animal than a police commissioner should have been. He played politics with his job, with his men, and with investigations, in an effort to expand his constituency inside the Congress Party and in the community. He would have played Amlani both ways, to limit him as a rival influence in the party but not so overtly that it would cost him Amlani's support when the time came for Jamal to make his move.

"He had Arvind call me when you were named to head the investigation," Jamal answered nonchalantly. "They wanted to know what kind of a chap you are."

"And what kind of a chap did you tell them I am?"

"I told them you would run a clean investigation—and I mentioned you have a weakness for good whiskey and . . . interesting women."

Sansi grunted. He remembered Amlani's offer of a *stengah*, which had preceded the offer of a bribe.

"Is that all?"

"It was enough." Jamal looked amused. "I didn't know you were going to jump into the minister's cot, Sansi. That was your idea, not mine. All you did was convince Amlani I was right and save him the trouble of setting you up with one of his girls."

"*Bhagwan*," Sansi muttered. "And now you are afraid of Amlani. You know it's only a matter of time before it's your turn."

"He is getting too big, Sansi. He was supposed to have stepped down by now, but the bigger his companies get, the more power he acquires, the more he wants. It is becoming less and less likely that he will ever step down."

"What has he asked you to do?"

"Nothing I haven't been able to handle—so far. But I am not prepared to let it continue to the point where he thinks he can tell the government what to do all the time."

"Well, naturally, I will do anything I can to help," Sansi said tartly.

"You are an investigator, Sansi. Investigate."

"You told me you knew who was trying to kill him."

"I think I know where it is coming from," Jamal said. "But I don't know who it is coming from."

"Why don't you just step aside and let whoever it is get on with it?"

"What do you think I've been doing this past year?" Jamal said.

Sansi stopped in mid-stride. "What do you want me to do, find out who it is and see if I can help?"

"Would you?"

Sansi's mind reeled; it took him a moment to recover. "Who do you think it is?"

"It is somebody inside Renown, the same person who has been feeding Rao information. I think it might be somebody in Amlani's family."

"His sons?"

"They both have reason to hate their father," Jamal said. "It was supposed to be Arvind's company now. He ran it for a year after his father's stroke. Then Amlani came back, bolder than ever, and he won't go away. He keeps putting off the date of his retirement. Arvind has to be wondering if he is going to live long enough. And of the two boys, he is the one most like his father—perhaps he got tired of waiting."

"And Joshi made the mistake of getting involved with Anita Vasi," Sansi said.

"From what I understand, the whole family is split over it," Jamal added. "You know Amlani took out a contract on her? Joshi had to smuggle her out of the country. You don't kiss and make up after something like that."

"Johnny Jenta can't have been too happy with it either."

"Jenta is a consideration," Jamal acknowledged. "There has been more than one attempt on Amlani's life. They could have come from different sources. But this latest attempt has the look of an inside job."

They came to the end of Marine Drive, where the food stalls gave way to sand flats and street kids played an endless game of cricket under lightbulbs strung from bamboo poles. Jamal scrunched the empty bani puri bag into a tight ball and lobbed it to the boy with the bat. The boy grinned, swatted it away and turned his eye back to the bowler. Sansi and Jamal turned and retraced their footsteps.

"What other information has Rao been getting?" Sansi asked.

"He knew about the scramble to cover up the Varanasi spill—you had Amlani more worried than you realize—he knew about the Renown Trust, that Amlani was going to try and buy you with it." Jamal paused. "He might have known there was going to be an attempt on the life of your witness."

Sansi groaned softly.

"Nothing was spelled out," Jamal added. "Rao had no idea where it was coming from. It was all hints, tips, anonymous typed notes on scraps of paper."

"Why didn't he do something with it?"

"You can't guess?"

"I want you to tell me."

"He had been burned badly by Amlani—twice. He thought it might be a trap, a setup of some kind."

Sansi sighed.

"I think whoever was feeding Rao the information wanted him to use it too—to hurt Amlani in the market, spoil the merger with Dumont, something. When nothing happened, they took matters into their own hands."

"And now you want me to talk to Rao to find out who it is?"

"The problem with Rao is he doesn't know how much he knows," Jamal said. "And neither do I. You are the only man in India who knows it all, Sansi. You are the only one who can put it all together—quickly."

"Why does it have to be done quickly?"

"Because if this merger between Renown Industries and Dumont Chemical is allowed to proceed, it will be a disaster for India. The amount of money it will put in Amlani's hands is . . ." He gestured hopelessly. "What will he do with it all? What could he not buy? He will be too big, Sansi, too powerful—and he will have given the Americans a presence in the political life of this country that will be of benefit to nobody but them."

"Ah,"—Sansi waggled his understanding—"and no benefit to you either?"

"Find out who is trying to kill Amlani," Jamal pressed.

"You didn't answer my question."

"What question?"

"What do you want me to do if I find out, help them?"

"You help me, you help your country—and you help yourself."

"And how do I do that?"

"If you find out who is trying to kill Amlani, we use it to split Renown Industries apart, we drive a wedge between Amlani and the Americans. We stop him . . . anyway we can."

"If that means standing back and letting him be killed?"

"Do you really have a problem with that, Sansi?"

Sansi felt suddenly isolated among the noisy, cheerful faces swarming past them on the pavement. He stopped and looked at Jamal, his face disfigured by the serrated shadows of the palm fronds.

"I will need the protection of Crime Branch," he said.

"Do this for me, Sansi, and I will do better than that."

Sansi waited.

"I will give you Crime Branch," Jamal said.

"What do you mean, you will give me Crime Branch?"

"When this is over you will come back to Crime Branch as a chief inspector. In two years I will make you my deputy. When I become chief minister, you will be joint commissioner of Crime Branch."

Sansi swayed under the impact of Jamal's words. The commissioner had set his timetable for his move on the chief minister's job—but first he had to get rid of Amlani.

"I need somebody I can trust to watch my back," Jamal added. "You have no reputation to worry about anymore, Sansi. You might as well be a policeman."

CHAPTER 32

"I didn't know you were an Oxford man," Imilani Rao said. "Which college?"

"Magdalen," Sansi answered.

"Balliol," Rao announced with the self-importance of a man who had attended Oxford's most distinguished college. "Which years?"

" 'Sixty-five to 'sixty-eight."

"I was there in 'fifty-four," Rao said. "Were you there on scholarship?"

"My father," Sansi said.

"Of course," Rao said. "The blue eyes."

One way or another Sansi was damned. He might have some money and he might be an Oxford man, but he wasn't the best sort of Oxford man and, of course, he had no caste, something money could never buy, even in India.

"From Banbury, desirous to add knowledge,
To zeal, and to be taught at Magdalen College . . ."

Rao orated grandly then waited for Sansi to finish.

> "The River Cherwell doth to Isis run,
> And bears her company to Abingdon,"

Sansi concluded obligingly.

"John Taylor," Rao said. "Jolly good."

" 'Thames and Isis,' " Sansi named the poem. Then he returned the compliment.

> "Balliol made me, Balliol fed me,
> Whatever I had she gave me again . . ."

A panicky look came into Rao's eyes. " 'Balliol made me, Balliol fed me.' Yes, I know it, I know it . . . I just can't quite . . ."

Sansi waited just long enough then concluded:

> "And the best of Balliol loved and led me.
> God be with you, Balliol men."

"Yes, of course," Rao said, chastened.

" 'Verses,' " Sansi said. "Hilaire Belloc."

They sat in Rao's office atop a decomposing, six-story Victorian relic whose gargoyles had long since succumbed to the leprosy of pollution and regularly dropped claws, noses, and ears onto the passing traffic of Victoria Road. The building, once the Asian headquarters of a long forgotten British merchant bank, had been home to the Rao Manufacturing Group since Rao's grandfather bought his first mill in 1911.

Rao's office appeared to have changed little in the intervening years. Its walls were paneled with dark mahogany, and the furniture was shabby and grand and smelled of rot. The pictures on the walls were portraits of heavily whiskered British and Indian gentlemen from a bygone age, though there were a few prints of Oxford. The only modern touches were the telephone, a fax machine, and what looked like a television cabinet in a corner whose shelves were lined with flaking, leather-backed books.

Rao was plumpish and smooth-faced, with fleshy lips and white teeth. His wavy hair sparkled with gel, and the suit he wore was a fine gray gabardine whose Savile Row cut suggested British tailoring rather than one of his own factories. His tie bore the Rao crest of a gold-embossed elephant and howdah on a red background; a matching silk handkerchief hung elegantly from his breast pocket. Rao's taste was English in every way but one— he had the Indian weakness for jewelry. He wore a gold and ruby tiepin, shirt cuffs fastened with gold ingots, a Piaget watch faced with diamonds, and several rings.

"Would you take a cup of tea with me, Mr. Sansi?"

"I am rather pressed for time," Sansi apologized.

They spoke English rather than Hindi, and Sansi noticed that, like him, Rao had no accent, though unlike him, he spoke an outdated English that few Englishmen spoke anymore.

"Oh come, Mr. Sansi, a gentleman never hurries," Rao said. "Surely it is better to arrive late than in disarray."

"I would hate to keep Mr. Amlani waiting for his day of reckoning," Sansi responded.

"Quite so."

"I wonder if I might see the material you received anonymously this past year concerning our mutual friend."

"I told Commissioner Jamal there wasn't much to it," Rao said. "I never attach much importance to anonymous information."

Sansi began to understand why Rao was the head of a rapidly dwindling empire.

"Sometimes we learn something from the language used," Sansi said. "The wording and structure, the paper, the printers or typewriters they came from."

"Of course you can," Rao responded crisply, as if he had known it all along.

He pushed a button under his desk and a wall panel slid back to reveal an old brass-legged safe Sansi thought must have been there as long as the building. There was no combination, only a double lock for which Rao had the keys in a drawer. He took a large brown envelope from the safe, gave it to Sansi, and waited while Sansi shook the contents onto the desk and studied them.

There were five notes, all written in English, three on common computer stock, a couple on colored notepaper; all looked like copies. It appeared that several different typewriters or printers had been used, one a laser jet, the others daisy wheels of various type and vintage. The daisy wheels would be easy to trace if the machines were still at Renown House. But the messages took the form of questions and might easily have been interpreted as spite—or entrapment, as Rao apparently believed—unless the reader was closely acquainted with the events they addressed. In the light of what he knew now, Sansi found them infuriating.

The first said: *What is it worth to know Renown American refinery meets no emission control standards Mexico or India?*

The language was correct if terse, so there was some attempt at disguise, and the spellings were correct, which indicated the author was educated.

"The first one I thought was an attempt to get money out of me," Rao said. "I still don't know why I kept it."

The second note said: *What does Dumont want with Amlani?*

"I had no idea what that was supposed to mean," Rao said. "It came before anybody knew Amlani was borrowing from Dumont."

Sansi sighed but said nothing.

The third note said: *What would Dumont like to know about Patna?*

"That is when it all started getting too mysterious," Rao said.

Sansi couldn't help himself. "It didn't occur to you that these questions might be trying to tell you something rather than asking you something?"

"Yes, of course." Rao looked stung. "But what precisely was I supposed to think they were trying to tell me, Mr. Sansi? What value was I supposed to attach to gibberish like this?"

The fourth note was on yellow paper and showed that a certain amount of frustration had begun to creep in. It read: *Tell Varanasi commission to look closely Patna memos on emission upgrades.*

Sansi struggled to be polite. "Do you remember when you got this? Did you keep the envelopes? Do you remember the dates you received them, any dates at all?"

"I didn't see the envelopes," Rao answered. "I can't be sure. I know I mentioned that one to Jamal because we played bridge after we played tennis and it was the day the Varanasi inquiry opened. I must say, we all wished you well but we thought you rather had your work cut out."

Sansi waggled his head. At the time, he and Chowdhary were already looking closely at Agawarl's memorandums between Patna and Renown. But to have known that someone was leaking information in Bombay about the exact same memos at the exact same time—at the very least they would have known somebody at Renown was trying to warn them of a conspiracy to discredit the Agawarl memorandums.

But it was the last note that brought a gasp to Sansi's lips. It consisted of only three words: *Agawarl to die?*

The question mark was like a hook into Sansi's heart. It suggested the note had been sent before Agawarl was killed, that the murder didn't have to happen, that it was planned but there was still time to do something about it. If the note had been brought to Sansi's attention when it mattered, Agawarl might have been saved. He would have lived to give evidence at the commission. Amlani would be in jail by now—and Rupe would still be alive.

Sansi forced himself to keep his voice level. "Do you mind if I take these away for forensic examination, Mr. Rao?"

"With my blessing, Mr. Sansi. Anything you can do to punish the scoundrel."

Sansi put the notes back into the envelope and dropped the envelope into his briefcase. He got up to go and Rao offered his hand. Sansi had to hide his distaste as he shook it.

"Mr. Rao, you have experienced a great deal of difficulty with Madhuri Amlani over the years," Sansi said, unable to resist. "You know, if you'd mentioned any of this to the Americans, any of these notes, they might have had second thoughts about the type of man they were getting involved with."

"What makes you think I didn't, Mr. Sansi?"

"I thought you mentioned them only to Commissioner Jamal?"

"I thought they were worth a phone call to the Americans." Rao added, "I thought Dumont might like to know the kind of thing Amlani was caught up in."

"They didn't believe you?" Sansi said.

"Oh yes," Rao answered. "I spoke to a man called Grayson, the man who set the whole thing up. He believed me all right. And do you know what, Mr. Sansi?"

Sansi waited.

"I think it only persuaded them further they were getting involved with the right man."

■   ■

The drive north out of Bombay to Juhu Beach took an hour, and by the time Sansi's taxi dropped him in front of the Juhu post office, he still wasn't sure how he could ask Johnny Jenta what he wanted to ask him and get out alive.

First he had to get in. Sansi had timed his arrival for midday, knowing Jenta's nightly exertions with his harem made him a late riser. The phone rang for a long time before somebody answered, a wheezy male voice he thought deserved to be Jenta's but wasn't.

Sansi said simply: "My name is George Sansi. I am a lawyer. Tell Mr. Jenta I will be at his house in one hour to speak to him about Anita Vasi."

He hung up without waiting for an answer. Jenta had no reason to see him, and he wasn't going to make it easy for Jenta to say no.

Sansi spent the next hour strolling the pastel streets of Juhu testing his memory, identifying the heavily guarded villas of Bollywood's rich and famous, recalling the sex crimes, drug deaths, and other crimes of passion that had taken place behind the wisteria-scented walls.

Around twelve-thirty he found himself outside Jenta's house, a windowless white rectangle on cement posts a block back from the Holiday Inn where so many of Jenta's girls practiced their skills on the tourists while waiting to be discovered. The house was surrounded by a wall of cookie cutter cement blocks through which Sansi could peer inside. He saw a couple of cars and a half-dozen motor scooters parked in the shade.

Sansi was surprised to find the entrance ungated and the two guards so involved in their own conversation they waved him inside without a second glance. He felt slighted. He walked across the shaded parking area underneath the house to the only obvious access, which was a wide cement staircase with an iron railing coiled around the main support pillar. There were a half-dozen security guards smoking and playing cards on kitchen chairs near the bottom of the stairs. He continued past them and started up the stairs; if any of them noticed him they gave no sign.

Sansi found it astonishing that a gangster of Jenta's notoriety had survived so long with such careless security. Then he turned a corner at the top of the stairs and was confronted by a red metal door that looked strong enough to stop rockets. He realized security was a lot heavier than it seemed. The whole house was a bunker—no windows, no balconies, no weak points, and only one obvious way in and out. A security camera in a niche over the door gazed down at Sansi, relaying his image inside. If someone didn't like what it saw, Sansi would be unable to go forward. To go back he would have to pass the guards at the foot of the stairs. Jenta's house was a fortress and a trap, a trap that could be sprung on the word of the man inside.

Sansi pushed a button beside the door and heard a distant buzzing sound. A metallic voice from the camera niche asked him what he wanted. He repeated his message about Anita Vasi. After several minutes without a response Sansi thought he might be going no farther; then the door buzzed loudly and swung outward. He stepped into a dimly lit passage that led to another shorter flight of stairs. The floor, walls, and ceiling were unfinished cement painted black with only one weak light behind a metal grill. It had the utilitarian smell of planned violence about it. Sansi thought people had been hurt, perhaps murdered in this mean, black space. He liked it less when the door buzzed and closed behind him.

He moved cautiously through the gloom, remembering all the reasons why it had been a mistake to come. Then the door at the top of the stairs opened and an enormous purple figure beckoned him inside. Sansi walked up the steps and into a world of perpetual twilight. It was a room with recessed strip lights at ceiling height which cast inverted cones of light down walls covered with mauve flocked wallpaper. The floor was covered with embossed black vinyl tiles that felt sticky underfoot. There were mauve velvet curtains at each end of the room, and the only furniture was a couple of benches with mauve velvet padding. Loud music played somewhere and the room smelled of stale perfume and cooking ghee; the crepuscular, vaguely threatening feel of a sleazy nightclub in the daytime.

Jenta's goon wore a mauve silk shirt and pants and had frizzy shoulder-length hair in a ponytail. He smelled of onion, and when he spoke his voice was wheezy, the voice on the phone. He gave Sansi a lazy pat-down then pulled back a heavy curtain at one end of the room and waved Sansi through.

Sansi stepped into a room that was bigger and darker than the one he had left, though there was light from a television set and an open doorway, through which he saw a smoky, well-lit kitchen, a *bai* cooking at a stove, and a couple of young women fixing themselves lunch—or breakfast. The goon brushed past Sansi and went to the kitchen to rejoin the forage for food.

Sansi peered around, waiting for his eyes to adjust. He saw the same flocked wallpaper, furniture, flashing pictures of women on the wall, photographs of starlets reflecting the light from the TV.

"I want to know something," a voice said out of the darkness, a man's voice with a heavy Marathi accent. "How much did you get to throw the case against Amlani?"

The TV flickered and Sansi saw faces at a table against the wall, a girl and a man with gray hair. He approached them slowly, trying not to trip, till the light from the TV gave them some outline. Jenta was sprawled on a divan strewn with cushions, the girl beside him, their faces turned toward the TV. There were plates of partially eaten food on the table in front of them. Jenta's breakfast nook.

"Whatever it was, I hope it was worth it," Jenta added without taking his eyes off the TV. "Because the whole country saw you get fucked."

"Why do you assume it's over?" Sansi asked.

"You won't get him now," Jenta answered.

"I don't have to," Sansi said. "Somebody else is trying to do it for me."

Jenta didn't answer. He picked up a remote and shuttled rapidly between Star, Doordashan, Zee TV, CNN, and the BBC.

"Nothing on the foreign news," he said.

"He is not a head of state," Sansi said. "All evidence to the contrary."

Jenta smiled slightly, put down the remote and looked at Sansi for the first time.

"You here to offer the movie rights—Anita want to play herself?"

"Can I see 'Baywatch'?" the girl said. She wore studded jeans, a carefully torn T-shirt, and looked fifteen.

Jenta handed her the remote and she turned back to Star; the screen filled with images of the California master race. Tired of waiting to be asked, Sansi pulled out a chair and sat down.

"A lot of people have reason to want him dead. Me, Anita Vasi—you."

"Why me?" Jenta said, unruffled.

"You had a lot of money invested in her."

"Had," Jenta added. "Not anymore."

Sansi had used the name Anita Vasi to gain entry. He had no idea what else it would get him except trouble if Jenta realized how little he really knew. Jenta had to know Anita Vasi had been to a party at Sansi's apartment. What he might not know was that she and Sansi had never exchanged more than a dozen words.

"Anita thought she could count on you for protection," Sansi said.

Jenta glanced at the girl beside him. She gave no sign she was listening.

"Anita ran out on me," he said. "She lied to me, she took money from me, she left debts."

"She ran because Amlani wants her dead," Sansi said. "She was afraid, she still is."

Jenta looked unimpressed. "I would have protected her. If she had been honest with me, she would still be here, she would still have a career, because I would never have allowed her to get involved with an Amlani."

"Why don't you protect her now?" Sansi said. "So she can come back to Bombay?"

Irritation sparked in Jenta's eyes. Beneath his cap of gray

hair his skin was the color of dark grape, his face narrow and ophidian. The velveteen folds of age had the gleam of cobra scales, as if they had been oiled. A life of sunless debauchery suited him, Sansi thought.

Jenta snatched back the remote and shut off the TV. The girl looked at him in dismay.

"Go and watch it with the others," he said. She was about to argue then thought better of it and left. Sansi watched her go; the hips of a woman, the petulant step of a child. The moment she had gone, Jenta leaned forward and said angrily: "You go back and tell that fucking houri I owe her nothing."

"She wants to come back," Sansi said.

"That's her problem."

Sansi was glad of the gloom to hide his growing unease. "She needs money," he said, fumbling for a new way to unlock Jenta's secrets.

Jenta wasn't buying it. "Did Joshi dump her? Is that what this is about?"

"He's an Amlani, what would you expect?"

Jenta leaned back and seemed to relax. "It was only a matter of time before he found out what a bitch she is." He paused. "He told her about the money and now she thinks that's what she's worth."

Sansi shrugged.

"That's my money," Jenta said. "Joshi came to me because he is a businessman and I am a businessman and that's how we settled it. The money he paid was for her debts and her contract and he did it out of respect for me. It had nothing to do with her. I only got back what I put into her."

"There must be something she can do to make peace with you," Sansi said.

"She was always more trouble than she was worth," Jenta said. "She was lazy, she was late, she couldn't act, she couldn't dance. She didn't even like to fuck." He leaned forward. "Now she's had a kid and she wants to come back? Nobody wants an actress with a kid. Tell her to stay in New York, there's nothing for her here."

Sansi lowered his head as if discouraged. Perhaps Jenta didn't have a motive to kill Madhuri Amlani. But Joshi did. And Anita Vasi was no longer pregnant, she was the mother of Amlani's grandchild.

"The best role she ever played was gold digger," Jenta went on. "Joshi Amlani was in love with her, he would have done anything for her. But she couldn't keep up the act, not even to save her own skin."

Sansi got up to go. "She always said you were her harshest critic."

Jenta's oily skin folded into a smirk. "Consistency," he said. "That was her biggest weakness. In her whole career I never saw her give a consistent performance. Consistency is the key to good acting, Sansi, that's something you should know."

Sansi looked thoughtful.

"I will pass that on when I see her," he said.

CHAPTER 33

Sansi turned the corner from the Rajput Hotel into Lodi Road. He stayed on the west side of the road and walked in the direction of Amlani's Delhi house, the site of the car bomb explosion a few days earlier.

He was dressed like a tourist, with a camera on his shoulder, which made him a target for every beggar on the street. He did what every wealthy Indian did. He looked through them knowing if he parted with a single paise he would be swarmed.

The wreckage of the car had been cleared from in front of Amlani's gray marble palace but the road was scarred. There was a wide scorched area, the pavement cracked, blasted, and pitted. As he drew closer Sansi saw glinting fragments of metal embedded in the curb and footpath; a twenty-foot section of fence was missing.

There were still few details available from the Delhi police, and the wreckage, bomb fragments, and explosives residue were all at the forensic laboratory. Sansi knew the car had barely made it out of the driveway before it exploded. It reinforced Jamal's theory of an inside job. The bomb had been planted while the car was inside the grounds of Amlani's house and supposedly safe, but the bomb had exploded prematurely.

Sansi took out his camera and reeled off a few shots of the blast site for his own reference.

"Sahib, shit on shoe, sahib, shit on shoe."

Sansi sighed, looked down and saw a large glob of excrement atop his shoe. A few feet away a scrawny man in a ragged singlet and shorts helpfully proffered his shoeshine box. The monkey man.

"Did you put that there, salah?"

"No, you think I crazy man, sahib? You come, sahib, I clean for you."

"How much?"

"What you like, sahib." The monkey man grinned.

Sansi followed him reluctantly to the side of the road and put his fouled shoe on the box.

"What you doing, sahib, making holidays?" the monkey man chatted amiably.

"You live on this street, don't you?" Sansi said.

"Oh yes, sahib. I live here three years now."

"Were you here the other night when the car blew up?"

The monkey man grimaced and shook his head. "Very bad, sahib. Two peoples I know killed, many wounded."

"Very bad," Sansi agreed. "Were you here the days before it happened?"

"I here all time, sahib," the man answered. "Day, night, all time."

Sansi reached into his camera case and took out some pictures. He held them, one at a time, under the man's nose.

"You know any of these people? You see them at the house across the road in the days before the car blew up?"

The monkey man stopped working and looked up at Sansi. "You policeman, sahib? Detective policeman?"

"Something like that."

"How much you pay, sahib?"

"Do you know that man?" Sansi brandished a picture in front of him.

"Oh yes, sahib, that rich man, Amlani, who own big house. The man they try to kill."

"The man who tried to kill?" Sansi said.

The monkey man shrugged. "Peoples, sahib, bad peoples."

Sansi showed him another picture. "Do you know that person?"

"How much you pay, sahib?"

Sansi took out a hundred rupee note and held it between his fingers. "You tell the truth, I give you another hundred. You tell lies, I send the police back to throw you in jail."

The monkey man waggled his head.

"You know that person?" Sansi showed him the second photograph.

"*Nahi*, sahib."

"Are you sure? Look again."

He did as he was told and shook his head a second time.

"What about this person?" Sansi showed him another picture.

"*Acha*, sahib," the monkey man said. "I know this man. He was here two days before." He pointed to a second picture. "And that man, sahib. He was here too."

Sansi walked back up Lodi Road with clean shoes. He remembered what Amlani had said when they watched a similar scene from the house across the road six months ago.

A little shit goes a long way, he had said then.

■   ■

"The only crime I have committed is to be too successful," Amlani said. "And now they want to kill me for it."

His wife, Gauri, sat on the sofa opposite, plumply demure, hands folded in her lap. The only times her husband invited her to his quarters at Ocean View were when he wanted something from her, usually something to do with family. The last time had been to see if she could help find Joshi a suitable wife. That had been before Anita Vasi. The actions Amlani had taken since then had driven a wedge between himself and his youngest son that threatened to tear apart the entire family.

"I am tired, Gauri," Amlani said with uncharacteristic pathos. "I can't go on fighting wars on every front."

Gauri took a breath before speaking. She knew what she was about to say had been unacceptable to her husband in the past—but something had happened that might make it acceptable now.

"I think he loves her, Madhuri."

Amlani grimaced. He knew it was true. What was mortifying was that he hadn't been able to put a stop to it.

"It has been eight months now and he still won't see sense," Amlani said. "Now there's the kid, and it has made him more stubborn than ever. I warned him, you know. I told him she would get herself pregnant, but he still doesn't listen."

"I only met the girl once," Gauri said. "She seemed very nice. Ramshi says she is nice."

"She's a houri," Amlani grumbled. "She's working her way to respectability on her back."

Gauri didn't think the dowry system was much better. She lowered her gaze so her husband couldn't see the look in her eyes.

"You know what he told me last night?"

Gauri looked back up.

"He told me he is leaving to be with them. Did you know about that?"

"He hasn't said anything to me about that." Privately she was surprised her youngest son had waited this long.

Amlani grunted. "You're all on his side, aren't you? Only Arvind has any common sense. Only Arvind knows how to follow his brain, not his . . . heart."

"What would you like me to do?" Gauri asked.

"Everything I have done, everything I have built, was to be handed on to my sons. . . ." Amlani shook his head in despair. "Now I am betrayed and attacked from the inside and the outside." He paused as if the words stuck in his throat. "Go and talk to him. Tell him he can bring the girl and the kid back."

Gauri gave a discreet waggle of her head.

"At least we'll have them all here under the same roof," Amlani added. "If the girl behaves herself, if she looks like she will make a good wife to my son, well, we will see . . . perhaps in time."

"It is the decision a father would make," his wife said.

Amlani eyed her suspiciously, unable to tell if she was mocking him.

CHAPTER 34

Champagne was the taste of triumph.

Amlani emptied his glass and surveyed the smiling faces that filled the boardroom; directors summoned from every corner of the Renown empire for a vote that had taken less than a minute. Those nearest Amlani started to applaud and it spread quickly through doors left open so secretaries and staff could see history being made. Waiters brought more champagne to fill empty glasses.

Within minutes the result of the vote would be relayed to Dumont in Philadelphia, where Ray Kemp waited anxiously for confirmation of the merger that had eluded his company for so long and proven so costly to accomplish. Since Grayson and Towne were no longer with the company, they would have to read the news in *The Wall Street Journal*.

What made the moment especially satisfying for Amlani was the presence of both his sons at the table. At the moment of its greatest triumph the Amlani family was united again. Another few months and Amlani would be able to step down in confidence. In another few months, when the paperwork was signed,

Renown Oil would be stable, and Renown Industries would be secure for the twenty-first century.

There was a blinding flash of light, a company photographer taking pictures.

"Please, Mr. Amlani, sir." Prasad ushered the photographer forward. "May we be having a picture of you now?"

Amlani smiled broadly and waved his sons to join him.

"It has to be the three of us," he said. "The old generation with the new."

Arvind and Joshi were propelled forward through the crowd. Amlani pulled them boisterously to him and stood them one on each side, arms around their shoulders. Arvind smiled as easily as his father, though Joshi was solemn and self-conscious. The camera flashed and there was a renewed burst of applause accompanied by loud cheers. Amlani's brothers, Prakash, Nusli, and Haresh, pressed forward to shake hands and to embrace their kin. Nothing had been said openly but no one who was there failed to recognize the importance of the moment, the first public proof of reconciliation.

More pictures were taken of all the Amlani men together and then of Amlani with each director of the company. The celebration spilled out of the boardroom into the corridors and offices outside, the beginnings of a party that would go on through the afternoon and continue well into the night at Ocean View.

For everything that had been said about him, for all the assaults on him and his name, the charges he had rebuffed, the hatreds he had endured, Amlani was assured his place in history. He had taken Renown from nothing and in a single extraordinary lifetime, by his own will, turned it into India's first billion dollar company.

When the photographer was finished, Amlani took another glass of champagne and threw himself into the party, determined to immerse himself in the pleasure of the moment, to relish the enormity of his success. As he moved exuberantly from one group to another he was not aware of the odd, creeping silence that began outside and spread like a poisoned tide throughout the floor till it spilled into the boardroom and the only remaining sound was his own voice.

Engulfed by the sudden silence, Amlani turned to its source, the open doors of the boardroom, where a wall of khaki uniforms had appeared—and with them a man he never expected to see again, George Sansi.

Amlani stared as if he were witnessing the resurrection of a corpse. He put down his glass and moved through the still and apprehensive crowd till he was within a few feet of Sansi. He glanced around at the policemen, at least thirty of them, some with rifles, some with lathis, as if they expected to put down a street protest by common thugs. His own security guards stood helplessly by while armed police officers took up positions by the elevator, in the corridors and doorways. Sansi had brought a small army, an occupying force, into the heart of the Renown empire.

"Whose men are these?" Amlani asked, more curious than alarmed. "Are these Jamal's men?"

"They're my men," Sansi said.

"Your men?" Amlani said disbelievingly. "You think you are going to arrest me?"

"Of course not, you are immune to prosecution," Sansi said. "I have come for your son."

Sansi raised his hand and flexed his index finger ever so slightly to Chowdhary, who stood beside him in his inspector's uniform. "Take Arvind Amlani into custody, would you, inspector."

Amlani was still unable to believe Sansi was serious. "Don't any of you take one step forward," he commanded.

But Chowdhary brushed past him, two men close behind. There was instant uproar; Amlani's directors jostling the advancing police officers, secretaries screaming, trying to get out of the way. A tray of glasses crashed to the floor. Amlani shouted to his security guards to throw Sansi out. A couple responded halfheartedly and were easily restrained. Prakash and a few directors gathered protectively around Arvind, who looked panic-stricken. Scuffles broke out; lathis and rifle butts started to fall. Amlani looked on, stunned.

"Do you clear the room or do we?" Sansi said, his voice cutting through the commotion.

"This is an obscenity," Amlani said, his voice an enraged whisper.

"Yes," Sansi said. "It seems wrong somehow, doesn't it?"

Amlani struggled to bring his temper under control. He looked toward Arvind and gestured reassuringly.

"Go along with them for now," he said, a slight tremor in his voice. "I will have you out in an hour."

The mood in the room swung back into precarious balance. As everyone watched in amazed disbelief, a half-dozen policemen took Arvind Amlani into custody, led him out of the boardroom, across the office, and into a waiting elevator.

Then Chowdhary and his men began clearing everyone else from the room, everyone but Sansi and Amlani. When they were finished Chowdhary nodded to Sansi then closed the doors behind him and took up position outside. Sansi had what he wanted. He and Amlani were alone in the Renown boardroom together, and no one would be allowed to leave or enter unless Sansi said so.

Amlani appeared to have regained his composure. He returned to his chair at the head of the boardroom table and sat down. Around the room several chairs lay on their backs amidst broken glass and puddles of spilled champagne, making the sanctity of the Renown boardroom seem soiled, violated.

"On whose authority did you bring those men here today?" Amlani asked.

"They are here on my authority," Sansi said.

He walked around the table and stopped halfway down, beside the windows with their view of the city. From here, Sansi thought, everything looked safe and distant.

"You don't have any authority," Amlani said. "I don't know

what you told Jamal but if he knows anything about what is going on here today he has destroyed himself with you."

"I am here to do business," Sansi continued evenly. "The kind of business you understand."

Amlani swiveled his chair to face the windows, so he could look out over the city he dominated.

"You are nothing," he said. "You have nothing to negotiate."

"I have your son," Sansi said. "Give me Ramani and you can have your son back."

"Is that what you promised Jamal?" Amlani said without looking at Sansi. "That you would deliver him Ramani?"

"He will have the nation's gratitude."

"It will be brief."

"Perhaps he knows something."

Amlani sniffed. "Ramani is dead. The world knows he is dead."

"I can connect Ramani to the bombing of Rupe's aircraft," Sansi said. "I can also connect him to the murder of her husband. What should concern you is that I can connect your son to them too. So you decide. Which one do you prefer to give up— Ramani or your son?"

"You can't prove anything," Amlani said. "And if you could, who would listen to you?"

"Did you know that all explosives leave a signature?" Sansi continued. "Something about impurities peculiar to the place of manufacture getting into the constituent parts of the explosive and fusing together. Sand from Surat, for instance, turning up as silica in a bomb in New Delhi. According to the federal forensic laboratory in Delhi, the explosives used to bring down Rupe's aircraft were manufactured at your plant in Surat. But what is particularly interesting is that the signature of the bomb used to kill Rupe is an exact duplicate of the signature found in the explosives used to kill Mani." Sansi paused. "You are quite right, it doesn't prove anything conclusively. A good lawyer could present it as simple coincidence if it ever got to court. But a lot could go wrong before it ever got to court. A lot could happen to your son while he is in custody—heart attack, suicide, attacks by other prisoners. You know what a dangerous place a jail cell can be, no matter what precautions you take to keep a prisoner safe."

Amlani's gaze swiveled back to Sansi.

"Of course, the evidence we need to convict Ramani isn't anywhere near as much as we would need to convict an Amlani," Sansi added. "I am reasonably certain Ramani's former comrades in the military would be able to extract a confession. And, of course, when he no longer has your support—"

"I've wasted enough time on this," Amlani said. "I'm calling the governor now. My son won't be in a jail cell for one hour."

"Actually, I think you might have a little difficulty reaching the governor this afternoon," Sansi said. "I believe he is away from Bombay for a few days, visiting in-country, I am not exactly sure where. And by the strangest coincidence, Commissioner Jamal and the chief minister both seem to have been called away on urgent business that should keep them occupied for, oh, at least a couple of days—and that is all the time we need."

He took a few steps closer and leaned down so he could look directly into Amlani's face.

"Either you give me Ramani or I give you the body of your son in the morning."

Amlani's color deepened as fear and rage pushed his blood through his constricted veins. "You're not capable of something like that, Sansi," he said dismissively, though there was an unsureness in his voice that hadn't been there before.

"You made me a man who could do something like that," Sansi said quietly.

Amlani looked up into Sansi's face, searched his eyes and was appalled by what he saw there. "This is inhuman . . ." he began, his voice wavering.

"It is, isn't it?" Sansi said. "It's what happens when there is no more law, no more civilization. We are all reduced to the level of jungle animals. I can come in here with a group of armed men, into this place where you think you are safe, and I can do whatever I want to you and your family. There is nowhere for you to hide, nobody who can help you. There is no justice, no mercy. This is where you have brought us—and I must tell you, I feel comfortable here. Everything is so much simpler."

Amlani began to sweat. It started as a sheen then coursed down the creases and crevices of his massive forehead in rivulets till it soaked his shirt. The smell of it infected the air around him.

"I don't know where Ramani is," he said. "He left weeks ago. He could be anywhere."

Sansi said nothing. He knew the satisfaction that came from a hard won conviction, and he had known no regret when he sent a man to the gallows and seen the extinction of evil, but he hadn't known anything quite like this—the pure intoxication of revenge.

"You will pay for this, Sansi, you and Jamal," Amlani blustered.

"Not as long as you have a child left alive," Sansi said.

Amlani had to struggle to control the quaver in his voice but at last he said: "He bought a house in Cochin. I don't know if he is there now."

"Pray that he is," Sansi said, and slid a pencil and a Renown notepad across the table.

Amlani scribbled down the address and pushed it back. Sansi tore off the top sheet, went to the boardroom door, and passed it out to Chowdhary. Then he returned to his chair.

"It could be a long wait," he said. "Why don't we have a spot of tea?"

■ ■

In the next three hours Sansi watched Amlani, hostage to the terrors he had unleashed, erode and crumble like a sandstone monument winnowed by the wind. A little after four Chowdhary returned and he and Sansi had a brief, whispered conversation. Then Sansi returned to his chair, expressionless.

Amlani waited wretchedly.

"Captain Ramani seems to feel betrayed," Sansi said. "He is saying all manner of unflattering things about you and your family. I suspect Commissioner Jamal's file on you is going to get much fatter, don't you?"

"If you have harmed a hair on my son's head . . ." Amlani's voice was hoarse, desperate.

Sansi got up to go. "He never left the building. He's downstairs, in the janitor's quarters, I believe. We'll send him up on the way out."

Amlani grunted as if in pain.

"You see what happens when you create so much hatred and fear?" Sansi said. "It is so easy to think the worst of everybody."

He turned to go then stopped, as if remembering something. He took a sheaf of folded documents from an inside pocket and dropped them on the table in front of Amlani.

"You might want to read these later," he said. "They are copies of messages that went out anonymously from this office to Imilani Rao. To make it easy for you, we have enclosed a list of the make and model of the printers they were printed on. You'll probably find they all match printers in this office. Someone close to you is very much opposed to the idea of your going into business with the Americans." He smiled slightly. "Spies have a way of turning up in the most unexpected places, don't they?"

Sansi continued to the door then paused, drawing out Amlani's misery.

"By the way, we did an analysis on the explosives used to blow up your car. They came from your plant at Surat too, from the same batch of explosives used to blow up Rupe's airplane. It is probably just another coincidence, the kind of circumstantial evidence that is so easy to get thrown out of court. You can decide for yourself what importance you want to attach to it. But while we are on the subject of coincidence, perhaps you might like to ask Arvind and Ushar what they were doing at your house in Delhi two days before the bomb was planted in your car. Perhaps you knew they were there, they probably both have a reasonable explanation. . . ."

"Get out . . ." Amlani said, his voice a tormented moan.

"Personally, I don't think Arvind is at all happy about this merger with Dumont," Sansi went on. "He knows the Americans and I think he's afraid of them. He's afraid that once you bring them on board with all their money and expertise, the company will never really be his. He knows it is only a matter of time before they take it away from him completely. I think your son will do just about anything to stop you putting your name to that merger—I don't think you will live to sign those papers."

Amlani groaned softly.

"Of course, it is all probably just a string of coincidences and doesn't prove anything. I certainly wouldn't feel confident taking it to court. And you don't have to believe any of it. After all, he is your son. You made him what he is. You know better than anybody what he's capable of doing."

Sansi opened the door, stepped outside, and closed it softly behind him.

Alone in the boardroom, alone at the heart of his empire, Amlani wrapped his arms around himself and rocked slowly back and forth in his chair. Somewhere in the pulsing narrows of his carotid artery a blood clot trembled, detached itself into the bloodstream and started toward his brain.

CHAPTER 35

Joshi stirred from a deep slumber and looked at the bedside clock. It was after eight. He should have been up and dressed, he had a full workday ahead. But it had been a late night. Anita was awake till midnight with their son, and when she came back to bed he hadn't wanted her to go back to sleep immediately. As always, she had not denied him.

He watched her for a minute, her face cradled in a nest of dark hair, lips slightly apart, snoring softly. He adored her. She was the most exquisite creature he had ever known, a loving wife and a devoted mother. She spent so much time with their son, the nurse had to drive her from the nursery sometimes for fear she would be out of a job.

Joshi climbed out of bed and started toward the nursery when he heard something that made him stop—a cry of some kind, not a baby's cry, a man's cry. He heard it again, a scream, long and agonized. It was too close to be the street. It had to be the roof. His father.

The second stroke had left Amlani a cripple, unable to go anywhere without help. But he liked to go to the rooftop to watch the sunrise and to watch Arvind swim in the pool. After the stroke, the natural assumption of power by Arvind, and the cancellation of the Dumont merger, Arvind had taken over his father's role completely. Arvind ran the company now, Arvind made all the decisions, assumed all the responsibilities—and privileges. One of those privileges was Ocean View and its rooftop pool.

Every weekday morning Arvind went up to the roof and swam through the heavens just as his father had. Except now his father sat in a wheelchair and watched, his movements feeble and uncoordinated, his speech slurred and indistinct. But all those who saw him swore that when he watched his son swim, his eyes were filled with love.

The screaming turned loud and shrill. Joshi pulled on a robe and ran from the bedroom, out to the lobby. He pounded on the elevator button and the elevator grunted its lethargic response, but he couldn't wait and ran barefoot to the fire stairs that led up to the roof.

When he reached the rooftop and threw open the fire door he stopped, appalled by what he saw. His father was slumped motionless in his wheelchair, shrouded in a white terry-towel robe, staring blankly at the pool. Arvind was submerged at the center of the pool. A servant stood at the pool's edge with a long pole, holding Arvind under while he struggled and clawed weakly to be free. Around him was a spreading pink stain.

Joshi ran down the steps, screaming at the servant to leave his brother alone. The servant dropped the pole and ran toward him. They met at the water's edge as Joshi was about to throw himself into the water. The servant wrapped his arms around Joshi's waist and pulled him down at the edge of the pool, holding him there. Joshi screamed and struggled to be free but the servant held him fast.

"Please, sahib!" the servant pleaded. "Acid, sahib. Acid in the water."

Then Joshi smelled it. A harsh, chemical smell. He struggled to his feet and saw that the servant's hands and forearms and feet were blistered and bleeding where he had tried to pull Arvind out of the water. He looked at his brother's body slowly turning in the pool, the skin eaten down to raw flesh, barely recognizable as human anymore. The blue-green of the water turned a darker red.

"I try, sahib," the servant whimpered. "He struggle too much. I burn my hands, my legs. Pool full of acid, sahib. Full of acid."

Joshi remembered his father, hurried to him and knelt down so he could look in his face. There was nothing there, no expression, only his dark eyes staring blankly at the pool. It was impossible to know how much he had seen, how much he understood.

On a rooftop a hundred yards away Raffee put down his binoculars and turned away. It had taken a long time and more than one attempt. But he had kept his promise. His journey was done, his pilgrimage complete.

ABOUT THE AUTHOR

Born in England, PAUL MANN lived in Australia and Canada before settling in Maine, where he now lives with his wife and children.